Also By
William A. Cimino

Manifestations of Apprehension, A Memoir

MORE BOOKS FROM THE SAGER GROUP

Chains of Nobility: Brotherhood of the Mamluks (Books 1-3)
by Brad Graft

The Deadliest Man Alive: Count Dante, The Mob and the War for American Martial Arts
by Benji Feldheim

Death Came Swiftly: A Novel About the Tay Bridge Disaster of 1879
by Bill Abrams

Sing Sing Follies (A Maximum-Security Comedy): And Other True Stories
by John H. Richardson

Going Home to Die No More: A True Kentucky Story about a Train Robbery and a Hanging after the Civil War
by Russ Witcher

Who She Was: My Search for My Mother's Life
by Samuel G. Freedman

On the Run with Mad Bombers, Outlaw Lovers & Movie Stars: True Stories
by Daniel Voll

Lifeboat No. 8: Surviving the Titanic
by Elizabeth Kaye

Hunting Marlon Brando: A True Story by Mike Sager

Miss Havilland: A Novel by Gay Daly

Our Washington, DC: America's Hometown in Transition
Edited by Susan Sheehan

Saloon Man: A German Immigrant Battles the Limits of Liberty, 1870 to 1915
by Robert Mugge

See our entire library at TheSagerGroup.net

THE DREAM

A Novel of Race, Trust and Enduring Friendship

WILLIAM A. CIMINO

The Dream: A Novel of Race, Trust and Enduring Friendship
Copyright © 2025 William A. Cimino

All rights reserved. No part of this publication may be reproduced,
stored in a retrieval system, or transmitted, in any form or by any
means, electronic, mechanical, photocopying, recording, or otherwise,
without the prior written permission of the publisher.
Published in the United States of America.

Cover design conceived by William A. Cimino
Cover design & art and interior design by Siori Kitajima, PatternBased.com

Cataloging-in-Publication data for this book
is available from the Library of Congress.

ISBNs:
eBook: 978-1-958861-79-0
Paperback: 978-1-958861-80-6
Hardcover: 978-1-958861-81-3

Published by The Sager Group LLC
(TheSagerGroup.net)

THE DREAM

A Novel of Race, Trust and Enduring Friendship

WILLIAM A. CIMINO

*To Fran: A teacher, school counselor, and loving wife of
fifty-eight years who shares in making
our dreams into realities*

CONTENTS

Author's Note

As a young boy growing up in Brooklyn, New York, until I was nearly fourteen, I can remember the multicultural environment surrounding my neighborhood apartment during my kindergarten and elementary school years. Whether you called it a melting pot, a salad bowl, a kaleidoscope, or some other cultural mix, the common denominator was the assimilation of numerous racially and ethnically diverse populations. Those who immigrated from Poland, Ireland, Germany, and other European nations lived a few steps away from my family of Italian ancestry. To me, they were all just people.

I do not recall many Black families in my neighborhood, even though migration from Africa, the Caribbean, and the South during different timelines beginning in the early 1800s, contributed to Black communities in Brooklyn, especially in the Crown Heights, Brownsville, and East New York sections.

From my perspective, everything seemed to be in harmony. Neighborhood families greeted one another, and the children played together, enjoying activities such as stickball, roller skating, snowball fights, and sledding. Family gatherings, especially Sunday dinners, played a significant role in fostering our close-knit relationships and traditions. There was always a celebration whenever someone had a birthday, regardless of age. It was a happy time that overshadowed any prejudices or racial tension that may have existed.

In 1959, having moved to Nassau County on Long Island, I commuted to a small all-boys Catholic high school about thirty minutes to the east in Suffolk County. The school had approximately four hundred students, all of whom were White. It wasn't until I attended St. John's University in Jamaica, Queens, New York, that I began to recognize the social aspects and issues of race. Low percentages of students of color attended the university, all of whom were pursuing their specific degrees of interest. This was the four-year period 1963–1967, and like a burst from holiday fireworks, along with the escalation of the war in Vietnam, was the ever-present scourge of racial tension and the civil rights movement in the news media.

Four years of study flew by, and significant events unfolded quickly. Two weeks after graduation, I married a student I met in my first semester. Eleven days after our wedding, I entered the US Air Force and attended Officer Training School in San Antonio, Texas. I returned home to retrieve my bride and headed back to Texas for more training. It was during the trip west through the Southern states that racial unrest amplified what I had observed and learned while in college.

Signs of racial prejudice were everywhere, flashing like a bright neon sign. You could not unsee it! Maybe we were naïve, but we discussed the distasteful, explicit hatred that took us both by surprise. The expressions were not so evident in the northern cities of the Eastern Seaboard, where racial discrimination existed, especially in housing and employment. It was like driving into a different world. To borrow a few lines from *Manifestations of Apprehension, A Memoir*, a book I previously wrote:

> As we drove further to the south and west, it was disturbing to see signs of racial discrimination: "No Colored Allowed," "White bathroom only," and similarly divisive statements. That did not sit well with us. We would learn that there are not only open displays such as these but even more subtle ways to discriminate, discredit, and alienate African Americans and other people of color.
>
> When I reflect on all the years of my service and beyond and the diverse composition of the men and women in the military, while it has its share of social problems, it has been an environment of teamwork, mission-oriented actions, and devotion to duty and country from all members—Black, White, Latino, Asian; the list goes on.

Serving in the military was one way to gain exposure to diverse ethnic and racial groups—people from all over the country. It was a force function that thrust many into the mix. This predominantly racially inclusive environment confirmed that there are ways to work together, to understand cultural differences, to appreciate what everyone can contribute to objectives, and to act jointly as a unified human family.

While the racial tensions in the early 1960s resonated in my mind, the struggle for civil rights, widespread segregation, police brutality—particularly in the South—limited opportunities for African Americans—not only in housing and employment, but also in education—were evident. The civil rights movement—most notably led by figures such as Martin Luther King Jr., and highlighted by a march on Washington, DC, in 1963, and King's iconic "I Have A Dream" speech—offered nonviolent resistance tactics such as sit-ins, protests, and boycotts. More young activists led the vocal demand for change.

Fast-forward to 1993, when I retired from the Air Force and entered the civilian workforce. My experience and various roles in multiple information technology and defense companies have provided me with continued exposure to and appreciation for a multicultural environment. Once again, teamwork among the diverse employees contributed to company goals and shared success. Yet, while these harmonious interactions served us well within a contained workspace, the forces for widespread change against racism in America moved the needle slightly despite significant steps.

Earlier events, in addition to the March on Washington (1963), led to the cause for the elimination of racism: Brown v. Board of Education of Topeka, Kansas (1954) was a landmark Supreme Court case led by Justice Earl Warren that declared racial segregation in public schools violated the Fourteenth Amendment and was, therefore, unconstitutional; the Montgomery Bus Boycott in Alabama (1955–1956) was led by Rosa Parks and Martin Luther King Jr., protesting segregated seating on public transportation; sit-ins (the late 1950s) were nonviolent protests where African Americans would sit at segregated lunch counters; freedom rides (1961) were conducted by interracial groups who rode buses through the South to challenge segregation on Interstate highways, bridging protests across states; and the Civil Rights Act of 1964 resulted from federal legislation that prohibited discrimination based on race, color, religion, sex, or national origin.

In the commercial world, where competition is fierce, hope is often viewed as a poor strategy for securing opportunities to grow a business. Dedicated analysis through SWOT—strengths, weaknesses, opportunities, and threats—is a strategic planning tool that provides a framework to evaluate a company's competitive position. In society, however, hope *is* essential, and when accompanied by the aforementioned legal strategies of antiracial proponents and other causes throughout the decades to the present day, it contributes to the fight to eradicate racism.

Despite these efforts, the advancement in social media continues to communicate racism and demonstrate that this scourge lives on in America through racist language, coded racist messaging, targeted harassment, and amplified White supremacist views. As an example to draw attention to racism, the July 2013 Facebook posting by Alicia Garza used the phrase "Black Lives Matter" following the acquittal of George Zimmerman in the shooting death of Trayvon Martin. On the other hand, social media can transcend certain boundaries that divide us and foster a sense of global solidarity, reinforcing the importance of civil rights in America and worldwide.

I do not propose that I am anything near an expert on Black history, slavery, racial discrimination, or the civil rights movement. I don't claim to fully understand every facet of racism, but I've grown to appreciate its depth—the way it shapes lives, communities, and legacies in ways that aren't always visible. I probably know as much as the average American. I could never say that I "walked in a Black person's shoes," but what I have come to recognize is that racism is not merely a matter of individual bias, but a deeply rooted system that's woven into history, institutions, and everyday interactions. Its complexity demands not just awareness, but a willingness to listen, learn, and confront uncomfortable truths.

I value our diversity and view it as a characteristic of our country that offers merit more than divisiveness. Embracing diversity or division is a matter of choice that requires action. We must act in a way that explores and exploits the merits of a rich variety of backgrounds, perspectives, and experiences that all individuals bring to society, extinguishing the mindset that differences among people justify inequality.

When we accept diversity, we foster inclusion—by creating an environment where everyone feels accepted, valued, and empowered to contribute their best without fear of discrimination or bias; we encourage collaboration—by integrating diverse viewpoints and solving problems more creatively; we promote equality—by valuing diversity means actively addressing inequalities and ensuring that all individuals have access to opportunities and resources; and we strengthen communities—by allowing diversity to enrich our shared experiences, helping us build stronger connections and understand different perspectives.

I am proud of my Italian heritage, the customs and culture passed down from my ancestors, and the fact that I occasionally enjoy sharing them with those from other backgrounds. If I expect them to accept me and how I'm different from them, how could I not treat them accordingly?

I admire the many great works by distinguished authors and scholars devoted to Black history and the plight of the Black community. I offer a story based on a relationship established early in youth, which created a bond and grew stronger in the face of the intertwined forces of prejudice and adversity, and resulted in a representation of a better social construct.

The Dream is a story of hope. Two boys, one Black and one White, form a relationship marked by young innocence, friendship, and mutual support, despite the ongoing hatred and turbulent societal shifts around them. Through their deeply enriching bond of genuine empathy and strength amid a world of racial separation, they affirm that we can hope . . . we can dream.

PREFACE

In the interest of the integrity of events and figures in *The Dream*, I have preserved the accuracy of core historical content and notable individuals during the tumultuous years of civil unrest in the 1950s through the 1970s.

The locations and grade levels of Public School 91 (PS 91) in Brooklyn during this period have been altered slightly to fit the story's plot without compromising the overall historical integrity of that period.

For example, in reality, PS 91 was located in the Crown Heights section of Brooklyn and taught kindergarten through sixth grade. Students progressed to junior high school for grades seven through nine, and to high school for grades ten through twelve. In this story, PS 91 is located in the East New York section of Brooklyn and teaches kindergarten through eighth grade, which is followed by four years in high school.

The location of Thomas Jefferson High School and the 75th Precinct of the New York Police Department is accurately set in the story's East New York section of Brooklyn.

Fictitious names are used for hateful, organized network members who contribute to civil unrest. I have chosen to represent their disgraceful description of Black individuals by substituting the term "N-word" where appropriate.

Cast of Characters

Chapter 1
- Margaret Lopez (Maggie)—PS 91 first grade teacher
- Taylor Washington—Black student, first grade, PS 91
- Nicholas Greene (Nick)—White student, first grade, PS 91
- Dr. Mary Carpenter—PS 91 principal

Chapter 2
- Mary Greene—Nick's mother
- Kevin and Jimmy—Nick's school playtime friends
- Makena Washington—Taylor's mother
- Jonathan Greene—Nick's father, an accountant
- Michael Greene—Jonathan's older brother, killed in the Korean War
- Julie Greene—Michael's wife
- Mikey and Jenny Greene—Children of Michael and Julie
- Kathleen Greene—Jonathan's younger sister
- William and Sarah Greene—Jonathan's parents
- Donna Sweeney—PS 91 eighth grade teacher, school counselor

Chapter 3
- Gracie Benson—PS 91 fifth grade teacher
- Gloria Rivera—PS 91 seventh grade teacher
- Angela Mancini—PS 91 second grade teacher
- Jamal Brown—Black man, PS 91 janitor/maintenance

Chapter 4
- Eddie—PS 91, Taylor's school playtime friend

Chapter 5
- Shamus O'Reilly—75th Precinct officer, NYPD
- Maurice Kessler—Black student, Jefferson High School
- David Ozersky, White student, Jefferson High School
- Francis O'Reilly—Father of Shamus, former NYPD officer
- Samuel—Francis O'Reilly's friend
- Emily Smith—Jefferson High School nurse

- Evan Walters—Jefferson High School principal
- Buddy Mason—Senior, Jefferson H.S.
- Henry Mason (aka Sabre)—Buddy's father, warehouse worker
- William Handly—NYC Superintendent of School Buildings
- Frank Moretti—Grocery store owner
- Reggie "Smokes" Johnson—Black worker, grocery store, janitor, night watchman

Chapter 6

- Isabella "Izzy" Garcia—PS 91 second grade teacher
- Conan McGuire—75th Precinct sergeant, NYPD
- Johnny Baker—75th Precinct officer, NYPD
- Sonny Mason—PS 91 eighth grade, Buddy's younger brother

Chapter 7

- Henry Williams—PS 91 eighth grade, younger brother of Trevor Williams (Jefferson High School)
- Amira Jackson—PS 91 eighth grade, younger sister of Lucas Jackson (Jefferson High School)
- David Smith—PS 91 seventh grade

Chapter 8

- Mike Nelson—75th Precinct officer, NYPD
- Tom Baker—PS 91 eighth grade
- Richie Valentine—PS 91 eighth grade
- Billy and Frankie Lynch (twins)—PS 91 eighth grade
- Donald Foster—75th Precinct officer, NYPD
- Peter Goodwin—75th Precinct officer, NYPD
- Sean O'Neill—75th Precinct officer, NYPD

Chapter 9

- Isaac Washington—Taylor's father, a pharmacist
- Destiny—Sitter for Taylor

Chapter 10

- Francis O'Rourke—75th Precinct captain, NYPD

Chapter 11

- No new characters

Chapter 12

- Kevin Jackson—Amira's father
- Wanda Jackson—Amira's mother

Chapter 13
- Vincent Gallo—Vinnie Gallo's father
- Vinnie Gallo—PS 91 eighth grade
- Elana Sanchez—Sofia Sanchez's mother
- Sofia Sanchez—PS 91 eighth grade
- Thomas Malcolm—*Brooklyn Eagle* reporter

Chapter 14
- Trevor Williams—Black senior, Jefferson H.S., older brother of Henry Williams (PS 91)
- Lucas Jackson—Black senior, Jefferson H.S., older brother of Amira Jackson (PS 91)

Chapter 15
- No new characters

Chapter 16
- Jethro Paine (aka Cue Ball)—Yonkers, NY, resident
- Demon—Paine's dog
- Butch Brady (aka VenoM)—Mississippi resident
- Rhett Walker (aka Cyclone)—Syracuse, NY, resident

Chapter 17
- No new characters

Chapter 18
- Ben Rogers—75th Precinct officer, NYPD surveillance
- Evan Campbell—75th Precinct officer, NYPD surveillance
- Liam Doyle—Chief, Yonkers police
- Sean Ryan—Lieutenant, Yonkers police

Chapter 19
- Tyler Barnes (aka X-ray)—75th Precinct administrative clerk, NYPD
- Brian Savage (aka Bullet)—Brooklyn pawn shop owner
- Ricky Miller (aka Deadman)—Yonkers, NY, resident

Chapter 20
- Helen Mason—Deceased wife of Henry Mason
- Theodore "Ted" and Amelia Cooper—A PS 91 student's parents

Chapter 21
- Marty O'Shea—Detective, NYPD Bureau of Special Services and Investigations

Chapter 47
- No new characters

Chapter 48
- James Jones—Black student, seventh grade, PS 91

Chapters 49–53
- No new characters

Chapter 54
- Jenny Wilson—School secretary, PS 91
- Rafael Vargas—Sergeant, US Marine Corps

Chapters 55–58
- No new characters

Chapter 59
- Kenneth Washington—Isaac's older brother
- Samira Washington—Kenneth's wife
- Darnell and Sadie Washington—Isaac and Kenneth's parents
- Kenneth Washington Jr.—Kenneth and Samira's son

Chapters 60–62
- No new characters

Chapter 63
- Dr. Clair Cartwright—White, renowned geneticist, Rockefeller University
- Dr. Zora Caldwell—Black, geneticist, Cold Spring Harbor Laboratory (CSHL)

Chapter 64
- Lila Greene—Jonathan and Mary's daughter
- Edward and Susan Moore—Mary's parents

Chapter 65
- No new characters

Chapter 66
- Alan Lefkowitz—Engineering instructor, Brooklyn Technical High School
- Marty Fanning—Science and biology instructor, Brooklyn Technical High School

Chapter 67
- No new characters

Chapter 1

EAST NEW YORK, 1957

Summer was over for the elementary school children, whose mixture of happy and sad faces was greeted by numerous eager teachers under an early-morning warming sun at PS 91, at the corner of Albany and East New York avenues in the heart of a residential neighborhood in the eastern section of Brooklyn. Margaret Lopez gathered her first-grade students and directed them to the classroom she had so diligently prepared for their big year ahead.

She worked especially hard to create thoughtful touches to make her classroom an inspiring environment where her students can thrive academically and emotionally. She desired that their first steps into the classroom would be a warm, inviting world designed to spark curiosity and joy in young learners.

Her classroom was a model of bright, themed walls in a cheerful color palette of murals that would inspire stories and learning. There were interactive bulletin boards—welcome boards, which displayed the students' photos paired with their names, and learning displays—with the alphabet, numbers, shapes, and colors.

The cozy reading corners were fitted with bean bags or small chairs, creating a magical space for story time. The overall ambiance was one that blends fun with learning.

Lopez had recently graduated from the School of Education at St. John's University in Jamaica, New York. She wore a conservative mauve dress with light blue flowers on her slender frame, which stood at five feet four inches. Her rich, long black hair flowed past her neck in natural waves, and her beautiful brown eyes and warm smile framed her flawless, light brown complexion. She radiated with enthusiasm.

After completing her challenging coursework, student teaching internships, and fulfilling the rigorous state certification requirements to secure a position in the New York City Public School system, she was excited about her new role and dedicated herself to a career in education.

The children scrambled to find the wooden desk of their choice in the classroom, which had about thirty-five students. Lopez quickly brought the room to order, directing the students to settle down and pay attention, and she introduced herself. She scanned the room, which contained a roughly fifty-fifty mix of boys and girls, and noted the diverse ethnic tapestry before her. She already had a good understanding of her class makeup based on previous enrollment statistics and information, but seeing it represented by real little kids brought a huge smile to her face and a realization that *I'm here . . . with my students . . . this is wonderful!*

The population in East New York changed from the late 1950s to the mid-1960s, with a previously predominant composite of mostly working-class Italians and Jewish residents, giving way to an increasing number of working-class Black people and Puerto Ricans. The classroom of first graders accurately reflected the local population. Lopez enthusiastically asked, "All right, students, are you ready for your first-grade year?"

About half the class shouted out, "Yes!" With their elbows on the desk and faces planted in their hands, the other half mumbled something unintelligible. They seemed lost in the summer that they wished would never end.

Lopez observed this and asked again, "Okay, now, everyone, are you ready to begin a very exciting year at school?"

"Yes," bounced back much better this time.

Lopez addressed her class again. "Students, please look around the classroom. These are your classmates whom you will get to know, become friends with, and help one another to do well in school. You will share learning, activities, and playtime with them." As she continued to address the class, preparing them to accept their classmates with open arms, her voice began to fade from their hearing. They drifted a bit. They focused more on the human characteristics of their classmates, including differences in ethnic backgrounds, skin color, hair, eyes, and physical size.

Taylor Washington was sitting in a front-row seat and gazed around until he paused and held a focus on Nicholas Greene, sitting a few aisles across from him. Nicholas, in turn, stopped his head swivel when he noticed Taylor's stare. The two boys seemed locked in a state of suspended time, frozen and unmoved.

Lopez was still speaking to the class, and most students returned to reality as her voice grew louder and captured their attention. After what seemed like forever, Taylor slowly raised his hand slightly as if to say "Hi" to Nicholas. He did not smile when presenting this gesture but held his gaze firm. Nicholas did not immediately react, but as he had a pinpoint view of Taylor's hand, he thought Taylor meant it for someone else, perhaps someone behind him. So he turned his head to see if anyone returned Taylor's gesture of friendship. He didn't see anyone and turned back to this Black student, who now smiled and pointed as he mouthed the words, "No, you." Nicholas slowly raised his hand in reply but maintained a somewhat confused look.

A few seconds later, Lopez took complete control of her class. "Okay, let's get started!" The school halls were now quiet as Taylor and Nicholas' class, along with all others in PS 91, initiated a kick-start to the new school year.

School principal Dr. Mary Carpenter planned to chair a quick but crucial session in her conference room at the end of the day. She was well-known as an anomaly in the New York City public school system, as most principals were men. She was fifty-seven years old, short in stature, with a blend of brown and silver hair styled fashionably. Her glasses drew attention to her hazel eyes, which reflected wisdom and empathy. She earned her teaching degree at Hunter College in New York City and taught students across multiple grade levels in the 1920s and 1930s.

Carpenter was a widow, and while she loved children, she could not have any of her own. Her husband was killed in the Japanese attack on Pearl Harbor on December 7, 1941. She dedicated the remainder of the 1940s to honing her credentials as an educator. She earned a master of science in education at Teachers College, Columbia University, and focused her learning on counseling and curriculum development. A few years later, she continued her studies at Columbia to earn a doctor of education degree. She had the respect and admiration of her entire staff for her dedication, intelligence, and authority.

Her team included teachers who specialized in different grades, assistant teachers who helped teachers with larger class sizes, a nurse who provided healthcare and first aid, a cafeteria staff, a librarian, a counselor for student guidance and support for academic and personal issues, administrative staff including secretaries and office managers for administrative support, and a janitor responsible for maintenance and cleanliness of the school.

Lopez established some basic classroom rules. As part of her teaching degree requirements, she participated in student training sessions, gaining hands-on experience in actual classroom settings under the supervision of certified teachers. There, she learned that the critical job of first-grade teachers was to create schedules and routines that help the young students pace themselves, organize their energy and active ideas, and get them to the end of the day happy, albeit perhaps a bit exhausted. She knew that predictable routines have proved beneficial in maintaining energy and enthusiasm.

Lopez had carefully planned an up-and-down pace for the day, providing active engagement periods and sustained quiet work. She had given her students expectations for their daily routine, including singing, reading, basic math, writing, recess/playtime, and basic science and social studies. Her students would learn to participate individually and interactively—essential skills to build self-confidence, social appreciation, and acceptance of their classmates.

Taylor and Nick were very attentive, but occasionally, they would exchange a mutual glance as if their first encounter was a primer for further curiosity. Nick was an only child and had always been a bit shy, a reticent boy who was more interested in observing the world around him than initiating conversation or sharing his thoughts and emotions. He needed the comfort of a slow-developing bond before he opened up to any level of interaction. He was content listening to his parents and often playing alone more than with other children during his earlier years, but now he faced Taylor, a Black student who seemed to persist in getting his attention. He asked, *"Why is he looking at me again? What does he want?"*

Lopez noted the quiet "communication" between Taylor and Nick but ignored it as other children in the class were also occasionally distracted away from her. This appeared to be the usual behavior of youngsters thrust into a new school-year environment. Everything around them, including their classmates, piqued their curiosity and attention.

As the day progressed, Lopez's class was excited about recess and playtime outside. There was a designated area for them to comingle and engage in various structured activities. Some of the kids made instant friendships, while others took a bit more time to warm up to one another.

Taylor gravitated toward a few other Black students but then spanned the area to find Nick, noting that he was talking with two other White boys. Nick would occasionally turn his attention from them to search the area for Taylor as if to ascertain if Taylor would still try to get his attention. Their eyes did not meet as they were in a simultaneous rhythm of just missing each other.

After the outdoor break, the children returned to their class-room, having expended some level of energy and now faced more time with quiet concentration, as Lopez initiated a short talk on what makes her class very special. "I hope you had a nice time during playtime outside and got to meet some of your classmates." The children smiled and nodded in unison as they searched the room for the others they had met. "You know, you are all very special kids! We have a class with many different-looking kids, but we are all here to learn together, treat one another nicely, and help one another when someone may need it."

Lopez transitioned to a curriculum subject as she did not want to go any further than this basic introduction of mutual respect. She determined this was enough for the young minds to absorb for now. The rest of the afternoon was focused on simple math and some fascinating science that captured every student's attention. They would be excited to tell their parents about what they learned on their first day of first grade.

Chapter 2

PS 91, An Essential Staff Meeting

The bell rang, and day one of the school year ended as children lined up to be led outside to anxious parents. They were eager to get home to a sense of normalcy—their room, their toys, their pets. The day remained sunny and calm, which added to the cheerful atmosphere. Adults carried on light conversations with one another, some who knew each other and others total strangers—a mix of ethnic and racial representation that reflected the composition of students across all grades.

Mid-sentence, Mary Greene interrupted, "Oh, so nice talking with you . . . there's my son, Nick. I hope to see you again soon." She darted away before the other woman could answer. "Nick, Nick, over here!" Nick ran into his mother's arms as she asked, "Well, how was your first day in first grade?"

Nick replied with one word as he was somewhat relieved to see his mother, "Good."

"Did you like your teacher, Miss Lopez?"

"Yeah, she's nice."

"Did you make some new friends?"

"I played with a couple of kids outside at recess. I think their names are Kevin and Jimmy." Before his mother could respond, he blurted out, "There was this one boy, a Black boy, he kept looking at me!" His expression told his mother that Nick was somewhat uneasy.

"Oh? Did he tell you his name? Do you see him here outside?"

"Yeah, he's right over there." Nick pointed to Taylor being led away by his mother, Makena Washington. She waved goodbye to several other Black mothers as they quickly dispersed with their children. The separate clusters of all-Black and all-White parents and students rapidly dissolved as if comingling would have a pernicious outcome.

Mary just glanced at them, not seeming overly concerned, then turned to Nick. "Well, let's go home. I want to hear more about what you did today in class, what new things you learned, and what you liked." Nick quietly walked hand-in-hand by his mother's side. His light brown hair swept across his blue eyes as he occasionally looked in the direction where he last saw Taylor; his curiosity about the other boy seemed to have a firm grip on his focus.

Mary and Nick walked home. They lived in a three-story apartment building just a few city blocks from PS 91. Nick's father, Jonathan, and Mary had decided to move to the apartment because it was within walking distance of the school. East New York in Brooklyn was a working-class neighborhood with residential and industrial areas. The streets had modest row houses, small apartment buildings, and occasional single-family homes. Many residences were built in the early twentieth century, featuring brick facades and stoops where neighbors would gather and children would play. The neighborhood had numerous local shops, bakeries, and delis scattered along commercial streets that catered to the diverse population, which included Italian, Jewish, and Black families.

Churches and synagogues were central to the community's social life, hosting events and providing support to residents. Public transportation, including buses and elevated train lines, connected East New York to other parts of Brooklyn and Manhattan, making it convenient for workers to commute to jobs in the city. However, the area also faced challenges, including economic disparities and the beginnings of urban decline.

Jonathan's parents, William and Sarah, had emigrated from Europe in 1918 at the end of WWI, were married in early 1920, and raised a family of three children. Jonathan was the second oldest of the siblings. Jonathan's older brother, Michael, was killed in the Korean War in 1952, just two weeks before he was to return to the United States. His wife, Julie, and two children, Mikey (the oldest) and Jenny, lived nearby and heavily depended on their family support system. Jonathan's sister, Kathleen, younger by three years, was single and lived in Manhattan, where she worked in the fashion industry.

Jonathan's parents worked in a coat factory early in their marriage and, over nearly seventeen years, had become naturalized citizens of the United States. Like many other immigrants from across the pond, they worked hard and were proud to assimilate their family into the American way of life while preserving traditions and customs.

While the New World provided opportunities, it also presented a melting pot that offered divisions and clashes. As the population of the United States worked through the 1950s, it experienced the emergence of one of the most divisive and tumultuous times in world history. As they shifted toward the sixties, the civil rights movement, the Vietnam War and antiwar protests, countercultural movements, political assassinations, and the emerging "generation gap" took center stage. Families across the country would face the challenge of navigating through these tough times.

Once all student-parent matchups were made, the teachers reentered the school for the principal's meeting. Dr. Carpenter greeted the group. "Good afternoon, everyone. I trust you had a good first day of our new school year. Our preschool meetings last week allowed us to focus on the year ahead, but we must continue addressing some of the issues raised. As you know, last year several students' parents brought our attention to racial incidents that plagued not only our school but others throughout the New York City metropolitan area. We need to give that our full attention and effort."

The staff's attention perked up a bit as they sipped more coffee than they had consumed in the morning, but with head nods, they quickly confirmed the need for discussion. They were all familiar with incidents that ranged from verbal harassment and bullying to violence and were eager to find ways to prevent or mitigate, as necessary, any reputational damage for PS 91 built on these heinous activities. Donna Sweeney, an eighth-grade teacher who also served as the school counselor, quickly added, "Yes, although you are all somewhat familiar with much of this, I am ready to summarize the areas of most concern for our school."

Dr. Carpenter interjected, "Yes, but I first want to emphasize, and I know I am repeating myself because it is worth repeating, that we are obligated as a team to work together in the best interest of all our students. They are here under our care for a good part of their day, and we must ensure they bring home the values and lessons we do our best to provide them." She added emphatically, "We must especially impart respect for one another among our students and build on their appreciation for others in their class, regardless of their background, color, religion . . . you know the rest. And, it is our duty to gain the trust of their parents and guardians."

Again, more head nods and turning to one another as if it were part of a ceremony to confirm what they already knew. "Before I hand it over to Donna, I want to remind everyone of some key schedule items. First, we have Parents' Night in three weeks, our first formal opportunity to share our recognition of students' progress and identify any issues with their learning and behavior. We will also begin other key meetings focused on school events throughout the year. So, we cannot delay preparing for these. Okay, Donna, please proceed."

Donna opened a file on the table and handed out a two-page incident report related to issues of concern. "I am sure these will reignite your fury as it does mine. Over the years, I have been in contact with several other school counselors and, more recently, at some of the borough's pre-school-year meetings. This is a widespread problem and only appears to be getting worse."

The teachers nodded in affirmation.

"As you know, it was only three years ago when racial segregation in public schools was declared unconstitutional by Brown v. Board of Education of Topeka, Kansas. Yet, we often witness a disrespect for that Supreme Court decision as incidents continue to rise. Recent local and national news media contain reports of violations of the decision."

Carpenter chimed in, "Inequalities continue to exist." As if she were a history professor giving a lecture on civil rights, she emphasized, "Even with Blacks serving in WWII and the Korean War, we still see racism. In this decade, while certain levels of open bias and racism have decreased, we still hear and witness bullying, verbal harassment, and incidents in the streets. And, I won't even get started on parallel movements in women's and gay rights, or problems in housing and job opportunities." The dutiful staff gave their full attention.

As Carpenter's meeting proceeded through the agenda, and the day was getting long, everyone had heard all they needed to commit to action. They emphasized the spirit of friendship among their students, who have so many differences. And they would raise their attention to the slightest hint of trouble. They all hoped for a year of solid relationships among students, harmony, and educational achievements—none of this would come easily, as hope is never enough of a strategy.

Chapter 3

JAMAL BROWN WEIGHS IN

It was only one month later, September 19, 1957, when Donna Sweeney rushed into Carpenter's office with a headline news story. "It's terrible! A seventeen-year-old Black student entered an American History class at a high school in East New York and threw a bottle of lye at a White student. The corrosive liquid exploded and spattered eighteen other students and the teacher." This incident appeared on the front page of *The New York Times* and sparked a debate, as well as a grand jury statement in favor of uniformed police officers in public schools across the city.

Carpenter replied, "I just heard from the superintendent. Awful! As I mentioned in our weekly staff meeting following Parents' Night just a week ago, parents across all grade levels expressed concerns about the rising racial tensions in our educational community. We must immediately get the word out to our teachers and support staff. We need to be proactive." A bit choked up but determined to do her part, Donna nodded and left hurriedly to draft an agenda for a later meeting.

Dr. Carpenter called a short special staff meeting for the end of the day. She did not want to waste any time addressing key points. She was a seasoned educator who had witnessed a wide range of behaviors in her thirty years of experience. The teaching staff and support personnel at PS 91 were informed of the racial incident, and after the "Oh my God, here we go again" and similar expressions of grief and despair, they tried to comprehend the challenges ahead. *How do we prevent this in our school? What have we learned, and how can we use our collective effort to keep racism out of our school?* They gave their full attention to the person they respected highly.

Carpenter offered some of the racist incidents she witnessed over the years, but quickly turned to preventive measures. She began, "We need to be specific in addressing this issue across our student body. Our kids range in age from six to thirteen, and therefore, their comprehension will require careful consideration regarding how and when we discuss racism. We have the perfect audience for this with our range of ethnic and cultural children, and we need to put all our energy and talent to work." She glanced at Donna to ensure she was ready for the highlights of the meeting. "Donna."

Donna nodded at Carpenter, scanned the conference room filled with serious-looking faces, and began, "Mary and I met late this morning to decide how best to address this today and to add specific frequent meetings throughout the school year focused on racism. We broke the age range into three groups: six to eight, nine to ten, and eleven to thirteen. We considered the expected comprehension levels for each group and compiled a short list of subjects to integrate into the curriculum for each." She handed a stack of pages to Gracie Benson, a fifth-grade teacher seated to her right. "Gracie, please take one and pass them to the others."

The teachers glanced over the handout, and before Donna could continue, Gloria Rivera, a seventh-grade teacher who recently transferred from a school in another area of Brooklyn, raised her hand and simultaneously said, "In Bedford-Stuyvesant (often nicknamed 'Bed-Stuy'), we experienced a huge amount of racial tension."

The Bed-Stuy section evolved from two middle-class communities in nineteenth-century Brooklyn: Bedford (to the west) and Stuyvesant (to the east). These communities contained German, Jewish, Italian, Chinese, Greek, and Irish immigrants. Blacks continued to move into the area; by 1940, Bed-Stuy was about 25 percent Black. After World War II, it became mostly Black. Now, the mixed communities are faced with economic decline and racial tensions, due to disparities in job opportunities, education, housing, and medical care.

Other teachers were ready to add their knowledge on the subject as Carpenter raised her hand to signal a pause. She was a true diplomat and never intended to make anyone uncomfortable or unnecessary. "I appreciate that you all have some valuable experience to share, and as we continue to meet on this subject, I want to ensure that you will have your turn telling your stories. But since it's the end of the day, let's quickly get through what Donna has prepared." Everyone understood and accepted their leader's request.

As the handouts made their way around the table, each teacher gave them a quick scan. Donna explained the approach for future meetings and the subject material: "We decided to conduct a monthly meeting to report any incidents in the wider educational community so that we remain aware of racist activity. We won't delay the meeting if we observe any racism in our school. It should be reported immediately so we can initiate action quickly." There were more head nods, no interruptions.

Carpenter emphasized, "Yes, immediately!"

Donna shifted into interaction with the other teachers. "Please look at the category columns and the bullet points under each for a moment. While this was the first cut between Mary and me, we want your feedback. Your experience with these age groups is invaluable, so any refining will be helpful." The teachers' faces brightened slightly as they heard their opinions mattered.

There was not one Black teacher among them. Yet, they understood that they needed to consider that they could "walk in one's shoes" to appreciate what needed to be done to comprehend any racist behavior and its effect fully. Dr. Carpenter had made this point clear in the past, as she would always call on any Black perspective that may have been available. She always tried to consider the Black community's view as much as possible.

Donna proceeded, "Okay, age group six to eight. Young minds have a good sense of right and wrong, but transitioning to the 'age of reason' varies among children in their development. It is widely accepted that the 'age of reason' is five to seven." This being the first bullet under the age groups, she turned to the others. "Ages nine to ten generally have a clear sense of right and wrong. And, finally, ages eleven through thirteen have a clear sense of right and wrong and an increasing ability to apply logic."

These definitions appeared to be widely accepted, as some teachers interjected with, "Yes, in general, this seems to be the case" or "Works for me."

Before going any further into the actions for each group that teachers would employ, she initiated a short discussion of how each age group would react to the story of the bottle of acid thrown by a Black student, or if they witnessed this terrible act.

Lopez quickly reacted, "Oh goodness, I think my first-grade kids would be horrified, very scared, and probably cry if they saw such a thing!"

Second-grade teacher Angela Mancini agreed but added, "I think my students would ask, 'Why did he do that?' They would be confused as well as scared."

Gracie Benson said, "My fifth-grade class would probably have some sense of racist activities, especially if they observed something in the news on TV or witnessed racist acts in a playground, store, or other public location." She added, "They may not fully understand the reasons for such behavior."

Rivera added, "In my previous seventh-grade classes in Bed-Stuy, we had several occasions to discuss racial violence; the students were well aware of the tensions of our times and were generally in favor of eliminating racism. However, I also observed students who felt otherwise and were perhaps influenced by their parents' attitudes. Not everyone wants to see civil rights extended to all."

"Okay, good points. Anyone else?" After a short pause, Donna worked her way down the handout. "Tiny steps. Ages six to eight need tiny steps when it comes to teaching and enforcing good relationships among their classmates. Consider their minds and comprehension, especially of right from wrong. Racism is complex. We all know that. We must also communicate our approach to their parents and emphasize that they should continue with tiny steps at home. This would be important to bring up at the next Parents' Night. So, please work that into your meetings with the parents."

The meeting progressed well up to this point, but comments became more intense as the discussion shifted to the next age group.

The janitor, Jamal Brown, a sixty-year-old, was also in attendance at the meeting. He was the youngest of nine children in his family. His mother thought he was the most beautiful of all her babies and aptly named him "Jamal," meaning "handsome" or "beautiful." Carpenter considered everyone on her staff to be important, and since Mr. Brown was Black, he might have a perspective at the meeting that others could not provide.

Brown smiled as he looked around the table. "Well, if I may?"

Donna and Carpenter replied, "Yes, Jamal, please go ahead!"

"In all my years, I seen some bad stuff, Whites and Blacks at each other, fightin', cussin', using bad language and name callin'. I even seen it in our school here, in the halls 'specially. But I don't say nothin', I mind my business."

Carpenter looked at Brown with a smile and said, "Mr. Brown, you do not need to be concerned here. Like everyone else, you are part of this school, and your opinion matters. You have better insight than most, and we believe you can help, so please go on."

Brown was not used to such acceptance in his past, but realized times were changin'. He said, "Thank you, Dr. Carpenter. I know boys get bad upbringin' 'cause they say things that they say they heard from their parents. That their White daddy says, like, 'don't mix with them Black boys. They just get you in trouble,' or Black kids saying the same thing about White kids." He made a point of distinction that seemed to resonate with the previous age group analysis. "I don't mean the little kids, just the older ones. They gettin' bad learnin' from their folks."

At this point, Donna asked, "Mr. Brown, what do you think we should do for these older kids?"

"Not sure I got the answer, but I know when I was growin' up, my momma and daddy always told me and my eight brothers and sisters to treat others the way we want to be treated, nice and respectful like. I seen with my own eyes that many times that worked, but there always be exceptions. What you all said about 'tiny steps' makes sense to me. Start young, even with babies a few years old, before school. I think they learn a lot before we even know it!"

"You are absolutely right, Jamal."

Hearing Donna call him by his first name again made him feel even more important and accepted at the meeting. Otherwise, it would be counterproductive to the meeting objectives.

The discussion continued as the dedicated group felt they were taking some reasonable first steps for their school. Everyone participated in some short side stories that lent credibility to their thoughts on the breakdown of age groups and associated actions. They wanted to make a difference. They were all in!

Chapter 4

THE SPALDING

During playtime one afternoon for Lopez's class, the day was bright and warm, and the children were engaged in several activities. One group of girls was at the swings and seesaws; another small group of boys and girls was running around the grounds in an apparent race to a designated finish line. Nick was playing catch with the two White friends he had previously met. Taylor was with three other Black boys separated by some distance as they tried to bounce a pink Spalding high-bounce ball with black lettering to one another. They laughed as they tried to see who could bounce it the highest.

"Whoa, that's really high," said one boy. Taylor tried to catch it, but he dropped it. He picked it up. "I can bounce it higher," he said. He put all his strength into launching a winner, and his buddies acknowledged that he did.

"Wow, that *is* higher," said another boy. He shouted, "My turn," as heads from many of the other kids turned in response.

Eddie grabbed the ball and gave it everything he could. He hurled it into the ground, and the Spalding took on a new shape as it rebounded upward. All eyes were on the pink sphere as it ascended in an arc that finally gave way to gravity. Taylor was in a position to catch it, but realized it would go behind him as it descended. What appeared to be everything in slow motion suddenly ended quickly, as Taylor, eyes focused on the ball, backed up abruptly, moments away from a catch, and bumped hard into Nick, whose back was turned. They both fell to the ground. The young crowd saw the impact and stared in silence.

Nick's friends stood motionless and wide-eyed. Taylor's friends, likewise. Nick slowly got up and rubbed his left arm. It had been bruised slightly due to the fall. Taylor saw his friends looking at him as he raised himself from the ground. Neither boy had seen the other at this point, but as they stood up fully, they now faced each other by mere inches, eye to eye. They were the same height. The Spalding came to rest a few feet from them.

Lopez had not seen the collision. Her attention was averted briefly as she engaged in conversation with another teacher. But the abrupt silence got her attention, and she began to approach Taylor and Nick. Her mind was immediately full of questions: *What happened? Did someone get hurt?* She saw a White boy and a Black boy facing one another at close range. They were not smiling. *Oh no*, she thought. With about twenty feet between them, Lopez stopped in her tracks. She observed something that eased her mind and piqued her curiosity.

After what seemed like an eternity, Taylor smiled and extended his hand for a handshake with Nick. Nick looked down at the gesture and returned his eyes to Taylor. He then broke into a smile of his own. Smiles and handshakes intact, the other children returned to their own activities. Lopez gave a sigh of relief, smiled, and returned to her post. She glanced at the group, and especially at Nick and Taylor again to verify what she had just witnessed. She would want to relate this to the other teachers at some point, as she was very proud of Nick and Taylor's behavior.

Thoughts swirled in the heads of Nick and Taylor. This was a new experience for both. The "accident" was neither of the boys' fault, nor were there any bad feelings that resulted from it. They were having fun, and now, all of a sudden, they were thrust upon one another in the next phase of their relationship, moving from curious stares on day one to handshakes and smiles on day 2. Nick glanced away to the other Black boys now standing closely behind Taylor. Taylor observed this as he, in turn, shifted his focus to Nick's friends. The two groups continued to silently watch for the next thing to happen: a fight, yelling at one another.

Taylor shifted into the verbal phase, hands still in an embrace, smiles still traded. "Hi, I'm Taylor. Did you get hurt?" as he noted the bruise on Nick's left arm.

Nick looked at his arm, "No, just a scrape; I'm okay. When I got up and first saw you, I thought you were gonna hit me."

"No, why would I do that?"

"I don't know." Nick couldn't quite explain why he had that thought.

"I wouldn't hit my new friend!"

Nick's smile broadened as he replied, "I like being your friend!"

Taylor matched Nick's new level of smiling, "Good, me too!"

The White and Black groups overheard and gasped at the dialogue between Nick and Taylor. Whatever thoughts they may have had about people of color other than their own, they were briefly put aside as they saw the birth of a friendship emerge, committed by a White boy and a Black boy! The two groups slowly became one as they expanded the games of "catch" and "bounce the ball the highest." The class was coming together in a relationship as Lopez had hoped.

The bell rang; playtime was over. As the children settled in for the afternoon, they looked around the classroom, especially at Nick and Taylor and the other groups that seemed separate but were now becoming one. These young minds could easily grasp and accept the spirit of friendship. Nick and Taylor didn't realize just how much their behavior influenced their classmates.

Chapter 5

SLAMMIN' SAM

Police officer Shamus O'Reilly slammed the door on Maurice Kessler, a Black student from Thomas Jefferson High School who decided it would be fun to give a classmate, David Ozersky, a White student, a facial acid bath, and in the process, injured several others who would have permanent reminders of the incident. O'Reilly was a proud member of the 75th Precinct and, like many other police officers serving the community, was a veteran of World War II. He was committed to waging war on racism and gang-related activity in his neck of the woods.

After a long interrogation, he could not determine any specific motive for the attack other than it occurred during the period of heightened racial tension in New York City schools. The attack sparked a citywide debate about juvenile delinquency and school safety.

Shamus' father, Francis, a retired New York City cop, gave him his first name as "a shamus," which was slang for "police officer," and he had hoped his son would follow in his footsteps. Francis had a good friend and Black partner cop named Samuel, who became Shamus's godfather. Francis honored Samuel by giving his son, Shamus, the middle name Sam.

In the course of Shamus's twenty-one years of service, he had earned a reputation for locking up more punks and hoodlums than anyone could count—Black, White, Latino—and it didn't matter if it was a minor skirmish or an all-out rumble in a gang war. As the statistics piled up, he was embellished with the title "Shamin' Slammin' Sam," or for those who preferred to shorten it, "Slammin' Sam."

The jail doors did indeed slam loudly and faster than the criminals' realization of the error of their ways. Shamus would always follow his door-banging ritual by peering into the eyes of the new residents behind bars with, "Get comfortable, morons, you ain't goin' anywhere anytime soon!" He would accompany his words with a few solid taps on the jail bars with his nightstick, better known as a billy club, for a little extra communication and intimidation.

Two other racially motivated incidents happened the same day, and the precinct was on high alert for further criminal activity in East New York. The less serious of the day was also at Thomas Jefferson High School, where a fight broke out between White and Black students in the halls between afternoon classes. After some investigation, it was determined that some White boys did not like their Black classmates talking with White girls. Shouting and name-calling rapidly escalated to racial slurs, shoving, hurling fists, and kicking those who ended up on the floor, while other students who shouted in support were equally met with those who shouted, "Stop fighting!"

The school nurse, Emily Smith, was notified immediately and was prepared to treat several boys from both sides. The high school principal, Evan Walters, ran to the fight scene as several teachers broke up the melee and escorted the wounded to the nurse's station. "What have we got here?" He could only anticipate the wrath that would come from the students' parents, whether their sons were involved or not. *How could Jefferson High allow this to happen?*

Emily did a quick superficial examination of five students and, after asking each of them questions, determined that most of them appeared to have minor cuts and bruises. Fortunately, the injuries were nowhere near as severe as the acid bath a few days ago. However, one student, Buddy Mason, was having trouble breathing. Emily suspected a broken rib or ribs and called the closest hospital. Buddy had received most of the kicking and was moaning from the pain. As Walters got on the phone to call Mason's parents, his mind prepared him for the storm to follow.

After the shock of the news and an outburst from Buddy's father, Walters tried to calm him down. "Mr. Mason, I can assure you that your son is in good hands at Beth-El Hospital in Brownsville. It appears he may have broken ribs from the fight, but we don't know yet for sure. We are monitoring his status closely. I assume you will make your way to the hospital. I can meet you there."

Henry reacted as Walters expected, "How can you allow something like this to happen in your school? The hospital just called me and told me they are taking X-rays and said it is highly likely that he has broken ribs! I intend to find out who injured my son, and you can expect to hear from me soon." Before he hung up, he said slowly and loudly, "Do not meet me at the hospital!"

Walters' "I'm sorry, Mr. Mason," was interrupted by the click. He knew he'd better advise the superintendent ASAP. William Handly did not receive the news well.

"Walters, I am getting more and more calls across Brooklyn about racial tensions ranging from classroom brawls to gun violence, and just the other day, some Black kid throwing acid at a White kid! I want a full report by the end of the day on the actions you intend to take. It better be comprehensive: your plan to prevent this from happening again, or any other racially motivated violence; your interaction with the parents to assure them that Thomas Jefferson High School will be proactive; and particularly with the entire student body, that this behavior is wrong and will not be tolerated. I expect some expulsions to come from this!"

As Walters winced in silent pain as he dared not interrupt Handly, he could only squeeze in a "Yes, sir," before he heard the second abrupt telephone click of the day. He called a crucial meeting immediately, as did Dr. Carpenter at PS 91. He could only think, *This crap is getting worse and worse in our schools and community!*

The first step Walters took was to get on the school's public address system just ten minutes before the bell signaled the end of classes for the day. "Teachers and students, this is Principal Walters. At the end of class for today, remain in your seats for an important announcement. It will only take a few minutes. Thank you."

There was no mystery here. Everyone by now had heard of the Jefferson H.S. fight, the rumors about who was involved, and that someone had been taken to the hospital. They knew what was coming. The bell rang. Teachers reminded their students to remain seated as some instinctively jumped at the sound of the bell. Now, all settled, albeit impatiently, they listened to Walters.

"Today is a sad day in our school. The fight between White and Black students does not represent the character and mutual respect of the majority of our students. You are all entitled to a safe environment while attending class. That being said, everyone's responsibility—teachers, other staff members, *and* students—is to ensure that safety is maintained. It took a few irresponsible individuals to escalate a preventable incident into a fight that injured some and sent one student to the hospital. Our school will now be under the microscope, and parents will all wonder who among you will be the next perpetrators or victims. You do not want a stain on your record. I will contact the parents of all involved and all parents to assure them that this will not happen again here at Thomas Jefferson. I request and urge you all to do your part. Dismissed."

The students wanted out of there and quickly departed their classrooms. Some students knew the boys involved in the fight, but even more importantly, they knew they were part of wider groups, young and upcoming gangs that were the seeds of more considerable trouble ahead.

The second incident was worse as it involved weapons of the day— knives, metal pipes, baseball bats. These seemed to provide more satisfaction than guns to the givers of hate. Three White men entered a grocery store where a Black man worked one of his three jobs—the others being a part-time janitor and a night watchman at a warehouse storage facility, one of the last standing as "urban renewal" encroached the area. The White gang suspected the grocery man of stealing from them at the facility where they worked and decided to teach him a lesson.

While one man raised a steel pipe that held the owner, Frank Moretti, positioned at the cash register at bay, the other two chased and cornered Reggie "Smokes" Johnson. "Smokes" was an apt name as he was rarely observed without a cigarette in his mouth, even now as it dropped to the floor in his haste to escape. While one man stabbed Reggie in his stomach, the other one picked up the cigarette and applied burns to Reggie's arm and face before they cracked the baseball bat across his shins and knees and made a quick escape. Reggie was bleeding out and couldn't move.

If it were not for Moretti, who quickly called the police and went to aid the victim by applying some severe pressure on his abdomen, Smokes may not have survived. Although he went through some problematic nicotine withdrawal while hospitalized for several weeks, he managed to pull through after surgery. He returned home in a wheelchair with casts on both legs and eventually transitioned to crutches. He kept his job at the grocery store and expanded his janitorial services, ensuring he would never return to the warehouse again. Nor would he ever walk the same again.

While Smokes had to fess up to the theft at the warehouse and face some charges that were dropped, he at least had the satisfaction that the police could make quick links to the crime and arrest the three thugs.

This was not the East New York that its law-abiding residents clamored for, as crimes, especially those racially defined and gang-related, grew exponentially. Difference, discrimination, and power fueled the division and hatred, not only between Black people and Whites, but between Whites and Puerto Ricans, Jews and Gentiles, and other groups.

A reminder of interracial tension and related crime that would capture the attention of Brooklynites and NYC in general, would be related to the Romeo and Juliet-inspired story—*West Side Story*, where rival teenage gangs struggle to control the streets in their neighborhood.

Officer O'Reilly somehow found his way into these racially-motivated incidents, as he usually geared up to add to his statistics in the "Slammin' Sam" category. Billy club at the ready, he loved his job!

Chapter 6

"It Doesn't Sound Like Nothing Serious!"

As the school year progressed toward winter, the children at PS 91 were well established in a learning routine, interacting with new friends inside and outside the classroom. They looked forward to holiday celebrations and hoped the magic white stuff would blanket the hills that would become their sledding playground.

Taylor and Nick continued to be the glue that unified the kids of different colors. Color didn't matter to them, as these six-year-olds enjoyed the fun of being together, whether it was learning, singing, or bouncing the Spalding outside. In fact, since Taylor and Nick's collision, more kids have been interested in the game. Pink balls were flying all over the playground. The two young boys emerged as leaders. The others observed and imitated the friendly relationship that defined their behavior—kids molded by kids, innocent and simplistic.

Lopez had a front-row seat for this development and could not be happier with how the school year unfolded. Except for the occasional query from some parents regarding slow learning in one or two areas, her communication with the parents went very well, and she assured them she would give full attention to improving those who needed it. She would use Taylor and Nick's encounter to express, "All her students embraced ethnic and racial differences in her class; they are learning and interacting in harmony with one another." This was in no small part due to how Lopez used Nick and Taylor's relationship for her class to reinforce the importance and benefits of friendship, and interracial harmony.

PS 91 was on track for a good year so far, without the scourge of racism that had been popping up at other schools in the area. However, the parents were a little more than concerned about it spreading to their children. They had heard Dr. Carpenter speak at Parents Night and learned about the proactive steps to prevent racist behavior at their school. But they were also aware through the news media of the recent racial incidents at nearby Jefferson High School and the grocery store encounter. Adding to this, the wider NYC area did not have any lack of frequent racial outbreaks and gang violence. *West Side Story* seemed to spread from upper Manhattan to all five boroughs.

The Jefferson High School students involved in the recent hallway brawl received severe reprimands from the school and some of their parents. No one was expelled from school or even suspended, as it was considered a first offense. Not all parents believed their kids were to blame. After the police investigation of the incident, it was determined that Buddy Mason initiated the fight by taunting some of the Black kids. When the Black kids' parents heard this and knew he ended up at the hospital, many would say to themselves, *Good, he deserved it!*

Henry Mason seriously considered filing a lawsuit against the New York City Public School System, but reconsidered once the police notified him of their findings. He complained to the law enforcement authorities that his son could have been killed by "those Black bastards." Still, they informed him that the school superintendent told the police that the school system might file a countersuit against the Masons if necessary. Eventually, no one wanted a lawsuit on their records, and the whole issue deflated quickly. Parents just wanted this behind them. Some students, however, thought otherwise. Their minds could not contemplate "Let bygones be bygones." That would only be a sign of weakness, spinelessness, and frailty. Instead, both sides planned their revenge. *This was not over.*

Most of their parents would agree that it was best to put the incident behind them, but a few held onto intense, home-grown prejudices throughout their lives. Their parents had instilled in them a hatred for anyone unlike their kind, and they "dutifully" passed those repugnant signs and behaviors of hatred to their children, usually by example rather than a lecture on the subject.

Just like the seeds of cancer are often undetectable, the seeds of hate and discrimination can be indolent and insidious. No one knew that a few of the boys involved in the Jefferson High incident had younger siblings at PS 91 and that these "big brothers" had imparted the same thoughts about racial and ethnic differences they believed to the younger ones. The upper-grade students at PS 91, whose older brothers served as their "inspiration" for these civil injustices, brought the seeds that would soon become visible.

The younger children's camaraderie, especially Nick and Taylor's relationship, would be tested as the environment at PS 91 would change dramatically. Dr. Carpenter and her staff's efforts would be challenged in terms of their ability to withstand the trouble on the horizon.

It was a week before the two-week Christmas holiday break. Students and teachers were looking forward to a well-earned respite after giving their best effort to education. The weather report predicted snow, adding to the excitement of the season. In everyone's mind, *there was nothing but fun ahead!*

On Friday, December 13, Nick and Taylor's class assembled in the gym for playtime as the temperatures outside had dipped too far south for anyone's comfort. They had the usual activities they normally enjoyed outside in the gym, as well as some additional indoor game equipment. Nick and Taylor created a new game involving the Spalding ball that combined their outside bouncing game with basketball.

Isabella "Izzy" Garcia, a second-grade teacher, accompanied Lopez, whom she called "Maggie," to the gym to oversee the children's activity there. Izzy graduated in the same class as her friend at St. John's and could easily have passed for her twin sister except for her slightly darker complexion, brown hair, and shapely figure.

Their group grew to about twenty Black and White boys and girls, lined in a semicircle facing the basketball net. Each member would bounce the ball toward the net and score a point if the ball went through the net. Whoever reached five points first was the winner. They were halfway through the period when they heard screaming in the distance. Everyone froze. The teacher's attention shifted from the kids in the gym to the commotion down the hall. Lopez shouted, "Did you hear that?"

Isabella replied in horror, "Yes, it sounded close, like maybe in the lunchroom!"

"I'll go and look if you stay here with the students."

"Okay, I hope it's nothing serious." Although Isabella thought to herself, *It doesn't sound like nothing serious!* Kids were screaming as they ran down the hall toward the gym. Lopez ran toward them but abruptly changed direction and ran alongside them.

"What happened?" she shouted at the horrified upper-class students in their apparent attempt to seek refuge.

It sounded as if all thirty-plus students were responding simultaneously, "They have knives; they have wooden sticks," followed by more screaming. "I think one of them has a gun!" The young children were severely shaken and confused by this sudden burst into the gym.

"Oh, my God!" Lopez entered the gym, slammed the door closed, and peered through the glass enclosure of the door as she told Isabella to get something to barricade it. Her first instinct was to protect the children in the gym, but she was also worried that others might be trying to flee and find safety. "Keep an eye on the hall for any others running this way. Whoever started this has knives, sticks, and possibly a gun!"

"A gun!" Isabella put her hand to her mouth. She began to cry. Many of the children were crying.

"Izzy, our first job is to make sure our kids are safe! See that room across the gym?"

"Yes?"

"Run over there and see if that room will hold everyone and can be locked from the inside!"

Isabella ran promptly without answering while the children in the gym were all wide-eyed and frightened at the turn of events. "Children, Miss Garcia may call you to the room over there, so please pay attention. Everything will be okay," Lopez hoped.

Lopez carefully looked through the glass and saw several teachers and Carpenter responding to the screams in the lunchroom. The lunchroom door was barricaded. They could not enter, but they could look through the glass enclosures. They were horrified. Several children, Black and White, were on the floor with various injuries. There was blood. It was Carpenter's worst nightmare. She directed Donna, standing beside her, to contact the police. Images of incidents in her past began to swirl in her head, but her first and only action right now was to prevent any further injury, or worse, at PS 91.

The police response took about five minutes, as some patrol cars were nearby. At first, two patrol cars arrived, and four officers entered the school. Once they communicated with Carpenter, they requested additional resources and quickly assessed the situation, paying particular attention to the barricaded door.

The surrounding residential community could not avoid hearing the police sirens, and most certainly could not unsee the growing police presence at PS 91. While some officers entered the school, others directed the onlookers to a greater distance as they were unsure if the threat would extend outside the school. Establishing a "safety barrier" for the inquisitive neighbors was imperative. It would not be long before word reached the press, and they would arrive at the scene. Neighbors bombarded the police with questions that they could not answer without further information.

"I'm Principal Carpenter. We heard screaming from the lunchroom! About twenty-five to thirty kids ran out and went toward the gym. The door is locked or barricaded; we can't get in. It looks like several students were injured, and I don't know how serious their injuries are. There are still many others trapped in there!" She was beginning to hyperventilate and looked as if she would faint.

Sergeant McGuire put his hand on Carpenter's shoulder, "Okay, Mrs. Carpenter, take a deep breath. We are here, with other police officers outside, and more are responding. Johnny, escort Mrs. Carpenter and these others outside the school. Keep everyone back."

"Yes, sir. C'mon, ladies, this way, please!"

McGuire got on his two-way radio, "This is Conan. I am just outside the school lunchroom in the hallway. The door is barricaded. I can see injured kids on the floor, some blood, and others being held by five or six White males who are waving knives and clubs at them. Call for ambulances. There are windows on the north side of the room, so get over there ASAP. Let me know when you are in place!"

"Yes, sir, on our way!"

"Someone, bring me a megaphone!"

"On the way, sir!" McGuire had the megaphone in his hand in less than thirty seconds.

"This is Sergeant McGuire with the New York Police Department. The school is surrounded by police. We don't want any further injuries. Drop your weapons and approach the hallway door immediately! Open the door, come out with your hands up, and keep them up!"

The perpetrators turned toward the hallway and the windows and observed the growing presence of the cops. They did not move as they turned their attention from taunting the students to slowly lowering their devices of hate.

"I will not repeat this before I have every cop here bust into the room and take you by force if necessary. Drop your weapons and come out with your hands up!"

The power shift from wild, evil-minded youth turned to reluctant submission as they realized their *"well-planned escapade"* was coming to an end.

The apparent leader, Sonny, now dejected, turned to his cohorts in crime, "Guys, we're busted." He dropped his knife, and the others released their weapons.

In a calm voice over the megaphone, McGuire said, "That's the right thing to do, boys; now approach the door, open it, and get those hands up high." Several other police officers, weapons drawn, now accompanied him.

Outside, the curious observers noted that some police officers were returning from the other side of the school building. Questions began to fly as they pushed forward. "What's happening? What happened there? Is anyone hurt? Why are there so many police here?"

The police there responded as they have always been trained to do in these situations. "You will know more once we investigate and get all the facts. Please stand back." This did not quell the crowd.

"My daughter goes to that school. I demand to know if she is all right!"

"Yeah, my son attends this school too. We need to know if they are safe! What happened in there?"

"It appears the situation is now under control. We will get a report within a few minutes and update you!"

"What update? How can you update anything when we have no information to update?"

"Please, sir, be patient. We have implemented procedures that have eliminated any further . . . " He hesitated, as he did not want to use the word "injuries," as that would probably worsen matters. "Worries."

The crowd was not appeased. The police outside stopped answering their probing questions, accompanied by rising voices. As the distant sirens approached, the crowd turned their attention as they grew closer. The worry level escalated as soon as they recognized the vehicles as ambulances.

"Oh no!" Several of the parents attempted to run toward the school. Panic was about to erupt.

One officer said, "The ambulances are just a precaution, folks. There is no indication of any serious injuries!" He knew this was a lie but felt it was the only way to keep the crowd in line.

The lock on the lunchroom door clicked, and the door opened. As the boys exited their crime scene, the police quickly handcuffed each one. McGuire directed the officers to take the boys down the hall to a room where they could ask questions. He also got on his two-way and asked for the status outside and for a paddy wagon to transport the young mob to the police station.

"Sir, the crowd is getting out of control, especially when they saw the ambulances arrive! The paddy wagon is on the way."

"Okay, keep those civilians under control! Do you need reinforcements?"

"No, there are enough of us out here. How's the situation in there?"

"We have all the thugs handcuffed and escorted to a temporary holding area. We'll begin preliminary questioning, but I want them taken to the precinct ASAP! I'll direct one of my guys to get with the principal to prepare a carefully crafted statement that we can jointly address to the public outside. Make sure the paddy wagon approaches the school out of view of the spectators, perhaps around the opposite end of the school. I don't want them to see who we will load. Once we determine who these kids are, we'll notify the appropriate parents."

"Understood, sir."

The boys sat silently and eyed one another, some slightly shaking their heads as if to say, "No talking." The police officers noticed this nonverbal communication and notified McGuire. "We think they might be planning to keep any information close and not reveal anything."

McGuire had seen this tactic before. "Find other rooms, separate them. We get them alone, and they won't have any certainty about what the others may have revealed. Where's my paddy wagon?"

Moments later, McGuire got the message that the paddy wagon was parked behind the school unnoticed by the crowd outside. "Thanks, we're sending them out." He turned to the assisting officers. "Okay, boys, the paddy wagon is outside the back door. Load 'em up. Johnny, I want you in the wagon with these idiots. Make sure there is no talkin' or communicatin' in any way!"

"You got it, sir!"

"I'm going to meet with the principal and catch up with you at the station."

The remaining officers snapped in unison, "Yes, sir!"

A police officer was with the principal, Donna, and other teachers in Carpenter's office. He briefly spoke with McGuire and then left to support the officers outside the school. Their outlook on the Christmas break went from cheerful expectations to downright depression as they were consumed by feelings of sadness, tearfulness, anger, frustration, hopelessness, and irritability, especially after all their efforts to avoid such incidents. *How would they approach the last week of school before the holidays? How could they even celebrate the holidays?*

Chapter 7

A Burdensome Day

Several EMTs were tending to the injured children who remained on the lunchroom floor, bloodstained and in apparent shock. Two Black eighth-graders, Henry Williams and Amira Jackson, and a White boy, David Smith, a seventh-grade student, had multiple stab wounds and also suffered from blunt force trauma. They were all moaning and writhing in pain. The EMTs stabilized their wounds and asked them questions to determine the extent of their injuries. They remained conscious as they were eventually moved and transported to the ambulances outside the front door of the school.

The crowd reacted as expected when they saw three stretchers emerge from the school, each attended by EMTs. Sergeant McGuire and Principal Carpenter emerged shortly after and positioned themselves at the top step of the school entryway.

Shouting from about fifty residents filled the street with a barrage of questions: "What happened in there? Are those kids okay? Is that my kid? Why is this school not safe?" It took a few minutes to calm down the crowd as McGuire and Carpenter extended their hands in an up-and-down motion. McGuire raised the megaphone to speak, and the crowd responded with less noise.

"We responded to a call that Dr. Carpenter and the teachers heard screaming in the school. They reacted immediately to determine the cause and found a group of students being held and threatened in the lunchroom. The door had been barricaded; they couldn't get in. They observed several boys with what appeared to be clubs and a knife."

The crowd gasped, and the shouting began again. "Our kids are not safe! Who are the kids with clubs and knives? Where are they? They should be expelled from school! Why can't you protect our kids?" More questions, all directed at the policeman and principal, were flying at them like darts.

"We have the boys in custody. They were transported to the police station and will be interrogated. We'll get to the bottom of this. We will not release any names of the boys or the victims until we notify their parents."

More shouts and pointed questions: "Were any of the boys Black?" "Were any of the injured kids Black?" "Was this a racist thing?"

McGuire knew if he gave too much information now, he might have another crime scene right here outside the school, perhaps a riot. "Please, everyone, we have just begun our investigation. We will determine all the facts of this case in due course. Until then, we request your cooperation and understanding." McGuire's police resources were strategically located around the crowd in significant numbers.

"At this time, I would like to turn it over to Principal Carpenter for a brief statement. Dr Carpenter."

"We are all appalled at this incident, as you are, I can assure you. Some of the teachers reacted to the screams and took brave steps to ensure the safety of many students. If it weren't for them, we might have had more injuries. We take great pride in remaining aware of any racial tension that might be present in PS 91, and we have implemented a program of education among our entire student population focused on preventing racism."

One man from the crowd yelled, "Well, it isn't working, is it?" The crowd was energized again and became loud.

"All I can promise you is that PS 91 will do everything we can to learn from this terrible incident today and work hard in the best interests of all students. We are committed to that end."

Before the crowd could add any further displays of displeasure, McGuire took the megaphone from Carpenter. "Okay, folks, it's getting colder out here. Please return to your homes and let us do our job. The police will ensure that the boys who caused this incident today are held accountable. Thank you."

After Carpenter and McGuire reentered the building, some of the crowd dispersed; others continued to express their complete lack of trust in the police and school staff to one another. They could only think of the numerous other clashes broadcast in the news around the New York City metropolitan area.

After any remaining discussion between McGuire and Carpenter, he returned to the precinct where the questioning would begin.

Carpenter gathered her staff and directed that all students be released after notifying their parents. She did not find comfort in anticipating the subsequent flood of questions that would be thrown at her.

"Everyone, this has been a burdensome day. We all work so hard to prevent what happened here today. And what happened here today will not stop us from continuing our efforts to prevent it from happening again in any form. Enough said. Please ensure that the students reach their parents safely and return home. We have one more week before the holiday break. We must carry on next week with as much normalcy as possible."

The teachers were emotionally and physically exhausted and found no reason to add to Carpenter's comments. They all slowly rose from their chairs and went to carry out their duties.

Chapter 8

A Mason Link

The boys who wielded the clubs and knives were detained at the precinct in separate rooms. Slammin' Sam did not get a chance to do his thing but did take the opportunity to quickly visit each boy and bang his billy club on a table mere inches from them. These boys reacted with smirks and careless attitudes. They did not yet understand the seriousness of their actions. To them, Slammin' Sam was more like *West Side Story*'s Officer Krupke, a police officer whose bark was bigger than his bite, but that would not last long, as they would soon learn otherwise.

As if it were a synchronized swim, five officers entered the rooms that detained the wise-ass wannabes to begin their questioning. Officer Nelson paired up with one eighth grader.

"What's your name, son?"

"Tom Baker"

"Okay, Mr. Baker. Are you a student at PS 91?"

"Yeah," said Baker, with a smug attitude.

"How do you know the other punks that caused all this trouble at the school today?"

"They are in my eighth-grade class."

"Oh, so you all decided that it would be fun to cause a whole lot of commotion and scare and injure other kids in your school?" Baker did not answer.

"I asked you a question, Baker!"

"Yeah, I guess."

"You guess? You guessed wrong, son. You and your moron friends are in deep trouble! You know that, right?" Again, Baker did not answer.

Nelson pounded the table, got into Baker's face, and asked loudly, "Again, I asked you a question! You better answer! Whose idea was it to turn to crime rather than learn somethin' in school today?"

Baker began to see that this would not end well if he didn't cooperate. "I'm not sure; it was either Richie or Sonny. Frankie and Billy were added after the three of us started talkin'."

"Just to be sure, you mean you, Richie and Sonny concocted this great idea?"

"No, I didn't make up this idea. Like I said, it was either Richie or Sonny."

Officers Donald Foster and Peter Goodman, in the other rooms with twins Billy and Frankie Lynch, respectively, questioned the eighth graders similarly. The twins said they suspected it was a plan by Tom Baker and Sonny.

Richie was bigger than Tom and the Lynch boys, and he was not about to reveal much. He stated, "I'm no snitch. I'm not talkin'."

Officer Sean O'Neill said, "Richie, the less you talk, the bigger your trouble!"

McGuire faced off with Sonny. "You the one with the knife?" Sonny kept his mouth shut. "What's your name?"

"Sonny."

"What's your last name, Sonny?"

"Mason. I'm Sonny Mason."

"Okay, Mr. Mason, why did you and your stupid friends . . . wait a minute. Mason, . . . Mason. Are you related to a Buddy Mason?"

"Yeah, he's my older brother."

"The Buddy Mason who attends Thomas Jefferson High School?"

"Yeah."

"I'll be right back, punk!" McGuire left the interrogation room and rounded up the other officers to meet in a conference room at the precinct.

"Gentlemen, I just found out that the boy I'm questioning, Sonny Mason, is the younger brother of Buddy Mason, the Jefferson High kid who started trouble there, a racial incident. I think it was late September. Let's check that. There may be a connection with what happened today. Get ahold of Mason's parents ASAP! Contact all the parents of these idiots!"

"Yes, sir. Yes, sir." The other officers responded in unison, snapped up, and headed to the files and phones.

Beth-El Hospital's ER received the injured students and quickly assessed their conditions from the stab wounds. Henry Williams's wounds were superficial, as he was able to defend himself well enough to avoid any deep punctures or injury to any vital organs. Both Amira Jackson and David Smith had more serious wounds that resulted in a dangerous loss of blood.

Amira suffered a deep wound to her abdomen; she was immediately taken into surgery after the hospital notified her parents. Seventh-grader David was exceptionally big for his age and tried to fight off the gang. He managed to strike two of them hard enough to cause them some harm, but he was quickly overcome by the other three. He took a severe slice to his arm before the boys backed off. He was being treated in the emergency room.

The officers back at the precinct assembled again in the conference room after collecting the files from the Jefferson High School incident. They confirmed Buddy Mason's name in the case and that he was the instigator in the hallway fight. They set out to call Buddy's father, Henry Mason, or, if necessary, bring him to the police station. Through their earlier investigation, they knew that the father was belligerent with Jefferson High School principal Evan Walters over the incident.

"Okay, guys. Let's get back to questioning these spoiled brats and find out how their extracurricular activity got started." The officers returned to their respective rooms.

McGuire opened the door to where a smiling Sonny had his feet on the table. "Get your feet off my table. This is no country club! You're in serious trouble. We are trying to contact your father as we speak." The feet came down, and the smile disappeared. "Who put you up to this? Your brother, Buddy? He started a fight between Whites and Blacks at Jefferson High School in September. Seems like the Mason family has it out for Blacks! That sound about right?"

Sonny just looked at the wall and said, "I ain't saying nothin' 'til my father gets here."

"Fine, have it your way for now, but I can guarantee you, it's gonna get a lot worse for all of you!" He left the room to check with the other officers and find Henry Mason's whereabouts.

It was now five p.m. Carpenter and her staff quickly met with the police to coordinate a joint meeting of school staff members, police, and the students' parents. After quickly dividing up the complete list of parents by their children's grades, they set out to notify the parents of the meeting, scheduled for Tuesday, December 17. As calls were made, parents were naturally horrified to hear the news; they had many questions that would take the school staff way too much time to answer. This was one week before Christmas. *Just what every parent needed, a somber topic right before the holidays! And worry about their child's safety at school!*

On this terrible day, the parents of PS 91's students would have a different conversation around the dinner table and, most likely, into the evening. Like most others, Nick's and Taylor's parents wondered, *How do we even talk about this with our kids? Will they be afraid to go back to school?*

Chapter 9

"I Don't Want to Go Back to School"

Makena and Isaac Washington exchanged glances and sighed as they paused after the last hour, trying to encourage their son, Taylor, to discuss what happened at school. He was a sensitive child who had learned to be friendly with others and usually took the initiative in conversations. However, today was different. He did not respond much to his parents' questions and merely repeated, "I don't want to go back to school." The screams in the school, the rush into the gym, and the frantic efforts by teachers Lopez and Garcia were terrifying. Their fear quickly spread to Taylor and the other children. It was a shocking experience—calm and fun one moment, pure chaos the next.

Taylor's mother said, "Well, let's have dinner . . . okay? Maybe we can talk about it later, Taylor. Would that be . . . okay?"

"Okay," came back in a very low voice.

Taylor's dad tried to change the subject. "You know, son, Christmas will be here soon! Are you excited about that? Santa Claus knows you are a very good kid, and I'm sure he will bring you lots of presents! Right?"

"Yeah, I guess so."

"So there's just one week of school left before you get a break from school, and . . . "

Taylor interrupted, "I don't want to go back there!"

Mom interrupted, "Okay . . . let's not think about school right now, just Christmastime and hope for some snow so we can go down some hills on the sled together!" Taylor showed a glimmer of a smile for the first time since he got home. "Let's say grace." The Washington family held hands and whispered a short prayer together before dinner.

Before they could take one bite, the phone rang. Makena got up from the table and answered, "Hello?"

"Hello, Mrs. Washington?"

"Yes, this is she."

"Mrs. Washington, this is Donna Sweeney from PS 91." She had taken a list of students from Lopez's class to contact by phone.

"Oh, Miss Sweeney . . . may I call you Miss or Mrs.?"

"Please call me Donna. I am calling about the incident that happened at PS 91 today, and to inform you that we have worked all day today to plan a meeting with the parents on Tuesday evening, December 17, at 7 p.m."

"Oh my gosh! We have been trying to get our son, Taylor, to talk about what happened. He was in the gym at the time, but he didn't want to say anything other than that he didn't want to go back to school. What happened? And please call me Makena."

"Mrs. Washington . . . I mean Makena, I am so sorry to hear that, and I am sure many young children like Taylor have been . . . traumatized." She hesitated to use that word due to its implied severity, but couldn't think of a suitable alternative.

"Unfortunately, I cannot get into any details . . . actually, we know very little about what caused the incident. We are working with the police, and they will be at the meeting to provide the parents with as much information as possible and what their investigation revealed."

Makena was about to ask if anyone was hurt, but was interrupted by Sweeney, who said, "I'm so sorry, Mrs. Washington, but I need to drop off. We still have many calls to make this evening. I hope to see you there." She hung up before Makena could say goodbye.

"Isaac, that was the school. They are having a meeting for the parents next Tuesday night at 7 to talk about the . . . thing at school today. The police will be there too."

Before she could go further, Isaac said, "Okay, let's get our sitter for Taylor so we can both go!"

"I'll call Destiny; she's always available during the week."

Dinner was now cold.

Jonathan and Mary Greene, on the other hand, could not keep Nick from talking about what happened at school. As a quiet boy who was primarily an introvert, his reaction to the spontaneous eruption at school changed his usual calm and placid nature; he was practically nonstop repeating what he had witnessed.

He described every detail as if it were unfolding again in real time. The screams, the reaction of Lopez, her direction to Garcia, and Lopez running out the gym door, only to return quickly with a bunch of screaming kids who were very afraid of something. And all the details that followed, which culminated in the police presence and the evacuation of the teachers and children from the school. *A lot of commotion, but no clear understanding of the cause.*

Nick added a new detail that was unexpected: "I think some White kids and Black kids were fighting in the school." His parents did a double-take on this and turned to Nick, after looking very concerned at one another.

Jonathan asked, "Why do you think that? Did you see anyone fighting?"

"No, I didn't see them, but when we came out of the school, I heard some people sayin' that."

Mary asked, "What else did they say?"

"I don't remember, but there was some 'ambalances.' I heard the sirens from the 'ambalances.' "

Jonathan quickly asked, "Ambulances? Did you see anyone who got hurt? Did you hear anybody say anyone got hurt?"

Nick thought briefly, "I don't remember; I don't think I heard anybody got hurt, Daddy."

Just when Jonathan wanted to probe further, they received a call from Lopez. Mary answered. "Hello, this is Mary."

"Good evening, Mrs. Greene, this is Miss Lopez. How is Nicholas doing? I'm so worried about him and all his classmates . . . what they experienced today."

"Miss Lopez, Nick has been talking about it since he got home. He's usually very quiet, as you know, I'm sure, but . . . how are you doing? I'm sure this has been difficult for you and the other teachers. Can you tell us anything . . . did anyone get hurt? Nick said ambulances were there!"

"Well, I'm calling to notify you of a meeting next week." Lopez provided the same carefully crafted information that all the other school informants had given to the parents. She was halfway down her list of calls, and Friday had been a long and stressful day.

Mary explained the call to her husband, adding, "We have to go to that meeting!" He nodded in agreement. *They wouldn't miss it.*

Chapter 10

THE BROOKLYN SHACK

Captain Francis O'Rourke summoned his lieutenants and sergeants for the status of the investigation of the PS 91 incident. It was Saturday, December 14, and the interrogation of the five boys made little progress other than their accusing each other of contemplating the heinous deed.

He directed them, "Well, stay on it! Put the pressure on those brats! I have grandkids who are in elementary school, and I am pissed that young kids like that become victims of stupidity and hate! I've been in contact with Principal Carpenter at PS 91. They are working with the school staff over the weekend to coordinate a meeting with the parents. I . . . um . . . believe they are targeting Tuesday evening, December 17. I plan to attend the meeting and want a few of you who responded at the school to be there with me."

A unified "Yes, Sir," echoed back strongly.

O'Rourke was a proud officer who did everything he could to prolong the long but waning history of Irish contributions to the NYPD. He worked his way up the ranks, beginning as a community liaison officer, engaging with the community, moving quickly into forensic and crime scene investigation, and eventually, as a patrol officer and detective in the force. He was highly decorated for his actions and success. His record and leadership inspired others to follow in his footsteps.

The investigative team decided to move some police assets to "The Brooklyn Shack," a rented storefront office located in nearby Prospect Heights at the intersection of Bergen Street and Sixth Avenue. It was a shared space for newspapers and police reporters where criminal activity could be gathered and disseminated. Elements of the *Brooklyn Eagle* and the *Daily News* were always present, eager to be the first to report the up and coming in the world of crime.

McGuire and others started populating a chalkboard of suspects, named as such only because they were yet unsure who actually inspired the plan for the incident at PS 91 and who had inflicted the injuries. They were hell-bent on getting to the bottom of it, and they would eventually transition from investigation to corroborating with the Department of Corrections, whose mandate was the custody, care, and control of individuals arrested and awaiting trial or serving short sentences in the city's jail system. The NYPD was responsible for law enforcement, maintaining public order, and investigating crimes. While separate, the NYPD and DOC worked together toward one goal—to eventually move criminals to a state of unhappiness behind bars.

The interrogation officers of the five boys shared the information they had garnered during their initial discussions with them. They had names, now listed on the chalkboard, but conflicting answers as to who thought up the idea of attacking the students at PS 91 or what the motive was. They established that Sonny Mason was the younger brother of Buddy Mason and suspected that there may be a connection between the incident at Jefferson High School and PS 91. *But what was it?*

At the top of the board, they chalked in the name "Henry Mason" with arrows directed to his two sons. By this time, they had contacted all the boys' parents except for Mason. They could not reach him or Sonny's mother. They had the addresses where each boy lived and went to Mason's house, but he was not home. They checked with neighbors who mostly said Henry Mason kept to himself and did not converse much with anyone. They also said they never saw the kid's mother . . . never saw her.

One neighbor, however, said that when he first met Henry, he mentioned that he worked at a Bush Terminal warehouse in Industry City, located at the Upper New York Bay waterfront in the Sunset Park neighborhood of Brooklyn. He also said he believed the mother had died a few years ago. Police dispatched a patrolling unit to check the terminal and determine if Mason was present.

"Ten-four, on our way," was the reply.

In its early days, the terminal had six warehouses and a pier on Twenty-Fifth Street. Over time, it grew into a sixteen-building complex, so there was a lot of ground to cover to find Henry Mason or information about him. The initial patrol unit requested a few extra resources, if available, to cover the area. They arrived within twenty minutes.

Chapter 11

THE RED AND WHITE 1956 CHEVY BEL AIR

The police team for the investigation worked through the weekend, and it was now late Monday afternoon. They wanted to uncover the motive and details of the perpetrators, which would result in accountability and justice, and also to provide answers to anxious, and most likely, angry and worried parents.

McGuire addressed the team, "Okay, so far, we all know that these kids, as young as they are . . . all thirteen years of age, are buttoned-up tight. Not sayin' much. What I sense is an attitude of hate. It's not anything they said because they ain't said much. I just can't put my finger on it."

Officer Nelson said, "I was putting the pressure on the Baker kid, and he finally came back with, 'Talk to Sonny.' I told him, 'when I asked you who was behind this before, you said it was either Richie or Sonny,' so . . . who is it? He then repeated, 'Talk to Sonny.' "

Slammin' Sam jumped in. "I been questionin' Sonny. Real snot-nose kid. Scoffs a lot like this is some kinda party. Anyway, I pressed him about his brother, Buddy . . . that he was found guilty of startin' the fight at Jefferson High. That made him a bit uncomfortable . . . I sensed I hit a nerve. I asked him if his brother had anything to do with what happened at PS 91. He shifted in his seat and looked a little attentive for a change. Anyone been able to reach the father or Buddy?"

As he heard the last portion of Shamus's report, Captain O'Rourke entered the room and said, "We've been lookin' for Henry Mason all weekend, at his home, at his place of work at the Bush

Terminal warehouses. We had several of our guys go through the entire complex over there and speak with several workers. No one knew the whereabouts of Mason, but they all said he was one 'weirdo,' kept to himself most of the time, but that there were some other men who come to pick him up now and then while he left his car, a red and white 1956 Chevy Bel Air, at the warehouse where he worked. We need to follow up on that more with some surveillance. We returned to his house, and neither Senior Mason nor his son, Buddy, was there—no sign of Buddy's mother either. A source from Mason's neighborhood said he believed she died a few years ago. Some of you may not know that Buddy was released from custody due to a first-time offense. He is under the microscope at Jefferson High, and he knows it, being really careful, I suspect. Keep at it!"

"Yes, sir," was loud and clear.

Officers Foster and Goodwin, who interrogated the Lynch twins, reminded the team that the boys initially pointed the finger at Tom Baker and Sonny Mason, but that they, too, now separately implicated Sonny as the leader.

McGuire summed up a few less relevant points for the team and ended with, "Okay, all of you except Shamus, go home, get some rest, kiss the wife, hug the kids, go back to life as it should be. We'll tackle this again tomorrow morning. We'll get surveillance on the Masons. Thanks." The team departed, and Shamus approached McGuire.

"What's up, Conan?"

McGuire said with a grin, "Let's you and I go pay a visit with 'eejit' Sonny." Shamus grinned back as he appreciated the proper way for Irish to pronounce "idiot. "Oh, and bring your famous billy club!" Shamus's grin got wider. *It would be a long night for one Sonny Mason.*

The Washingtons, the Greenes, and several hundred other parents were relieved to hear that Monday at PS 91 was as typical a day as could be expected after the storm inside the school the Friday before. There was a police presence, but it was not easily visible. The dedicated staff, under the leadership of Dr. Mary Carpenter, did an excellent job of keeping the students' attention at every grade level focused on their learning.

Naturally, some students, especially those who shared classes with Henry Williams, Amira Jackson, and David Smith, were full of questions. The teachers answered them with brief replies but also with veracity. They disclosed that all three were treated at the hospital and were doing well, with Henry being released after treatment and David the next day. They also said that Amira needed surgery, but she was so fortunate not to have internal damage to the extent initially believed. She was being cared for in the hospital for a few more days, maybe the rest of the week.

At the end of class, over the school's public address system, Principal Carpenter briefly repeated the status update that the teachers had given and concluded with, "You should see them again soon," which sparked a loud cheer throughout the school. *Normalcy, how nice it feels!*

Chapter 12

PS 91 School Meeting, December 17, 1957

It was twenty minutes before 7 p.m. at PS 91. Parents arrived in droves for the meeting they were anxious to attend with the educational staff and police. Captain O'Rourke planned to attend the meeting but was called to the police chief's office for another meeting.

The parents wanted answers. *What really happened here last Friday? Are the children who were injured okay? Is my child safe?* While some children were in direct contact with the five-boy attacking team, they could only disclose to their parents what they experienced. That, coupled with the brief call from the school about the meeting, left more questions than answers.

Signs read "SCHOOL MEETING, 7 p.m., IN CAFETERIA." Once inside, other signs with arrows directed the public to the room. The cafeteria, although smaller than the gym, which had only limited rows of bleachers, was chosen due to its ability to accommodate more seating for the expected number of attendees.

The cafeteria was nearly full minutes before the top of the hour, with several hundred people engaged in a loud discussion. At that point, a call was made over the school PA system for Amira Jackson's father. "This is Principal Carpenter. Is Mr. Kevin Jackson at the meeting? If so, please come to my office immediately!" Most parents, by now, have likely heard about Amira Jackson's injury and surgery through the grapevine, but were unaware of her current status. *There was a group gasp. Hope this is not bad news!*

The room fell silent as Jackson, seated at one of the lunch tables, quickly stood and shouted, "Here, I'm Kevin Jackson! Where is the principal's office?" His face could carry no greater worry.

He was led to Carpenter's office, where his wife, Wanda, was on the phone, anxious to talk with her husband. "Mr. Jackson, it's your wife calling from the hospital. She said it was urgent but that your daughter was okay." She wanted to give him that information immediately to ease his mind about any unnecessary worry regarding Amira.

Jackson grabbed the phone. "Wanda, how is our baby doing? Principal Carpenter said you had something urgent!"

Wanda spoke in a low whisper, "Honey, Amira told me something I think you should know right away, and since the police are at the school, you should probably tell them!"

"What . . . what is it?"

"Amira said that she remembers now that the boy who stabbed her with the knife said, 'Me and my brother hate you . . . ' " She paused and said, "He used the N-word. She said he grabbed her by the arm, pulled her close, and then drew the knife from his pocket or somewhere, but he said it quietly. She doesn't think anyone else heard it."

"That son of a bitch! . . . Mrs. Carpenter, please excuse my language!" Carpenter realized his emotions were high and just nodded back. "Did she say his name?"

"Yes, she said it was a boy in her class, Sonny Mason. Go tell the police!"

"Okay, hug and kiss our baby for me, and tell her I will see her soon." They both said their "love yous" and "goodbyes."

Jackson looked at Carpenter and said, "Thank you, Ma'am. I need to get back to the meeting. I may have important information for the police." He quickly exited her office, and she was not far behind him as he sprinted back to the cafeteria.

The inquisitive crowd was waiting for Principal Carpenter. All the teachers and some support staff were seated at a table that faced the parents. Sergeant McGuire and several fellow patrolmen, including O'Reilly, were angled adjacent to the teachers at a separate table. Carpenter entered, picked up a microphone, and was about to begin the meeting. She noticed that Jackson whispered something to McGuire, and they were in a conversation that no one else could hear. She waited until Jackson was seated. He nodded at her in appreciation for her patience.

Dr. Carpenter took a step toward the audience before her. You could hear a pin drop. "Dear parents, thank you for coming here tonight. As you can see from your turnout, our school presence, and police representation that we all take the incident that occurred here at PS 91 last Friday very seriously." Some murmurs were heard throughout the room.

She continued as the murmurs dissipated. "Our top priority . . . our most important priority (she felt it needed emphasis), is always the safety of your children while they are in our care here at school. Education comes next, and I want to assure you that all our preparation, planning, and actions are always toward those ends. You will all have the opportunity to ask questions of me and any of the teachers who have your children in their classes. We will do our best to answer those questions. I will then turn it over to the police. Sergeant McGuire is here with his team. Sergeant McGuire and some of the other officers were the ones who quickly responded on Friday and kept this terrible incident contained." She nodded at the policemen as she said this. McGuire nodded back.

She amplified the order of information to follow. "I will give you my account of the incident and our reaction. I will then call on Miss Margaret Lopez to recount what she heard and what followed because many of the children ended up in the gym where she and Miss Garcia were overseeing the first- and second-grade children there. Hopefully, this information will address some of the questions you have.

"In the early afternoon on Friday, approximately 1:20 p.m., we heard screaming. It appeared to come from right where we are tonight, the cafeteria. The later lunch group of upper graders would have just finished lunch here. Most other classes were in their respective rooms, except for the first- and second-grade children, who were in the gym. We did not conduct their playtime outside due to the frigid weather. Several other teachers and I immediately ran toward the cafeteria, where a group of students came out of the door screaming and ran toward the gym. The door quickly slammed shut and was barricaded. We could not get in. I directed Miss Donna Sweeney, one of our eighth-grade teachers and school counselor, who was with me in my office when we heard and responded to the screams, to call the police immediately. The police responded within about five minutes.

"I want to turn it over to Miss Lopez now so she can explain how things unfolded from there. After she is done, we will take your questions and then move them to the police. Miss Lopez." Carpenter handed the mic to her.

Lopez was nervous. She was a novice in her first year of teaching and was bombarded with tragedy in a place she considered safe, a place she considered beautiful, a place where only happiness was expected. She took a deep breath and regained her composure as she recalled what Carpenter told her while preparing for this meeting: "Maggie, just be yourself and tell precisely what you observed and did. You and Izzy should be proud of your instincts and actions to protect your students. I am proud of you both."

Compliments and encouragement to young teachers never hurt; they go a long way toward building self-confidence. Carpenter knew that; her years of experience taught her that.

"Good evening, everyone. I teach first grade here at PS 91. I was in the gym for student playtime." She turned and held out a hand gesture toward Izzy Garcia. "Izzy, . . . um, . . . I mean Miss Garcia was with me in the gym. All the children were playing and having a good time as they always do. They all get along very well." She smiled for a moment.

"We heard something and didn't know what it was at first, but as we looked through the glass on the gym doors, we saw a bunch of kids running toward the gym, screaming. We also saw Principal Carpenter and some teachers at the cafeteria door, but they couldn't get in. I went out to run toward the kids to see why they were running, but they wouldn't stop; they almost all passed me. I turned back with them, and we closed the gym doors and locked them. I asked Miss Garcia to check a room across the gym to see if it was big enough for all the kids and if it had a door lock to keep them safe. She ran over to check and waved at me to send the kids. I directed them to the room, but before joining her, I looked down the hall to make sure no other students were left out there. The next thing I knew, the police were there. Thank you." There was sporadic clapping from the parents, which escalated to almost the entire audience.

Carpenter reclaimed the mic. She hoped that the narrative she and Maggie shared would eliminate many questions, but she also sensed that realism would prove otherwise.

Chapter 13

THE FAMILIES MEET

During the presentations by Carpenter and Lopez, McGuire had leaned over to O'Reilly's ear and quietly disclosed what he had heard from Amira's father. He also told him that he had asked Jackson not to bring that up at the school meeting and that the police were investigating the connection between the brothers. O'Reilly turned, looked at McGuire, and smiled. He whispered back, "We were right, Conan. That little bastard had some inspiration! Our instincts on a connection between those two were right on. Want me to call the captain?"

"He should probably know this right away, so we can track down Buddy and his old man as soon as possible."

O'Reilly snapped back as he rose to make a call, "Copy that."

Carpenter addressed the group, "Okay, ladies and gentlemen, we have some teachers throughout the cafeteria with microphones so anyone asking a question can be heard clearly. I ask that we do this in an orderly fashion, one question at a time, and we will do our best to answer each one."

The father of an eighth-grade student raised his hand and was given a microphone. "Dr. Carpenter (he knew her with this title since his son came up through the grades at PS 91), I am Vincent Gallo. My son, Vinnie, is in Mrs. Sweeney's eighth-grade class. He was in the room when several boys attacked the other kids in here. Did you see any of the attacks and the injured kids?"

"When we arrived at the cafeteria doors and looked in, we saw two boys and a girl on the floor, and the ones with weapons that looked like clubs and knives were threatening others up against a wall. We did not see the attacks as they happened."

Before she could go any further, Kevin Jackson raised his hand and requested a mic as he shouted, "I can add to that!" McGuire was about to come unglued as he thought Jackson would spill the beans on the language used by Sonny Mason while attacking his daughter. Jackson noted McGuire's uneasiness and held up a hand toward him.

"My daughter, Amira, was the student who received the most harm. The two others, boys, were injured less seriously and were released from the hospital. Amira is doing okay after surgery. She suffered some damage to her internal organs, but the doctors at Beth-El Hospital did a great job! She will be there for a while, but she is safe and recovering." The crowd clapped, accompanied by encouraging comments and best wishes.

A woman in the audience raised her hand and asked for the mic. "Hello, my name is Elana Sanchez. My daughter, Sofia, is also in eighth grade. She has been at PS 91 since the fourth grade, when we moved to East New York. She was not in the cafeteria when the incident occurred. She was talking with her classmates today, and they said they all thought this was aimed at the Black students, even though a White boy was hurt. Is that true?"

McGuire immediately stood and spoke before Carpenter could respond. "Mrs. Sanchez—Dr. Carpenter, please allow me to answer that question."

Carpenter replied, "Please, Sergeant McGuire, go ahead."

"We initiated an investigation immediately after we returned to the precinct after the incident. The investigation is ongoing, and it would be premature to make any statements or conjectures as to the motive at this time. I will say that there is information that supports looking at this incident from a broader perspective. In other words, it may have been conjured up by others outside PS 91. That's all I can say and will say at this point." He hoped that it would suffice, but it didn't.

Thomas Malcolm spoke next. He stated his name and said, "I am a reporter with the *Brooklyn Eagle*. I don't have any children at this school, but I'm here in the public's interest. The implication of a wider conspiracy in this incident, especially as it may pertain to Black students, has caught my attention. I was one of the reporters who covered the story back in March 1954 about a gang war that was prevented. This decade has been one where gang wars over turf and girls, where the ages of gang members are between twelve and nineteen and are more or less divided into ethnic groups, are spreading across Brooklyn, Manhattan, and the Bronx. Sometimes, these gangs recruit younger members, a so-called 'junior' gang beneath them. We just might have that here."

As he was about to go further and imply that gangs may be specifically targeting Black people, the noise level intensified so no one could understand the person beside them. Realizing that Malcolm was introducing way too much for this crowd to digest at this time, McGuire got on the mic. "Everyone, please calm down. Please, take your seats. What Mr. Malcolm stated is valid up to a point. Gang activity is on the rise, but at this point, there is no absolute connection to the incident that occurred here at PS 91. As I said, we have some leads that may bring us to others, but there is no certainty that it is a gang, as he described. It could be someone who put the kids here up to the attack. We don't know yet . . . but we will get to the bottom of this."

As he said this, he thought of Buddy Mason but did not mention him or the incident at Jefferson High School. Luckily, no one brought that up, even though some parents knew, through their kids, that Sonny Mason had a brother in that school. McGuire said, "I am handing the mic to Principal Carpenter." Holding his hand tightly on the mic to prevent what he whispered to Carpenter from being overheard, he said, "Ma'am, you should probably bring this meeting to a close."

Just as quietly, she said, "Okay."

Principal Carpenter said calmly, "Parents . . . and others here, the night is getting long, and I think you have heard everything we can tell you. I assure you that what you heard here tonight is everything I know about the incident and what the police have told me. Let's let them do their job. As I said earlier, our top priorities at PS 91 are the safety and education of your children. We are dedicated to that, and I hope you can entrust us with keeping that promise. While distracted by this incident, your children have shown today that they are looking forward to the holiday break and are excited to celebrate. Let's all work together to make it as good as possible. Please have a good and safe rest of the evening. Thank you for attending, and good night."

McGuire and Principal Carpenter expected more pushback, but, to their surprise, most of the crowd slowly dispersed with a civil level of conversation remaining among them. A few parents were still having conversations with others they had just met. The Washingtons and the Greenes were seated next to one another. They didn't talk about their sons during the meeting and didn't realize the friend their son talked so much about over the last couple of months was the other's son.

Makena Washington said, "Our son, Taylor, didn't want to talk about what happened here last Friday, and he didn't want to return to school, but we said everything would be okay. Up until then, he was very happy in first grade and could not stop talking about his new friend, Nick. They play these games with a rubber ball . . . all the kids love it."

Mary Greene said, "Wait a minute! Our son's name is Nick, and he said a boy . . . a Black boy . . . looked at him and waved on the first day of school, and they later became friends, playing that game with the pink ball. What is it called?"

Both Isaac and Jonathan responded at the same time, "A Spalding!" They followed this with laughter.

Jonathan added, "Nick is very happy being friends with Taylor, and they seem to have brought the kids—Black and White—together, something Miss Lopez communicated to us. Nick is usually very quiet and reserved, but he could not stop talking about last Friday."

Isaac said, "I guess things like this affect children differently."

Teachers were now kindly asking the parents to leave the school. *After all, they will be back there tomorrow morning.*

The couples brought their conversation outside for a few more minutes with a commitment to get together soon, both thinking, *Our sons get along well together; their relationship is worth nurturing; the younger, the better.*

Chapter 14

YOUTH GANGS AND TURF WARS

While the school week came to an end as the PS 91 dismissal bell rang in mid-afternoon on Friday, December 20, 1957, prompting every student, this time screaming joyously, to make their exit, the police team at "the Shack" was reviewing the progress they had made in the last few days. The children and school staff turned their attention to the holidays. The police focused on casting a wider net on the root causes of the school incident.

Captain O'Rourke had a full agenda for the day, but wanted a quick update on the potential connection between the PS 91 and Jefferson High fights. McGuire presented the status with summary sheets in hand and stood next to the chalkboard.

"We now believe that Sonny Mason led the incident at PS 91. Shamus and I put extra pressure on him when we returned to the precinct after Tuesday night's school meeting. When we told him we had a witness that overheard his words directed at the Black female student he stabbed—Amira Jackson—his 'face looked like a smacked arse,' " prompting some laughter, especially from the Irish cops who knew the slang meant Sonny had a red face and was embarrassed. "We didn't tell him that the witness was Miss Amira."

O'Rourke then asked, "What were the words?"

McGuire pointed to the chalkboard. Under Sonny Mason's name was WHITE, PS 91 8TH GRADE, KNIFE ATTACK—VICTIM, AMIRA JACKSON, BLACK, 8TH GRADE. Under Amira's information were the words in quotes: "ME AND MY BROTHER HATE YOU N-WORD."

"His brother is Buddy Mason, who started the fight with Black students at Jefferson High. Further investigation revealed that some of them have siblings at PS 91, and they were in the cafeteria when

Sonny and his four morons attacked them. The sibling relationship is shown here on the board."

Lines were drawn between Trevor Williams, a Black senior at Jefferson High, and his younger brother, Henry Williams, the injured eighth-grade student at PS 91, and between Lucas Jackson, a Black senior at Jefferson, and his sister, Amira, at PS 91.

McGuire explained: "Our previous investigation of the fight at Jefferson revealed that Buddy Mason and several of his friends initiated the brawl because Trevor and Lucas were talking with White girls, and it seems the relationship between these kids was getting to a point that irritated Mason. We believe it goes deeper than that. We think there is outright hatred of Blacks and a penchant for racism."

O'Rourke said, "So if I can jump ahead here. Do you think that this was Buddy's way to get retaliation against Trevor and Lucas . . . have his kid brother attack their siblings at PS 91?"

McGuire came back: "Yes, sir . . . precisely what we believe. But then we asked, 'Was Buddy ending up in the hospital enough incentive for him to want to retaliate in this way?' We came up with possible answers. One, he didn't want to be in any more trouble at Jefferson. Henry Mason's father got head-to-head with the principal there and threatened a lawsuit. Buddy's fault was brought to light, and he knew he was lucky getting off so quickly on a first offense. Two, Buddy has not been in class at Jefferson since the attack on Friday at PS 91. We have been unable to locate him or his father at their home or the father's place of work at the Bush Terminal in Industry City. And . . . none of Buddy's classmates who were involved in attacking the Black kids know where he is. They swear to it."

O'Rourke stood up and began to exit the room. "Okay, men, good work so far. Stay on it. I need to leave for an appointment. Oh, one more thing. Do we have surveillance set up?"

"Yes, sir, I was about to mention that just before you got up. We have surveillance posted at the Mason house and the Terminal. We noticed his car was there the other day, but it went missing. We have an APB out through teletype and radio channels in the wider NYC metro area."

"Good, we'll get them sooner or later. I'd like it to be sooner! 'Slán go fóill.' " O'Rourke said as he abruptly left the building.

Conan McGuire, Shamus O'Reilly, and a few other Irish cops laughed as they observed the confused looks on the non-Irish cops.

"We Irish always try to keep a little of the old language goin'," Shamus said. "It means 'Goodbye for now!' " Conan and Shamus laughed; the other cops just shook their heads.

McGuire said, "Okay, boys, enough lessons on Irish gabberin'. Let's take a look at the other information we collected on the gang and racism activity in the NYC area."

Officers Nelson and Goodwin placed some folders on a table and pulled out several documents they would summarize for the team. Nelson handed copies to everyone and began.

"In this decade, Brooklyn—in fact, the entire NYC metro area—has experienced racial tensions and discrimination," Nelson said. "There's not much we see in Brooklyn schools, like what happened recently at PS 91 and Jefferson, including the acid attack there. We see it more in gang activity and isolated incidents like the grocery store attack on Reggie Jackson . . . usually several attackers against a lone Black person.

"Nonetheless, there has been a lot of debate about assigning police to the schools regularly, something that would stress our force severely." He thought momentarily.

"Okay, I'm getting a little off course here with some politics. Back to basics. We collected information about gang activity, including its internal organization and structure, methodology and goals, territorial turf wars, and other relevant details. Pete has done a deep dive into the details, so let me turn it over to him . . . Pete."

Officer Peter Goodwin had focused much of his investigation over the last few years on the explosion of gang activity.

"There are hundreds of gangs across the city with numbers of members in the thousands," he said. "Many are ethnic groups of Puerto Ricans, Blacks, Italians, and, sorry to say . . . Irish; sometimes, they are mixed. They are juveniles, usually between the ages of twelve and nineteen. They are well-organized: There's a 'president,' usually the smartest, and one with leadership skills; a 'vice president' who supports the 'president,' or takes over if something happens to him; and a 'war counselor,' who sets up rumbles, scouts enemy turf, and keeps an inventory of weapons."

McGuire asked, "What's the latest on types of weapons?"

Goodwin replied, "These gang members live in the projects and run-down tenement buildings. They can't afford handguns, so they use their fists, chains and clubs, knives, rocks, whatever, even pointed and cleated shoes. They sometimes use 'zip-guns' . . . homemade devices that are crude and sometimes backfire. They have proved to be too risky."

McGuire said, "I recall there was a murder in the summer . . . the uh . . ."

Goodwin knew.

"Yes, the Michael Farmer murder. It was in the *Times*. Poor kid had polio when he was ten years old, had a limp. Stabbed at a swimming pool. Another kid had serious injuries but survived. There were several gangs involved . . . had White and Black members."

McGuire asked, "What, if anything, can we relate between these gangs and the incident at PS 91?"

Goodwin held up a finger and said, "Ah! I was expecting this question. It is one we all have. Some of the larger gangs often have a smaller gang, referred to as a 'junior gang,' beneath them. Lately, we have seen these lower groups engage in what they call 'japping,' where smaller numbers, maybe three or four, attack lone rival gang members. They prove their worthiness to eventually 'graduate' into the 'senior' gang."

McGuire interjected. "So if I can draw a possible conclusion here, it would be that we think Sonny Mason may be working his way up to some senior level, that his brother, Buddy, is in?"

"It's undoubtedly worth verification. The thing is, we don't have any confirmation that Buddy is a gang member. No supporting evidence at all!" Goodwin then looked around the room at each officer with a shrug of his shoulders and his hands held out, his face expressing, "We don't know."

McGuire felt they had made good progress despite some critical answers pending. "Let's call it a day, men. Good work! After hearin' all this, I sense we continue focusing on the father, Henry Mason. It may be that his son, Buddy, is inspired by something he may be involved in, and the 'hate' is trickling down. 'Slán abhaile.' "

The non-Irish cops looked at McGuire as officer Donald Foster said, "More Irish? Really?"

McGuire laughed. "Be well and safe!" The other officers grinned but still shook their heads. *How much more of this?*

Chapter 15

MORE SPALDINGS

The holiday lights and decorations combined with a gentle falling snow to create a beautiful and joyous atmosphere across the city. Depending on where you were in Brooklyn, you heard the music and songs of the season over loudspeakers near shopping areas. The very popular Elvis Presley singing, "Here comes Santa Claus, here comes Santa Claus, right down Santa Claus Lane." A little further away, it might be Bobby Helms belting out "Jingle Bell Rock" or songs from Frank Sinatra's *The Sinatra Christmas Album*.

Christmas was a few days away, and Taylor and Nick couldn't contain their excitement. Their young minds had all but forgotten the event on December 13, and the thought of school itself did not even create a blip on their horizon. They also could not wait to get together because their parents had arranged a meeting during the holidays and told them about some planned activities. They thought, *This is the best Christmas ever!*

The magical morning arrived. Taylor woke up and hurried from his bedroom to the Christmas tree he and his parents had decorated a week ago. Only this time, it wasn't just the beautifully lit tree that was there; it was accompanied by lots of presents. The jolly ol' guy came through!

Like a pent-up spring let loose from a Jack-in-the-Box, Taylor ran to his parents, who wished they could get a few more minutes of sleep. "Mom, Dad, Santa Claus came! Come and see all the presents!"

Happy and smiling, albeit reluctantly, Makena and Isaac rose, donned their robes, and joined Taylor by the tree.

"Wow," said Makena. "I think Santa knew you were a good boy all year!"

Isaac said, "Of course, he knew! Well, son, what do you want to open first?"

Taylor had so many choices. He looked like he wanted to open them all at the same time!

"Um . . . this is a really big one . . . I'll open this one first." It was a box as big as he was. *What could it be?* He tore at the wrapping so that it would never be reused. The box inside slowly revealed something he had hoped for . . . a Flexible Flyer classic wooden sled!

"Yay, a sled! I can't wait to ride on it! Can we go today?"

His mother said, "Yes, we can go later after we go to church and before Christmas dinner with Grandma and Grandpa."

His father, anxious for some coffee, said, "Taylor, let's see what else Santa brought you!"

The boy opened a few more presents and loved each one: a baseball bat and glove, more Spaldings, a Slinky, Play-Doh, army men, and a cap gun. There were more to open, but he seemed focused on these for now.

Makena said, "Well, dear, do we get to exchange some gifts?"

"Uh, coffee first?"

"Okay, if you insist."

The Christmas morning at Nick's home played out in a similar fashion. The holiday spirit embraced the Greene family with the excitement of the long-awaited day.

As if reading from the same script as the Washingtons, Mary said, "Looks like you were a good boy, Nick! Mommy and Daddy knew Santa would be good to you!"

Nick was the epitome of cuteness in his red pajamas and fuzzy slippers, with a smile as wide as the Hudson River. His hair, which had grown a little longer for the winter, was flopped over his eyes, which were laser-beamed at the gifts beneath the tree. "Can I open this one?" It was a box almost as big as the one that contained Taylor's sled.

His father said, "Go for it, Nick! I wonder what that is." He winked at Mary.

Nick was about to open a present that he could build upon in the years ahead. "Oh boy, a Lionel Train set . . . just what I wanted!"

His father helped him open the box and take out the contents: train tracks that could be connected in an oval shape, a steam locomotive with smoke pellets, a gondola car, a refrigerated milk car, and a red caboose. It also had a small electric transformer that could be wired to the tracks to control the train's speed in forward and reverse movement and even blow the train's whistle. Nick was through the roof . . . so excited!

Nick eventually turned to open a few more gifts he had hoped for: an Etch-A-Sketch (he loved to draw), a Davy Crockett coonskin cap, and a baseball bat and glove. Little did he know there was some coordination between the Washingtons and his parents on the baseball gear.

Mary said, "Okay, guys, let's get some breakfast, and we'll come back and open some more presents," as she raised her eyebrows and curiously looked at the ones with her name on them. "We are going to Grandma and Grandpa's house later for dinner . . . and maybe more gifts!"

Nick jumped up and down, "Yay!" He loved the sound of that!

As Mary and Nick headed for the kitchen, Jonathan pulled out a 78-rpm vinyl record to place on his RCA Victor phonograph. He joined them as the velvety-smooth baritone voice of Perry Como sang "The Twelve Days of Christmas."

Chapter 16

Yonkers, Westchester County, New York

Four men sat around a card table in the basement of a dilapidated home a few miles northeast of the George Washington Bridge. The outside represented the best possible weed overgrowth, and remnants of trash were scattered throughout the yard, which was partially fenced in by decaying stakes. Jethro Paine and his slovenly friends were drinking beer and chain-smoking cigarettes.

Paine had a long, partially gray beard and was about 250 pounds, with a belly that hid his belt. His head was bald, with long, straggling, dirty-looking hair hanging from right over his ears to his shoulders. His clothes, jeans that weren't washed for quite some time and a red flannel shirt, reeked of cigarette smoke. Two of his pals looked like him; the other one was skinny, with sunken eyes in an ashen face, and looked as if he would die at any moment.

It was 8:00 p.m. on December 27. "Where the hell is he?" One of the men was getting impatient as he growled this to Jethro.

Jethro just growled back with a stern expression. "He should be here soon. He had to hole up at one of the guys' houses in another section of Brooklyn. The police have been staked out at his house. Somethin' to do with his kid at school. You want somethin' stronger than that beer to keep you calm?"

No answer, just a "uh huh."

Twenty minutes later, the Chevy Bel Air rolled up and parked in the carport, which looked ready to cave in at any moment. Jethro called out, "Henry, that you? We're down in the basement."

Paine's dog jumped up and barked at the sound of the car. Paine shouted, "Demon, shut up!" The dog, with its matted fur and scruffy appearance, sat down. It growled lowly, then settled down as it returned to gnawing on a now-flavorless bone. Its eyes were hidden by overgrown hair, and its character, sadly, reflected considerable neglect.

"I gotta hit the head . . . be right down." As Henry walked through the kitchen toward the bathroom, he noticed the dirty, piled-up pots and dishes in and around the sink, the small table that was so cluttered there was not one square inch of free space, and the floor that looked like it hadn't been cleaned in a decade. Henry took his sweet time in the bathroom, annoying the group even more.

As he descended the steps and entered the smoke-filled room, all eyes were focused on him as Jethro said, "Well, it's about time, we . . . why is he here?" He pointed at Buddy. They had no idea Henry's son would be with him.

Henry answered, "Well, Merry fuckin' Christmas to you, too! He can't be home; I can't be there either. I suspect the police want Buddy and maybe me; they have surveillance at my house and work. I dropped off the guy I'm staying with in Brooklyn, a block away from the Terminal, in the wee hours one morning to get my car. He was lucky enough to get it without them noticing . . . dumb cops. They probably fell asleep or were eating too many donuts to notice."

Jethro asked, "Well, what happens when he goes back to school?"

Buddy answered, "I ain't goin' back. I hate it there!"

Henry added, "Maybe it's a little earlier than I planned, but he's one of us now. Where's the beer?" Jethro pointed; Henry got one for himself and his son.

Henry filled in the group about Buddy's fight at Jefferson High and the plan they had devised to retaliate against the Blacks at the school. "My sources told me that the police participated in a meeting at PS 91, where our plan to injure some Black kids there—younger siblings of the ones that sent my kid to the hospital—was carried out. I had my friend go to the school on the night of the meeting to see if they were checking any list of parents. It seemed they just let parents and any other interested members of the public in for the meeting, so my friend sat in. The attack happened two weeks ago. We drew some Black blood, gentlemen!"

The group raised their beers and shouted, "Way to go, Buddy, you're an up-and-comer! '*N-word*' beware!" Buddy smiled and guzzled down the whole bottle, followed by a loud, gross belch. The group followed through with crafted belches of their own. Henry just smiled and looked in admiration at what he had created.

Henry looked at Jethro. "Before we start the meeting, I want to give you more of what me and Buddy plan in the Brooklyn area. I think the heads in Syracuse will love it, and it fits right in with their wider plans."

Jethro looked anxiously as he opened another beer, "We're all ears!"

"The gangs in the city area are growin' like mad, as you know. There's like thousands of gang members. They're poppin' up every-where. They are usually formed by different groups—I-talians, Spicks, some '*N-word*' in some of them too. They fight one another and target some lone people, but there ain't a whole lot goin' on in the schools. Recently there was a few school incidents that we would be proud of."

Jethro, anxious, interrupted, "Good enough for now. Can we get to the meeting? . . . Wait a second, don't you have another kid . . . Sonny, right? Where is he?"

"The police held him for a while, then tried to contact me. He's stayin' at a friend's house in Brooklyn, one of his classmates. The parents said they would take him in for the holidays since the police couldn't find me."

"How do you know this since you ain't been home? Did the kid's parents talk with you?"

"We have someone on the inside who keeps me informed."

"Someone on the inside . . . the inside of what?"

"The 75th Police Precinct!"

"Holy shit! Really? Who?"

"I . . . I can't say. Just drop it for now." The unruly group was wide-eyed in astonishment.

Mason hesitated momentarily, then said, "Alright, I've been in touch with Butch Brady in Syracuse. He was sent from Mississippi to help organize the Klan upstate with Rhett Walker. They notice some elements of civil rights activists beginning to take effect, and we plan to counter that in every way we can. So get ready, get off your asses, and buckle up!"

Chapter 17

A HOLIDAY DIVERSION

The Washingtons and the Greenes planned a surprise get-together for their sons over the holidays. As they both left their homes at about 1:00 p.m. on Saturday, December 28, Taylor and Nick were curious and had many similar questions: Where are we going? Can we make a snowman? Did we go there before? They were dying to know.

It was sunny, but the temperatures were in the high twenties, with a mild breeze that made it a few degrees colder. Nick was bundled up, looking like the Michelin Man with a heavy coat, snow boots, a scarf wrapped around his neck and face, mittens, and a thick, woolly knit cap with earmuffs.

They approached Prospect Park, a 526-acre playground in Brooklyn, west of East New York, with natural and recreational attractions. The public park contained many highlights, including hills for sledding, ice skating ponds, and a zoo known as the "Brooklyn Zoo." The adults discussed trying to cram all of this in for their sons for a few hours of fun.

Nick and his parents arrived at a designated point in the park and waited. As he looked around, Nick said, "Why are we waiting here?"

His father said, "You'll see in a minute."

As if on cue, the Washingtons came within view. Mary said, "Look, Nick, look who's here!"

Nick turned, and when he saw Taylor, they ran to each other, yelling their names. Taylor's father carried the Flexible Flyer and said, "You guys ready to do some sledding?"

The boys were overjoyed, and they could see other kids propelling down a nearby hill, some making it to the bottom, while others fell and tumbled through the snow, enjoying every minute of it. The Washingtons brought a thermos of hot chocolate and some paper cups. Makena offered, "Would anyone like some hot chocolate? It's cold out here!"

The adults sat on a park bench as they watched their kids having the time of their lives riding the sled together. Down, up, down, up . . . it continued for about thirty minutes. They handled the rides like pros until near the end, as they got a bit tired and finally fell off the sled and rolled side by side down the hill, laughing all the way. They retrieved the sled and approached their parents for much-needed sips of hot chocolate.

Jonathan said, "You guys did great! How was it?"

Nick and Taylor responded in unison, "Good!"

They rested there for a few minutes as the boys talked about their Christmas presents, and the adults learned a little about each other. Isaac was a pharmacist at a local drugstore, having earned his bachelor of science degree in pharmacy at Long Island University's pharmacy program on DeKalb Avenue in Brooklyn. He was lean and exercised regularly to stay in shape. He loved sports, especially baseball, and was an avid Dodgers fan.

Jonathan was an accountant with the WAC Tax & Accounting firm in the Brownsville section of Brooklyn. He earned his bachelor's in business administration with a concentration in accounting at City College of New York in Harlem, Manhattan. He also loved baseball but was a die-hard Yankee fan. This gave the men much to discuss and debate.

The women had drifted into their own conversation, but as it got close to 2:00 p.m., Nick and Taylor were ready for the next adventure. The adults offered two choices: ice skating or the zoo.

"The zoo, the zoo," came back strong from the two boys, who seemed to be in sync with everything. They sipped the last of their hot chocolate and headed to the Brooklyn Zoo on the eastern side of the park off Flatbush Avenue. It contained a well-populated array of animals in its 12-acre confines.

The boys loved every minute together as their outing drew to a close, but were physically exhausted. It was close to 4:00 p.m., and it was time to call it a day. Before they parted ways, the Washingtons and Greenes briefly discussed more opportunities to meet again.

They observed how well Nick and Taylor bonded and how much fun they had together. They both commented to one another that it was important for these young kids to grow and benefit from their relationship, which is not always achieved among people of different colors. During their conversation, they exchanged constant head nods, indicating understanding and agreement among them.

Just before they separated for home, Isaac said, "You know, boys, in a few months, when it's warmer here at the park, there's an area for picnics and sports, like baseball." He was referring to the Long Meadow section, which featured areas for baseball, other recreational games, and youth leagues. They were all aware by now that the boys had received baseball bats and gloves for Christmas. And Isaac and Jonathan agreed they had much to discuss about baseball! The women had also bonded through their warm and engaging conversation. *The Washingtons and the Greenes had something special to look forward to!*

Chapter 18

WHERE IS HENRY MASON?

Captain O'Rourke was furious when he heard the surveillance had let Mason's Chevy slip away unnoticed. "Why didn't you two see that red and white car when it was taken? It's January third . . . we had surveillance set up nearly three weeks now!" This outburst got everyone's attention in the precinct.

Officers Rogers and Campbell were on surveillance. Rogers nervously reacted to O'Rourke's outburst. "Sir, Campbell had to take a leak; I looked down for just a minute to . . . uh . . . read something, and . . . uh . . . the Chevy was very dirty and in a lowly lit area, at night, and . . . "

O'Rourke interrupted. "All bad excuses. You realize that, don't you?"

"Uh . . . no, sir . . . I mean, yes, sir . . . uh."

"Find that car! Find Mason!" O'Rourke stormed out of the room. The officers in the room fell silent, but one minute later, Sergeant McGuire entered with an update on the surveillance.

"Where's the captain?"

Campbell said, "He was just here . . . headed down the hall."

McGuire said, "Okay, I'll find him and fill him in later. We just received a response from our APB on the car. Came from our brothers-in-blue in upper Manhattan. The Chevy was seen leaving a gas station just south of the Westchester County line. We followed the car, no sirens, but it left our jurisdiction. We contacted the Yonkers Police Force."

Just then, O'Rourke reentered the room. "Sir, I'm glad you came back. I just gave an update on the surveillance on Mason's car and was about to find you." He repeated the information for O'Rourke.

The captain said, "Yonkers area, huh? I know the Chief there, Liam Doyle. We went through training in the city together back in the late '30s. Not much to it back then . . . basic law enforcement skills, some physical fitness, and firearms proficiency . . . " His thoughts drifted as he recalled, "Yeah, as long as you can read and write English . . . medical tests were no big deal, and background checks were a joke."

The younger officers in the room and administrative staff were all ears as they put their feet up on the desk or leaned forward, one hand raised to hold up their head, as if they were listening to a police fairy tale.

O'Rourke, now dredging up more information from yesteryear, continued, "Yeah, Liam and me, we came up through the ranks. He made it to chief. We seen a lot together. Two-way radios came on the scene after the War in the late forties. Really helped improve our communications and response times. Civilian uproar over so-called 'police brutality and discrimination' by the NYPD, so much so that the department formed a Civilian Complaint Review Board in '53 to address so-called 'excessive force' used by the police. Liam and I were part of a task force on the subject. All spun up by the civil rights activists, the media, community groups. Everybody bringin' attention to police misconduct and demandin' accountability. The NYPD fixed that. Put three deputy police commissioners on the board to investigate the complaints and decide on disciplinary action." In reality, there was very little correction by the police; civil rights groups continued a call for an independent civilian board.

O'Rourke woke up from his self-reminiscence, looked around the room to see some officers asleep, some gazing in amazement, and realized he had sent them off into "la-la land."

"Okay, men . . . uh . . . enough on that. Get back to work; I'll call Chief Doyle." He left the room abruptly, again. Everyone snapped back to police work.

O'Rourke got on the phone with Chief Doyle. After explaining the reason for the call, they discussed old times, which was a more extended version than the one O'Rourke gave his officers.

They had much more to catch up on, but before it went further, Doyle said, "Frank, hang on one second." He called out to his lieutenant, "Sean, check that APB we got from the NYPD on a red and white '56 Chevy Bel Air, owner Henry Mason. The car was recently seen entering our neighborhood from a gas station near the Washington Bridge." He observed Lieutenant Sean Ryan rise to take action. "Sorry, Frank, where were we? How's the family?" It went on from there for about thirty more minutes as two proud Irish officers shared memories and updates.

The Yonkers Police Force was now on the lookout for the car. In the APB, they also had a rough description of the father and son provided by neighbors who were interviewed by NYPD patrolmen near their house. Yonkers Police expanded the search in all directions over the county.

Just before the end of the two-week school break, the 75th Precinct police followed up with the parents caring for Sonny over the holidays, as they had been unable to contact his father. They wanted to make one more attempt to see if Sonny knew where his father and brother were, but the kid said he didn't know, that he hadn't heard from them. The parents wondered the same thing since school would be back in session on Monday, the sixth of January, and they were beginning to regret their offer to take Sonny in over the holidays. Watching over him was getting old, especially since the brat was teaching their son some bad behavior. *One snot-nosed kid cultivating his attitude on another.*

Chapter 19

HUDSON HOUSE, YONKERS

A young man walked to a nearby phone booth, opened the folding door, and once inside the sanctuary of privacy, dropped a dime into the slot to make a call. After three rings, another man answered.

"Hello?"

"Bullet, this is X-ray! I got somethin' important!"

"Hang on a minute . . . " The South Brooklyn pawn shop owner waited as the sole patron exited the shop so he could flip the door sign from "Open" to "Closed." Back on the phone, he said, "What's up?"

X-ray checked 360 degrees around the booth before he said, "I can't get a hold of Sabre. I need to contact him. The police are on the lookout for him and may be getting close!"

Bullet replied, "I know where he is. I can contact him. Any details?"

"I just overheard a sergeant and the captain at the police precinct talking about a hit they got on an APB out for Sabre's car. Seems like it was spotted up near 'Hudson House,' and the captain contacted the police up that way to find the car. They might be closin' in soon!"

"Thanks, I'll call them right now. Be careful. Anybody see you leave the building?"

"No . . . um . . . I don't think so. I told them I had to run an errand for my mother. They just waved me out. I checked all around before I called you."

Bullet wasted no time, "Adios."

Bullet was proud of his nickname, which he earned by stating, "I got a bullet for every 'N-word' in Brooklyn." He always relished the thought of expending as many of the projectiles as possible into the heads of his targets.

X-ray received his code name due to his ability to "see" into things that others could not, specifically, the information he could overhear at the 75th Precinct. It gave him great pleasure to be in a position that no other Ku Klux Klan member could hold. It made him feel very important. His simple administrative duties there easily cloaked him from the police, who were laser-focused on files, updates of information, and carrying out assigned responsibilities in the ever-growing war against crime.

Bullet called Hudson House. Cue Ball answered, "Yeah?" He wasn't as proud of his code name as some others were, since "Cue Ball" described his bald head, which he hated since its rapid birth many years ago.

"It's Bullet. You guys need to leave there now! I just heard from X-ray . . . uh . . . I . . . " He realized he should not have mentioned the informant's code name. *Well, I spilled the beans now!* He just continued the message and said the police spotted Sabre's car near Hudson House, and they may be closing in. "Tell Sabre I think we need to contact Cyclone."

Cue Ball said, "Who's X-ray? Never heard of him." Just then, as Sabre overheard the question, he realized he would need to provide some intelligence for Cue Ball and the others.

After Cue Ball told Bullet to hold, Sabre said, "Alright, guys, X-ray is my guy in the 75th Police Precinct in Brooklyn. Keep that to yourselves for now." He got a thumbs-up from the other three men.

"Yeah, right now. We're outta here!" Just as Cue Ball hung up the phone, the skinny dude returned from getting gas for the Chevy. Cue Ball screamed at him. "Where the fuck did you go for gas? The police spotted you in upper Manhattan. There are millions of gas stations near here! The police spotted you, and they are looking for the car right now!"

"Dead Man" (so appropriately code-named, not only for his facial features but potentially for his near-term status) wondered, *How does he know the police saw me . . . the car.* He mumbled back, "Uh . . . I . . . uh, wanted to drive the Chevy a little before I gassed it up. Guess I didn't know I crossed the county line."

"You're an idiot! Quick, everyone outside! Cover up the Chevy with everything you can find and put some of the crap out there to block it from view; we can't risk the police spotting the Chevy if we try to drive away now!" Sabre and the others darted outside to conceal the car. Cue Ball sneered at Dead Man as he followed the others. "You dumb shit!"

About twenty minutes later, the code-named group watched the streets from the reeking kitchen as they hunched to a window above the sink, knocking over the filthy pots and dishes. They were lucky. A Yonkers Police Force patrol car was slowly passing Jethro's house just a few minutes after the car-concealing task was done, and the frantic men returned inside the house.

They retreated to the basement. Paine lit into Dead Man again. "You almost got us in big trouble, you moron! If the police got to this house and found Henry, it could have been a bust for our planning and operations . . . for all of us. Tentacle-E would not be happy!"

"Tentacle-E" represented the East arm of "Octopus," one of the key secret planning and oversight centers in the network to create havoc and suffering among the Black population in the country. Cyclone, the head of Tentacle-E in Syracuse, was hosting a visit from the head of Octopus, who was aptly named and written as "VenoM," where the capital "M" stood for the location of Octopus—in Mississippi.

The clandestine activities of the KKK had a resurgence in the South due to civil rights activities that aimed at racial segregation and discrimination. The KKK increased violence and intimidation tactics that included bombings, murders, and other acts of terror to suppress the movement. White supremacy was the goal. The plans for increasing KKK influence in New York, especially in NYC, where there was a high Black population, were in the making among the members of Hudson House and their leaders, like Sabre and Bullet.

Hudson House provided a remote planning location outside NYC to provide insulation from the NYPD. Perhaps, now, its lifespan was coming to an end with the Yonkers Police Force on the prowl.

The focus was on priming younger members to create incidents in schools, whether they were elementary or high school, against Black students and to enable gangs to "rumble" and, worse, to inflict injury and death. Civil unrest already existed in the city, but the KKK wanted more.

The network for terror consisted of some very intelligent men, but also some real nitwits who joined out of curiosity and a lack of commitment elsewhere. Mid-to-upper management also used coercion and intimidation to ensure that some of the nonstrategic jobs could be carried out.

A prime example would be X-ray's task as the eyes and ears at the police precinct. Mason recruited him about a year ago from a civil rights rally where he observed him chanting against Black people. Tyler Barnes, aka X-ray, wasn't as pathetic as others; he had a high school education, which was good enough when he applied for a job as a clerk, with Mason's prompting, with the NYPD. Over the years, he advanced to administrative duties, which enabled him to be closer to daily activity and information within the precinct.

Henry Mason was considered a mid-level manager with the authority to seek out such individuals to help the network in its crusade against the Black community. The network used code names to minimize the risk of member identification, and some, like Henry Mason, had the privilege of choosing their own name. It usually represented something each member could identify with, representing each individual's inner hate.

Henry Mason, aka Sabre, loved the image of a pointed metal weapon whose likeness stood for how he desired best to inflict up close and personal harm to Blacks. Brian Savage, the pawn shop owner, chose his name, Bullet, to implement his hate. VenoM, is the code name for Butch Brady, "Grand Dragon," a state leader of the KKK from Mississippi, spreading poison as he managed Octopus, and who aspired to be an "Imperial Wizard." Rhett Walker, the "Grand Dragon" and state leader code-named "Cyclone" in Syracuse, managed Tentacle-E. He was dedicated to creating a racist storm.

They were members who represented a wider group of the elite in the network dedicated to the beliefs and ideals often found in written declarations that espoused White supremacy and racial purification, deeply harmful and hateful ideology.

The members, such as Jethro Paine, aka Cue Ball, and Ricky Miller, known as Dead Man, had part-time jobs: Paine worked at the factory complex along the Saw Mill River for the Smith and Sons Carpet Company, and Miller was a stock boy at a local hardware store. They were considered too dumb to manage anything but were helpful in the network.

Members like X-ray, who held sensitive roles or were at risk of being compromised, were isolated from other members to protect sources of information. Whatever level it was, the network, from menial tasks to the strategic direction of the Imperial Wizard, was all in support of hatred, racist activity ranging from verbal abuse to physical violence, and White supremacy.

After a sigh of relief for having successfully camouflaged the car and escaping the police, Henry and Buddy shifted their thoughts, looked at one another, and said simultaneously, "Sonny!" Henry knew he had to do something to get his other son to remove him from any link the police might use to locate his father, and worse yet, infiltration into secret activities. He thought for a minute. "I have a plan!"

Chapter 20

THE RETRIEVAL OF SONNY MASON

It was the weekend before school would begin its session in the new year. Henry called Tyler Barnes at his home in Brooklyn at about 7:30 a.m. Tyler had to report to the precinct for a reduced workday. "Hey, it's Henry. I'm stayin' here at Jethro's house for a while. I wish I didn't have to do that; his house is a pig's sty! I have to get my kid back before school starts on Monday. The police might try to monitor him to see if he gives them any possible information that could compromise my location and, ultimately, our plans. I don't know if Sonny will think of the Yonkers location, but he might. He knows I have been in Yonkers occasionally, and we can't afford to let that happen."

Barnes said, "I'm not supposed to know, but I overheard someone. I know where he is . . . stayin' with this family not far from here, whose son is in Sonny's class.

"I can go over there and show them my precinct ID and say the police want to question him, that I need to take him to the precinct."

Henry thought for a moment. "Uh, if they're suspicious and won't let him go with you, get their phone number, tell them the police have his father and that I will call them to release Sonny to you, that I made arrangements for his care and return to school while the police hold me. Let me know if that's the case, and I'll call them."

Barnes said, "Sounds good, I'll call you after I try that."

Henry hung up, and his mind went to this turn of events—he was on the run and both of his kids would be out of school. He wondered how they would assimilate into a new environment where most others were older. He couldn't risk returning to his house or job. He was stuck at Jethro's filthy house. The use of his car was a risk, and he needed to devote time and effort to the cause. The world felt a whole lot heavier on his shoulders. *How do I manage all this?*

About forty-five minutes later, Barnes had Sonny and was headed back to his apartment. He told Sonny he would call his dad and that he was expecting the call. Once there, Barnes called Henry. "Henry, Sonny's here at my apartment with me; the other kid's parents let him go with absolutely no question." *That little creep! They were thrilled to get rid of him.*

Henry said, "Good . . . thanks. Let me talk to him."

"Dad?"

"Yeah, Sonny, you okay?"

"Yeah, where are you?"

"I'm up at the house in Yonkers. I need to get you up here for a while. You can't go back to school or the house because the police might use you to connect with me here and learn about some things you and I discussed."

"Dad, I don't care. I don't wanna to go back to school. I hate it there! I wanna be with you and Buddy. . . . He with you?"

"Yeah, he's here. Okay, I will call a friend to pick you up and bring you here. You won't like it here, but it's only temporary until we find somethin' better. His name is Brian Savage. Stay put with Tyler."

"Okay, Dad. I'm glad I don't have to go back to school." Sonny's immature mind could not comprehend the consequences of his statement. They hung up. Henry's thoughts drifted a bit deeper this time as he began to question himself, *What have I done to this kid? If Helen were here, it would be different!*

The delivery of Sonny to his father went according to plan, and Tyler entered the precinct seconds before his show time of 10:00 am. Happy to see his father and brother again, Sonny's smile quickly disappeared as he looked around the confines of Cue Ball's Yonkers estate.

Captain O'Rourke was growing increasingly impatient with the lack of any substantial progress on the PS 91 case. He had demanded that at least a minimum crew work over the weekend. Sergeant McGuire selected a few police officers and one administrative support staff member, Tyler Barnes, to be at the precinct with him for a short workday on Saturday, January 4.

The police thought they would make one more attempt at questioning Sonny Mason before school started again. They expected him to return to school and didn't think a long-term stay with the parents who watched him over the holidays would last. Sergeant McGuire directed a call, "Hey, Tyler, call that couple who are watching Sonny Mason . . . what's their names?"

Tyler reacted as he should, nervously, now that he suddenly realized his true identity could be compromised. "Uh . . . sure Sergeant. I . . . uh . . . the a . . . the . . . Coopers . . . yeah, the Coopers. I think it's Ted and Amelia Cooper." The precinct temperature was warm and comfortable compared with the outside, but the sweat rolled down Barnes's back as if he were hiking through Death Valley in mid-August.

McGuire noticed the uneasiness. "What's wrong, Tyler?"

"Uh . . . nothing. I . . . uh . . . I may be coming down with the flu. Just feeling a little sick. I need to go to the restroom. Can I call when I come back?"

"Yeah, sure. Hope you feel better. Get back to me ASAP."

"Will do, Sergeant."

This sudden predicament caused a severe state of confusion as to what to do next. Barnes went to the restroom for a few minutes, then carefully peeked out to determine if he could vacate the precinct through a rear door unnoticed. However, one police officer was monitoring maintenance personnel there who were attending to a work order to repair some leaking pipes. He couldn't risk any questioning why he was using the rear door.

He returned to his desk, sat down, and thought for a minute. *I could call the Coopers and just say that I am following up. Ask if they ever heard Sonny talk about where his father might be. Then, tell McGuire that they said someone picked him up but didn't have a name. I could say they gave me a description of the guy, then I could give a bogus description to McGuire. Or I could get the hell out of here because sooner or later they will learn I'm an informant!*

Just as these thoughts raced through Barnes's mind, McGuire walked through the area and saw Barnes sitting there deep in thought. "Well, how are you doing? Feelin' any better?"

"No, actually, I threw up in the men's room. But I feel a little better now."

"Listen, Tyler, I can get someone else to call the Coopers. You want to take the rest of the day off, go home, and get better?"

Barnes thought again. *If someone calls the Coopers and they give the police my description, and say someone from the precinct came to pick Sonny up, it's over. They will eventually know it's me!* "No, that's okay. I'll call them now." McGuire told him to inform him immediately after the call.

Barnes called the Coopers' residence. Amelia answered. His questions and her answers went exactly as Barnes had anticipated. Mrs. Cooper stated that neither she nor her husband had ever heard the mischievous demon say where his father might be, even though they had asked several times, hoping the kid would have a revelation.

Tyler knocked on the Sergeant's office. McGuire waved him in and said, "What did they say?"

"Well, I got ahold of Mrs. Cooper, and she said someone picked Sonny up this morning."

"What . . . who?"

"She didn't give a name, just a description." Tyler gave McGuire a bogus description of himself, hoping it would take some time before the police found the truth. He knew his time at the precinct was in jeopardy and would probably end in a manner not of his choosing.

McGuire mumbled to himself, but loud enough for Tyler to hear. "Mm . . . that's odd. How would anyone know that Sonny was stayin' with the Coopers? We had a strict protocol among the school, the Coopers, and us to keep that secret!" Tyler left the room and, at a distance, glanced over his shoulder to see what Sergeant McGuire might do next. *If he decides to call the Coopers himself and they give him my description, I'll be in deep . . . (as the Irish would say), "cac."*

McGuire was a seasoned officer. Something was off. He sensed it immediately. He had Dr. Carpenter's home phone number, called and asked her to notify him if Sonny returned to school on Monday. He said someone picked him up from Coopers' house this Saturday morning and that he might be in school. He then thought of calling the Coopers himself but hesitated. He closed the door and called Shamus to his office.

Shamus had nothing better to do at home and promptly went to the precinct to meet with his Irish buddy cop. They talked for a while in private, going over all the facts: the key students in the skirmishes at Jefferson High and PS 91, the Black sibling relationships of the students in both schools, the simultaneous disappearance of Henry Mason and his son, Buddy, police spotting Mason's car as it was driven into Westchester County, and today the disappearance of Sonny Mason.

McGuire said, "Shamus, we need to press the Coopers. They had Sonny there for two weeks during the holidays. They must have heard something. Maybe they didn't want to tell a stranger who came to pick him up, or tell Tyler, just a voice on the phone, anything they may know. I think a face-to-face is needed."

Shamus nodded, "I agree, I'll go."

"By the way, Tyler called; he got a description from Mrs. Cooper of the guy who picked up Sonny this morning. See if it's consistent with the same question asked of Mr. Cooper." McGuire handed Shamus the description he had written down.

"You got it, boss. On my way."

Chapter 21

"Oireann Sé Do Tyler Go Hiomlán"

"He was a tall, lanky young man in his early twenties. He had dark brown hair, neatly cut and combed, a white shirt and a very skinny, plain blue tie. He showed us his ID, but we didn't pay much attention to it; we couldn't wait to get that terrible kid out of our house. Do you know what he taught our son . . . he . . . " Shamus interrupted Mrs. Cooper as she was about to go on, with Mr. Cooper by her side.

"Ma'am, Mr. Cooper, did he tell you his name?"

Ted Cooper said, "No, and when he flashed his police credentials at us, all we saw was the police precinct label and his photo. His thumb covered his name."

"Okay, so just to be sure, again, you never heard Sonny Mason talk about anything that might point to where his father is, correct?"

"That's correct, yes."

Shamus gave them a card with the precinct phone number and told them to call and ask for him or Sergeant McGuire if they thought of anything else. He said, "Anything additional you might remember could be very important, so we can make sure this doesn't happen in your son's school again. Thank you both, and have a good rest of your weekend."

Shamus called McGuire immediately as he put the patrol car in gear and headed back to the precinct. "Conan, the Coopers did not know who picked up Sonny, but they gave me his description, and it is nothing like the one our young man, Tyler Barnes, gave you. In fact, their description fits . . ." He started to say their description fits

. . . to a T, but the Irish anger came out, and he said, "Oireann sé do Tyler go hiomlán (*fits Tyler to a T*). Tyler picked up Sonny!"

McGuire couldn't believe what he had just heard. He looked outside his office window and saw Tyler slightly glancing back at him. Their eyes froze on one another for a few seconds, and then Tyler turned away.

"Shamus, no wonder Tyler was acting so strange earlier. He's withholding information for some reason. I feel like grabbing his neck right now and shaking the truth out of him, but it may be better to track his movements. I'll put one of the guys on his tail. Son of a bitch! Stop by my office again."

"Ten-four."

McGuire was careful not to make it obvious he was focused on Tyler. He called one of his officers in, and behind closed doors, directed him to track Tyler's movements once he left the precinct for the day. "Make sure he doesn't know he's bein' watched and report back to me when you get in your patrol car ready to roll!"

"Yes, sir," said Officer Nelson, as he thought, *so much for working a short day today!*

A few minutes after Nelson left the building and reported back to McGuire, he went to Tyler and calmly said, "Hey, Tyler, I've been watching you and . . . why don't you go home now since you aren't feelin' well. Shift's almost over for today anyway. Go ahead . . . go."

"Oh . . . okay, thanks, Sarge." He tidied his desk and got up to leave.

McGuire walked back to his office. *You creep, what's goin' on with you? What are you hiding?*

Shamus returned, and McGuire called in the other officers at the precinct to divulge what they had just learned. They all paused for a moment of internal reflection. Suddenly, McGuire verbally summarizes what he knows. "Mr. Jackson, father of the little girl, Amira Jackson, at PS 91 who was stabbed by Sonny . . . remember, he told me Amira said when he stabbed her, he got up close and said, 'Me and my brother hate you,' and he added the *N-word*. Then, we can't locate the brother, Buddy, or their father. More than likely, they are all together, probably up in Westchester County, since we spotted the Chevy there. Somehow, the boys might have been delivered to the father."

Shamus added, "And you think Tyler knows where they are since he lied about who picked up Sonny?"

"Exactly what I think. What I don't know is why."

Officer Goodwin said, "Sonny's father must be into something big because he did not return to his home or his job at the Terminal. No one there has heard from him or knows his whereabouts. And for the kids to go missing . . . he may have them involved. According to all sources, they're not the most likable kids. In fact, most say they're terrible."

McGuire said, "Okay, look. I have Nelson tracking Barnes. Let's call it a day. If I hear from Nelson and need to round you up, you'll hear from me. I need to call the captain and fill him in. I'm sure he'll want to call his Yonkers police chief buddy, Doyle, and provide him with the latest information and descriptions of the Masons. We need to find them. They all have bad attitudes, and I have a bad feeling about what they may be planning."

"Oh, and I better call the PS 91 principal, Dr. Carpenter, and tell her we believe Sonny will not return to school on Monday. Go home, boys."

McGuire remained in his office. He contacted Nelson by radio and told him he would get surveillance relief by 9 p.m. Nelson's short workday was turning into anything but. He was intent on ensuring he would not repeat the screwed-up surveillance with Mason's Chevy at the Terminal by Officers Rogers and Campbell, which resulted in the captain coming unglued.

"Captain, it's McGuire. I got some good news and some bad news on the investigation into the Mason boys' school attacks."

"I hate hearing that! Okay, give me the bad news first. I want to end it on a good note, if possible."

"Yes, sir . . . uh . . . we identified a mole in the precinct, and . . . "

"What! A mole in the 75th? Who?"

"Yes, our beloved administrative support guy, Tyler Barnes!"

"Barnes! Are you kidding me? What did you find out, and how?"

McGuire regurgitated all the ugly facts to the captain: He had directed Barnes to call the Coopers to find more intel on Henry Mason's whereabouts through his son, Sonny, only to learn that someone picked Sonny up; he further explained how Barnes gave him a fake description of the person who visited the Coopers to throw the police off, and that Shamus' follow-up at the Cooper's residence revealed the true description. That it "Oireann sé do Tyler go hiomlán." He went through Barnes, feigning illness, and assigned Nelson to monitor him as he went home. He finished by saying, "He usually walks to his apartment, not far from the precinct."

O'Rourke said, "Well, I can't wait any longer . . . what's the good news?"

"Now that we know Barnes is linked with the Masons, in some yet unknown way, we can pressure him to open up and progress on the connection among the Masons—the father, both sons, and the school incidents. I think we are very close to some clarity on the causes."

O'Rourke pondered and said, "Don't have our guys confront Barnes yet. Keep an eye on him, and let's see what happens on Monday when he is due back to work. In the meantime, I'm going to call a contact I have at the Bureau of Special Services and Investigations (BOSSI) downtown. I think it's warranted. They have some good tactics when it comes to surveillance. I would rather have a plain-clothes detective watch Barnes. He may get suspicious if he sees a uniformed cop or a patrol vehicle."

"Copy that, Captain."

The BOSSI was established in 1946 and focused on undercover operations to monitor and investigate criminal activities. O'Rourke hoped that bringing them into the investigation would tip the scales in favor of the NYPD. The elite organization assigned Detective Marty O'Shea to the case. O'Rourke had requested him by name. The two had worked together on many cases and would always have Guinness together to celebrate solving every one of them.

Officer Nelson was relieved of his surveillance duties promptly at 9 p.m. Saturday. His replacement sat down the street from Barnes' apartment through the night and was replaced twelve hours later by another officer. The shifts continued through Sunday as Barnes stayed put in his apartment. He had tried all weekend to contact Savage over the phone to alert him of his dilemma but could not reach him. His calls to the Hudson House also went unanswered. *Where the hell is everyone?*

Chapter 22

THE STAKEOUT

School was back in session on Monday morning, January 6, 1958. As classes were about to begin at PS 91, students were noisily sharing their stories of gifts and holiday adventures. They had fun and now needed to adjust by putting the school year into second gear . . . and third . . . and fourth . . . to the homestretch in June.

Taylor and Nick couldn't wait until playtime to continue sharing their stories about Prospect Park, snow sledding, the zoo, and their Christmas presents, and to hear from the other students. There was so much to tell. Playtime would be in the gym again, not outside yet as it was still too cold. Lopez hoped the bad encounter in the gym on December 13 would not be recreated in the children's minds. She and the other teachers had discussed ways to divert their thoughts from that scarring memory.

Dr. Carpenter and the police remained in touch regarding any new developments in tracking down the root cause of the attack in the school cafeteria. She knew Sonny Mason would not be in class, as confirmed by McGuire's call over the weekend, and shared that information with his teacher. McGuire also told Carpenter that they checked with Jefferson High School and that Buddy was not in class either. This indicated to the police that, with their father missing, it gave significant substantiation to a conspiracy behind PS 91's scarring. Carpenter's head was spinning. *What is going on with that family?* She directed her administrative support to notify all teachers to attend a short end-of-day meeting so she could provide the information she had just learned.

Carpenter and her staff shifted to re-motivation and commitment. "All ahead, press on." *We can't change the past, only influence the future. Do what we do best: educate, cultivate, inspire, and set good examples. Do our jobs!* During the day, her thoughts would shift from her usual routine to the extraordinary: how to shelter the innocence of PS 91 students from social turmoil and prevent another December 13 at the school.

Classes got off to a great start. The good memories prevailed, and learning was being served.

The list of police officers staking out Barnes grew as he remained in his apartment through the weekend. Detective O'Shea replaced a uniformed officer around 6 a.m. Monday morning. Barnes did not intend to report for work at the precinct. Instead, he called in sick, faking a cough and stating he had a fever and was making an appointment to see a doctor. The receptionist at the precinct relayed this information to McGuire immediately, as he directed her to do if Barnes called.

At about 8:30 a.m., Barnes emerged from his apartment building and walked a few blocks to the subway station on Sutter Street. He wore jeans and a short, heavy winter jacket that appeared to cover several layers underneath. A woolen cap with earmuffs covered him. O'Shea immediately radioed to the precinct to say that he had spotted Barnes. He had a good description, but the clothing concealed his identity except for a small part of his face. The tall, lanky build convinced O'Shea he had the right guy. He exited his unmarked car and proceeded on foot.

Barnes went down the subway stairs to take the BMT Canarsie line, which connects to Canarsie in South Brooklyn. O'Shea, who looked like hundreds of other Brooklynites dressed for the cold, followed, and both entered the packed train. Every seat was occupied, and there was little standing room left, the usual commuting situation in Brooklyn and the other boroughs during rush hour.

Barnes took the train, passing three stations before it reached the terminus at Rockaway Parkway station. He exited the train, walked up the steps, made his way to Rockaway Parkway, turned southeast, and walked one block to Conklin Avenue. He turned right, went halfway down the block, and entered the Savage Pawn Shop. O'Shea stopped about fifty feet from the shop entrance and took in the irresistible aroma that captured his attention with its thick scent of warm dough, caramelized sugar, rich butter, and brewing espresso. He savored the freshly baked goods, including cinnamon rolls and bagels, displayed inside Cecilia's Bakery. He waited there for a few minutes.

"Brian, I been tryin' to call you all weekend! Where have you been?" Barnes was in an apparent state of panic.

"Tyler, what the hell are you doin' here? I was out of town for the weekend with my girlfriend. What's goin' on?"

Just then, O'Shea entered the shop as he could not miss their raised voices. They stopped and looked at O'Shea. Savage said, "Yes, can I help you?" Barnes walked away and just looked around the shop.

O'Shea calmly said, "Oh, I can wait. He was here first." He told Barnes, "Son, go ahead, you were here . . . "

Barnes interrupted him, "No, you go. I'm just lookin' around."

Savage stared at O'Shea. "Well, what can I do for you?"

"I'm just curious. My grandfather just passed away and left me some old coins. Said if I ever needed money, they might be worth something. I really need a short-term loan. Would you take the coins as collateral?"

"I don't know. Let me see the coins."

"I don't have them with me. I just wanted to know if a loan is possible. I can bring the coins in later."

"Well, anything's possible. Come back with the coins."

"Uh . . . okay, thanks." He slowly looked around the shop as he approached the door. "Thanks again, see you later."

Savage and Barnes stared at him, and once he was out of earshot, Barnes filled him in on all the details that led to his being a target of the police investigation. They got into a verbal quarrel. He couldn't hear the words as he looked into the shop from across the street, but O'Shea could tell it wasn't a pleasant conversation. He ensured he was hidden from view and called for immediate police backup on his walkie-talkie. Within minutes, police were posted near the front and back entrances to the pawn shop.

With everyone in place, O'Shea reentered the shop. "Back so soon?" Their tirade was interrupted.

O'Shea said, "I don't have the coins, but I do have another question."

"Yeah, what?"

O'Shea got closer to Barnes and asked, "Mr. Barnes, why aren't you at work this morning?" This caused wide-eyed astonishment, as they both realized they didn't need to continue their conversation. Savage took a quick glance at the access to the rear of the shop and bolted. O'Shea pulled his Smith & Wesson Model 10 .38 revolver on Barnes as he shouted to Savage, "You won't get far. Tyler, you are under arrest! Turn around . . . hands behind your back." Tyler complied and was handcuffed as two police officers escorted Savage back inside the shop.

"Thanks, officers. We're taking these two to the 75th Precinct. I'll radio ahead to Sergeant McGuire to expect them in a few minutes." They all walked out the front door. O'Shea flipped the shop sign to "Closed." They got in two patrol cars, and as they were about to get underway, O'Shea said, "Pull around to Conklin Avenue and stop in front of Cecelia's Bakery." He got out and returned after he bought some freshly baked treats for himself and the assisting police. "Okay, now we can go to the precinct!" All smiles. *Well, not all!*

Sergeant McGuire notified the captain, who was elated at the news. O'Rourke said, "Drill the kid and get to the bottom of what the hell he's involved in with this guy, Savage, and the connection with the Masons. The NYPD must show real progress in this case. I'll be at the precinct later."

McGuire was eager to get into a room with Barnes. He had many questions and all day, and possibly into the night, to get all the answers. He summoned Shamus, and his nightstick, to introduce themselves to Savage. Shamus was fired up as usual.

As Barnes and Savage were escorted into the precinct, all attention turned to them. You could hear a feather drop. McGuire walked over to O'Shea and shook his hand. "Thank you, Detective O'Shea. Frank will come by later if you want to stick around."

"Sure, I'll be happy to. Anything I can do in the meantime?"

"Yeah, why don't you accompany me with Mr. Barnes here and find out what he's been doing. Looks like he's sick, running a fever

. . . right, Tyler?" Tyler turned red and said nothing. *What could he possibly say?*

Shamus rapidly fired one question after another, each accompanied by a bang of the nightstick inches from Savage that caused him to come a few inches off his chair. The noise could be heard throughout the precinct as all the occupants broke into smiles as they shook their heads.

McGuire and O'Shea stared at Tyler for a long minute, making the Death Valley sweat return to the young man. "Why did you lie, Tyler?" Simple enough question, but one that, in the moment, made Tyler realize his life was about to change, and not for the better. He was silent.

"You know, son, we are going to be here as long as it takes for you to come clean, so get as comfortable as you are able." Tyler squirmed in his seat. "Why did you pick up Sonny Mason, and where is he?" Again, silence, more squirming, followed by the appearance that he was ready to talk, but didn't. "You know, this could go very badly for you, or it can result in less trouble if you cooperate. It's your choice. I think you're a smart guy, Tyler. I think you can decide the right way to go, but it better be fast. I'm losing my patience, and when the captain gets here, you'll be in for all hell breaks loose!"

Tyler was an intelligent young man, and McGuire emphasized that he had his whole life ahead of him if he chose to speak and face the consequences of his actions. It didn't take much longer for him to open up about his involvement. McGuire wanted to know the "what" but also the "why."

Tyler told McGuire about all the communications between him, Henry Mason, Brian Savage, and Sonny, his connections with Hudson House, and the limited elements of the plan he knew were devoted to racial hatred in the broader NYC area.

McGuire asked, "Where is Hudson House, and who are the players there?"

"It's in Yonkers. I don't know the address. If I knew, I would tell you."

"Think, did you ever hear anyone mention an area, a street, something identifiable near the Hudson House?"

Tyler thought for a moment and said, "I do recall someone mentioned a street . . . a . . . something with a 'W' . . . I can't think of the name."

McGuire turned to O'Shea. "Marty, would you please go tell that to one of my officers and see if you can locate all streets in Yonkers that start with a 'W' and have someone call O'Rourke with the information? He will want to call the Yonkers police chief there. He knows him personally."

"Will do."

McGuire and Tyler spoke for another few minutes. Once McGuire realized he had probably pulled out as much information that Tyler had, he asked, "Why, Tyler, why? You were part of the NYPD police. We fight crime; we don't contribute to it. I've watched you work in support of all our efforts, and now come to learn that you are an informant for a group that is contributing to the very crimes we are trying to prevent. I'm disappointed but want to know what led you to your actions."

Tyler sighed and began a lengthy story that led to his radicalization. He told McGuire that he was an only child and that he had always been obedient and respectful growing up. He did well in high school but didn't want to attend college, as his parents had hoped and were ready to support him. He told McGuire that he had thought about college but had determined it wasn't for him; he wanted to enter the workforce and become independent. He loved his parents but yearned to be self-sufficient.

His story shifted to when he attended a rally in Brooklyn against Black people and was approached by Henry Mason while there. Henry befriended him, met him often, and took him for breakfast or to the local drug store, where he bought him an ice cream soda. Tyler said his favorites were a root beer float or egg cream—a classic NYC original consisting of milk, seltzer water, and Fox's U-bet chocolate syrup.

"Tyler, I'm confused. If you had such a decent upbringing, were obedient, did well in school, etc., why did you attend the rally?"

Tyler shook his head in despair. "When I was in my junior year in high school, one weekend my parents left for a forty-mile drive up to Pleasantville in Westchester County to visit with some friends.

My father was in the Marines during World War II and had a buddy up there from the war in the Pacific. He and his wife became close friends with my mom and dad. Their names are Annie and Thomas Barnes."

He paused, recalling the tough part. "They left the house one evening and were driving through Harlem when their car broke down. This gang of Black kids . . . around six of them . . . beat up my parents (he choked a bit and took a deep breath) . . . robbed them. They didn't even have a lot of money on them, maybe thirty-five dollars. My dad fought hard and actually injured three of them seriously, but then, eventually, they overwhelmed him. There were too many of them. They hurt my mom too, really bad. She never recovered from their attack, physically or psychologically. I guess that impacted me in a way that I wanted some revenge for what they did, especially to my mother." Tyler looked down and began to cry.

McGuire took it all in before he walked over and put his hand on Tyler's shoulder. "I'm sorry for what happened to your parents. It seems like good people are often the victims. They're innocent. But one bad act does not get undone by another. Think of all the innocent Blacks that would become victims of violence if this hate were to continue into action?"

Tyler nodded his head. "I know, Sarge. I'm sorry; I messed up!"

"Alright, I'll be back in a few minutes. Can I get you something to drink?" Tyler just nodded as he continued sobbing. Just as he was about to exit the room, a police officer came to the door and whispered to McGuire that they had found something.

O'Shea and Officer Nelson met with McGuire. Nelson said, "We found two streets in Yonkers that start with 'W': Walnut Street and Warburton Avenue. Walnut is located in the northern part of the city; Warburton is several hundred feet east of, and parallel with the Hudson River."

McGuire, with a light-bulb moment, said, "Hudson House. My bet it's somewhere on Warburton!" Just then, O'Rourke arrived and saw Detective O'Shea.

"Marty, so good to see you. How's the family?"

"All good, Frank, you?" The rank didn't matter to these two; they were close buddies from the escapades of the past.

"Great. Let's catch up in a little while. What have we got?" They moved to McGuire's office to update the captain. Shamus joined them with all the information he "squeezed" from Savage. The picture was becoming clearer. O'Rourke got on the phone with Doyle at the Yonkers police and shared the same intel. They began a random search up and down Warburton for any information on the suspects or the Chevy. They now had photos and descriptions. *Someone must know something!*

The bell rang for playtime. The first- and second-graders ran to the gym. Some of the administrative staff accompanied Lopez and Garcia to ensure that all the kids were engaged in a happy time and would not recall any of the horror that had previously existed in the room.

Some of the kids were playing the traditional "bounce the Spalding," while Taylor and Nick were having a most exciting conversation. "My dad told me he might talk to your dad about you and me playing baseball together!"

Nick said, "Oh. I really like baseball. Sometimes, my daddy and me, we watch it on TV."

"My dad said we might go to a baseball game too! He always talks about Jackie Robinson. He used to be with the Dodgers."

The two boys spent the rest of the time in the gym talking about baseball, especially being together and all the fun they would be having now outside of school. The get-together during the Christmas break marked a new level in their relationship, one significantly advanced from the initial awkwardness of staring at each other on the first day of first grade. They considered each other best friends.

Chapter 23

THE SUBJECT OF BASEBALL

Isaac Washington worked hard to become a pharmacist, like his older brother. However, his four years of course study at Long Island University Pharmacy did not come without challenges. He was one of the few Black individuals to achieve an opportunity in the program in the late 1940s despite growing systemic racism and segregation.

He was acutely aware of barriers and discrimination that limited opportunities to people of color and was determined to prove, to himself more than anyone, that he had the fiber and stamina to succeed. He wanted a family and the means to provide a promising future for them. Achieving a higher education was the first step toward that objective.

He faced injustices at school and, afterward, at the drugstore pharmacy where he worked to serve his community. It was almost a daily occurrence. There was always someone who would try to discredit him or make him feel inferior. However, while raising awareness of the need for desegregation and equal rights, his attitude fostered friendly interaction, and he did his best to defuse any potential hostility.

He kept up with national and local news, especially regarding racism and civil rights. He religiously read the related articles in *The New York Times*, *The Daily News*, and occasionally in *The Brooklyn Eagle* and *The Brooklyn Chronicle*. He knew that much needed to be changed in the social order and was determined to do his part, no matter how insignificant someone might think it was.

Isaac was a good man, a good husband, and a good father. He considered that his top priority and kept his compass intact in those commitments. His mindset toward others, regardless of their background, was always focused on being positive. Meeting the Greenes through their sons' friendship offered an opportunity he recognized and discussed with his wife, Makena.

They both had a small group of Black friends, some of whom had young children, with whom they socialized occasionally. The excitement that Taylor brought home from his first day in first grade uniquely opened up a new potential relationship. Their meeting with Jonathan and Mary at PS 91, when the school staff and police addressed the attack in the cafeteria, was pleasant, free of any signs of prejudice or dislike.

The outing with Taylor and Nick at Prospect Park strengthened those feelings, and after Isaac and Makena had an enjoyable conversation about it, they decided to contact the Greenes to suggest some activities for the boys that would maintain their relationship with them. Several activities came to mind, especially with the warmer months ahead: baseball, park outings, visits to the city, fishing, and more that any kid—or adult for that matter—would enjoy.

It was Friday evening, January 10. "Hey, Jonathan, it's Isaac."

"Isaac, hey man, how's everything goin'?"

"Good . . . good. Hey, Taylor can't stop talking about all the fun we had over the holidays and his conversations with Nick this week in school. They seem to have bonded very well, and Makena and I are very happy about that." Jonathan was happy to hear it, but he thought he was about to listen to a "but" or something that would change Isaac's message.

"Uh-huh."

"Well, we were wondering if we could talk about reuniting again soon. We are thinking ahead a bit, and I remember you sayin' you're a Yankee fan." He laughed. "I won't hold that against you!" They both laughed. "I was thinkin' maybe we could plan to go to a game . . . the season will start in a few months."

"Yeah, sure, that sounds great! But, won't you miss the Dodgers? They left for LA."

"I know, what a disappointment. I'll miss them, but I don't mind goin' to a Yankee game; after all, I'm still a New Yorker!" They both laughed again.

Jonathan said, "Isaac, let's plan on it . . . would love it. You know Mary likes to watch the games also."

"Oh, so good to hear that. Makena is a big fan. I think she knows more about baseball than I do. At least she talks about it more than I!"

"Well, why don't we make it a family thing again? Maybe right after the season opens in early April. We can check the schedule and see what works for us."

"Yeah, yeah. Hey . . . uh . . . I also wanted to ask if you want to get the boys on a youth baseball team together. Look, I'll be frank, I know there's a lot of resistance to mixing . . . you know . . . uh . . . "

Jonathan said, "Isaac, our boys love each other. I don't care what anyone says or thinks. Let's do that. They would love it. I know Mary and I would love it. It would give us more opportunities to get together with you and Makena, watch our sons learn the game, and learn what it means to be on a team, all working toward a win."

This was music to Isaac's ears. He was comforted by Jonathan's words. "I am so glad to hear that! I'll tell Makena; she'll love it!"

"Okay, Isaac. It's a plan! Thanks so much for calling us." The two men hung up, feeling they had accomplished one of the most important things in their lives. Perhaps they did.

Isaac thought for a moment and remembered that he had mentioned to Taylor the possibility of him and Nick playing on a youth team together. He had regretted that because he was unsure of the outcome after speaking with Jonathan. The Greenes may have just been courteous and would not want any relationship to go further. This would result in disappointment for Taylor. On the contrary, all turned out much better than he expected.

Jonathan went into the TV room, where Mary watched one of her favorite programs, the real-life sitcom about the Nelson family, *The Adventures of Ozzie and Harriet*. She also liked *Lassie*. She and Nick watched it together every week. Nick thought all dogs were as smart as Lassie.

"Mary, I just got off the phone with Isaac!" He told her all about their conversation. "He's a nice guy! I was going to ask if he liked fishing and if maybe we could go together sometime, but I didn't want to push too much. Maybe later."

"That sounds great! Nick would love that, and I would like to get to know Makena better. She was charming to talk with, and I think we hit it off. I prefer a friendship more than what we hear and read about all this racism, segregation, and crime. It makes me sick. We should encourage Nick as much as we can to keep his friendship with that nice boy, Taylor. He's a sweet kid."

Jonathan said, "I agree, absolutely agree! I'm going to see if I can find the baseball season schedule." Mary returned to watching Harriet Nelson, wearing her apron, as she baked cookies in her kitchen. *She could never make enough for her sons, David and Ricky.*

Chapter 24

MRS. DANIELS, YOUR FRIENDLY NEIGHBORHOOD SPY

The Yonkers police patrolled Warburton Avenue from south to north and back again several times during the week. The road was lined with a mix of residential, commercial, and industrial buildings. Some areas contained homes in disrepair; others were more upscale. The Chevy was nowhere to be found, and no one had seen anyone who resembled Henry Barnes or his two kids.

Doyle was in frequent contact with O'Rourke. "Frank, we haven't turned up anything yet. We are going to do a house-to-house query. It may take some time, but we'll get it done."

"Thanks, Liam. I appreciate all the help."

"Anytime, my friend. You only need to ask."

"Likewise. I look forward to hearing some good news. I know you won't rest until you find somethin'." They hung up.

Back at the precinct, the police continued to hold and question Savage and Barnes separately, and especially pressured Savage for more information by leveraging Tyler's information. "We know about Hudson House, Savage. Where is it exactly in Yonkers? Might as well tell us. The Yonkers police are searching, and they'll eventually find Mason's Chevy and whoever is involved up there. The more you keep it secret, the worse it will be for you. What is Mason up to? Who else is involved in this hate group? We know what Barnes knows, and we'll find out more."

Shamus hammered away at Savage, literally and figuratively. He added a little extra thought. "You can consider your pawn shop permanently closed if you wish." Little did he know that the police were combing every square inch of his shop. When they took breaks, they stopped by Cecelia's.

Savage had been involved with Mason for years, but he was now beginning to doubt his involvement with him and his future. Shamus observed the wheels spinning in Savage's head. "Think about it. I'll give you some time." Shamus left the room and wouldn't return for hours. *Let that "scatach" contemplate his situation for a while.* He grinned as he thought of the Irish word for "scumbag."

Late on Saturday, January 11, the Yonkers police caught a break. A patrol car searching Warburton stopped at a small house and knocked on the door. An elderly woman came to the door but did not open it. She shouted, "Who's there?"

"Ma'am, it's the Yonkers police. We need to ask you some questions." She opened the door slowly, the chain, which could easily be snapped by the slightest force, still intact. "Good afternoon, Ma'am. We are looking for someone who has a red and white Chevy that might be somewhere in this neighborhood, and we were wondering if . . . "

Mrs. Daniels interrupted, "Right over there." She pointed to the house about fifty feet down the avenue on the opposite side. "I seen that car there. It was very dirty, but I know the color. There were people from that house coverin' it up very fast the other day, like they wanted to hide it. But it ain't there anymore. I watch outside all the time; not much else for me to do. My husband died ten years ago, and I live here alone. Sometimes, my daughter comes to see me from Poughkeepsie." She went on for another minute, and the police had to interrupt her this time.

"Ma'am, this is very important. Do you know when the car left that house?"

"Uh . . . it was on Thursday . . . Thursday afternoon . . . not sure of the time."

The policeman showed Daniels a photo of Henry Mason's kids that the school had provided to the police at the 75th Precinct in Brooklyn, who had passed them on to the Yonkers police. "Please look at these photos. Did you see . . ."

"Yes, yes. I saw both of these kids. One kid showed up there a couple of weeks ago, a day or two after Christmas. I think the younger one came about a week later, around Saturday." The woman had a pretty good mental calendar. "They were with two men when they all left that house." She gave one description that most likely fit Henry Mason. She described the other as "a creepy fat guy with a bald head and hair over his ears down to his shoulders." She heard the cop mumble something that sounded like "kooball."

"What did you say, kooball?"

"No, nothing, Ma'am, just thinking out loud. Was there anyone else?"

"No, not when they left, but there are two other men over there a lot. One looks like the fat slob with the bald head; the other one is real skinny and looks sick all the time. They are always yellin' at him for somethin'."

"Ma'am. You have been very helpful. Anything else you can tell us?"

"Yeah, the men and the older boy loaded the car, and I saw them put rifles in the trunk!"

"Okay, thank you. Have a good day." *Watching everything that goes on in this crappy neighborhood 24/7!*

Officer Phillips radioed his headquarters with all the information that Daniels provided. Within minutes, it worked its way to Chief Doyle. He was elated and excited to call Frank O'Rourke with the update.

"Liam, that is fantastic news! You and your men are to be commended! This is very helpful. You found Hudson House! We have two key suspects in custody and are beginning to piece together a network that is linked to two recent attacks on Black students in our schools. And we think their plans go well beyond that! I owe you your favorite bottle of whiskey! A Jameson, perhaps?"

"Ah, my friend, you know me too well. A Jameson will do just fine, but I will only have it if I can share it with you!"

"You're on. Take care!" *Making progress is always something to celebrate with whiskey, even though the case has more to go!*

O'Rourke met with Sergeant McGuire and several police officers to review the information and coordinate a joint effort with the Yonkers Police to raid Hudson House. In the meantime, Shamus would revisit Savage to tell him what the Yonkers Police had learned, and that Hudson House was no longer a secret. No one would disclose that an eyewitness in the neighborhood provided this treasured trove of information.

McGuire and O'Reilly went back to work on Barnes and Savage, respectively. They retrieved them from their cells, returned them to separate interrogation rooms, and laid it on thick.

"We found Hudson House, Savage, on Warburton Avenue. We know that Henry Mason, his two sons, and another one of your filthy group are on the run. We'll find 'em. If you help, we'll consider reducing the long jail term you're facing." Shamus and Savage stared at one another. "I can give you some more time to think about it. You can stay right here and enjoy that hard metal chair you're sittin' in all night if you want."

Savage said, "I was thinking about telling you about Hudson House. I . . ."

Shamus yelled, "Well, it's too late; we already know about it, so no brownie points for you! Give us something we don't know, something valuable. And I'll decide if it's useful or not!"

McGuire filled Barnes in on Hudson House and asked him what else he knew of Mason and his pals' plans, where they went, and why. Tyler reiterated that he would completely cooperate with the police and their investigation, but was limited in what Mason and Savage shared with him. "Think, Tyler, think. Any mention of a place other than Hudson House? Another code name, an area, a city?"

Tyler thought hard, reaching into the depths of his memory. Something was on the tip of his tongue. "Uh . . . uh . . . Syracuse! I remember Henry Mason saying something about Syracuse. He had to go to Syracuse. I remember it because he was supposed to meet me again at the drugstore. He promised me an ice cream soda. He called me at my house the day before and said he couldn't make it."

McGuire thought, *Syracuse? What the hell is in Syracuse? We finally made some progress, and new questions pop up!* No news to him, really. This is the nature of police work. You find out the answers when you find out.

"What else, Tyler? Anything you can recall in your conversations with Mason? What he and the others were planning? Why he would go to Syracuse? Does anything connect with the incidents in Jefferson High School, where Buddy attended, and PS 91, where Sonny went? Both of Mason's sons were involved in attacks against Black students. Did Mason say anything that you recall that ties all this together?"

"Uh . . . Mason would sometimes talk like he was in a dream . . . about the limited scope of activity against the Blacks in the NYC area and the network he wanted to build, especially in Brooklyn, with the help of others like those at the Hudson House. He often called Hudson House a safe haven and steppingstone."

"A steppingstone? A steppingstone to what?"

"I'm not completely sure, but he talked about using the knowledge and experience of the South, and that it was spreading to the Northeast, that he wanted to move up in the 'grand scheme of things' . . . his words. He never fully explained that, so I'm unsure what it all means. I'm sorry. I just got wrapped up too much with him because of the hate I developed for the Blacks . . . what they did to my parents. I am so stupid."

"Tyler, I think this is extremely helpful. I appreciate your willingness to help the police. I wish you never got into this mess. I will put in a good word for you and hope it helps, but you should know it's not up to me or the captain."

"I know. Thank you, Sarge."

More pieces of the puzzle and more questions!

McGuire shared all the puzzle pieces with the team, including Captain O'Rourke. After the group thought about all the data, some light bulbs lit up. "Limited scope of activity against the Blacks in the NYC area and the network he wanted to build" . . . "Knowledge and experience of the South, and that it was spreading to the Northeast" . . . "Steppingstone." Hudson House to Syracuse, perhaps.

Several team members said it all at once. "Ku Klux Klan?"

O'Rourke said, "Boys, that's a pretty good guess as far as I'm concerned. And, if it's true, we've got a much bigger problem." He quickly notified Chief Liam Doyle and jointly decided they would contact the Syracuse Police Department. This case jumped from a Brooklyn issue to a Brooklyn-Yonkers one and now, possibly, statewide *or more.*

Chapter 25

DEMON BECOMES DAMON

While the country was eager to put WWII and the Korean War in the rearview mirror, it searched for stability, focusing on family values and conformity, where men and women observed strict gender roles that met society's expectations. The growth of the civil rights movement in the '50s often contributed to countering racial segregation in schools, housing, and employment. Segregation was made into law several times in the nineteenth and twentieth centuries.

Some people believed that Black and White individuals were incapable of coexisting. However, in May 1954, the Supreme Court ruling in Brown v. Board of Education of Topeka, Kansas, held that the "separate but equal" doctrine, as applied to public education, was unconstitutional. African Americans gained the right to attend schools alongside their peers in primary and secondary education. Despite this landmark case in Black history and other civil rights movements, some people didn't accept it or care.

The NYPD had enough on its plate with organized crime, where the Mafia and other groups were heavily involved in illegal activities such as gambling, loan sharking, and racketeering; narcotics and drug-related crimes that were on the rise; property crimes, including burglaries, thefts, and vandalism of residential and commercial areas; and violent crimes—murders, assaults, and other offenses.

Street gangs were prevalent and grew into the hundreds, with members in the thousands. The police knew that the gangs were generally divided along ethnic lines and were primarily involved in street violence to claim their turf. Gangs like the South Brooklyn Boys fought the Chaplains, an African American gang, and the

Jokers. The Mau Maus emerged as a Puerto Rican gang. *West Side Story* wasn't just a movie; it was acted out in real life in the streets. The NYPD employed various strategies to combat these crimes, including increased patrols, undercover operations, and community policing tactics. They also collaborated with federal agencies as needed.

Given the information from Tyler Barnes and the trickle of answers that were quickly turning into a waterfall from Brian Savage, the criminal landscape for the NYPD immediately got greater, as it now needed to consider a White supremacy factor that would generate hate and violence against the Black community in the NYC metropolitan area.

Savage had opened up about Hudson House and its connections in Brooklyn and Syracuse, revealing that radical leaders, predominantly from the South, were providing inspiration, methodology, and tactics. He didn't have names or codes—at least any that he would care to divulge, fearing future retribution. Still, he did explain the overall objective of inspiring the younger population to take action against the Blacks. He completely threw Henry Mason under the bus, noting that since his wife, Helen, died, he had transitioned from one who merely had a dislike for Blacks to hating them and choosing violence. He raised his sons to be just like him, *unfortunately*.

Just before Captain O'Rourke called Chief Doyle in Yonkers, he told his officers at the 75th Precinct, "We may have to call in the FBI. I'll bring that up with Chief Doyle and get his opinion, but if this is as big as we are beginning to learn, if it does include elements of the KKK, it would be negligent if we didn't." Everyone nodded in agreement. *Of course, he was their captain.*

O'Rourke decided he would call Doyle and request a face-to-face meeting with him. They set a time to meet on Monday morning as soon as O'Rourke could get through all the city traffic. O'Rourke just said, "No problem, Liam. I'll keep the siren on all the way there!"

"Okay, I'll listen for the siren! See you Monday."

Shortly after Doyle ended his conversation with O'Rourke, Officer Phillips notified him that Mrs. Daniels had called to say she saw two individuals enter the house across from her. Doyle ordered Phillips to investigate and to take Officer Denten with him.

The two police officers drove by Hudson House. There was no car, and no one was in sight. They continued and stopped at Mrs. Daniels' house. She opened the door and invited them in before they could knock.

"Mrs. Daniels, this is Officer Denton. We received your call. What did you see?" She invited them inside and asked if they wanted some tea she had just prepared. "Uh, no, Ma'am, but thank you. You said you saw two men. What did they look like?"

"They were there many times before. They came in an old pickup truck and went inside, and it wasn't two minutes later when they both came out, and the fat guy, who looked like the owner, was yelling at the skinny guy. They remind me of Laurel and Hardy, you know, some people call them 'Skinny and Fat'. I sometimes watch their movies on TV."

"Could you hear what he said?"

"No, but the skinny guy got back in the truck and left. The fat guy is still in the house. That was about twenty minutes ago." Just then, the officers could hear some commotion nearby. They went to the door, looked outside, and saw that the truck was there, and the fat guy was yelling loudly again at the skinny one.

"Where did you go for dog food . . . Jersey?" The only thing the police could hear from the skinny one was mumbling as they reentered the house.

"Mrs. Daniels, you have been a tremendous help. Thank you for calling us. We need to see what's going on over there."

"Oh, you are both very welcome. Next time, stop by for some tea." Both officers tipped their hats, got in the patrol car, and slowly and quietly approached Hudson House. They slammed on the door with their nightsticks.

"It's the police! Open the door!" The fat guy came to the door, opened it slowly, and was about to say something when Phillips and Denton pushed their way in as they drew their weapons. "Where's the other guy, the skinny one?" They looked around the kitchen and thought they would gag, but they hung in there; *they had a job to do!*

"He . . . he's down in the basement feedin' the dog . . . what's . . . what's goin' on?"

"Call him to come up here, now!"

"Ricky . . . Ricky, get up here!" Deadman came up the stairs with a bag of Gaines Meal dog food. He dropped the bag when he saw the uniformed police. He stood there wide-eyed, which indicated that he actually was alive.

Phillips demanded, "What is going on here? Where are the others?"

"We came to feed the dog. The owner had to leave town, and we said we would take care of him. Only, shit-for-brains here forgot the dog food!"

Ricky said, "I told you I thought you had it in the truck!" They both started shouting at one another again.

Phillips looked at Denton and said, in a low enough voice that only his partner could hear, "Yep, Laurel and Hardy!"

"What . . . what did you say?"

"Nothing. Where is the owner of this shithole of a house, and Mr. Henry Mason, and his two sons, Buddy and Sonny?" This question took both "dog-food forgetters" by surprise, resulting in blank stares and dropped jaws. "We know they were here. Where are they?"

Both answered that they didn't know where they were going or when they would be back. "Wrong answer. Turn around; you're both under arrest!"

"For what? We didn't do nothin'."

"Double negative, which means you did do something. Let's go!"

"Double what?"

"Someday, we'll explain it to you. Let's go!" As they made their way to the patrol car, Denton asked Phillips, "What about the dog?"

Ricky said, "What . . . you gonna arrest the dog too?"

As the two cops laughed, the fat man said, "Shut up, Ricky!"

Phillips said, "We can contact some shelters in the area." They returned to the police station and locked Deadman and the fat one in the same cell. *Maybe these two will get to know one another better and appreciate how stupid they both are!*

Officer Phillips had Daniels' phone number and called her to say again how helpful she was and that they had arrested the comedic team. They would look for the others, but didn't expect them anytime soon. They also told her that a dog had been left at the house, had been fed for a while, and that the police would attempt to contact a shelter to pick up and care for the dog.

"Oh, I love dogs! I had a cute dog, but it died about the same time as my husband. It had the cutest eyes that would twinkle, so we named her Twinkles. You know, I could take care of the dog. I'm always here, and it wouldn't be a burden. I live just fine on my husband's pension and Social Security. My house mortgage is paid off. I would take good care of it. What is it . . . uh, him, her? Is it male or female?"

"We didn't see it, Ma'am, but, uh . . . we'll see what we can do. Thank you again."

When O'Rourke and Doyle met and discussed all the details to date—the school attacks, the suspects, the victims, the information from Tyler Barnes and the others, and the raid on Hudson House, they agreed that they should contact the FBI. They first called the Syracuse Police Department to determine if they knew of any KKK activity in their area. If Henry Mason and others were headed that way, it could be to link up with a KKK element that Tyler Barnes hinted about.

Hearing feedback from the Syracuse chief, Spencer Miles, confirmed for O'Rourke and Doyle that their instincts were correct, that there was KKK influence there. They had been tracking some known operatives for over a year but lacked evidence in other investigation areas. They remained in communication for the next week as searching for the red and white Chevy was a high priority and possibly the best link to locating Mason and company because no one in Brooklyn and Yonkers had any solid leads on where in Syracuse to look.

But the week also contained something good. The Yonkers police had initially worked with a local animal shelter to take Demon just before his food ran out. They linked Mrs. Daniels with the shelter, and they were happy to turn the dog over to her adoptive care. Due to limited resources and overcrowding, Demon was probably due to be euthanized before too long.

Daniels called the police to relay her heartwarming story. She said, "That dog was a mess, neglected by his owner. He should be ashamed. Before the shelter turned him over to me, they gave the dog some medicine and shots and cleaned him up a bit. I took . . . " She paused, with her voice cracking, then said, "The name tag on the dog was 'Demon!' I took that name tag off and threw it in the garbage! Who would ever name their dog that? I changed his name to something that sounded close so he would know I was calling him. I named him 'Damon,' . . . got him a new name tag, gave him a nice bath, and brushed his coat of hair. I can see his eyes now, too . . . those big, beautiful brown eyes! He's a big guy and loves belly rubs. But I think he loves jumping up on my lap the most and looking at me with those eyes! We just look at each other, and he loves my hugs, too! I can't thank you, fellas, enough!"

The entire Yonkers Police Force eventually heard her story. *And the woman and her dog were much happier!*

Chapter 26

NUMBER 42, BROOKLYN DODGERS

The joint efforts of the combined police organizations made little progress over the next few months. Wherever Mason and others were in the Syracuse area of the state was still a mystery, and the information coming from Barnes, Savage, and the Hudson House creeps was exhausted. It remained difficult to track known KKK members, and there wasn't any known meeting place for the nefarious group. However, the police's interface with the FBI during this time matured as they shared intelligence that was gaining ground.

The FBI's Counter-Intelligence Program (COINTELPRO) used wiretapping, informants, and physical surveillance to gather crucial information on criminal activity. They intercepted some chatter that indicated meetings at "the cabin," sometimes with further designations, such as "Cabin 1" or "Cabin 2," and others. Still, the locations were yet unknown, and the dates and times were always in code. But the FBI staffers felt they were closing in; they needed a break. They needed to hear someone say something that would lead to one of the cabins . . . they needed to locate the red and white Chevy . . . they needed to match a face with a photo.

The 75th Precinct police did not provide any updates on school attacks to Principal Carpenter at PS 91 or Evan Walters at Thomas Jefferson High School. Dr. Carpenter dutifully kept her commitment to monthly staff meetings focused on avoiding racism in any form in the school. The police decided to inform them only when they had successfully solved the causes of those crimes. As far as they knew, the educational staff at both locations focused on teaching, not crime solving, and would likely prefer to leave the past behind.

The police focused on the increasing plague of intimidating gangs that wreaked havoc on them, civic leaders, teachers, and the population in general. The Bishops, The Hawks—who even had a membership card, "Hawks Social Club," with a phrase, "Til death do us part"—The South Brooklyn Boys, The Majesties, The Garfield Gang, and many more continued the teen warfare rumbles among their greased-duck-tailed, switchblade-wielding members, who would often produce headlines in the *Brooklyn Eagle* and other local newspapers.

Jonathan checked the baseball season schedule. He knew the Brooklyn Dodgers had their last season in Brooklyn and announced their move to Los Angeles on October 8, 1957, leaving the New York Yankees, the only baseball team in town. He would gloat a little when he called Isaac one evening.

"Hey, Isaac. I was following up on our plans to go to a ball game. Not much choice, you know . . . Yankees . . . Yankees . . . or Yankees." He laughed.

"Okay, Jonathan, go ahead. Rub it in, but I will still follow the Dodgers, even if they're in LA now."

"I hear you. So sorry they left Brooklyn! What do you think of attending the first Yankee weekend game in April? They will play the Baltimore Orioles on April 19 at Yankee Stadium. You think Makena might like to go too? Mary loves the game and watches them on TV with me."

"Yeah, Makena will. Let's make it a family day at the stadium. I'm sure the boys will be excited to go!"

"Okay, I'll reserve tickets for that day. I kinda wish we could see Whitey Ford pitch that game, but he's pitching the day before, and the boys will be in school, and we'll be at work. So this is the next best day."

Isaac said, "I can't wait. Let's hope for good weather. Even though my heart will be with the Dodgers and one of my favorite players, Jackie Robinson, I'm sure I will have a great time there with you and your family."

"Ah, Jackie Robinson! I love what that guy did for baseball and what he stands for."

Isaac was elated to hear Jonathan praise Robinson. "I agree. He had so many challenges, you know, being a Black man, facing all kinds of criticism, some from his own teammates, if you can believe that." This generated a comprehensive conversation about Robinson as a ballplayer and a man who made civil rights history.

Jonathan added, "Yes, I can. I have followed the news on Robinson for a while now. Being the first Black player in the history of Major League Baseball, how he faced racist abuse through the seasons, but with dignity and grace."

Isaac's quick reaction added more substance to Jonathan's remarks: "He sure did. He showed that he and his fellow Black players belonged in the game by his actions and ability on the field. He was so good that he was named the first-ever Rookie of the Year in 1947."

"I remember that! That was big news! I can't remember who he played for before the Dodgers, though. Do you know?"

"Yeah, he was a shortstop with the Negro League in Kansas City—The Monarchs, where he demonstrated his speed around the bases and his great at-bats at the plate.

"The Dodgers' team president, Branch Rickey, wanted to sign a Black player to the game, despite MLB Commissioner Kenesaw Mountain Landis' strict segregationist policy. When Landis died, Rickey made it happen. He wanted to make the Dodgers better than their poor baseball record and to bring Ebbets Field back to life. Robinson's talent, youth, and emotional strength set him apart from other aging athletes. He signed with the Dodgers in 1946 for a year in the minors, then moved up to play second base. Sometimes, he played the other bases."

"Wow, Isaac, you know a lot about him!'

"Yeah, Jonathan, he is one of my role models. He was not only a Rookie of the Year but an MVP in 1949, and he helped the Dodgers win the World Series in 1955. Uh . . . I have to add that it was against the New York Yankees." He laughed.

"How well I remember that! But I also remember the Dodgers losing to the Yankees in Game 7 of the World Series in 1956. I think that was Robinson's last game, too, not taking anything away from him, of course." He wanted to make that clear.

"That was painful to watch! But I think of number 42, how he took abuse, faced opposing players on the field, base runners who stepped on him as they ran the bases, balls thrown at him by pitchers, racist chants from the stands, and opposing dugouts. He was bigger than all of that by resisting the urge to fight and demonstrated his contribution to the team. I guess I could go on and on. Sorry to lay it on so thick."

"Isaac, you don't need to apologize. I'm with you. I agree with everything you say. I admire Robinson. I don't look at his skin color. I look at the man."

That conversation, and especially Jonathan's last remarks, between a Black father and a White one not only strengthened their relationship but also established a basis for mutual respect and appreciation that would trickle down to their sons. They couldn't wait for the day at a baseball game in the Bronx!

Chapter 27

CABIN 1, OTISCO LAKE

In a remote section of Otisco Lake, the easternmost of New York's Finger Lakes in Onondaga County, smoke rose from a cabin occupied by ten men—men who have or had other jobs, some respectable, and who even looked nonthreatening. *But, looks can be deceiving.* The cabin was a simple design constructed from local logs, stones, and rough-hewn timber that blended with the natural surroundings. They referred to this in their communications as "Cabin 1." It was the main headquarters for Tentacle-E.

The other cabins were dispersed in other lake sections and around the neighboring Skaneateles Lake. They were built in the 1940s by the Walker family and used extensively for vacationing, hunting, and fishing. The family's ownership dates back to the Revolutionary War, when lands around the lakes were granted to soldiers as compensation for their service. Rhett Walker was the property's sole heir, and he often secluded himself at these locations to engage in those activities. But more recently, he was there to conduct the planning and operations of the evil empire he was so proud to be a member of.

Butch Brady led the meeting. He was a vicious man with a deep-rooted anger for Blacks. As the Grand Dragon of Mississippi, known as "VenoM," he led the Octopus component of the Klan. He led many cross burnings to intimidate and terrorize Blacks in the South, as well as occasional lynchings, although the frequency of these crimes had decreased compared with earlier decades. New York was an opportunity for White supremacy growth, and he especially yearned to target the "Black-rich" population of NYC.

Mason, Paine, Walker, and local Syracuse residents sat around the room as the fireplace provided warmth on the remaining cool days of early April. Brady began, "I'm here for a week and need to get some information on your progress and guide you on how we proceed with making NYC our playground." Everyone laughed as they fully understood. "But first, I understand that some of you are on the run, and the police may have captured some of our guys . . . no contact with them in Brooklyn?"

Henry spoke up first. "I have not been able to contact X-ray, our informant inside the 75th Precinct of the NYPD in East New York, or our guy, Bullet, in South Brooklyn. They have gone dark, which is very unusual. I would always phone them at their homes or Bullet at his pawn shop."

Jethro Paine added, "My guys at the Hudson House are also unreachable. They were supposed to feed my dog, but I have no idea where they are and if my dog is still alive."

Brady stared at them briefly, and the uneasiness among his listeners was clearly visible. And it was apparent that the dog meant nothing to him. "This reminds me of other times when some of our men went missing. It usually means they were intercepted, but some have abandoned our cause. Is there anything we should be concerned about them tipping off the cops about our location?"

Henry answered, "I think we are safe . . . here. As far as I can remember, I never disclosed the Syracuse component to anyone. They absolutely would not know of the cabin locations."

Rhett Walker said, "We know the Syracuse cops are working with the FBI and that they have tracked some of our guys. We also have a few informants placed around the cop community to give us the upper hand as much as possible. But no one has been anywhere near these cabins."

"Good, let's keep it that way. We need to keep moving, never in one place too long, and never leave any evidence of our group or what we are planning. Understood?"

A complete round of "Understood" echoed in the cabin.

"First, let's discuss recruitment. I understand, Henry, that your boys have been active in their schools. I heard all about the attacks on the Black youth there. Where are they now?"

Henry's thoughts briefly returned to his self-imposed questions about what he had done to his sons' futures, even though the inspiration of the cause overpowered him. "Yes . . . Buddy and Sonny both led the attacks in the schools. They came to Syracuse with me and are with one of our members' family and their sons. They won't be returning to school in Brooklyn, maybe not anywhere. They are dedicated to our objectives." His regret did not show, but he felt it big time internally.

"Great to hear. We will need more young up-and-comers like Buddy and Sonny. Anyone else?"

Walker spoke next. "We have several of our local guys grooming their teenage boys and expect they will be able to do the same in the schools here."

"Good, good. However, we need to ramp up the activity in Brooklyn, our best target area in the city. And now, since we lost that capability with Mason's boys and other assets, we need to regroup and connect with anyone else in that area."

Mason and Paine knew that would be difficult, but didn't add anything to the conversation. Brady went on. "Well, more on that later. Let's look at the specific targets, especially the gangs that are at war with one another. We should recruit inside the gangs that fight that Black gang . . . what is it called?"

"The Chaplains," said Henry. "They are fierce rivals with the Puerto Rican gang called The Mau Maus." The conversation continued for another hour to solidify specific steps for infiltrating the gangs to achieve the best effect. However, they realized it would take time to reestablish their footing due to those who needed to flee the area or were perhaps no longer available due to police intervention.

They transitioned to discussing the weapons inventory, which primarily included firearms and explosives. Walker said, "We keep everything spread around Cabins 2, 3, and 4. So we have a fallback stash if one gets discovered or raided." Walker continued to go over the inventory quickly, item by item.

Brady seemed happy but added, "Okay, protect it and make it all count. If you run low or get busted, we might be able to run some supplies through our interstate channels. Let me know."

The men took a break for a quick lunch and guzzled down some beer or something stronger before pulling out maps of the area, marked with detailed escape routes from each cabin and also depicting where they had set booby traps. The discussions continued for two more days to ensure that everyone was aware of their latest status and responsibilities. Henry and Jethro knew they could not return to their previous homes and jobs. They were now committed to serving Tentacle-E and depended on it for survival. This realization manifested itself in self-doubt as their work in the evil empire was now their full-time job. *And Henry would need to manage his two teenage sons as an added bonus!*

Little did they know that a few days before their meeting, a Syracuse police officer was posted and hidden from view along US Route 20 West. He observed the red and white Chevy and followed it at a distance, among other vehicles, to remain unnoticed. He relayed his position and transferred the information on the Chevy to other police further west and around the county. The Syracuse police also notified the FBI in the area, and together, they established an unmarked vehicle network along all major roads around a twenty-five-mile radius. They noticed that the car exited off Route 20 and took secondary roads toward Otisco Lake.

The law enforcement team of Syracuse police and the FBI was well aware of the 75th Precinct informant and that he tipped off radical members of the Klan's network. They had a strict protocol that maintained secure intelligence among a limited task team to avoid any similar warning signals to Walker or the others. Chief Doyle in Yonkers and Captain O'Rourke in Brooklyn also had access to the most updated information. *And, as far as they all knew, it was working. They were closing in.* They decided to monitor the area and avoid any immediate confrontation that might trigger warnings to others. The objective was to contain the threat, and once they felt confident that they had it cordoned off with adequate resources, they would strike. All the effort from late January was about to pay off. *Thank God for red and white Chevies!*

Chapter 28

GAME DAY, APRIL 19, 1958

The Greenes and the Washingtons met at the corner of Sutter Avenue and Rutland Road at noon to take a 45-minute subway ride from the Sutter Avenue subway station to 161st Street in the Bronx to see the New York Yankees play the Baltimore Orioles at a 2:00 p.m. game. They had walked from their nearby homes on this mild spring day, with temperatures between 50 and 60 degrees, with partly cloudy skies. Nick and Taylor had baseball gloves with them as they dreamed of catching a foul ball.

The parents gave each boy a fifteen-cent subway token, a solid brass coin featuring "NYC" in the center and the "Y" cut out, to deposit into the train's entrance turnstile. They were excited about going to the game together, and using the unique coin for the subway ride was part of the fun. Having to go through many stations and stops generated several "Are we there yet?" questions from the curious boys. The train was crowded as usual, offering very few seats, but one man rose to offer Mary his seat. She and Jonathan thanked him, but then Mary offered it to Makena, who said, "Oh, no thanks. It's okay, you go ahead."

The man said, "Hey, lady, I offered you my seat, not this . . . " He hesitated as Jonathan and Isaac were about to intervene, but Mary looked him in the eye before speaking.

"You offered me the seat, so it's mine. I offered it to my friend. End of story." The man now had four sets of eyes staring at him—two at eye level and two from Nick and Taylor below. *And also from an inquisitive crowd inside the packed train.* The man slowly turned away and slithered through the crowd toward the end of the subway car. He fully realized he was outnumbered. Shortly after that, another man rose and offered his seat to Mary. *Well, this day is getting off to a good start!* The boys seemed confused by this disruption, but the smiles on their mothers' faces put them at ease. *Back to baseball!*

The train came to a stop at 161st Street–Yankee Stadium. Along the way, it became more packed, if that were possible. But when it's a Yankee game, people will become sardines in a can for their home team! The crowd exited and made their way to the stadium. Lots of baseball chatter, families and individuals, high hopes for a win, and searching of pockets for entry tickets.

Jonathan had purchased the tickets, and although Isaac offered to pay him for his family, Jonathan just said, "No, we got this. Why don't you get food and drinks? We can swap next time!"

Isaac said thanks but wanted to confirm, "Okay, but don't forget now. Next time it's on us!" He got a thumbs up and a smile, which was all the verification he needed. They followed the signs to Section 217, which was situated near first base and between the lower and upper sections. It would provide good views of the game. It was around 1:20 p.m., with sufficient time to stop by the restrooms and peruse the gift shops for any pregame souvenirs. Isaac bought Yankee baseball caps for the boys, and they picked up some hot dogs and drinks before they proceeded to their seats. The growing boys were especially starving at this point.

While baseball was a sport for everyone, and especially with the noteworthy contributions from Jackie Robinson and other Black athletes, there were still incidents of racial segregation and discrimination at Yankee Stadium and other ballparks, as in many aspects of American society. Black ticket holders were sometimes relegated to specific sections of the stadium or subjected to hostility from other spectators. The efforts and actions by Major League Baseball and role models like Robinson were a step forward, but they did not eliminate racial tensions at sports venues across the country. It still existed and would manifest itself again today, helping to spoil a planned day of fun, at least for the Washingtons and the Greenes.

Jonathan led the others as they descended to the middle of Section 217. He had the ticket stubs for six seats, one of which was right next to the stairway. The crowd noise was minimal as the game had not yet started, and the Yankees' defense was warming up on the field. As they continued down the steps, a voice rang out, "Hey, you're in the wrong section. You belong up in the Black section way up there." He pointed across the field up toward the nose-bleed seats. The voice came from a middle-aged White man, flanked by his buddies, who laughed and pointed as he did.

They chanted, "Up there, up there."

Isaac turned and faced them. "Look, guys, we are here today just like you . . . to enjoy the game. So, if you don't mind, please keep your racist comments to yourselves. We have every right to be here. We spend our money here just like you." Makena and the others stopped for a moment but did not interrupt.

"Yeah, well, we don't have to like it."

Jonathan said, "C'mon, our seats are down a few more rows."

Isaac was turning to join the others, but responded, "No, you don't have to like it, but we are going to sit in our paid-for seats. I hope you guys enjoy the game." He left as the others jeered at him. Isaac just ignored them and went to his seat.

"Dad, why did that guy say that? Why was he mean to us?" Taylor was upset; his day began to ruin. Nick was also disturbed by the foul and unsportsmanlike behavior.

"It's nothing, son. Some people just like to make trouble. Don't worry, look, the game is almost ready to start!" The diversion tactic slowly took effect as Taylor and Nick, seated next to each other, pointed at the players and tried to identify the ones they knew. Isaac and Jonathan spoke quietly to one another, trying to put the incident behind them. They scanned the seats in every direction to note where other Black spectators may be seated. Seats were filling with predominantly White fans, but there were occasional men, women, and children of color, including some Black individuals. The one thing in common among everyone was that they were all there to enjoy a baseball game, root for their team, eat hot dogs, hopefully catch a foul ball, and go home after witnessing a win, not getting into fights with other fans. *At least for most fans!*

As the game started, Jonathan and Isaac could still hear an occasional racist comment from the rows above. Still, it was primarily statements among the group to one another rather than directed (but perhaps intended) at the Washingtons. The two men looked at each other and shook their heads, focusing intently on the game.

"Play ball!" It was 2:00 p.m., and the umpire had sounded, officially beginning the game.

The crowd noise was at a whole new level as each pitch, swing, miss, hit, base running, and fielding was in play. Boos and cheers took their place where appropriate for the fans on each side as the game progressed through a couple of innings. Nick and Taylor did their share of noise, as did their parents. The day unfolded better than when it started on the train, and while approaching their seats in the stadium. The incidents were in the past and out of mind.

Four innings were completed before the Yankees took the lead in the fifth, and led the game by 2-0 by the end of the sixth. Makena was long overdue for a visit to the ladies' room and said she would be right back. Mary immediately said, "I'll go with you. You boys all okay?" They almost didn't answer as they were engrossed in the action on the field.

Jonathan answered without turning his attention from the field. "We're all good."

The two women climbed the steps, Makena a little slower than Mary. When they approached the row containing the harassment team, the slovenly-looking man in the end seat, next to the stairs stuck out his foot just as Makena was to take the next step. She tripped on it but did not fall. Mary shouted, "I saw that. That was no accident; it was intentional!" The nearby crowd averted its attention from the game to the commotion. Isaac and Jonathan clearly heard Mary and turned their heads to see the women face to face with the guy holding a huge beer, whose leg was still outstretched.

Isaac rose from his seat. "Jonathan, please stay with the boys . . . be right back." He darted up the steps and got between the women and the beer man. "Look, if you insist on continuing to be an asshole and making trouble, you can deal with me, not these women." Before the beer guy could respond, Isaac continued. "I'll be happy to take this outside with you if needed so you don't continue to disturb the people here who came to see the ballgame and not hear you make trouble and an ass of yourself. Now what's it gonna be?"

The guy was definitely under the influence and pondered what Isaac had said momentarily. But as he looked at the lean and muscular physical specimen of a man, and it made no difference that he was Black, he was not drunk enough to make the wrong decision. He sat down without an apology and drank down his beer. Isaac looked down at him and said, "Good decision; keep it that way! Ladies, can I escort you to the restroom?"

They decided they could make it on their own, although Makena showed signs of unsteadiness. She and Mary ascended the steps arm in arm. Isaac returned to Jonathan and the two little boys, who again were traumatized by unsociable behavior. The game and the day were unnecessarily interrupted again.

The women were in the ladies' room, trying to unwind after their third encounter of the day. Mary noted that Makena seemed off. She understood how abusive this could be for her, but she had come to learn that Makena was a strong woman who was not easily intimidated.

She asked, "Makena, are you alright? I don't know how you and Isaac can face all this racist stuff. You okay?"

"I'm fine, really. I'm just a bit tired today," she said as she continued to show slight but noticeable signs of weakness.

Mary hesitated but asked, "Makena . . . uh . . . it's probably not my business, but . . . are you expecting?"

Makena smiled, looked at Mary, and said, "Yes, I'm . . . due in late September!" Mary smiled back, and they both hugged one another tightly.

"Does Taylor know?"

"Not yet. We'll tell him soon when I start showing more. He's very observant and won't miss my growing belly, so we'll need to tell him soon. If you tell Jonathan, that's okay, but please don't tell Nick yet. I want us to be the first to tell Taylor."

"Of course. You have my word."

"Thanks. I'm okay. I'm ready to go now."

"Okay, hold onto me. And if that pig gives you or us any more trouble, I'll take care of him myself!"

Makena laughed. "Oh, I hope I don't see that . . . for his sake!" More laughter came as they left the ladies' room. Returning to their families was uneventful as the racist pig was dead drunk on his ass and had passed out. His buddies elected not to be as stupid as he was and remained silent.

The rest of the game became more exciting as Mickey Mantle hit a single home run in the eighth inning. The Yankees scored another run before going into the ninth. They had a 4-0 lead over the Orioles. However, the Orioles tried to make a comeback and scored three runs in the ninth. The game ended with a Yankee win, 4-3. The fans went wild! Nick and Taylor went wild!

The two families joined thousands of others as they exited the stadium. Most made their way to the subway, which would be packed again. The two families rode the train back to East New York and had good conversations, most focused on the fun and very little on the not-so-much-fun. They did not witness any further racial discrimination of any kind. They had had enough of that earlier. Hearing the boys talk about baseball and their desire to play together on a youth team was enlightening and something to plan ahead.

They reached the subway exit in their neighborhood and spoke a little more as they ascended to the street level, where they would part ways for home. Isaac reminded Jonathan, "Remember, my friend, next time tickets are on me." Jonathan gave a thumbs up, and Mary, making sure no one saw her, gave Makena a smile and a "zipped lip" sign. Makena, smiling back, mouthed the words, "Thank you."

Chapter 29

A Guinness, a Jameson, or Even an Amaretto

Butch Brady contacted a trucker he knew who used to run illegal contraband from the South up the East Coast and points north. It was Sunday morning, April 20, when they linked up on an obscure road midway between Cabin 1 and Syracuse for his return to Mississippi. Walker had dropped him off earlier at a designated location. While he looked forward to returning to the South, he contemplated his few days with his fellow Black haters. He felt he had done everything he could to support their crusade but was disappointed to hear of the setbacks, including the loss of critical resources in Brooklyn and Yonkers. While hopeful, he also had an intuition from experience, a sense that things were about to go wrong. He couldn't be more right!

The joint undercover surveillance operation between the Syracuse Police Department and the FBI was in place. Their experience had taught them that patience, although time-consuming and frustrating, usually pays off. Over the next three days, the collaborative efforts of the local police and the FBI worked toward closing the net. Specific chatter coming from suspects and containing the words "Cabin 1," "Cabin 2", "the next lake," "venom is on his way to octopus headquarters," and "cyclone finalizing tentacle-e plans," all contributed to previously collected intelligence on the group that the FBI has been following for months.

From this point, the FBI took the lead and called for more resources as the puzzle pieces eventually pointed to specific areas sparsely populated with cabins around Otisco Lake and "the next lake," which they determined to be Skaneateles Lake. The cabins in these areas were isolated from one another. It would be a delicate situation to pinpoint the ones that offered comfort and relaxation to innocent vacationers who were hunting, fishing, hiking, or simply enjoying a getaway from their daily work routine, amid the nests of evil. However, the agents assigned to this case had previously dealt with similar encroachments. They would invade with the utmost precision and safety.

They would especially use all the information and tactics they gained from a raid the year before, on November 14 at the home of American Mafia mobster, Joseph Barbara, in Apalachin, New York, four and a half miles north of the Pennsylvania border. More than one hundred mobsters from the United States, Italy, and Cuba attended a meeting, and the FBI made many arrests of highly ranked Mafia members.

All major roads were heavily fortified at the points of entry from secondary roads in the county, and checkpoints further up each significant road served as secondary barriers to any escape. FBI special agent William Coppola was in charge of field operations. He reported to Angelo Bruno, supervisory special agent at the Syracuse office, who managed specific cases or operations and was involved in planning and overseeing the cabin raids.

In the late afternoon on Wednesday, April 23, an FBI agent in a camouflaged surveillance vehicle reported the red and white Chevy's movement on a dirt road, they code-named "DR Alpha," from an isolated cabin area to a narrow gravel road that partially loops the northeastern end of Otisco Lake. The FBI took up positions several miles in both directions on the gravel road. As the Chevy made its way north to link with a connecting route to Skaneateles Lake and the other cabins, the unmarked car with Special Agent Coppola and an assistant quickly blocked the car's path from a distance of about fifty feet. Coppola remained in the vehicle, using a bullhorn to warn the occupants of the Chevy. "This is Special Agent Bill Coppola with the FBI! We have the roads blocked in all directions. You are surrounded. Get out of the vehicle with your hands up . . . up . . . high."

Henry Mason, Jethro Paine, and Rhett Walker were in the Chevy on their way to one of the other cabins to pick up some weapons and other supplies, as they had planned to stay at Cabin 1 for a while. They had each brought a few weapons with them— handguns and rifles, but did not have the level of an arsenal they would need if found by the authorities. The others had remained at the cabin, waiting for their return to refine the plans they discussed with Brady.

Mason slammed on the brakes, and ground dust partially obscured the Chevy from Coppola's view. As Coppola repeated, "There's nowhere to run! Come out of the vehicle . . . " Before he could finish, Mason spun the Chevy around and went as fast as he could, throwing up gravel and a curtain of dust behind him. Coppola chased and radioed other vehicles in the vicinity. "We are in pursuit of the red and white Chevy. It is headed back toward the cabin on DR Alpha."

Mason had already determined that the other end of the gravel loop road was blocked, and their only chance for escape would be to retreat to Cabin 1, fight the FBI, and escape if possible. Paine and Walker hung out the car windows and began firing their weapons at Coppola. One bullet pierced the front windshield between Coppola and his assistant. They dropped back and radioed that they had received gunfire but were okay.

It was getting dark as the tall pines masked the sun, which was on the verge of disappearing altogether. Mason and his riders arrived at the cabin, grabbed their weapons, and ran inside to alert the others. The perfect hideout was no longer perfect. The occupants scrambled to get their guns and took defensive positions inside the cabin. Other forest flora that surrounded the cabin would contribute to the complexity of any approach in this isolated area. The agents' dark clothing would be an advantage in masking them if they decided to approach the cabin.

Several other vehicles arrived on the scene in minutes, while others were positioned in stages on roads emanating from the cabin area. The FBI also had a patrol boat offshore. Their entire team had .38 caliber revolvers and submachine guns. Everyone tightened the net gradually until the cabin was virtually a world unto itself. The special agent in charge, Michael Romano, was linked to the site via special communications. It was often a comical time at the Syracuse Field Office, as everyone referred to Romano's group as the FBI's Mafia because most of his agents were of Italian descent.

Darker now, with temperatures getting cooler and a slight rainfall, Coppola got on his bullhorn again. "Listen up! This is the FBI! We have your cabin surrounded! There is nowhere for you to go. Quit while you can. Firing at us . . . again . . . will only make matters worse for you. We know who you are and what you are planning. We have intel on your activities in Brooklyn, your operations from Hudson House, two of your guys from there, and some of your members in this local area. We have some of your members in lockup; the informant inside Brooklyn's 75th Precinct, the pawn shop in South Brooklyn, and . . . "

As Coppola had more words of wisdom, Walker and the others opened fire. Shots rang out, and the FBI took cover. They observed that one of their agents had taken a bullet to the leg, but he was immediately dragged to cover by another agent. The FBI returned gunfire and pierced through most of the windows on the front and sides of the cabin. The exchange lasted for another fifteen seconds, and then there was a pause.

It was pitch black outside and inside the cabin. The rain intensified, now much heavier, accompanied by a crack of lightning and a roar of thunder. In the momentary light, agents observed two men running from the rear of the cabin into the woods. When the pair heard, "Halt. Stop running. You won't get far," they fired their guns, only to receive return gunfire that caught both of them. One dropped with a wound to the mid-section; the other was dead before he hit the ground. Three agents quickly closed in to take the injured one into captivity. Handcuffed and moaning, he was removed from the brush he had hoped would conceal him. The other was carried to a vehicle equipped to handle the ones that didn't make it out alive.

Walker, Mason, Paine, and two others made a last attempt to fire at the well-trained, highly experienced agency, whose primary mission is to uphold and enforce federal laws, investigate crimes, and protect the United States from various threats, including terrorism, espionage, and organized crime. It was no contest! They received a barrage of machine gun replies that clearly communicated the battle was over. Walker did the honors. "We are coming out! Don't shoot!"

Coppola bullhorned back, "Hands up high! No surprises, or we'll open up with the machine guns again!" With powerful lights focused on them, the five men exited the cabin. The agents approached slowly, with their weapons ready for anyone else who might have remained in the cabin. Agents came through the back door and windows, signaling that the structure was clear. Everyone was soaked to the bone. Most didn't care and could hear the accolades and cheering from the main office on their radios. The others experienced a range of emotions quite differently: anger, fear, shock, anxiety, and perhaps relief.

Once the captives had spent most of the night being interrogated, they were thoroughly exhausted and shoved into their separate cells. The FBI learned about some of the planning that was underway, but over time, they would perceive the much bigger picture from senior Klan members. The wounded agent was given a thumbs up by the physicians who removed the bullet from his upper leg and told him he was lucky it didn't hit a bone or a major artery. He would return to duty within the week. The criminal with the mid-section wound was in surgery.

It wasn't long before FBI special agent Romano notified Chief Miles of the Syracuse Police Department of the raid and capture that had already provided significant intel on the inner activities and plans of the KKK. Miles, in turn, notified Chief Doyle in Yonkers and Captain O'Rourke in Brooklyn. They would soon have a much clearer picture of the demonic plans that would have contributed to an already existing racially unstable environment. *Nonetheless, it was undoubtedly time for a Guinness, a Jameson, or even an Amaretto!*

Chapter 30

THE SCIENCE PROJECT

Sergeant McGuire informed the principals of PS 91 and Thomas Jefferson High School of the recent raid and capture of "domestic terrorists" who had been responsible for the coordinated and planned attacks at their schools. They were shocked at the scope of the crimes by young students whom they initially had thought had committed random acts. They would hear that while the police had gleaned a lot of important information from the criminals behind the attacks, they had uncovered a much broader strategy from Henry Mason that had helped to avert similar incidents citywide.

They also learned that the students involved in the school attacks would receive a range of punishments consistent with their participation, their previous record, if any, and their willingness to accept responsibility. Some were placed on probation. However, Buddy and Sonny Mason, leaders and instigators molded by their father, ended up in juvenile detention, where hope remained for their rehabilitation. Time would tell. The principals passed the welcome news to their staff, who turned their attention back to an exhilarating second half of the year with summer on the horizon.

Eventually, the news that the principals had received would spread to the parents, who had all but forgotten the attacks from back in December, either intentionally or as a natural progression of life and daily routines. They were more focused on their children's schoolwork performance.

On Monday, after the game, Isaac noticed that Taylor had put on the Yankee ball cap as he was ready to walk to school with his mother. He asked him why he didn't wear the hat he always wore before, the Dodgers cap. Taylor said he and Nick decided to wear the Yankee hat to school, and they did every day since the weekend game they attended. Isaac thought, *This may be a new era in baseball in the Washington household!*"

The baseball caps hung on Nick's and Taylor's coat racks with their jackets. Lopez informed the class that they would work on a science project and team up with a partner. Nick and Taylor immediately looked at one another and secured their team with head nods and okay signs! Science was one of Nick's and Taylor's favorite subjects, and they both demonstrated a strong affinity for the subject.

She told the kids that they would work on the project over the next two weeks and then present the class with what they had learned. This activity was designed to be both fun and interesting, promoting curiosity and teamwork. The students were all in, as they recognized that this new activity nourished their inquisitive minds.

Lopez provided a few examples of the projects and said she would help them. She offered the following ideas for the projects: plant growth, magnets, mixing colors, types of bugs, simple machines with levers or pulleys, growing crystals, balloons, static electricity, and even homemade volcanoes (which she realized could be messy but was willing to give a try). The kids' eyes lit up when they heard the list, and they began chatting.

Lopez said, "It sounds like everyone is excited about doing a science project, so I'll give you a few minutes to decide your teams, and tomorrow you need to let me know what your project will be. Tell your parents about it, and if you want to do a project I didn't mention, you can tell me tomorrow." She had already prepared notes that each student could give to their parents, communicating the same message she had said, because she knew not everyone would remember. She happily witnessed a new level of interest in her class. Later, she shared her excitement with Izzy Garcia, who also promoted a science project for her second-grade students.

After dinner, Makena called Mary. "Hi, Mary, it's Makena. Do you have a few minutes?"

"Hi, yes. Is everything alright? Are you okay?" Her only thought when she heard Makena's voice was her "condition."

"Oh, yes, I'm fine. Thank you. Did you get Miss Lopez's note about the science project?"

"Yes, Jonathan and I were just talking with Nick about it. He is so excited and said he and Taylor are a team for the project. We were talking about the ones Miss Lopez listed, but Nick said he and Taylor were thinking about something else . . . something Taylor suggested."

"Taylor told us that he and Nick wanted to do a project on the human body . . . and . . . uh, you know, what they all do, what the body parts do!"

"Yeah, I heard that! Where did they come up with that?"

"Well, Taylor has always been interested in basic . . . uh, medicine, human physiology, if you can believe that. He talks a lot with Isaac, especially since he's a pharmacist and deals with medicine. It's quite a stretch, don't you think?"

"Uh . . . no, not really. I mean, if he is interested, that's a positive thing. And apparently, Nick is also interested, not that he's expressed it before as Taylor may have, but . . . I think it's great that they want to work together on it. I'll tell Jonathan, and will you tell Isaac?"

"I will. I think he will be thrilled! Uh, so . . . do you want to get together to work on this with the boys? They have two weeks. Seems like plenty of time."

"I love it! Jonathan and I will brainstorm ideas and call you back in the next day or two. Please call me if you have any ideas."

"Sounds good, will do. And thank you again for your concern about me." They hung up and became even more cognizant of the friendship that was developing, growing.

The Washingtons and the Greenes got to work, independently, and spent some time that evening sketching out possible elements for the project—a model of the human body that they would outline and identify with significant parts, *most parts*, that their sons would explain in tag team fashion *to some degree yet to be determined!* The boys were overjoyed after learning their parents were cooperating on the school project. It was almost as much fun thinking about it as going to a Yankee game, without the racist distractions, of course.

After a couple of days of creative thought by both families, Mary called Makena to see if she, Isaac, and Taylor had any ideas. Makena told her that Taylor was the most vocal when describing his thoughts. Mary said, "That's interesting. Nick also had some ideas and wouldn't let Jonathan or me get a word in edgewise. He was so excited!"

"Hmmm, okay, I'm curious. What did Nick say?"

"He already drew an outline of a person's body and showed it to us. He said that he and Taylor could tell the class all about the body's organs, like the heart, lungs, stomach, and brain."

Makena laughed. "Taylor said they could color the organs on a piece of paper, cut them out, and put them on the body. I think these boys have been talking in school and are way ahead of us adults. What do you think?"

Mary laughed and said, "Yeah, those two, what rascals. They don't need us very much, do they? I guess all we need is maybe some poster board or a large sheet of paper, crayons or markers, and let them do the rest."

"Taylor has some of the poster boards in his room. He likes to use it for different things, and we have many color markers."

Mary laughed again, and Makena asked, "What?"

"I was just thinking. Maybe we should, uh . . . limit the parts of the body to certain ones . . . if you know what I mean!"

Makena's laughter seemed like it wouldn't stop. "I agree. I don't think Taylor and probably Nick would mind going into further detail. But I'm not quite sure if Miss Lopez is ready for that for her class!"

"Me neither. Why don't we just wait and see how much intelligence these boys want to share with their class?"

"Sounds like a plan. I'll let Isaac know so he doesn't do anything unnecessary."

"Me too with Jonathan. Check back in a few days?"

"Will do. Thanks for calling!"

The science project was off to an unexpected start. The parents thought they would need to advise and direct, but it was more like listening and observing. The first-grade tag team had everything under control!

Chapter 31

BIG MAN

The FBI and the collaborative police teams had celebrated a victory with the capture and initial interrogation of Walker, Mason, and others. They realized that refining shared information from all sources enabled the successful raid at Otisco Lake, with only one minor, non-life-threatening injury to the good guys. However, they put a plan in place to better understand what all the chatter they gathered over many months really meant, how it tied to these individuals, and how it spread into Brooklyn.

Rhett Walker, Henry Mason, Jethro Paine, and the other captives were charged under federal law and would, therefore, be detained in a federal facility while awaiting trial, which could take considerable time. Armed federal agents transported them in secure vans to the Ray Brook, New York Federal Correctional Institution, located 194 miles northeast of Syracuse. They determined that this Adirondack region facility was the best for the nature of the charges, domestic terrorism, and the jurisdiction.

Through preliminary interrogations, the FBI determined that Walker would likely be the primary source of information, as he had been in the area for a long time and meetings were often held at his cabins. He had answered some questions but was hesitant and tight-lipped for others. Informants can work both ways, and the FBI had established its own at the Ray Brook facility. He was single, had experience as an informant for the FBI, and possessed the ability to draw others out in conversation. His appearance fit the role. His clothing, hairstyle, a week's growth of facial hair, and demeanor aligned well with Walker's, and he was gifted at sharing plausible stories and experiences that insidiously led to a trusting relationship. Jack "Big Man" Henderson was ready for duty.

After processing, the doors behind Rhett Walker slammed shut, awakening Henderson in the cramped cell they would share for the unforeseeable future. "Hey, I'm trying to get some sleep here." Henderson's voice was booming with anger. "Put him in another cell, would ya?"

The guard disregarded Henderson, smiled, and told Walker, "Enjoy your stay, and get comfortable." Walker said nothing as he eyed his roommate occupying the bottom bunk bed with his feet overhanging the end. He realized that the upper bunk was his obvious new resting place—*if resting was even possible with that beast below me!*

Walker tried to initiate some basic introductions. "My name's Rhett Walker. What are you in for?"

Big Man replied, in no uncertain terms, "I don't care what your damn name is, and it's none of your business. Shut up, and let me get some sleep!"

Walker didn't get the message loud and clear or any other way. He said, "Well, we may be here a long time together, so I just wanted . . ."

Big Man rose out of his bunk, stood up—all six feet seven inches and 240 pounds of him, every bit of it pure muscle, with arms bulging from his shirt—and got within a very uncomfortable distance to Walker, looked down on him, and said, "If I hear one more word out of your mouth and have to get up again, you're gonna wish you were never born. Now, shut up!" Message received!

The following day, Walker was shocked to hear Big Man greet him as they rose for breakfast. "Walker, the last guy that shared a cell with me wasn't very friendly. He annoyed me, and I took care of that!" Walker's eyes widened. "I was in one of my moods yesterday, and I gotta tell ya, I turn a bit belligerent if things don't go the way I think they should go, especially if I need sleep, so just warnin' ya. But . . . I'll give you a chance, so . . . we can do a restart. My name's Jack Henderson. Everybody calls me Big Man."

"Big Man? I can see why. No trouble from me. Just wanna get along, no trouble." As the jail cell opened, nothing more was said, and they proceeded to breakfast. The first few days contained minimal conversation between the roommates. Walker thought this was probably a good thing until the lack of conversation and any human interface by the end of the week was wearing on his sanity. It was too quiet, even with the threat of an irritable big man in the room. He didn't realize this was the precise tactic that Henderson would use to get him to open up.

While most prisons had a strict schedule for meals, outside exercises, work assignments, and access to reading materials, the guards had told Walker that for the first few weeks, he would only be allowed outside his cell for meals. This was an intentional tactic to get him to wonder what "the first few weeks" meant and to realize life would get pretty dull.

Walker thought he might break the ice again when he observed Big Man shift from his usual downcast eyes and angry expression to a hint of a grin and a "mornin'." It took him by surprise as he was beginning to think he would spend a considerable amount of time in complete silence. *Maybe this is what solitary is like without a massive warm body nearby!*

"Uh, mornin'. If you don't mind my askin', did they keep you from going anywhere except for meals when you first got in here?" Henderson knew what the guards had told him and played along to confirm his inactive environment. He could leave the cell for several hours during the day, leaving Walker alone to ponder his destiny.

"Yeah, I was here for over a month before I could leave the cell. They wouldn't even give me anything to read. Just sit in here and do nothin' but think. I complained, but no one listened or cared." He was going to ask Walker where he was from, but experience told him to be patient and ask at the right moment.

Walker listened, clasped his hands in front of himself as he sat on the floor against an opposite wall, looked down, and said, "Yeah, I wish I was back in my cabin by the lake right now, not this hellhole." There it was. The entrance to the conversation that would follow. Henderson nodded his head slightly as he looked at Walker. *Here we go. The hook is set. I just need to reel him in carefully!*

"Your cabin, huh? Sounds like somethin' nice, somethin' you enjoy, or should I say, enjoyed?" This was the transition question, the one that would open Walker up. It was not too direct, like "Where is it," or "What did you do there?" He knew Walker would tell him that in due time on his own because it was clear that Walker was not a friend of silence.

Walker gave limited information about the cabins and his activities there. They had been in his family for generations; his great-grandfather had built the cabins and passed them to his grandfather and father since the Civil War. He told Henderson he was the only heir, never married, and liked to hunt and fish. These were all very general in nature, but at least he was talking, and Big Man was listening. *Thank God, the silence is broken!*

Days passed, and Henderson would listen mostly but occasionally raise a question. "I guess the Walkers loved the cabins, the outdoors . . . how did they make a living, raise their families?" Innocent enough and not prying too deeply, thought Walker. But he decided to turn the questions toward Big Man.

"Well, you know a little about me. What about you? Or are you gonna turn, uh . . . 'belligerent' again?" Walker chanced a mild laugh. Henderson looked at him and exposed a slight smile.

This was the next step in Henderson's plan. He was making progress. "I got here about six months ago. I'll spend a long time here unless I can figure a way out, but this is a tough nut to crack."

"I don't know how long I'll be here. Waitin' on a trial. You?"

"I already had a trial. Sentenced to twenty years. I was involved with a group in the South and got caught when we carried out some activities against the government up here in New York. I might have some years after I get out, but that seems a long way out there."

Walker took it all in and felt he had someone he could relate to, precisely what the FBI wanted him to feel. Plan on track. Over the next two weeks, the cellmates progressed to the "buddy stage" and gave up more details of their backgrounds and crimes. Henderson would whisper an update as he walked by one or two of the guards, who were also informants in the prison and would pass the information to FBI management.

The FBI did not anticipate the depth of the information Walker would reveal. He began with his ancestors, who were among the early members of the Ku Klux Klan in the South, dating back to 1865. After that, they moved northeast to spread their faith. They believed in "frontier justice" for minorities and Jews rather than the rule of law and the courts. Then he briefly discussed the three periods of Klan strength in American History—the late nineteenth century, the nineteen twenties, and the current decade, when civil rights were at their height. Henderson began to understand Walker's commitment to the organized group.

Walker talked about his intention to "make his father and grand-fathers proud" of his devotion to the "way things were in the South through slavery," and even though that was no longer possible, he would do everything in his power to spread terror and hate. He eventually revealed more details—the Tentacle-E "arm" of Octopus, the network spreading into the New York City metropolitan area, especially in Brooklyn under the leadership of Henry Mason, and the fallback location of Hudson House, including the recruitment of youth, the next generation, and the revival of ages gone by.

The era of "Black codes" occurred in states like Mississippi and Florida after the Civil War, when laws were enacted to control the newly freed Black population and to maintain a social and economic order that was much in accord with the antebellum South's forced labor and racial subordination. He went on to explain how White supremacy emerged as a fundamental creed of the Klan through the Nashville Klan convention to create a chain of command for the organization. Despite this development, he mentioned there were elements in the Klan that fought one another, as he described a Nashville gang of outlaws who adopted a Klan disguise and became known as the Black Ku Klux Klan.

Henderson sat there mesmerized as Walker continued as if he were the most educated man on Earth about the Klan's origins and emergence through historical periods: birth, transition, rebirth; old Klans and new Klans; essential figures in the history of the Klans; power struggles; violence of lynchings, shootings, whippings; losing ground and gaining ground. It was as if he had a PhD on the subject.

The next day, a prison guard came to remove Henderson from his cell. Walker looked on and asked, "What's goin' on? Where you takin' him?" The guard ignored him, and the two men left. Big Man had all but completed his assignment. He was headed to the FBI headquarters in Syracuse to provide the information he skillfully acquired.

Butch Brady had hoped that Walker would be an influential disciple of the Klan in the Northeast and would contribute to its resurgence. He would soon learn otherwise and begin looking over his shoulder to determine if the FBI was closing in on him. Who knows what the captives might say about his visit to Syracuse and his status in the Klan? Uncertainty is disruptive.

The FBI gave Henry Mason one privilege. He was permitted to call each of his sons in juvenile detention in Syracuse. He had the opportunity to explain what had happened, to apologize for getting them involved, to acknowledge that he had ruined their future, and to encourage them to try to change their lives. But he didn't do that. He just complained about being caught, that the Klan would go on, and that they should "carry the flag" for the next generation. While he had his moments of doubt and regret, they were short-lived. His hate was so deep-rooted that he couldn't even produce a trace of encouragement for his sons and their future.

Buddy was just like his father. He had many years ahead of him, but his thoughts and actions would likely parallel those of his father and possibly even Rhett Walker's. Sonny, being only thirteen, was not subject to the longer indoctrination that his older brother had undergone. Whether he realized it or not, he had a chance to rehabilitate himself into a better life.

Chapter 32

"This is a Job for Your Father! Isaac!"

Lopez was halfway through her science class on the first Friday in May. "Now, class, we will listen to Nicholas Greene and Taylor Washington. They will tell you about their science project, which is about the human body." The students all clapped, as they had done before and after each presentation. Nick set up an easel so that Taylor could place a poster board with a simple outline of a body that resembled a man more than a woman, solely because it lacked any indication of hair on the head. While Taylor adjusted the board, Nick opened a bag containing several paper cutouts resembling body parts to be added to the board. He also took out a small bag of colored pins. Ready for action!

Taylor started, "Today, my friend, Nick, and me . . . I mean, Nick and I would like to tell you all about the human body, your body!" They had the class's full attention, and Lopez was seated at her desk and smiling. "Human 'anomy,' . . . 'antomy,' . . . uh, I mean, 'anatomy' is all about the human body." The class laughed a little and also tried to get the word out with similar trouble, but after hearing it again from Taylor, they finally got it right.

Taylor continued, "The body has three main things: cells, tissue, and organs. Oh, and it has 206 bones, but that would take a long time to talk about. Maybe another time. Now, Nick will tell you about the cells first." Nick walked to the display, holding a pointer he had borrowed from Lopez. He looked at the class and took a deep breath.

He swung the pointer all over the outline as he explained. "The human body has a lot of cells, all kinds of cells. Some are muscle cells, nerve cells, and blood cells. There are other cells too, but we, Taylor, and me . . . I mean, Taylor and I don't know too much about them yet. The muscle cells help your muscles move. The nerve cells work all over your body, especially in the brain and spine. We have those . . . you will see them soon. The organs are pretty cool; we will show you those too." Some kids were soaking it all in with their elbows on their desks and hands holding their heads. Others were nodding in affirmation of what they were hearing.

Taylor took the pointer from Nick and said, "I will now . . . " One kid interrupted the presentation and said, "What about the blood cells?"

Nick quickly grabbed Taylor's pointer and answered, "Oh, I forgot. Yeah, the blood cells . . . there are red ones and white ones." The kids' eyes lit up, and they exchanged glances. *When I see blood, I only see red ones!* "Red cells have oxygen in them, and white cells help against infections, like from cuts or scrapes." *Okay, now it's Taylor's turn.*

Taylor's first-grade presentation on tissue sounded more advanced than even Lopez expected. He briefly covered epithelial (which he pronounced correctly), connective, muscle, and nervous tissue. Lopez wondered, *How does he know that?* She was duly impressed.

The two boys then added and described the major organs, switching back and forth to pin them to the body and telling the class what they do in the body. The colorful cutouts of the heart, lungs, brain, kidneys, stomach, and other organs contributed to an enjoyable and straightforward illustration that the class appreciated, which they applauded loudly. Lopez also clapped as she added her compliments of praise and admiration for the boys' effort. She recognized that they had worked hard to give an excellent presentation, demonstrating knowledge, and showing how people can work together effectively.

In the remaining weeks of May and into mid-June, Nick and Taylor, along with their class and the remaining upper classes at PS 91, completed the school year with a nasty experience behind them. Dr. Carpenter and her staff continued to monitor any evidence of racial bias or tensions through their monthly meetings.

Lopez had accomplished a great deal with her first class, laying the foundation for their future success. The core reading and writing skills included mastering the alphabet, phonics, simple reading, and mathematics, such as counting, number recognition, addition, subtraction, shapes, and patterns. Her art and music lessons lent to each student's creative expression, and the physical education and activities rounded out their learning with practices for good health. Overall, it turned out to be a good year.

With the summer break approaching, Nick and Taylor could only think of all the activities they would do, especially together, based on what they had learned from their parents' discussions. There would be so much: more MLB games, youth baseball at Prospect Park, subway rides to New York City, more tokens to drop in the turnstiles, museums, fishing at Sheepshead Bay, Canarsie, and even at the lake in Prospect Park, and Coney Island with its attractions and rides.

But the beginning of the summer revealed another exciting thing to look forward to. Taylor did not observe the occasional first-trimester symptoms of nausea and fatigue his mother experienced, but it was trimester number two, and the baby bump was impossible to hide. One morning, he said, "Mom, what happened to your belly?" For him, all of a sudden, it appeared . . . out of nowhere!

Makena smiled at him and said, "Taylor, I'm going to have a baby! You're going to be a big brother!" Taylor's understanding of babies growing in their mothers' wombs was developed to some maturity. He just wasn't sure how they got there in the first place. He had friends with little brothers or sisters, but he still wasn't sure he had the whole story. So he asked.

"How did it get in there . . . in your tummy?" Taylor's question thrust him into the broader curriculum about human biology.

Makena said, "Just a moment . . . Isaac? Isaac, come in here, please!" She told Taylor, "This is a job for your father! Isaac!" Isaac entered the room, observed his wife pointing to her stomach, and heard her say, "Honey, please take Taylor inside and explain this!" Isaac's expression made Makena smile as she walked into another room and said, "Or you can stay right here!" *Now, I guess it's time to learn a little more about the human body!* Makena figured she had done her part; now it was time for Isaac to determine the age-appropriate explanations of reproduction!

Thomas Barnes met with Sergeant McGuire before he would visit his son, Tyler, held in custody for his participation as an informant for the Klan's plans, which targeted an opportunity in Brooklyn. McGuire contacted Barnes at Tyler's request and said that his son told him that he had to reconcile what he had done with his father. McGuire gave Barnes a very high-level summary of his son's crimes. Still, having worked with him in the precinct and spent considerable time talking with him after he was caught, McGuire felt that his son was a good person, young, and had a good chance at a normal life.

The elder Barnes asked McGuire, "How could he do such a thing? He's always been a perfect son, applied himself well in school, and has always been obedient and respectful. What changed him?"

McGuire said, "Sir, you will need to ask your son those questions. You can take all the time you need." He walked Barnes to the detention area of the precinct and announced their arrival to Tyler. "Tyler, your father is here to see you."

While the walk took only thirty seconds, Thomas Barnes' complex mix of emotions could have filled a book. He was struggling with his disbelief that his son had committed a crime, a serious crime. He was disappointed and angry and wondered if he was at fault for something he may have missed that could have prevented his son's actions. He wanted answers and hoped to get them from his son, with whom he had shared years of trust, mutual respect, and love. As a Marine, he faced some challenging situations, but this was something completely foreign and unknown to him, and he was torn between supporting Tyler and the need for accountability. His deep sense of grief was overwhelming. His image of his son was tainted; the life he envisioned for him was, at this moment, lost.

McGuire opened the cell door and let Thomas Barnes join his son. He closed the door and told him to call out when he was ready to leave. "Dad!"

"Tyler!" They hugged for a long while before Tyler spoke first.

"Dad, I'm sorry, I'm so sorry. I messed up." Tears welled up in his eyes, and they could no longer be suppressed as they streamed down his face. "I never . . . I never should have become so hateful that I would turn on the very people I looked up to, respected, worked with, and trusted. I'm an idiot!" He bent his head down as he sat on a cot and wrapped his hands behind his head, shaking it from side to side.

Thomas walked over to his son, placed his hand on his shoulder, and asked, "Why, Tyler? Why? What changed you? I never thought you could do anything like this. You have always respected the law; you worked for the law, contributing to their cause to fight crime, not . . . why?"

Tyler composed himself and began the story he had told McGuire, the transition caused by the Black gang attack on his parents and the need for revenge. He was angry that the attack happened, that his parents were innocent victims, and that his mother never fully recovered. It was something to reconcile. Accountability was important to him, but he recognized that he chose the wrong way to seek it. As he related all this, he suddenly realized he had not asked about his mother.

"Dad, how is Mom? She must be so disappointed in me. Please tell her I'm sorry, that I love her, please." His tears reappeared as he wondered how he would even face his mother if he had the chance. When would or could he see her?

"Your mother is heartbroken, as you would expect, but never think she doesn't love you. She had the same reaction I had when we learned you were arrested. She had the same questions and felt the same about perhaps missing any signs that would trigger concern. But there were no signs. I will arrange for your mother to visit you soon. I wanted to speak with you first to learn what happened and why. You will be okay. Sergeant McGuire told me the same thing. He also believes you will be okay."

They spent the next hour discussing the immediate future of serving time for mistakes and the period of adjustment back to an everyday, productive life. Thomas emphasized that Tyler had many years ahead to do the right things and compensate for the brief period in his life when things went wrong. He encouraged Tyler to return to the son he had always known he had, the son he was always proud of, and who would achieve whatever he set his mind to do. He knew his son had the deep-rooted values that he and his wife had instilled in him and that they believed he would ultimately navigate his way through this complicated reality.

Thomas Barnes' approach to his son's dilemma was diametric to the one Henry Mason used for his sons.

Chapter 33

"THERE'S A BABY IN THERE."

Taylor was at the second base position. He chose this because Jackie Robinson was a role model and usually played second base. Nick, who wished to emulate Mickey Mantle, was in center field. The boys were in summer mode with a good school year behind them. Now, it was all about a different dose of daily fun as they took up positions on the first game of the summer season.

The youth baseball club at Prospect Park included young kids who were new to the game or had a few years of experience. The fields were often formed into makeshift diamonds, where crude chalk lines guided the batters' paths around the bases, often no more than a patch of designated turf or a cleared area.

Local Little League squads and volunteers, who had learned the game's basics, coached the team players according to the kids' performance with flexible and adaptable rules. The focus was on learning rather than following strict rules. It was all about community and its love for baseball, the social development of youth, and a part of representing the cultural advancement in Brooklyn, which was crucial in providing children with opportunities to build skills, friendships, and memories that would last a lifetime.

Taylor's and Nick's parents shared a section on the sidelines with others who cheered for their kids and their team. Everyone enjoyed the game, especially observing their kids play, with little emphasis on any errors they may have made. The coaches focused on making it into a learning moment rather than something to be ashamed of. The sunny weather and surrounding park environment complemented what they would experience as a perfect day at the park. But things sometimes change in an instant.

Just before Taylor got up to bat, a group of White teenage boys assembled about fifteen feet behind the umpire at home plate. They were making noise and talking loudly as the pitcher wound up for his first pitch to Taylor. The boys began heckling him. "Hey, little Black boy, you can't hit nothin', miss, miss, miss." Taylor swung as the pitch landed right over the plate, resulting in a strike. The umpire turned and told the boys to keep quiet as their spectators yelled the same thing. They just laughed and waited for the next pitch.

Some of the boys said, "Ah, let's go." However, a majority of them chose to continue harassing Taylor. One boy shouted the *N-word* just as Taylor swung the bat to connect, hitting a ground ball that cleared the third baseman and remained in play, allowing Taylor to reach first safely. The umpire held up his hand and shouted, "Time out!" He walked over to the boys and reprimanded them. The cheering section was doing what they came to do, only this time, cheering for the umpire. The juvenile wannabes left the area and searched for another venue to contaminate.

While community events, like youth baseball, strived to bring people together, no matter what their backgrounds were, public places, like parks and sports fields, still gave those with deeply ingrained attitudes on segregation an opportunity to express their beliefs in offensive ways. The officials and parents at Taylor and Nick's game fought back to show their support for the team as a whole, including Taylor, rather than singling out anyone, as the hecklers had done. The game went on, resulting in a 6-4 win for the Brooklyn Sluggers, Taylor and Nick's team!

After the game and the cheerful conversation among the parents, coaches, and umpires ceased, Taylor asked why the boys were calling him the *N-word*. He didn't use the actual word that was represented by the term *N-word*, which his parents had taught him never to use, as it was very disrespectful and hateful. Nick jumped at the answer before anyone else.

"Because they don't like you, Taylor, like I like you. Because they're stupid and don't know that you're a good person." Taylor's and Nick's parents looked at one another. *We couldn't answer it any better than that . . . for now!*

They both said, "That's right. Nick is right." Hearing Nick made Taylor feel good. And he felt even better when they went for ice cream after the game to celebrate the win. Nick and Taylor didn't know that their parents would have bought them ice cream even if they lost.

They enjoyed the summer, especially when they were together. This allowed their relationships to mature further, with Nick and Taylor, Jonathan and Isaac, Mary and Makena, and each other, as well as the entire family. The Washington family continued to encounter racial discrimination on various levels, ranging from minor innuendos to outright verbal confrontation with the use of the *N-word*.

Fortunately, nothing ever escalated to physical assault. However, the frequency of incidents had an impact on the family and, most visibly, on Taylor. Mary and Jonathan were always there to support them and would actively participate in shouting back at the perpetrators when necessary, providing not only strength in numbers but also in racial composition.

The majority of the time when visiting the city, Nick and Taylor happily dropped more tokens into the subway turnstiles; marveled at the dinosaurs in the American Museum of Natural History, part of New York's cultural history for eighty-nine years; and enjoyed the scenes, landmarks, lakes and bridges, and most loveable of all, the zoo, in Central Park. On occasion, racial remarks polluted what would have been an otherwise perfect day.

In southwestern Brooklyn, they spent day-long occasions at Coney Island with thousands of tourists from around the world who would also enjoy the amusement park, boardwalk, and beaches. Nick and Taylor loved the carousels with hand-painted horses and other gentle rides. The boys thought about riding the Cyclone, an iconic wooden roller coaster built in 1927, but their parents said they could when they were a little older. They weren't sure if the long, adrenaline-charged ride would provide thrills or something else, like nausea . . . or worse. The boys would remind their parents that they wanted a Nathan's hot dog when they got hungry, which was often. They returned home on the subway, fulfilled but exhausted. *Having fun is hard work!*

Jonathan loved fly fishing for trout. He had learned the sport from his father, who took him to small streams in Westchester County, near towns such as Mount Kisco, Katonah, and Chappaqua, several of which had origins tied to Native American heritage. However, rather than flies, they used night crawlers—worms they captured at night in nearby parks using flashlights to see and grab them before they retreated underground. He asked Isaac if he was interested in going. He had never done any freshwater fishing before, but Isaac said he was willing to learn, yet knew nothing about the sport. Jonathan said, "Isaac, the only thing you need to know is that fly fishing is helpful whether you catch a trout or not."

Isaac, confused, said, "Uh . . . I don't know what you mean."

"It's the therapy of the water. Being outdoors, surrounded by nature, where it's quiet, and all you hear are the sounds of the flowing water bubbling nearby, the trees rustling, and the birds making their calls. It's where stress disappears, and you relax, forget everything else, and just take it all in through your senses. It's an emotional respite. And if you catch some trout, that will be a bonus! Maybe just you and me for now. Perhaps the boys might be interested when they get a little older. My dad started taking me when I was around eleven years old."

Isaac replied, "That sounds exactly like something I could use. When can we go?"

Jonathan and Isaac planned a weekend day in late June. Jonathan noted that the water would warm up and that it would become too late to fish for trout after that because they only thrive in cold water. They could go again in early fall if Isaac had a good experience and wanted to continue. Isaac said, "I'm already okay with the whole therapy thing, trout or not!" It was a bond-building step the men recognized and accepted, "hook, line, and sinker."

The women also spent more time together, especially shopping for baby items in anticipation of the new baby due in a few months. Should we buy pink or blue? That was the question, so it would need to be decided later. However, for now, the gender-neutral items would be onesies and sleepers in neutral colors, such as white, gray, and yellow. A crib, bedding, a changing table, blankets, diapers, bath items, bottles, and bibs were all on the menu. Makena had several close friends who were excited to help her, but she had chosen to include Mary in this activity more often. Seeing how Taylor and Nick did so much together, and now Jonathan and Isaac were gravitating to shared interests, it was only natural.

The Washingtons and the Greenes loved all that Prospect Park offered, but spending a few hours together at a park closer with playgrounds and space for a picnic lunch was also convenient. The boys were having fun on the swings, slides, seesaws, and monkey bars when Taylor saw something that made a light bulb go off. He watched a Black woman pushing a baby carriage and realized he had forgotten to tell Nick what he had recently learned.

He said, "Nick, c'mere! See that lady with the baby buggy?"

"Yeah?"

"There's a baby in there."

"Uh, yeah, I know."

"Do you know where the baby came from?"

"Yeah, it came from the mom."

"Yeah, but do you know how it got *in* the mom?"

"Uh, yeah, my daddy told me. I asked him how the baby gets inside the mom."

"What did he say?"

He said, "The mommy and daddy love each other, and the baby grows in the mommy."

"Yeah, but they always love each other. Sometimes they love each other, and there's no baby in there."

"Yeah, I guess."

"I know how the baby gets in there!"

"How?"

"The dad puts a seed in the mom, and it makes her egg have a baby."

"Oh! How does he put the seed in the mom? She has an egg in there?"

Taylor cupped his hand up close to Nick's ear and whispered into it. Nick's eyes lit up as he said, "How does he do that?" Taylor did more whispering, and Nick's eyes did a repeat performance, only bigger. They stared at their parents sitting on a park bench, talking. They giggled, and Nick said, "Your parents did that?"

Taylor said, "Yep, that's why my mom is having a baby soon!"

"Wow! Maybe my mommy and daddy can do that too; then we can have little brothers or sisters. What do you want?"

Taylor said, "I told my mom I want a baby sister."

"What did she say?"

"She said she didn't know if it would be a girl or a boy, but she would do the best she could for a sister."

"Oh, wow! I want a sister, too!" And it wasn't long before the Greenes learned their son had just leaped into an advanced understanding of life. They wondered at what point "the talk" would take place; now, it was practically all done for them. The two families anticipated the new arrival with constant questions from Nick and Taylor. This was almost as exciting for them as a Yankee game!

Chapter 34

EAST NEW YORK, 1958-1961

A summer filled with fun approached its end as Taylor and Nick spent a day with their fathers casting for fluke, sometimes called *summer flounder*, off the Canarsie Pier, a few stations away by subway. They could often see fluke hugging the bottom of the sand as the fish tended to move toward the shore during the warmer months. They filled a bushel before they wondered how they would transport it all home on the subway. They put about a dozen in a small, iced cooler and donated the rest to others on the pier who had bigger coolers.

It was time to prepare the boys for their next year at PS 91 as second graders. They would be in Garcia's class, and she would have many of the students whom Lopez taught in first grade. Lopez shared a great deal about her students with Garcia, mainly how they had matured socially and intellectually. By mid-August, the new academic year had put the summer fun behind them, and children, as they had a year ago, pondered it a bit longer before the routine of listening and participating in class became the norm.

All the preparations for the arrival of another human being in the Washington family were complete. Now, it was time to deliver the goods. Makena had survived through a hot summer that she thought would never end. *I'm ready, already!*

In the early morning of Wednesday, September 24, Makena told Isaac it was time. They had coordinated with the Greenes to care for Taylor that week, and possibly for an extended period if needed. They were thrilled to have Taylor stay with them, but no one was more excited than Nick. Sharing a room and working on their homework together, especially in subjects like reading, math, and spelling, was more enjoyable than doing it alone. Discussing everything they did together in the summer went way beyond their bedtime. When they heard, "Lights out, boys! Time for sleep," they would be quiet for a minute, then resume the chatter.

After a five-hour labor at Kings County Hospital Center, Makena delivered Ava Washington, a seven-pound, twenty-one-inch baby with wisps of black hair curled gently across her forehead. Her soft brown cheeks, deep brown eyes, and tiny curled fists expressed an attitude: *"Here I am, ready for the world!"* Isaac was relegated to the waiting room, which was aptly named as he thought waiting would never end. Hospital protocols called for clinical efficiency and a sterile environment; childbirth was a medical procedure, not a family-centered experience (yet). But attitudes were shifting, just not in time for this delivery. Nonetheless, Taylor got his wish. He had a baby sister. He was a big brother, a role and responsibility he was prepared to assume.

Mary, Jonathan, and Nick were elated to hear the news of little Ava and couldn't wait to see her. Mary immediately went shopping to buy something pink while contemplating her situation regarding children. Maybe this was the right time for a new little Greene in the family? She and Jonathan had discussed it in the past but had made no firm decision one way or the other. Maybe seeing little Ava would change their minds. But for now, it was time to celebrate with Makena, Isaac, and the new big brother.

Over the last year, Mary and Jonathan had enjoyed their growing relationship with the Washington family. It was a testament to how families could get along while being different in some ways. However, they witnessed the challenging systemic discrimination that intended to segregate their friends, often in public places where it was supposed to be fun and enjoyable. They often discussed how unfair it was and how the Washingtons must feel despite their apparent strength in those instances.

They fully agreed to be advocates and confront discrimination in any form, and especially to provide their support by speaking out against those harmful actions. They were unsure if Isaac and Makena would want to discuss their feelings in depth, but it appeared that the support Mary and Jonathan had provided so far was at the right level. They worried about how the boys would cope with the incidents, especially in the long term. They were young, impressionable, and exposed to social pressure.

Mary and Jonathan were intelligent and would react as the situation demanded. They would continue to provide Nick with parental guidance that focused on recognizing injustice and emphasizing the values of empathy and equality. They would describe the current climate of social inequities in the simplest of terms so that Nick could process what he may have witnessed. They would respect Isaac and Makena's right to do the same for Taylor. Still, they would look for opportunities to express their emotional support and actions that he would recognize coming from Nick and his family.

It was a delicate balance, navigating the risks of facing backlash or legal consequences. It was about building trust and amplifying Black voices, not overshadowing them. Emotional toil, frustration, and heartache were countered with hope and resilience. The bottom line was that the Washington family was important to the Greenes. And they realized the Washingtons felt the same way about them.

When Mary and Jonathan had Nick, born in 1951, they observed a decade that unfolded with an intensity of highly publicized single events of racial discrimination and the exponential growth of youth gangs. A one-line news article, now and then, in local Brooklyn newspapers, got their attention. They did not necessarily observe the more subtle forms in housing, particularly in Bedford-Stuyvesant, Brownsville, and East New York neighborhoods. Restrictive covenants, bank loan denials, and discriminatory real estate practices forced Blacks and other minorities to be in overcrowded areas that supported segregation.

Despite the US Supreme Court's 1954 decision in Brown v. Board of Education, segregation persisted across the country. Daily life had its share of discrimination in restaurants, shops, tourist areas, and sports venues. Job opportunities were also affected in the workplace, leading to economic disparities.

Brooklyn, the neighborhood of the Greenes and the Washingtons, witnessed occasional events and the ongoing, inherent, pervasive, and systemic inequalities that formed the groundswell for the fight for equality—the civil rights movement. The *New York Daily News* reported that crime had some of the highest rates in Brooklyn during the 1950s, especially gang-related activity. Amid these trends, and in contrast, the *Kings County Chronicle* and other local newspapers would identify East New York and Brownsville, in particular, as centers for business, fashion, politics, music, education, community events, clubs, organizations, art, culture, and sports entertainment. Iconic landmarks, such as the Brooklyn Bridge and Coney Island, along with economic growth, marked the borough's position globally. All contributed—the advancements and the compounded social challenges—to the chaotic mix of Brooklyn's DNA.

The intended infiltration of the Ku Klux Klan to enhance their presence and objectives in Brooklyn and neighboring boroughs was averted. The news hit *The New York Times* front page with praising comments from the city's mayor. Tyler Barnes provided crucial information that had enabled the collaboration among police forces and the FBI, which resulted in the arrest and conviction of suspects devoted to domestic terrorism. Tyler was serving a reduced sentence due to his cooperation, admission of guilt, and repentance. His future held hope, and he would benefit from the support of his parents and 75th Precinct police officers who wanted him to have a second chance.

Rhett "Cyclone" Walker, Henry "Sabre" Mason, Jethro "Cue Ball" Paine, and others were convicted and were serving long sentences in federal detention. In hopes of getting reduced time behind bars, they cooperated, to the extent they could, with the FBI to uncover the broader network that extended beyond New York State, and which led to the arrests of others closer to KKK central. Butch Brady did not have to look over his shoulder any further. The Grand Dragon of Mississippi was a title that had now become meaningless as he sat in a federal prison, serving a severe sentence in his home state. The Octopus component was severely gutted. Jack "Big Man" Henderson received a commendation for his work in extracting information from Walker. He was honored but felt that was his job, his specialty— no reward necessary.

Buddy Mason was serving a minimum sentence for his attack on Jefferson High School and his participation in support of his father's plans for further disruptions of racial discrimination and violence. The decision for a minor sentence was due to the coercion by his father, and not solely attributed to Buddy. Sonny would come to realize that there was a devoted rehabilitative team that would encourage him to change his behavior and attitudes in support of social harmony.

Nick and Taylor never faltered in their relationship, as they did more with each other in the next three years than they could have imagined. They continued to collaborate on more science projects, especially those involving the bones of the human body and the major organs. Eventually, they became more detailed in their explanations by adding the reproductive organs as their interest in the subject grew. By the end of the school year in June 1961, they also grew physically by about six inches, making them four and a half feet tall.

They did more fishing, learning to make lures and cast farther out into deeper water, and expressed an interest in fly fishing, which Jonathan and Isaac had discussed that the right time for them was coming soon. There were more youth baseball games, trips to the zoo and New York City attractions, and attendance at MLB games, primarily with their fathers and sometimes with the whole family, including little Ava, who was often seen wearing a Yankees uniform and hat.

Chapter 35

Dr. James Reed, New York University

When Taylor was in first grade, his instincts drove him to seek a friendship with Nick immediately. It didn't enter Taylor's mind that their skin color might have anything to do with seeking a new friend. He took the initiative, and despite accidentally bumping into one another during school playtime, the handshake and smile spoke volumes, laying the foundation for a strong relationship. It wasn't complex. It was a spontaneous and innocent social interaction that felt natural and correct.

Taylor's loving parents raised him to be obedient, polite, and respectful. As he matured to the age of ten and progressed through fifth grade, he had developed a clear sense of right and wrong. He fit perfectly into the category of understanding that PS 91 school counselor Donna Sweeney provided at the crucial meeting that principal Dr. Carpenter had summoned to address racial incidents and discrimination in Brooklyn, as well as how to address these issues, if necessary, with students in different grade levels.

Taylor hadn't yet reached the next level of maturity, of applying logic to the incidents he witnessed. He knew they were wrong, as he observed the reactions of his parents and Nick's parents. But he was confused. Hearing his parents answer his question about why some people acted a certain way with Black people didn't provide a satisfactory answer.

In the early 1960s, the civil rights movement gained traction and visibility as the struggle for racial equality entered the living rooms of many Americans, who watched frequent TV coverage of related incidents. Isaac and Makena would see the violent attacks on Freedom Riders in the South in 1961, who faced brutality after challenging segregation in interstate travel. The evening news also often depicted sit-ins and protests at segregated lunch counters. Activists faced hostility with courage.

Taylor occasionally saw the TV stories with mixed emotions and reactions to the civil rights movement. "Dad, why are those people fighting with Black people?" Isaac and Makena tried to balance his level of understanding with pride and inspiration, countering his fear and confusion. They explained segregation and discrimination as injustices and that there was something called the "civil rights movement" that aimed to make things right and just. It was a means, a fight to overcome them.

They did not necessarily want to bring up the racial discrimination directed against them so many times in public places. Still, they chose to use a few examples that would help Taylor understand why the civil rights movement was on the rise, explaining it in the simplest terms possible. "Taylor, remember when we took the subway to Yankee Stadium with Nick and his parents, and there was a man who didn't want your mom to have the seat he gave Mrs. Greene?" He went on to explain that the civil rights movement was aimed at preventing such behavior.

Taylor was only ten years old, but observant, and now he had more questions than ever before. As responsible parents, Isaac and Makena assessed that Taylor was ready for more in-depth answers. As the new decade emerged, he experienced confusion and, at times, fear. It was appropriate to address these emotions head-on.

Isaac also stressed that civil rights applied to everyone, not just a select group, and that the movement stood for a message of equality and justice that would represent a world without fear. It was a dream of a better future. Taylor seemed to understand what his father and mother told him. His reaction was what they expected, and his parents realized that if they lived in the South, it would be a different discussion based on the widespread brutality ever present there.

"And that's the way it is." Walter Cronkite, news anchor for the CBS Evening News, summed up his report that day on civil rights events, with words that established him as one of the most prominent journalists, along with Edward R. Murrow (CBS), David Brinkley and Chet Huntley (NBC), and Howard K. Smith (ABC). The news stations played a crucial role in documenting the civil rights movement. They kept Isaac and Makena, as well as the rest of the American people, informed by exposing the realities of segregation and discrimination and the courageous fight by activists for justice. Isaac and Makena knew this was important for a young Black child to understand as much as possible.

The Washingtons believed that childhood, regardless of race, should be filled with fun, excitement, learning, and emotional stability. Isaac and Makena stressed the need for Taylor to focus on things that would contribute to those objectives. They enrolled Taylor in sports activities, often coordinated with Nick's parents, so the boys would attend the same soccer skills sessions, gymnastics, and other sports, where they developed coordination and teamwork. They added stickball games, a popular street sport played in Brooklyn neighborhoods, where kids from the city block would spontaneously start a game, using a broom handle for a bat and just about anything to represent the bases and home plate.

Nick and Taylor became interested in model building, constructing airplanes with balsa wood, or cars from plastic parts. There were art classes and science clubs where their creativity would shine, and the families often worked together in social and civic activities, such as neighborhood clean-up projects, which instilled civic pride—a comprehensive approach to rearing children in a world that often presents counterproductive behavior.

Isaac and Makena did everything they could imagine would help their son to not only understand what Black people faced, but also enable him to be a kid, and enjoy life despite the seeds of slavery and the years of aftermath from its roots . . . and to be cognizant of the importance of the civil rights movement that shouted for all to hear, "It's time!"

Isaac and Makena came from families that were the exception rather than the norm. Isaac's father was one of the early Black men who became pharmacists, and Isaac followed in his footsteps. Education was a priority in the Washington family, and Isaac's parents worked hard to support his efforts to achieve his degree. Makena wanted to be a nurse, but when she met Isaac, they married soon after he graduated. Taylor entered the world soon after, so she was dedicated to being a full-time mother.

Isaac and his wife would occasionally talk about the issues that carved the Black population from the rest of society and that prevented equal rights for all. They would have lengthy discussions that would trace history to the present day to understand the scourge of slavery and all that would result from its origins. They understood that racial discrimination is not rooted in logic or reason, but that it stems from biases, prejudices, and social constructs that have been perpetuated over time. They knew that, at its core, racial discrimination contradicts the principles of fairness, equality, and human dignity.

They were intelligent enough to realize that having prejudices is not illegal, but that acting on them to the detriment of others was considered a hate crime that was racially motivated. They thought, *Everyone has prejudices of some kind! It was natural; it was human.*

They did their research, visiting libraries, compiling reading material that they would discuss between themselves, but also with some close Black friends who expressed more interest now than before because they recognized that the civil rights momentum addressed racism as more than just prejudice in thought; it was an oppression that limited the rights of Black people, and it was getting big airtime. They knew that the social construct of race historically classified human beings according to physical or biological characteristics, and that ethnicity is an acquired shared culture of language, practices, and beliefs.

Their conversations aimed to support Black people who were now encountering a new wave of attention. It was a social encounter, but more importantly, an educational one, a hopeful one. Many understood Black history, while others had numerous questions. "Well, how did slavery start in the first place?" One of Isaac's friends, James Reed, would address this question, which he had heard many times before.

Reed was a professor at New York University, where the school had begun to diversify its faculty to meet the growing demand for representation in various subjects, including Black history. The early rise of the civil rights movement influenced colleges to incorporate Black history and culture into their curricula, which were often taught by Black scholars, such as Dr. Reed. He was instrumental in establishing an Introduction to African American Studies, Diversification of Perspectives course and curricular reforms at NYU. Other universities would establish similar studies and programs, expanding the diversity of their history departments.

Dr. Reed could spend hours answering this fundamental question. Still, to promote conversation and not monopolize it, which is his classroom methodology, he gave a short answer that he knew would provoke more questions. "Slavery has been around for thousands of years. It began independently in various parts of the world, including Iraq, Egypt, Greece, Rome, and China. The transatlantic slave trade began in the fifteenth century when Portuguese and Spanish began enslaving Africans and transporting them to the Americas to work on plantations."

Wow! The history of slavery in a nutshell! The group was intrigued but did not immediately follow up with another question. Reed added, "However, historians believe that a significant starting point for slavery in America was in 1619, in the seventeenth century, when twenty enslaved Africans were brought ashore in the British colony of Jamestown, Virginia. A crew from a private vessel seized the slaves from a Portuguese ship. In the century, European powers—such as Spain, England, and the Netherlands—expanded their colonies in the Americas, Africa, and Asia." *The nutshell got bigger!*

Chapter 36

SATURDAY, APRIL 21, 1962, "QUEI MALEDETTI RAGAZZI!"

The Moretti family established several grocery stores throughout East New York and neighboring Brownsville and Cypress Hills. There were five Moretti brothers. Angelo Moretti was the older brother of Frank, who owned the store where Reggie "Smokes" Jackson was attacked in 1957. The brothers had a good reputation for their small, family-owned stores, which served the community. As his brothers did, Angelo took great pride in showcasing his store with large display windows filled with canned goods, fresh produce, and other essential items that every family craved.

The narrow aisles were packed with cans of Campbell's soups, boxes of Kellogg's Corn Flakes, and tins of coffee. In one corner, the butcher counter had marbled slabs of meat, thick-cut pork chops, and links of sausage. The smell of raw meat blended with the saltiness of brined olives, stacked in barrels nearby.

His store was an unspoken invitation, as the added scents of freshly baked goods, and citrus fruits blended to draw customers in to hear a radio humming softly from behind the counter playing a mix of Frank Sinatra and Motown hits.

Above the entrance was the sign Angelo had constructed and hand-painted himself, which read, Angelo's. Simple and personable. He was there to provide more than just his array of grocery items. Any customer would experience his friendliness and warm conversations as it was also a social hub where you got to know your neighbors, learn about their families, and listen to how their children were growing and advancing in school. His store was a neighborhood staple, where you would go to shop there and "stay a while."

Makena shopped there often, as it was on the corner of their street. Sometimes, on weekends, she would bring Taylor and Ava with her, as they looked forward to peering into the counters, especially for their favorite penny candy that Mr. Moretti would sometimes offer them for free. He showed the same respect and friendship to all his customers, greeting them by name, regardless of their ethnicity or culture, unlike the Italian one he was so proud of. And his customers loved him for that. He would always converse briefly with the kids, expressing his joy at seeing them with his captivating smile. He loved kids and had six of his own.

After he loaded the items for Makena into a paper bag, he said how good it was to see them and to say hello to Isaac. This happy man, with very little hair except for a thick mustache, and wearing his butcher's apron, waved goodbye to the kids and moved on to his other customers, who filled the aisles.

When Makena and the kids returned home, she realized she had forgotten to pick up some freshly baked bread. She said, "Taylor, honey, I forgot to get a loaf of bread. Here's a quarter. Please go back to Mr. Angelo and tell him we need one loaf of Italian bread." Taylor had gone to the corner store by himself many times, and it was a routine of merely getting on his two-wheel bike for a quick errand. The sidewalk traffic was light, with a few people going about their daily business, exiting or entering their apartments, walking their dogs, or conversing, sometimes in languages Taylor could not comprehend.

The store was just a few minutes' walk from the apartment and under one minute by bike. Seconds from the store, and in a section where there was no one else, Taylor was about to pass an alleyway when three White teenage boys jumped out and knocked him off his bike. They grabbed him and pulled him into the alley. Startled and afraid, Taylor shouted at them, "Stop. Why did you knock me down? Look what you did to my bike!"

His Schwinn bike was durable and high quality. The bike company was known for its craftsmanship, strong steel frames, and reliable components. Taylor didn't know if his bike had been ruined, but after seeing it on the ground, he wasn't sure of its condition or if he could ride it again. He didn't realize he had a nasty cut on the left side of his head from hitting the concrete sidewalk.

The boys just laughed and called him names using the *N-word*, and also called him a baby, "a little Black baby." "Are you gonna cry, little Black baby?" They pushed him until he fell again and kicked him in the back, stomach, legs, and face. It all took seconds before the young cowards ran down the alley unnoticed by anyone. They were so proud of how they took care of the "little Black baby" in their neighborhood. Taylor groaned on the ground, but eventually got up and picked up his bike to see if it was still rideable. The bike had a few scratches that ruined its overall appearance, but it remained functional after striking the ground.

As Taylor ached, he walked his bike to Angelo's. He didn't have the strength to climb onto his bike without pain. He walked into the grocery store when some of the customers and Moretti saw blood coming from his head. Moretti quickly came around from the counter that held the cash register. "Oh, mio Dio, Taylor, whata happen to you? You bleeding!" The customers looked on with obvious concern.

"Some White kids knocked me off my bike and beat me up! They kicked me and said nasty things. I think my bike is alright, but I didn't ride it yet." He took the quarter from his pocket and said, "My mom told me she forgot to get some bread. She wants a loaf of Italian bread, so . . . " He was interrupted when Isaac ran into the store and was about to tell Moretti that his wife said Taylor was taking a very long time to get the bread and that she wanted him to check on their son. He then saw his son with a bloody streak down his face.

"Taylor! What happened? Did you fall off your bike? Are you okay?"

Moretti said, "Isaac, he justa got here, and I was going to get a wet towel to wipa the blood. He said some Whita boys bully him . . . knock him down off his bike and they kick him!"

Isaac was furious and asked, "Taylor, what White boys?" as a store clerk came with a wet towel and some bandages. "Did you ever see these kids before? Who are they? Do you know where they live?" The store clients increased and now huddled around the father and son, interested in what Taylor knew. *This was big news in the neighborhood. Shopping for groceries was not.*

After the clerk assisted with the towel and bandages, Isaac thanked him and turned to Moretti as Taylor continued to moan from his injuries. "May I use your phone? I want to call Makena to tell her what happened and that I will take Taylor to the hospital."

Moretti said, "Of course, of course!" He then mumbled in a low voice, "*quei maledetti ragazzi!*"

As Isaac went to grab the telephone, he stopped and said, "Excuse me . . . what?"

Moretti said, "Oh, *Mi scusa*, sorry, I mean excuse me. I said, 'Those damn boys!' "

Isaac was dialing Makena, and looked at Moretti when he said, "Those damn boys . . . right! Their parents will hear from me. I will find them. I can take some racial abuse now and then, but when they attack my family, they gang up on my son, that's going too far! Makena?" Makena answered, and Isaac told her what had happened.

She screamed, "Oh, Taylor . . . is he okay?" Isaac told her that Moretti and his helper provided some bandages that seemed to slow down the bleeding, but that Taylor was complaining of pain in his stomach and back, that he had bruises on his face, and that he would call a cab to go immediately to the hospital emergency room.

"Bleeding? Bruises on his face! Oh, my God! Who did this to him?"

"I don't know yet, but I will find out . . . somehow. I'll call you from the hospital!" He hung up and called for a taxicab. He would have taken Taylor home to take their car, but he wasn't sure he should try to walk him even a short distance. The cab arrived, and he and Moretti helped Taylor into the backseat. Isaac thanked Moretti and his clerk again and asked one more question. "Would you mind keeping Taylor's bike here while . . . "

Angelo answered before Isaac could finish asking. "*Certo, certo!* I mean, of course! I put it in the back. It will be safe there in the storeroom."

Isaac shook Angelo's hand and sat next to Taylor in the cab. "Kings County Hospital, please. And hurry!" Isaac mumbled to himself, *Those bastards!*

Chapter 37

KINGS COUNTY HOSPITAL

Doctor Perry Hamilton spoke to Isaac. "Your son sustained several injuries, and he has visible signs of nausea and dizziness. The kicks to his face caused blunt force trauma, resulting in contusions—damage to blood vessels beneath his skin that caused swelling. We applied an ice pack to reduce the swelling. We'll continue to apply ice to the swollen area for about ten to fifteen minutes every hour for the first twenty-four hours. There are also minor cuts from the kicking and his contact with the ground. The bleeding from the head always looks worse than it is. We have treated those with clean bandages and some nonprescription pain medications."

"You said you will apply ice for the first twenty-four hours? You mean I can't take him home? Does he need to stay here in the hospital?"

"Yes. Upon our examination and his symptoms, he may have damage to internal organs as well, which we need to monitor for any warning signs. He's complaining about pain in his back and abdomen. I asked him where the pain was, and I checked his abdomen for any tenderness, swelling, or rigidity. Using my stethoscope, I did not hear anything abnormal in the digestive tract. His blood pressure and pulse are slightly elevated, but not dangerously high. I am going to order an X-ray to determine if anything is broken. At this point, I don't think anything is broken, but we need to be sure."

"Thanks, doctor. Anything else you can tell me?"

"Once I see the X-ray results and monitor Taylor over the next couple of hours, I should have a better idea of his injuries and treatment, and when he can go home. Oh, I also wanted to mention that Kings County Hospital is beginning to use new technology called 'ultrasounds,' which produce diagnostic images. We typically use it for obstetrics and gynecology, but we are expanding its capability to other areas. If the X-rays warrant, I may suggest doing an ultrasound. A combination of all this will give us a much better understanding of Taylor's injuries."

"Wow! Sounds like a lot! Thank you so much, doctor. I trust you will take good care of my son. His mother is so worried about him. I am so worried about him. Did you ask him how he got hurt? Did he tell you anything?"

"Mr. Washington, I'm glad you asked that. Taylor did say that some White boys beat him up. I think he's more worried about his bicycle than himself at this point, but I think you should know that we treated another Black boy about the same age as Taylor recently for also being attacked by several White boys. That other boy lives in the same general area where this took place, near Angelo's grocery store. Taylor told me he was almost there to pick up a loaf of bread when they knocked him off his bike and attacked him."

"Are you serious! Another kid was attacked? When, who? Can you give me his name? I want to track down these kids and have a word with their parents . . . maybe even file a lawsuit."

"I'm afraid I can't disclose any information, the boy's name, or his parents. I strongly suggest you contact the police. I believe the parents of the other kid reported it. The police would be the ones to connect these two . . . hate crimes. That's what I believe they are. Hate crimes."

"That is very interesting and great information. Thank you. You know, several years ago, when my son was in first grade, there were attacks in his school, and they even connected it to attacks in Jefferson High School, where White students attacked Black students. The students in the schools were siblings. It was a complex situation, and the police found out it was part of a widespread plan to increase racial discrimination and violence in Brooklyn. It appeared to be inspired by KKK activity that had spread to New York. It was reported in *The New York Times*, too."

"You know, I recall reading about that! What is this world coming to?"

"I think that question comes up now and then. Thanks again, doctor. I'm going to call my wife, then wait here at the hospital for any updates from you for the time being."

"I will let you know of anything new. Take care, and don't worry, we'll take good care of Taylor. He seems like a nice kid!" Isaac gave the doctor a thumbs up and went to make a call to Makena. *She's probably climbing the walls right now!*

"Honey, I just spoke with Dr. Perry Hamilton. He's a pediatrician here at Kings County Hospital. He gave me his immediate assessment of Taylor's condition. He seems very competent and thorough."

Isaac spent the next twenty minutes reviewing everything he heard from the doctor and trying to answer Makena's concerns. At one point, she started to cry, but Isaac assured her that Taylor was in good hands and that the doctor would report the findings from the X-rays so that they would know the next steps. He tried to turn Makena's attention a bit. "How's our little girl doing? I bet she misses her brother."

Makena laughed, "Yes, she keeps calling, 'Taylor, Taylor,' and she walks all over the apartment looking for him. We miss him," as she began to cry again.

"He will be okay. Can you notify the school? I don't think he'll return for a day or two, maybe a few days, but I'm not sure yet."

"I will. Oh, and I'll give Mary and Jonathan a call so they can tell Nick. I'm sure he'll be upset if he doesn't see Taylor in school on Monday."

"Okay, good. One more thing. You won't believe this, but the doctor told me that another Black boy was attacked by White kids recently in the same area. Probably the same kids, but not certain."

"Oh my God! Who are the . . . " Isaac interrupted.

"I asked the doctor the same question. By law, he can't disclose any of that information, but he did tell me the other boy's parents filed a police report, and that he advised us to do the same. The police will likely link the two incidents or investigate to determine if any connection exists, and then they may provide us with some answers. I'm thinking of filing a lawsuit . . . a lawsuit for a hate crime!"

"A lawsuit? We've never been involved in any lawsuit. What is this world coming to?"

"You're the second person who asked me that question today. And, I don't have the answer. I am so angry right now! You know, we live in a nice neighborhood, with nice neighbors; with our friends; with people like Mr. Moretti, who is also friendly, respectful and ready to help. And yet there are these punks who roam around with nothing better to do than attack someone and send them to the hospital. This is obviously racially motivated. It's a hate crime!"

The call ended with Isaac and Makena consoling one another. It was the fallback action that always defined the deep bond and mutual support in their relationship. Isaac reassured her. "We'll get through this together, for Taylor. I'll be home soon, and so will our son."

Makena smiled as she wiped away her tears. "I love you!"

"I love you, too!" Isaac returned to his seat in the waiting room to wait once again, and hopefully not as long as he had for the birth of Ava. Within one hour, Dr. Hamilton returned.

"Mr. Washington, good news! The X-rays don't show any signs of broken bones. He has bruises on other parts of his body, including his legs and back. They will disappear in a week or so. The facial swelling has subsided, and Taylor is complaining about being hungry, which is a positive sign. It appears his nausea and dizziness have mitigated. I recommend we keep him overnight to ensure there is nothing we should be concerned about internally. We'll monitor him frequently and keep you informed."

"That's great to hear, doctor. Can I see him?"

"Yes, I was just about to tell you, he's asking for you, so please."

Isaac smiled for a change as he approached Taylor, sitting in his bed with a white towel wrapped around his head. The towel was knotted at the top, and the two ends flopped to his ears. The towel held a bag of crushed ice against the remaining swollen area on his face.

"Taylor, how are you feeling? You look like the Easter Bunny with that towel around your head!" This made Taylor laugh, followed by a groan.

"Dad, don't make me laugh. It hurts!" He took a long, slow, deep breath to regain stability in his torso. "Is Mom worried about me?"

"Of course she is! I spoke with her just before the doctor came out to tell me that you will be okay. Mom and Ava miss you very much and can't wait for you to come home. The doctor wants you to stay here overnight so they can keep an eye on you and make sure everything is okay. I'll stay here in the hospital if you want, but if I go home, I'm not that far away. I can be here very quickly. You still feel very sore?"

"Yeah, my head and my stomach, but I'm . . . " He was just about to say how hungry he was when a nurse wheeled in some food. Taylor propped himself up a bit with his father's help to dig into the turkey, mashed potatoes, soft vegetables, and a cup of apple sauce. His father smiled, thanked the nurse, and set the food tray close to Taylor. *Now I know he's feeling better!*

Isaac was relieved to see Taylor take the first few bites, which brought a smile to his face. Sometimes, *food is good medicine.* "Taylor, take your time. Eat slowly. Is it good?"

"Yeah!" That's all Taylor wanted to say. Any further explanation would detract from the enjoyment of eating.

"Listen, I have to make a call. I'll be right back in a few minutes."

"Okay, Dad."

Isaac went to the nurses' station and asked if he could use a phone for a local call. She directed him to the public phone booth in the waiting room. He dropped a dime in and dialed the operator. "Yes, operator, can you please connect me with the police precinct in East New York?"

"Yes, sir. Just a moment."

"Hello, this is the NYPD, 75th Police Precinct. May I help you?"

"Yes, hello. I want to report a crime . . . a hate crime!"

Chapter 38

THE TIP OF THE ICEBERG

Jonathan and Nick went out to shop for birthday gifts. Mary's birthday was two weeks away, and the guys wanted to be prepared. They said they were going to the park to play catch for a while, but when Mary noticed that Nick's glove and baseball were still in his room, she had a pretty good idea what they were really doing.

The phone rang. Mary answered, "Hello?"

"Hi Mary, this is Makena."

"Oh, hi, how are you? How is everything?"

"Well, that's why I'm calling. Taylor is in the hospital."

"Oh, no! What happened? Is he alright?"

"Isaac is there with him at Kings County. On his way to Angelo's, some boys attacked him when he went to pick up something I forgot to get, just a few minutes earlier when he and Ava were with me."

"Oh, Makena! Attacked! I am so sorry. Who attacked him? Is he injured badly? I hope not!"

Makena gave Mary as much detail as she knew and told her that she wanted to call so they could inform Nick why Taylor would not be in school on Monday. It looked like he would be in the hospital for a few days. She said that Isaac was so angry that he was going to call the police and was even thinking of filing a lawsuit. Then she told Mary that the doctor told Isaac that another Black boy was attacked in the same area, and that the parents filed a report with the police. That was probably the only way they might be able to find out who the boys were. As far as they knew, there were no witnesses or way of knowing who these kids were or where they lived. There were three White teenage boys.

"Makena, I am so sorry to hear all this. I'm sick. Jonathan and Nick will be sick about this. I'm sure Nick will be very angry. Every time you and your family were on the receiving end of some racial discrimination, Nick would ask why it was happening. We would have lengthy discussions about it. And now, with the news about the civil rights movement in the country, it comes up more often. We don't always realize it, but Nick hears things, overhears news on the TV, or sometimes Jonathan and I talk. So he has a lot of questions."

"Taylor is the same way. I wonder if they talk to each other about it. It wouldn't surprise me. They're as close to being twins as you can get without the skin color, of course." Both women laughed because they had repeated it many times before.

"Makena, if you and Isaac need to be at the hospital together, please call me anytime. I can take care of Ava and anything else you need. And please keep us updated on Taylor. I feel so bad for him and hope he returns to normal very soon. Love you guys."

"Mary, thanks so much. I'll keep you informed. Love you guys too!" They hung up, and their sighs were almost loud enough to hear across East New York.

Nick and his father returned a couple of hours later. "We're home," Jonathan said.

Mary was apprehensive about telling them that Taylor was in the hospital due to the attack. She diverted to asking, "Well, how was the park?"

Jonathan and Nick looked at one another for mutual assurance that their answer to this question would be the same. "Good!" Mary put her hands on her hips, stared at them, and said nothing.

Jonathan said, "What?"

"That's it? A one-word answer, 'good'? You guys usually have so much to say when you return from the park to play catch. And how was the catching without your ball and glove, Nick?"

They laughed, and Nick said, "Mom, we can't tell you where we went. It's a secret."

Jonathan began to feel the heat. "Trust us," he said with a smile. "No more questions allowed."

Mary said, "Okay, you two, but I do have something serious to tell you."

"Oh, what is it?"

"Makena called me." She sighed. "Taylor was attacked by three White boys, teenagers, while he rode his bike to Angelo's grocery store. They knocked him off his bike and beat him so bad that he's in the hospital, at Kings County."

Nick was stunned. His jaw dropped and he shouted, "I want to go see him!"

Jonathan's expression went from smiling and *we can't fool her when it comes to her birthday* to widened eyes in disbelief. "What? In the hospital? How bad is he? Did she say? Is Isaac with him?"

Mary gave all the details to him and Nick regarding the incident and Taylor's condition. Their reaction was one of anger at first, but it soon turned to concern for Taylor and the Washington family. Jonathan assumed that the attack on Taylor was an attack on his family, if not directly, but at least by the fact that they were a Black family. When he heard that White boys recently attacked another Black boy in the same area, he asked, "What do you think they will do?"

Mary told them that Isaac was contacting the police to report a hate crime and hoped they could provide some information on the boys who hurt Taylor, that perhaps the two attacks were committed by the same bullies. "Nick, Mrs. Washington wanted me to tell you that Taylor will miss school on Monday, maybe even a few more days, and not to worry. The doctors are taking good care of him." Nick ran into his room and slammed the door shut.

Jonathan said, "I'll go in and talk to him. I know how upset he must be. I'm upset. This crap has got to stop, especially when it gets violent!"

"I'm upset too. I told Makena we would watch Ava anytime if they wanted to be with Taylor together."

"Okay, good, yeah, of course. I'll be back in a little while." He went and knocked on Nick's bedroom door. "Nick, are you okay? I'm coming in. I wanna talk with you." He heard a faint "Okay."

Nick was lying face down in his bed. Jonathan sat next to him and rubbed his back. "Listen, Nick. I know this is bad news, and we are all angry. The good news is that Taylor has some injuries that are not very serious, and he is getting very good care from the doctors at the hospital. His father is there with him."

"I want to go and see him, Dad."

"I know you do, and I'm sure Taylor would want to see you, but right now, we need to give him a chance to rest and for the doctors to make sure he gets well enough to go home. Tell you what. I'll check with his parents and see if there's a good time to visit if Taylor's going to be there for a few days. Okay?"

All Nick could think about was finding those kids who beat Taylor up and finding a way to make them pay. He expressed that to his father, who was ready to pounce on the idea, but thought for a moment before speaking with his son. "You know, I feel the same way." Nick sat up and looked at his father.

"You do?"

"I do. But revenge is not a good thing. It can get you in big trouble in many ways."

"What do you mean?"

"Well, if you were able to find those boys and get in a fight with them, no matter how angry you are, you could end up in the hospital like Taylor. And, if you went to pick a fight and they reported it, you could be in trouble with the police. Mr. Washington probably wants to bust those kids' heads, but he did the right thing. He called the police. They should take care of it."

Nick did what he always did: He listened to his parents and then asked a hundred more questions to ensure he understood everything, and more importantly, that he was satisfied with the answers.

"Why do they pick on Black kids like Taylor, Daddy? Why?" Jonathan pondered. *The answer to that question is one that can be short or take all night, and more, to answer.*

"That's an excellent question, Nick. People may answer it in different ways. Some will say that they were brought up wrong and turned out to be bullies, that they don't respect other people, that they want to force their power over others, and that they can only do it when they have many against one. Maybe their parents don't like Black people, and their kids just pick that up from them; maybe they saw their parents mistreat Black people. There are probably many more reasons I can't even think about right now. You know, when we saw what some people said or did when we went to the Yankees game the first time with Taylor and his parents, it wasn't right. People have been treating Black people, like the Washingtons, badly for many years. For now, it may be best to keep up with how Taylor is doing and look forward to when he's back in school and you guys can be together like before."

"Okay, but I still don't understand why so many people don't like Black people. Why don't they, Dad?" *The hundred-question kid was at it again.*

"Well, I think we can have more talks about this. Maybe a little at a time. And I know that you will learn more about Black people in school and especially with some of the things you saw on TV with what they call the civil rights movement, which is all about finding a world where we don't single out certain people—like Blacks, Jews and others—and show disrespect and hatred."

"I didn't know all that. I wonder how Taylor feels about all that."

"Well, you guys are good friends. I'm sure you and he can talk about it. He may be able to tell you things from his point of view, and that might be better than any answers I can give you. But remember, you can always ask me or Mom anything, okay?"

"Yeah. I wanna ask Taylor!" Jonathan knew this was the tip of the iceberg, for an in-depth conversation on racial discrimination, civil rights, the activists, the marches, the sit-ins, and everything else saturating the daily news in America, including the escalation of the war in Vietnam.

Chapter 39

A Place to Get Things Done

Sergeant Conan McGuire took charge of the investigation triggered by Isaac's call to the police. McGuire had explicitly been assigned to cases involving racial discrimination since his direct encounter with the racially motivated attack in PS 91 nearly five years ago. His experience with the aftermath of that incident and the prior attack at Jefferson High School kept him involved through the arrests and convictions of the individual who inspired them. Captain O'Rourke depended on McGuire's insight and ability to treat these crimes with efficiency and empathy.

"Mr. Washington, I am sorry to hear what happened to your son, and I hope he heals quickly. There is no place in Brooklyn, or anywhere for that matter, for these attacks. I want to get a full report from you. I can meet you anywhere it's convenient for you, or let me know if you can come to the precinct."

"Thank you, Sergeant. I just heard from a nurse that my son finished his dinner and is resting quietly . . . fell asleep, actually. She said that with the pain medication, he may sleep for a while. I can come there now if you're available."

"Anytime, Mr. Washington. I'll be here if you can come over now." Isaac said he would be on his way. He told the nurse that he would be gone for maybe a couple of hours and then return, and to please tell his son, if he wakes up, that his father would be back soon. The nurse nodded and said she would keep an eye on Taylor.

Isaac called Makena and briefly told her that he had spoken with Sergeant McGuire and was headed to the police precinct to give him a report. He mentioned that the nurse would tell Taylor that he would return to the hospital soon if he woke up while he was gone.

He paid the cab driver and exited the cab in front of the police precinct at 484 Liberty Avenue in East New York. He looked up at the structure. He had never been to a police station before. He paused as he observed this historic building, constructed in 1886, with Romanesque Revival architecture that emerged in the nineteenth century, with its rounded arches over the windows and doors, and thick stone walls with ornate columns that enhanced its image of stability, durability, permanence, and timelessness. It looked like a place to get things done.

A clerk took Isaac to Sergeant McGuire's office. McGuire said, "Thanks for coming in, Mr. Washington. Can I get you something to drink . . . coffee or a soda?"

Isaac suddenly realized he hadn't eaten anything since early that morning. "Uh . . . you know, I would appreciate a cup of coffee, thank you." McGuire called for his clerk to fetch a cup for Isaac. The clerk asked what he would like in his coffee. Isaac said, "Just black, please." The clerk was back in less than a minute.

Sergeant McGuire asked, "Mr. Washington . . . "

Isaac interrupted him and said, "Please call me Isaac. You know, I remember you when you came to PS 91 to talk with the parents about the school attack there in 1957. My son was in first grade then."

"Yes, I remember that well, and I have been working on racially oriented crimes ever since. Please tell me everything you know about the attack on your son."

Isaac was eager to do that, but first asked, "I understand that another boy was attacked in the same area recently, and that it might be the same boys who did it. The doctor at Kings County would not give me any information. He's the one who suggested I call the police."

"Mr. Washington. . . I mean, Isaac . . . before I can tell you anything related to the other attack, I need to know your details, and then we will investigate. We can provide more information once we have sufficient information and any link between the attacks. So I ask you, please, let's just focus on your son's incident right now."

"I understand. Thank you." Isaac disclosed everything he could remember he had heard from his son, Mr. Moretti, at the grocery store, and Doctor Hamilton. Sergeant McGuire listened carefully, took a few notes, and assured Isaac that the police would investigate his son's attack immediately. He already suspected a high degree of probability that the same boys were involved in both, but he felt it was premature to mention it.

"Isaac, thank you for coming in. Here's my number. If you recall anything else, please don't hesitate to call me. I will personally contact you with any updates from our investigation. Where are you headed now? Back to the hospital, home?"

"I will go back to the hospital. I may stay there the night, but I'm not sure yet."

"I will have one of my officers drive you there. I hope your son recovers quickly and gets back to normal. Good luck to you."

"Thank you very much, Sergeant." An officer dropped Isaac off at the hospital. He quickly ran to Taylor's room to find him still asleep. A nurse came in shortly after.

"Mr. Washington. I'll get Doctor Hamilton; he wanted to speak with you when you returned." She immediately left before Isaac could ask her why. Just then, Taylor woke up.

"Dad. I got up while you were gone and went to the bathroom. I peed some blood!"

"Blood! Did you tell the nurse or the doctor? How are you feeling? Does anything hurt?"

"I feel tired. It just hurts when I pee. I told the nurse, and she got the doctor. He came in and examined me and said he would talk to you when you got back."

The nurse returned and told Isaac that the doctor would be there to speak with him as soon as he finished up with another patient. Isaac couldn't wait and asked, "My son said there was blood when he went to the bathroom! What does that mean?"

According to Doctor Hamilton, the nurse said, "It's probably from his kidney. He mentioned something about doing an ultrasound. He'll discuss it with you, any minute now." She left just as quickly as she came in.

It was only ten minutes later, but seemed like an eternity, before Doctor Hamilton arrived. "Doctor, what is causing the bleeding my son is having? Is it internal bleeding? How serious is it?" This day was bad enough. He didn't want to hear any more bad news.

"I've ordered a urinalysis to confirm the presence of blood and check for any other abnormalities. If it comes from his kidneys, an ultrasound will show the extent of any kidney damage. Once we know that, we can advise you of the proper treatment. If it's a mild injury, it will heal with rest and hydration, and he should limit any physical activity to avoid further strain on the kidneys. In most cases, we recommend an over-the-counter pain reliever. If it's severe, we may suggest he remain here for monitoring. It is rare, but in some cases, surgery may be needed to stop the bleeding."

"Oh boy! This is getting worse!"

Doctor Hamilton assured Isaac. "Don't worry too much. I've seen many cases like this, and usually, it's a nonsurgical issue, but we need to be sure. Now that Taylor is awake, we'll move him to the lab for the ultrasound. All okay with you?"

"Yes, you know best. We want the best for our son. Whatever you think."

"Great! I'll set that up right now." Isaac made another visit to the waiting room and the phone booth to call Makena. It was turning out to be a nonstop day, paying attention to Taylor, meeting with the police, and now back at the hospital to learn of the next piece of news that would occupy his mind for the foreseeable future.

He called Makena to bring her up to date. Her worry level was rising faster than a sunrise in a sped-up movie. She said, "Oh no! Our Taylor! Does it hurt when he pees blood?"

"He said it just hurts when he pees, otherwise he seems to be okay . . . no pain. We'll know more when the doctor gets the urinalysis and ultrasound results. I'll call you as soon as I hear. Listen, I think I will just stay here with Taylor, at least for tonight. I will call my folks at the pharmacy to tell them I may need someone to cover for me for a few days."

"Okay. You must be exhausted. Have you had anything to eat since you left the house? You've been at this all day!"

"No. You just reminded me of how hungry I am right now. I had half a cup of coffee at the police station, that's it."

"I can see if Destiny can come over for a little while. It's a good thing she still babysits. She might be able to watch Ava while I bring you some dinner."

"Okay, thank you! If not, I can ask if there is anything nearby that I can grab quickly. I want to be here when the doctor has the test results. Just call the hospital when you find out about Destiny, and ask for me, that I'm meeting with Doctor Hamilton." Isaac returned to Taylor's room. He was gone, taken by the nurse to the lab for the tests. *More waiting, for test results, the doctor's report and recommendations, food, police work . . . and who knows what else!*

Chapter 40

Someone Must Have Seen Something

Destiny held little Ava in her arms as Makena kissed them both goodbye and carried the dinner of the previous night's leftovers for Isaac to her car. She had already explained what happened to Taylor to Destiny, and the babysitter did not hesitate to offer her support. The Washingtons loved Destiny. She reminded Makena of herself when she was her age.

She was the daughter of one of their closest Black friends, and they had used her babysitting services for the last five years. They expressed how sad they would be to see her leave after the summer to attend Howard University in Washington, DC, to major in communications and journalism, but how proud they were of her and happy about her success. She was the first person in her family to attend college. She loved storytelling, which always got Taylor's and Ava's undivided attention.

Makena delivered dinner to Isaac, who was still waiting for Taylor to return from the lab. The worried couple hugged and whispered, "I love you." Isaac said, "He'll be okay. I got a sense the doctor was not too concerned but just wanted to be sure with the extra tests."

Makena's eyes moistened. "I pray that he's okay—our Taylor. I've been so on edge, and now I'm beginning to get angry like you. I don't like being angry, but this is an exception." She wiped her eyes. "You better eat this. You must be starving!" Just as Isaac was about to take his first bite of the chicken dinner, a lab technician wheeled Taylor into the room.

Makena jumped up from her chair. "Oh, Taylor, honey, how are you feeling? Look at what they did to my son!" His face displayed cuts and bruises, with slight swelling, which was clearly visible as the ice pack had been removed before the lab tests.

Isaac put the fork, which still held the first piece of chicken, down before he said, "The swelling has gone down a lot. You should have seen it earlier!" Then he took his first, second, and third bite. He chewed and asked simultaneously, forgetting that his parents always told him not to talk with food in his mouth, "How were the tests at the lab?"

Taylor said, "Oh, it was okay; it didn't hurt or anything. There was a guy who told me what he was doing, and he was looking at a screen that he said showed pictures of my kidneys and that he would give them to the doctor. I had to pee again, in a small bottle. I still saw some blood, and it hurt a little."

Makena held Taylor's hand and hugged him with her free arm around him. The nurse came in and said that Doctor Hamilton had called and said he would be here in about twenty minutes. The Washingtons thought every bit of communication might have a good or bad outcome. *Why twenty minutes? Is it bad news?* Isaac finished his dinner and settled his hunger pangs for now.

Waiting . . . waiting . . . always waiting! Doctor Hamilton came into Taylor's room. Isaac said, "Doctor, this is my wife, Makena."

Hamilton extended his hand, "Mrs. Washington, nice to meet you, and I'm sure you are both anxious to hear the test results." They both gave their attention with eyes that would not blink while holding their breath. "The tests reveal that the kick to the lower back caused a contusion, a bruising in one of Taylor's kidneys, the one on his left side. This contributes to the mild to moderate bleeding. That's why Taylor has some blood in his urine right now. The good news is there is no laceration that could cause internal bleeding and would likely require any surgery."

Makena asked, "Was there anything else that these . . . kicks from these juvenile delinquents did to my son? Any other organs?" She could not hold back the anger.

Hamilton continued, "The kidneys are generally protected partially by the ribs and surrounding muscle tissue. The kick was forceful enough to transmit energy to the one kidney through Taylor's flank region. Nothing else was affected. The other kicks—we think there were as many as ten based on the surface bruising—did not extend to anything serious."

Isaac asked, "So what do we do about this bleeding, doctor?"

"It's pretty straightforward. We recommend adequate fluid intake, initially intravenously, so we should keep Taylor here for another day. Continue hydration at home, limit any activity for about a week, and make sure he gets good bed rest. I'll recommend adequate over-the-counter pain meds that won't stress the kidneys. We'll also want to follow up with lab tests to check Taylor's blood count, kidney function, electrolyte balance, etc. These can be done as an outpatient."

Makena asked, "Will Taylor be able to return to school soon?"

"I expect we'll release him from the hospital tomorrow, and he can return after resting at home for a couple of days. However, please ensure that he refrains from any physical activity until we conduct the follow-up lab tests and examine him again. After about a week, he should be able to do some mild exercise. This isn't something you should rush."

Isaac responded to all the information. "Doctor, this is good news. We were so worried it was a lot worse. Thank you for all the information and for taking care of Taylor." Makena also thanked him.

Hamilton went over to Taylor and put his hand on his shoulder. "Young man, you will be as good as new soon. Just listen to your parents, and don't try to do too much." He turned and wished the Washingtons good health before proceeding to his next patient.

Taylor had been thinking about Nick, school, and especially the science fair that was scheduled for June. It was established at PS 91 two years earlier and was a big hit with the students and parents. Taylor and Nick had decided on their exhibit, but had not yet started any work on it. Taylor was anxious about it and worried that his medical condition would impact the project start. "I have to tell Nick we need to start the project for the science fair."

Makena said, "Don't you worry. You boys have plenty of time, well over a month, and I'm sure when you and Nick put your heads together, you will be ready." Taylor smiled, probably for the first time in many hours, and nodded. He knew his mother was absolutely right.

After a couple of hours, Makena returned home to care for Ava. She gave Destiny the news about Taylor's injuries and treatment, emphasizing that it could have been a lot worse. She wanted to hear all about Destiny's plans for living in DC and her curriculum at Howard University. Isaac decided to stay with Taylor for the night. He promised to return home to freshen up after Taylor had breakfast the next day. He called Jonathan and Mary to ask if Nick wanted to visit Taylor on Sunday and said he would be happy to pick him up.

Mary answered, "Oh, Isaac, we have been so worried about Taylor. It's awful . . . those bullies! I hope the police catch them. How is Taylor doing?"

"The police will investigate. I went to the precinct to file a report of the assault. Taylor had some tests today, and he will remain in the hospital tonight. He had an injury to his left kidney. He has some bleeding, but the doctor said no surgery was needed. They are treating it with hydration, painkillers, and rest for now. Taylor got kicked many times in his face, back, and stomach . . . a lot of swelling, but that has gone down quite a bit. The worst was the impact on his kidney."

"Oh, my gosh! Nick has been so worried about him; we are all worried here. I'm so sorry this has happened. I hope the police catch those brats and they get what's coming to them. Oh, yes, Sunday. I think Nick would love to see Taylor. Can he bring him anything? Can we do anything?"

"I think when Taylor sees Nick, that's all he will need, but thank you. I can pick Nick up, say, between 9:30 and 10 tomorrow morning?"

"That sounds great, Isaac. I'll tell Nick. He'll be so excited to see Taylor. Thank you, and tell Taylor we are thinking of him and hope he recovers soon." Isaac thanked her, and they both hung up.

Nick was elated to hear he could visit his friend. He couldn't wait for Sunday.

Sergeant McGuire had assembled a couple of officers to check the neighborhood where the attacks on the two boys had happened to see if anyone noticed anything. Perhaps there was something someone saw about the attack in broad daylight, but was reluctant to report it. *Someone must have seen something!*

The Black boy who was attacked before Taylor's incident was treated and released from the hospital the same day. He had a few cuts and bruises from being pushed and beaten with fists, but was not on the ground where more injuries could have been the case. The parents of the previous attack mentioned to the police that their son said he saw some people across the street from Angelo's, looking out their first and second story windows just before he was attacked. The police conducted a query with people from the apartments in that area, but no one said they saw anything.

Brooklyn is a place where many people sit by their windows and watch the world go by. They are people who have nothing else to do. They're home all day, and it's more interesting to see everyone else's business than to be bored with their own. Often, the window hangers would talk to one another with those who were side by side, above, or below. There was always someone ready for a long, meaningless conversation, and the police knew that.

McGuire's team had a full plate of police work: suspects to question and more serious crimes to solve. They could not knock on any doors near Angelo's again until Monday or Tuesday. But they did call Angelo, and after some conversation about how his family and business were doing, they got to the point. "Angelo, this is very important. We are trying to find any witnesses to the attacks on the Black boys near your store recently. Can you tell us about anybody who watches the streets from their windows, across the street, on your side, anywhere?"

Moretti said that many people look out their windows and that, "He wasa sure thata somebody saw the boys beat up the Blacka boys." He said he knows all his neighbors by name because "They shopa atta my store."

"Okay, Angelo. We'll stop by your store to talk to you in a few days." Angelo always loved it when the police came to his store, for grocery business or police business. It made no difference to him what clothes or uniform they wore or how they combed their hair. He loved people, and they loved him. But now he felt something more, a sense of civic duty.

Angelo's father, Giuseppe Moretti, immigrated to the United States in 1915, one of three million Italians who were part of the "New Immigration" that began in 1890. He spent seventeen years becoming a naturalized American citizen, playing a vital role as part of the organized labor supply in America. He embraced citizenship with integrity. He always gave his sons good advice, and to him, the most important was, "*Non dimenticare mai le tue origini italiane, ma fai tutto il possibile per essere un bravo cittadino americano*" ("Never forget your Italian heritage, but do everything you can to be a good American citizen").

Angelo remembered that, and now his sense of civic duty was crucial because he might be able to help catch "*quei maledetti ragazzi!*"

Chapter 41

ANOTHER BLACK BOY

Isaac downed his coffee and a bagel still warm from a small café one block away, where he picked up a half dozen. He grabbed a quick shower to freshen up and kissed his wife and Ava before leaving to pick up Nick and proceeding to Kings County Hospital. Ava kept saying, "Is Taylor coming? Where is big brother?" She was holding one of the teddy bears that Taylor brought her when she was two years old. She and the bear were inseparable. Makena told her Taylor would be home soon, maybe after one or two more "nighty-nights." Ava processed this with just wide eyes as she looked at her bear and said, "Two nighty-nights."

Nick ran in and out of his room and through the kitchen before Isaac arrived. Jonathan and Mary observed this kid, who seemed to be on a mission. He finally went to the hallway that led to the apartment's front door, anticipating Taylor's father at any moment. His father and mother walked over to him. Mary asked, "Nick, what's all the running around about?"

"Uh . . . I got some stuff to bring to Taylor." He had a paper bag stuffed to the top.

Jonathan asked, "Nick, what's in the bag? You plan on staying overnight?" He and Mary laughed, but Nick looked a little . . . guilty. Then he laughed.

"Oh, just got some stuff I know Taylor will like. I got him some snacks from the kitchen, some comics he likes, some word puzzles, uh . . . some books; one is a joke book I have that he didn't see yet."

"Wow! That should keep him busy while he gets better!" Mary thought for a moment. "Nick, you better check with the nurse and make sure the snacks are okay for him to have while he's in the hospital."

Nick said, "Okay." But he was already thinking of how he would sneak the treats to Taylor.

They arrived at Taylor's room. He was wide awake, and a big smile spread across his face when he saw his best friend. "Nick, Nick!" He almost didn't notice his father was there, but after Isaac stared at him and put his arms out to the side in a gesture of *"Hey, what about me?"* Taylor said, "Oh, hi, Dad!"

"How are you feeling today, son? Any more pain when you, uh . . . you know?"

"You mean when I pee, Dad?" The boys laughed. "It doesn't hurt as much, and the blood is not as much as yesterday. The doctor saw me right after I ate breakfast, and he said that I'm getting better." His attention immediately focused on the bag. "What's in the bag?" Nick scanned the room and peeked out the door to ensure the big, nasty nurse was nowhere in sight.

He pulled out the snacks first and said, "Taylor, here. Hide these. Put them under your pillow; no, under the blanket . . . quick!" He checked for any potential confiscation again. *All clear!* Isaac just shook his head. Nick then followed with the other items that he knew Taylor would love. They both pulled them out of the bag, looked them over, and couldn't decide yet where to start. *Ah, wait. The joke book!* They both settled on getting some laughs *for a change.*

Isaac told the boys he would be right back. They were fully engaged in the joke book. He went to the nurse's station and asked if he could speak with Doctor Hamilton. The nurse nodded and said she would call him, and he should meet him in the waiting area. Isaac said, "Okay, thank you," and headed to the waiting room. *Why does he want to meet me in the waiting room?*

Twenty minutes later, Isaac was about to return to ask the nurse when the doctor would be available to meet him. *This waiting, waiting is driving me crazy!* As if a prayer had been answered, Hamilton approached Isaac and gestured for him to a private corner of the room. Isaac's frustrated face turned into one of concern. "Doctor, what is it? Is it bad news?"

Hamilton spoke in a low voice, only intended for Isaac. "Not for Taylor. He's doing well and recovering as expected. He should be able to go home tomorrow and rest on Monday and Tuesday. If he is feeling well enough, I see no reason why he can't return to school on Wednesday, but please ensure that he avoids any heavy physical activity for the next week."

Isaac was confused. "Well, I'm delighted to hear that. However, it sounds like there's bad news for someone! Who?"

"I didn't want to tell you this in front of Taylor. I just came from the emergency room. Another Black boy, a little older than your son, just got admitted here. A group of White kids also assaulted him."

"Oh my God! Is he gonna be okay? How bad?"

"He has some serious injuries; he's headed for surgery right now. Seems like there's an epidemic forming in terms of racial violence in East New York and other sections of Brooklyn. I have been getting notices from other doctors I know at other hospitals. I haven't seen this kind of violence with victims ending up in the hospital for some time. We notified the police. I have to go. The parents are on their way here. I'll see you tomorrow?"

"Yes, thank you, doctor. I hope that kid turns out alright."

Hamilton left quickly with a "Me too!"

When Isaac returned to see Nick and Taylor having fun with the bag of "medicine" contents, his mind was in a swirl—good news about his son, bad news about another Black kid who took a beating. He didn't think it was necessary to interrupt their visit together. He would tell Taylor the good news when the time was right. He would hold off on the bad news. Maybe it was better not to say anything about the bad news at all.

After an hour of exhausting all the bag items and sneaking in a few snacks, the boys discussed their science fair project. Nick said he would start to work on it. "Mr. Washington, when can Taylor go home and go back to school?"

Isaac said, "I just spoke with the doctor. He said you can go home tomorrow, Taylor, and return to school on Wednesday if you rest tomorrow and Tuesday." Both boys smiled at the good news and immediately returned to planning mode for the science fair. Isaac took this opportunity to call Makena with the good and bad news.

There hadn't been too many violent, racially based crimes in the area, at least nothing in the newspapers that Isaac could recall. However, he wondered if this was a new trend, especially with the civil rights movement gaining popularity and attention. The Greensboro sit-ins began on February 1, 1960, when four Black college students sat at a "Whites-only" lunch counter at a Woolworth's store in Greensboro, North Carolina. The peaceful protest sparked a wave of sit-ins across the South, marking a pivotal moment in the civil rights movement.

Shortly after, in April 1960, the Student Nonviolent Coordinating Committee (SNCC) was established during a conference at Shaw University in Raleigh, North Carolina. The SNCC became a pivotal organization in the movement, advocating for nonviolent direct action and later supporting broader initiatives, including voter registration and Freedom Rides. The Rides were organized by the Congress of Racial Equality (CORE) and began on May 4, 1961, departing from Washington, DC, and heading out to reach New Orleans in mid-May. The riders often faced brutal violence, especially in Alabama and Mississippi. However, their efforts received national attention.

Isaac had kept up on all the news and important stories related to the civil rights movement. It seemed like momentum was developing, and he was hopeful that America was waking up and that justice was on the horizon. There were so many other events that pointed to the promise in America. The dawn of the 1960s counterculture was aptly represented by Harper Lee's Pulitzer Prize-winning novel, *To Kill a Mockingbird*, one of Isaac's favorite books, which explored racial injustice, moral growth, empathy, understanding, and courage.

The space race, which unfolded in the mid-1950s between the United States and the Soviet Union, was underway. Likewise, trends emerged in youth culture, the music revolution, television and media, and fashion. All of these were defined in the early 1960s, and while they represented innovation, competition, social change, youth empowerment, and optimism, they also brought about turbulence. The era, marked by hope and promise, was overshadowed by the escalation of the war in Vietnam.

Isaac reflected on America's multifaceted nature. *What did it all mean? What kind of world will Taylor and Ava face as they grow up?*

Chapter 42

"Watcha da Store; I be Righta Back."

The police raised the priority of the investigation into the assaults on the three Black children. The frequency and suspected link among them could not be delayed any longer. They established a perimeter of several blocks surrounding the area where the attacks happened and assigned officers to use their patrol vehicles to make regular runs. They would increase the number of police and vehicles on the weekends as much as resources allowed because all three incidents occurred on a weekend.

The first boy, Charles Brown, was Taylor's age and was injured as he walked past the alleyway. All his friends called him "Peanuts" as a tribute to the character Charlie Brown. His parents, Michael and Shirley, and other family members called him Charlie. His parents were working with the police to identify the assailants, but there was little progress. Charlie attended PS 108 on Linwood Street in East New York. After a brief examination by a family doctor, Charlie was released and returned to school the next school day with a few bruises and Band-Aids to mark his experience and tell his classmates what happened to him.

The older boy, Tyrone Smith, was thirteen and was severely injured as he fought back hard. The sustained fighting only exacerbated the initial injuries. He also attended PS 108 and was attacked a couple of blocks from Angelo's grocery store. The Smiths, Tyrone Sr. and Sandra, were working with the police, but they also wanted to question their son. When they went to the hospital to see him, he was still under surgery, but a doctor who met them said he thought he heard Tyrone say he knew who attacked him.

He had said, "I'm not sure of his capacity to recall anything accurately when he spoke. He was in a lot of pain, and we needed to give him something to take the edge off before we considered surgery. It wasn't long after that when we all agreed that surgery was absolutely necessary. He had extensive internal bleeding." The Smiths had notified extended family members, who all quickly assembled at the hospital to offer support and pray together.

After two hours, the surgeon, Doctor Jacob Rosenberg, entered the waiting room. The family went silent as Tyrone's parents slowly approached the doctor. Sandra had a crumpled tissue that she had used to wipe her eyes. Tyrone Sr.'s furrowed brow and wringing hands were a silent plea for good news. Their hearts racing, they struggled to hold their composure, frozen in time and consumed with the fear of loss. Tyrone finally asked, "Doctor, our son . . . is he alright? Is Tyrone going to be okay?" The family held its collective breath.

"I will be honest with you. Your son lost a lot of blood, and I needed to address several internal organs that were damaged. He's not out of the woods yet, but we have stabilized him. We may need to follow up with more surgery, but I want him to rest for now as we monitor him closely to understand how he responds to what we have done so far. We'll complete a scan in a couple of hours and watch his vital signs throughout the night. I wish I had better news, but you need to remain hopeful. I am, and I'll do everything possible to free him from further danger."

The Smiths were in shock. One minute, they're at home watching sports, cooking, or discussing family, jobs, and upcoming summer vacations. The next is a state of worry and more prayers. A representative from the 75th Precinct was at the hospital and spoke briefly with the family, stating that there was very little information currently available and that the police would begin an immediate investigation. He did not mention the broader scope of the assault on Tyrone, which included Charles Brown and Taylor Washington. That would only generate many more questions that still had no answers.

Before the policeman met with Angelo, the shopkeeper took some initiative on his own, looking forward to helping them find out who the "damn boys" were. As he swept the sidewalk outside his grocery store, which he did faithfully each morning, he scanned the row of joined apartment buildings across the street. He noticed the usual—many people, mostly retired or simply tired, leaning on their windowsills, some with a pillow for added comfort. As their eyes met, they would wave at Angelo, and with the mastery of a vibrant trill of the "r," they shouted, "Buongiorno!" Angelo responded in kind but occasionally said "Good Morning" to emphasize he was also an American.

Angelo took a mental note of those potential witnesses to Taylor's and, perhaps, the previous boy's attack. *Chi potrebbe sapere qualcosa?* Who could know something? He went into his store and told his helper, Giovanni, to "watcha da store; I be righta back." He walked across the street and looked up at his friend, Salvatore Ricci, occupying a second-floor window. In his most beautiful and friendly Italian, he asked, "*Salvatore, come stai? Posso salire e parlarti per un minuto?*" Salvatore responded that he was well and that, of course, he could come up and talk for a minute. Being in America was one thing. Having the opportunity to chat with a friend in Italian was a welcome treat.

Angelo said that he wanted to help the police find the boys who beat up the Black kids. He said the police asked him if he could help and told them he was sure someone had seen something. Salvatore was hesitant at first, always thinking of the worst that could come from any information he might disclose. But Angelo was a long-time friend, and he trusted his instincts. *If Angelo asks for help, how can I refuse?*

Salvatore told Angelo that the three boys were about the same size and much bigger than Taylor and the other Black boy. He said that the one who knocked Taylor off his bike wore a black leather jacket and a red bandana around his head. He said one of the other boys had on a red baseball hat with a "C" on it and he didn't know what that stood for.

Angelo, who loved watching and talking "*bazaball*," said, "A redda capa? That's a Reds' cap! Cincinnati Reds! Why woulda soma one from Brooklyn wear a redda cap?" Salvatore, who understood

English as well as Angelo, just shrugged his shoulders. It made no sense to him either.

He asked Angelo why he even lived here: *"Perche vibe qui, poi?"* Angelo shrugged his shoulders as well. Angelo was happy. He determined this was very good information to give to the police. He figured that, at this point, he had more information on the case than they did. He was grateful to Salvatore and told him to stop by his store for some free fruit. He hastened back across the street and went immediately to his phone.

When he reached Sergeant McGuire, he gave the information he received from Salvatore. He told the police that out of all the window people, he knew he could count on Salvatore. He knew how perceptive he was, that his eyeglasses had just been renewed, and that he was confident Salvatore's vision was trustworthy. All this in broken English, which came across just fine.

McGuire was pleased and expressed his appreciation to Angelo. Now, they had something to look for that would identify the boys they were so eager to drag to a cell, and maybe even give Shamus an opportunity to slam his billy club again. He was getting close to retirement, so any slammin' would be welcome. Years ago, they looked for a red and white Chevy Bel Air; now, it was a red cap. Both to help find racial discriminators and eliminate any further violent intentions.

Everyone in Nick's class was eager to hear from him when Taylor was absent on Monday. Gracie Benson, their fifth-grade teacher, had been notified of Taylor's assault and his latest condition. She called on Nick to briefly tell the class what had happened because he had just seen Taylor the day before. Nick told everyone that Taylor would be in school on Wednesday. Everyone, including Benson, clapped. He spent more time telling them what he brought to Taylor, especially all the snacks he snuck in. Everyone laughed. It was happy news that overshadowed the downside.

Benson was well aware of the close friendship between Nick and Taylor. In her meetings with the other teachers, each would always share the strong points and those that needed improvement for every student who would pass from one teacher to the next. Whenever the conversation centered on Nick and Taylor, everyone knew that the two boys represented a special relationship that the students also recognized. Many had witnessed or had heard about the encounter that triggered the birth of their friendship.

Benson would say, "Good begets good." Or, as the saying goes, "You reap what you sow." And sometimes, "What goes around comes around." The phrases all serve as a reminder of the cause and effect between Nick and Taylor. The other teachers could not help but wonder where she had obtained the quotes, and because Benson used them so often, they affectionately named her "The Quotaholic." Others came up with "The Quotaphile." Benson loved it. It just inspired her to use more quotes.

When Taylor returned to class, he had followed the doctor's orders, which his parents ensured he would. He was rested and, while limited in his physical activity, was as good as can be expected under the circumstances of his hateful experience. Like all other racial discrimination and open displays of hate, he and his parents would put this behind them. Isaac and Makena talked in depth about a lawsuit but decided just to let the police do their job and not create any more anxiety in the family. If Taylor's condition had been worse, the decision might have been different. Peanuts' parents decided the same, but Tyrone's parents hired an attorney before their son's second surgery.

The two months remaining before the summer break consisted of continued learning, maturation, and celebrations, culminating in a school science fair that students and parents alike enjoyed. Everyone savored the exhibits and demonstrations from various grade levels, including simple electricity experiments, magnetic fields and magnets, solar ovens, and engineering projects such as bridge building, greenhouse effect studies, acid rain simulations, as well as Newton's cradle and momentum experiments.

When Taylor returned to school, he and Nick got busy collecting plastic tubing, balloons, Taylor's bike hand pump, and colored water that represented the blood. They constructed a working model of the human heart, where the balloons represented the four chambers, and the tubing represented the arteries and veins, showing the flow of blood. They used the hand pump to replicate the heart's pumping action. They also prepared an illustration board that explained blood pressure. Benson awarded them an "A" grade for their effort, which rounded out a very successful fifth-grade year. Their parents, naturally, were very proud of them.

Chapter 43

Pivotal Turning Points

Less than a week after the 1961–62 school year ended, kids and their families began their summer activities, vacations, and visits to local and distant attractions. Nick and Taylor had nonstop fun. And three boys, one with a very visible red baseball cap with a "C" logo, stepped up their version of summer fun. However, they didn't experience the thrill they had before. The police were ready for them, thanks to Angelo and Salvatore.

They were nabbed as they approached the same alleyway they had used before. The police would refer to them as "dumb criminals," returning to the scene of previous crimes. Sergeant McGuire contacted all of the parents of the victims of the attacks. Thanks to the boy with the red cap, three other sets of parents received a package handed to them, accompanied by the words, "You've been served." The Smiths wasted little time in filing a lawsuit as their son struggled through rehab. It was a close call while he was hospitalized and had four surgeries to repair severe internal damage. His family's prayers were answered, and they continued to support their son in numerous ways.

The Vietnam War and the civil rights movement competed for news headlines as they both drew national attention to rapid developments. In one of the news broadcasts, Walter Cronkite gave the American people a short history lesson on the origins of the war and significant events leading to the present.

He noted that the US Congress considers the Vietnam era to have begun on February 28, 1961. While most historians attribute the war's origins to the 1950s, the conflict in Southeast Asia started with the French colonial occupation in the late 1800s. Over the next half-century, a timeline of complex political and military issues among the United States, France, China, the Soviet Union, and South Vietnam contributed to the emergence of the war.

From the early 1950s to mid-1954, a founding principle of the Truman Doctrine was that US foreign policy would assist any country whose stability was threatened by communism. In January 1950, the People's Republic of China and the Soviet Union formally recognized the communist Democratic Republic of Vietnam. They provided economic and military aid to communist resistance fighters within the country.

In June of that year, the United States stepped up military assistance to France. In early 1954, the French were defeated, and their rule in French Indochina ended. President Dwight D. Eisenhower recognized that this defeat posed a severe threat in Southeast Asia and could lead to a domino effect of communist expansion throughout the region. This domino theory would guide US thinking toward Vietnam going forward.

The Geneva Accords established North and South Vietnam with a division at the seventeenth parallel and an agreement that elections would be held within two years to unify Vietnam under a single democratic government. The elections never happened. The United States began backing South Vietnam as North Vietnam built supply routes, later known as the Ho Chi Minh Trail, through Laos and Cambodia to support guerrilla attacks in the south.

In July 1959, the first US soldiers were killed during a guerrilla raid on their quarters near Saigon. In May 1961, President Kennedy sent helicopters and four hundred Green Berets to South Vietnam to perform secret operations against the Viet Cong, short for Vietnam Cong-san or Vietnamese communists. In January 1962, US aircraft began spraying Agent Orange in Operation Ranch Hand to kill vegetation that offered cover and food to guerrilla forces. Over the next year, South Vietnamese troops continued to be defeated as more civilians and Buddhist protesters fell victim to attacks. South Vietnam then went through a period of military coups and government replacements.

The trend in the war was in the wrong direction. The trend in the civil rights movement was in the opposite direction. The struggle for equal rights was very much alive as activists built on the momentum of earlier sit-ins and boycotts, local protests, and legal challenges that all forced the broader public and lawmakers to confront segregation and racial discrimination.

The efforts were characterized by community-led actions in cities across the South, fighting school segregation, discriminatory voting practices, and unequal public facilities. Local organizers worked relentlessly to challenge the status quo through nonviolent protests and legal battles, often at significant personal risk. The hope was that the attention would propel sweeping changes in American society.

Both the escalation in Vietnam and the intensity of the civil rights movement were defined by stages of gradual buildup, with pivotal turning points and far-reaching consequences. Each generated public sentiment and policy in its own way.

A Baptist minister with a blend of personal experience and religious conviction, raised in the tradition of moral clarity, often referenced the themes of liberation, justice, and the promise of equality in the Bible. These resonated with his perceptions of segregation and injustice, forming his moral foundation for activism. His speeches and writings proposed a vision of nonviolent resistance and racial reconciliation.

The Birmingham Campaign, where he participated in a series of nonviolent protests against segregation, took place in the spring of 1963 and intensified when coordinated sit-ins, boycotts, and marches brought national attention to severe racial segregation and police brutality in the city. He was confined for his participation in the campaign. He wrote the "Letter from Birmingham Jail" on April 16, 1963, which emphasized the strategy for nonviolent resistance and articulated the moral foundation for the broader Civil Rights Movement. His letter helped galvanize support for civil rights reform.

Dr. Martin Luther King Jr. drew upon these experiences to refine his understanding of the path to equality. His dream of hope and progress intertwines with his personal suffering and aspiration narrative. His introspection formed a foundation for continued action. His years of hardship, inspiration, community-led activism, theological insights, and political and social experiences created the potential for a pivotal turning point in American history.

Isaac, Makena, and their Black discussion group met again to assess the wave of news crashing down on America. They recognized it was history in the making, and it generated exciting conversations. It was hopeful news. They had all experienced the same treatment that Isaac and his family had over recent years, and they were tired of it. It wasn't right, and now there was one among many who were making noise in a most dignified, nonviolent, and intelligent way.

They would all spend more time than ever glued to the evening news and reading *The New York Times*. The 1962–63 school year passed in the blink of an eye as Nick and Taylor completed sixth grade. A few inches taller and eleven years old, they had entered Donna Sweeney's defined age range for developing the ability to apply logic and deductive reasoning to their mindset.

They took a step back from their gut reactions or habitual thinking to analyze their beliefs, assumptions, and decision-making processes systematically. They would witness the historic events that were unfolding for all Americans. Their newly formed intelligence, with its Aristotelian-like capability for deductive reasoning, applying the "if-then" framework and other syllogistic or categorical statements, would begin to answer some of the questions that had lingered and bothered them in the past.

Chapter 44

STRATEGY AND COLLABORATION

NYU Black history professor Reed played a significant role in preserving and advancing the ideals of the civil rights movement through education and scholarship. He and others engaged in research and teaching that supported civil rights ideals. They closely followed key figures in the American civil rights movement. NYU's Tamiment Library housed collections related to radical organizing and labor movements, which were closely tied to civil rights activism.

The Tamiment Library was founded in 1906 as part of the Rand School of Social Science, a worker-education institution sponsored by the American Socialist Society. It was donated and became part of NYU in 1963. NYU students were part of a broader wave of youth activism, and some may have participated in demonstrations or marches in support of civil rights.

Dr. Reed was in a perfect position to relate the movement's impact on America. The meetings between Isaac and others became more frequent, especially as news of a planned march in Washington, DC, became known. Links between NYU professors and march organizers were not well-documented, but the university's intellectual and geographical context likely contributed to some level of engagement with the civil rights movement. NYU's location in New York City, a hub of activism and intellectual exchange, provided opportunities for collaboration and influence among scholars and activists.

A. Philip Randolph and Bayard Rustin worked diligently to coordinate plans for a massive demonstration, known as the March on Washington for Jobs and Freedom. Randolph was a trailblazing labor and civil rights leader who founded the Brotherhood of Sleeping

Car Porters in 1925, the first African American labor union. He was instrumental in advocating for racial and economic equality. His efforts led to significant milestones, such as President Franklin D. Roosevelt's Executive Order 8802, which banned discrimination in the defense industry during World War II.

Bayard Rustin was a strategist and activist deeply committed to nonviolent resistance. He was a key advisor to Martin Luther King Jr. and the chief organizer of the March on Washington. His Quaker beliefs and his work with organizations such as the Fellowship of Reconciliation and the Congress of Racial Equality (CORE) influenced his approach to nonviolent tactics. The Randolph-Rustin partnership shared a vision for justice and equality in the fight for civil rights.

Their efforts and the growing academic focus on the study and understanding of the civil rights movement led to academic contributions of published works, which included civil rights activism and historical relevance; educational initiatives that engage students in advocacy, and organizing efforts that challenged systemic racism and explored abolitionist movements; and, development of courses dedicated to civil rights movement along other prominent African American historical events.

The American public sensed that something significant was on the horizon. Images of recent vivid news coverage where police used high-pressure water hoses, dogs, and mass arrests brought national attention to the plight of the Black population in the South. They intensified the resolve of civil rights leaders and activists across the nation. Organizations such as the Southern Christian Leadership Conference (SCLC), the Student Nonviolent Coordinating Committee (SNCC), and CORE mobilized behind the call for national action, setting the stage for a more significant unified protest.

Isaac, Makena, Dr. Reed, and now an expanding group of Black citizens from around Brooklyn, occasionally gathered on weekends throughout the summer to view and discuss the emerging, day-by-day-changing news. They would rotate the venue among the participants, who would provide light hors d'oeuvres and refreshments. When the meeting occurred at the Washington residence, Taylor wondered what all the excitement was about. He was about to get a dose of history that would leave an indelible impression.

Randolph and Rustin recognized that the movement's strength lay in unity. Coalition-building was essential. They brought together a diverse coalition that included civil rights organizations, labor unions, religious groups, and student activists united against racial injustice and economic inequality. Addressing the logistical challenges was also important. They worked closely with federal and city officials to secure necessary permits, plan a safe and symbolic route, and manage the flow of hundreds of thousands of demonstrators.

In the months leading up to August 28, 1963, intensive planning, collaboration, and a profound strategic understanding of symbolism and messaging unfolded. They chose a route that was practical and symbolic. They would begin at the Washington Monument, a site of national significance, and proceed along the National Mall to the Lincoln Memorial. It was not an arbitrary choice but one that traced the history and enduring ideals of American democracy. It highlighted the gap between the nation's founding promises and the reality of segregation and inequality. No other place in America could match this setting for historic change.

The message needed to be clear, addressing racial injustice and economic disparity. The organizers ensured that the event would be peaceful and reflect the nonviolent philosophy championed by leaders such as Dr. Martin Luther King Jr.

Evening news coverage in July 1963, leading up to the March on Washington and King's speech, focused heavily on the momentum of the civil rights movement. News anchors, such as Walter Cronkite, highlighted the march's planning and significance while emphasizing its goals of racial equality and economic justice. They covered the growing anticipation of the event, describing it as a historic moment in the fight for civil rights.

Coverage also included the challenges faced by the organizers, such as logistical hurdles and opposition from certain political groups. The media emphasized the march as an opportunity to push for the Civil Rights Act, which was being debated in Congress at the time. Chet Huntley and David Brinkley co-anchored NBC's *The Huntley-Brinkley Report*, which covered civil rights issues and offered insights into the broader societal implications of the movement. On ABC, Howard K. Smith also covered significant civil rights events and provided commentary on the challenges and progress of the movement.

Dr. Reed summarized how the stage was set for the march and speech to a receptive audience of friends at his home in Brooklyn in early August. It was another brief history lesson that everyone appreciated. Reed noted that there was a historical precedent for the march. "The idea of a large-scale march on Washington was considered as early as 1942 by A. Philip Randolph, who protested racial discrimination in defense industries. That march was canceled after President Roosevelt issued Executive Order 8802." He explained what the order achieved.

Isaac asked, "Is there any significance to the date of the march? Does it have any special meaning?"

"Great question, Isaac! I recently heard that same question from some students and colleagues. Yes, indeed. This year is the centennial of the Emancipation Proclamation issued by President Lincoln in 1863, declaring that all enslaved people in the Confederate states in rebellion against the Union were to be set free. As I'm sure you all know, it was a pivotal moment in American history, reshaping the war's purpose to include the abolition of slavery. Additionally, it also marks eight years to the day since the brutal murder of Emmett Till."

Another friend, Martin Adams, asked, "I was watching the news and heard about the roles Randolph and Rustin played in planning the march. Were there any other significant contributors?"

Reed was well-informed on all aspects of the march, drawing on a variety of sources. "Marty, yes. The 'Big Six' civil rights leaders also helped organize the march: A. Philip Randolph, Martin Luther King Jr., James Farmer, John Lewis, Roy Wilkins, and Whitney Young. Their collaboration brought together diverse groups and agendas under the unified theme of 'Jobs and Freedom.' "

The group was amazed by Reed's knowledge, and some were even taking notes to share with their families. It was like a free college course, compliments of a gifted NYU professor. They were cautiously optimistic about the historical march. They knew, as the general public did, that Martin Luther King Jr. would be one of the speakers at the March, but the exact content of his speech was not widely anticipated. King was scheduled as one of the final speakers, which reflected his prominence in the civil rights movement.

AUGUST 1963

On Monday, August 19, a new school year began. Nick and Taylor had just turned twelve and were in Gloria Rivera's seventh-grade class. The history curricula were established and included American and world history, aligned with state and national standards. The topics of American history included early exploration and colonization of the Americas, the American Revolution and the founding of the United States, westward expansion and its impact on Native American populations, and the Civil War and Reconstruction.

Curricula often took time to adapt to contemporary events, and the civil rights movement was still in its early stages of unfolding. In less than two weeks, events in Washington, DC, would have a lasting impact on history classes across the nation. While not yet a formal part of the history courses, it would be difficult to avoid discussing the significance of the historical year and the days ahead.

The summer had been a turbulent period in the Vietnam War, politically and socially. Protests against the South Vietnamese government, led by Ngô Đình Diệm, escalated. The Buddhist majority opposed his favoritism toward Catholics and his oppressive policies. On June 11, 1963, a Buddhist monk self-immolated in Saigon, drawing attention to the crisis. The US presence increased in South Vietnam with over sixteen thousand military advisors. The Kennedy administration faced growing concerns about Diệm's leadership and the effectiveness of US support. Political instability escalated. The question was, *What would be prominent in the news in the summer of 1963—the Vietnam War or the civil rights movement?* We were about to find out.

Isaac arranged to take a day off from work at the local pharmacy. He and many of his Black friends felt an obligation to follow the news coverage of the March on Washington and listen to the speakers' messages. They would gather at a local community center in Brooklyn, which was deeply involved in civil rights activism. It was one of several locations that served as a hub for activism, community organizing, and cultural expression.

Churches such as the Concord Baptist Church of Christ and Bridge Street AME Church played a crucial role in mobilizing the Black community by hosting meetings, rallies, and educational programs. The Brooklyn NAACP and local chapters of CORE advocated for racial equality and organized protests against segregation and discrimination. As the civil rights movement gained momentum, many Brooklyn schools and community centers became hubs for discussion and workshops.

The anticipation among the Black population was immense and filled with hope. The event marked a pivotal moment in the fight for civil rights, providing an opportunity to demand justice and equality on a national stage. Black communities organized, fundraised, and mobilized nationwide to ensure a strong turnout. Churches, civil rights organizations, and local leaders spread the word. They encouraged participation, envisioning what they hoped would be a unifying moment for people from all walks of life standing together. Many were eager to hear from the speakers, leaders who would articulate their shared struggles and aspirations.

The night before the march was filled with determination, camaraderie, and strategic planning among the leaders. Bayard Rustin finalized logistics, including organizing transportation, security details, and preparing the order of speeches, all to ensure the march's success. Martin Luther King Jr., A. Philip Randolph, John Lewis, and others met to align their messages, emphasizing economic justice, the Civil Rights Act, and the broader goals of "Jobs and Freedom."

President John F. Kennedy did not plan to attend the March on Washington in person but would closely follow the event from the White House. He was very supportive of the march and its goals. It aligned with his emphasis on civil rights legislation.

Before she dismissed her class for the day, Rivera reminded her students that the next day would be very important in America. She briefly explained the reason for the march and the gathering of critical civil rights leaders, saying, "Perhaps after tomorrow, we can discuss what happened and what it meant." The other teachers delivered a similar message to the one directed by Principal Dr. Mary Carpenter, as she anticipated that the historic day would underscore the teachings and emphasize the importance of just and equal treatment that students should have for one another.

Taylor told Nick, "My dad told me about tomorrow, too. He said that we would talk about it as a family. I can't wait to hear all about it!"

Nick said, "My parents said the same thing!"

Chapter 46

August 28, 1963

The weather was clear, warm, and sunny, with mild morning temperatures that would reach the mid-80s by midday. The march in Washington, DC, formed as participants arrived in the city by bus, train, and car from across the country, many of whom had traveled overnight. The Washington Monument marked the assembly area, where the atmosphere was one of unity and determination, with many carrying signs expressing urgency and aspirations that read, "Jobs and Freedom," "We Demand Equal Rights Now," "End Segregation in Public Schools," and others that emphasized civil rights, economic justice, and equality.

People assembled in thousands of other cities and towns to witness this historic day. Isaac walked a few blocks to the community center that would be filled nearly to capacity with other Brooklynites of varied ethnicities and races. Dr. James Reed and his colleagues were deeply invested in the civil rights movement, gathering in New York University's lecture halls to witness the day's events. Reed was well-connected with other universities, professors, and students who were active in the movement.

Students and faculty from nearby Queens College actively participated in civil rights activities. Howard University in Washington, DC, was a hub for civil rights activism. Many of them participated in the march. Dr. Charles Hamilton Houston, a political scientist at the university, contributed to the intellectual foundation of civil rights strategies. The professors and students at the University of Chicago were dedicated to social justice and were recognized for their involvement in protests and community organizing efforts.

The country was taking notice with hope, determination, and curiosity. While supporters were inspired by the unity and collaboration among civil rights leaders, White skeptics and opponents expressed concerns about the potential for unrest and violence. *Something could always go wrong!*

American history is replete with images of solidarity and unity. Photographs from the Women's Suffrage Movement, such as the 1913 Women's Suffrage Parade in Washington, DC, showing women marching with banners demanding the right to vote, demonstrated unity in the fight for gender equality. "We Can Do It!" posters featured Rosie the Riveter, utilizing propaganda to encourage solidarity among Americans in support of the World War II effort. The March on Washington, DC, was in line to add to these iconic visuals.

An estimated 250,000 people marched peacefully from the Washington Monument along the Mall to the Lincoln Memorial. Once everyone was assembled, the first official act was singing the "National Anthem" by Camilla Williams, an accomplished opera singer. The formal and patriotic tone of the gathering was set.

Washington's Archbishop Patrick O'Boyle emphasized the march's unity and moral purpose in his invocation. Renowned performers added a musical element that inspired the crowd. Marian Anderson sang "He's Got the Whole World in His Hands," emphasizing spiritual undertones in the civil rights struggle. Mahalia Jackson sang a gospel classic, "How I Got Over," that aroused emotions and determination.

An opening address by A. Philip Randolph set the stage by calling for justice, equality, and economic opportunity, a frequent and rhythmic message. John Lewis was one of the youngest leaders in the civil rights movement and a key figure in organizing activism focused on voting rights and desegregation in the South. He was the chairman of the Student Nonviolent Coordinating Committee (SNCC). His presentation particularly critiqued the federal government's civil rights bill and called for strong protections against police brutality and voter suppression.

Roy Wilkins's speech also highlighted the fight for civil rights and economic justice. He was best known for his role as the executive director of the National Association for the Advancement of Colored

People (NAACP). He was often referred to as the senior statesman of the civil rights movement, particularly due to his notable achievements in landmark cases such as Brown v. Board of Education (1954).

Bob Dylan's "Blowin' in the Wind," which questioned societal injustices, and "If I Had a Hammer," a song about justice, freedom, and love, resonated with the march's themes as Peter, Paul, and Mary sang them. Joan Baez sang "We Shall Overcome," the unofficial anthem of the civil rights movement, and "All My Trials," a spiritual folk song that reflected struggles and resistance.

The day's events so far captured an entire nation's attention with consistent messages executed peacefully. They all contributed to the march's powerful emotional and cultural aspects, focusing on equality and freedom. As Isaac and those around him watched with undivided attention and enthusiasm, Dr. Reed and his colleagues took mental notes of the day and how it would be incorporated into their curricula.

The Black population and many others who stood with them all felt something similar. *This is what we need, what our country needs, what we've been waiting for! Our dreams can become a reality! Unity and perseverance can achieve our goals!* There was a collective sense of triumph and happiness, although many realized that the fight wasn't over. There was more work to be done, and more influence was needed. The best was yet to come.

Randolph briefly introduced Martin Luther King Jr. with profound respect and admiration. He referred to King as the "moral leader of our nation," emphasizing his dedication to justice and equality, as well as the significance of his role in the movement.

King had the attention of a quarter of a million people assembled at the heart of American democracy and civic expression, standing in the shadow of the Lincoln Memorial, facing toward the Reflecting Pool, and beyond to the Washington Monument and the Capitol. It symbolized a bridge between the ideals of equality laid out by Lincoln and the ongoing struggles for justice in 1963. He had the attention of millions more, who were glued to the news media coverage of the scene in the nation's capital.

King's gift of weaving references from the Bible, the US Constitution, and other significant and recognizable sources enabled him to deliver one of the most iconic speeches in American history. Unlike his fellow speakers, the text of his speech was not ready for advance distribution by the previous day. After arriving at his hotel room later that evening, he sat down to write it and finished a draft after midnight.

His speech lasted approximately seventeen minutes and concluded around 4 p.m. Despite its brief duration, its impact on the civil rights movement and American history proved immeasurable. He spoke of Abraham Lincoln, who signed the Emancipation Proclamation, and said that it represented hope to "millions of Negro slaves." He pointed out that after one hundred years, "the Negro still is not free." He emphasized that the promise for all men "would be guaranteed the unalienable rights of life, liberty, and the pursuit of happiness." In his own eloquent way, he said that did not happen and that "the bank of justice is bankrupt."

The nation's people heard King's key points, emphasizing the urgency of making democracy a reality for all God's children and that Black people should have the same citizen rights. His oration spoke of police brutality and change, especially in the Southern states. His speech gained momentum when he explained that he had a dream. The elements of Martin Luther King Jr.'s "I Have a Dream" speech captured the essence of what it meant for America to represent the land of the free through many visuals that he described for his listeners. One by one, they created a tapestry of love among all people across the United States. It was undoubtedly singled out as the highlight of a triumphant march.

The New York Times and other major news media nationwide described the impact of King's words, which gave hope to making "the kingdom real." It was a crowning achievement that would become a legacy.

Isaac, his friends, Dr. Reed, his colleagues, and people of all colors and faiths clearly understood that King's speech called for racial equality, justice, unity, hope, optimism, and urgent action. History was made on this day.

Chapter 47

"We May Think We Can, but We Can't."

After dinner, the evening news programs would begin and be filled with images and commentary on the historic day in the nation's capital. The march, the songs, the speeches, and the entire atmosphere of hope for justice and equality rang out loud and clear in a dignified manner. It would become a primary topic of conversation among the public, especially the Black population, for weeks to come. Many families who had faced racial discrimination or violence had their spirits lifted. Their horizons brightened with the hope that change was in the air.

Isaac told Taylor and Makena about the day he and others spent at the community center and the brief and enthusiastic conversation that followed before people left for their homes. Makena told him that she watched most of the speeches on TV as she waited for another mother to bring Ava home from kindergarten. A group of them took turns transporting the youngsters to and from school.

Isaac wanted this historic day to serve as a teaching moment for Taylor, fostering a deeper understanding of a Black boy's perspective. His comprehension would be shaped by what his parents had taught him over the years, complemented by the events in Washington, DC, that had occurred earlier in the day. There was a lot to consider. *Where do I start?*

With Taylor's maturity and ability to engage in more intelligent conversation, he thought it would be best to recall some of the family's past experiences with racial discrimination. He asked, "Taylor, do you recall any past instances where someone confronted us and said or did hurtful things to you? What things made us feel threatened?"

Taylor thought for a moment to reach back into the recesses of his mind that contained subconscious thoughts and feelings that were perhaps difficult to understand completely. "Uh, yeah, I remember those guys at the Yankees game when we went with Nick and his parents. They were annoying us, and you almost got into a fight with them."

"Okay, is there anything else that comes to mind?"

"Well, yeah, of course. When I got attacked by those White boys, I had to go to the hospital for a few days. Why?" Makena observed and liked where this was going. Ava sat on the floor with her toys, lost in a completely different world.

"The march in Washington, DC, today and the speeches, especially the one given by Martin Luther King Jr., were very important to our country and its people, for all people." He went on to explain the most significant themes that likely emerged. "There was anticipation and unity among many people as they expressed excitement about the event and hoped it would bring about change in America, change that would eliminate behavior against Black people like you and our family experienced."

"Wow. Do you think that will really happen?"

"I sure hope so! Many people are sharing their reflections and struggles, which are similar to our own experiences with discrimination. They admire leaders like Martin Luther King Jr. and his dedication to action, which significantly contributed to the movement in many ways. When the news comes on, let's listen to his speech together. It was less than twenty minutes, but he said a great deal in that short amount of time."

Taylor had seen his parents excited about many things, but this seemed like a whole new level of enthusiasm. Something special got their attention, and they wanted him to feel the same way. In a few minutes, the evening news would begin.

Jonathan and Mary knew how important this day was, especially to their friends, the Washingtons, who, over the years, sustained verbal and physical abuse. They also knew that Isaac had occasionally met with other Black friends in a discussion group and had attended a community center today to observe the march and speeches. Jonathan thought about asking if he could join him, but decided that maybe a White guy didn't need to be there.

He told Nick that this day was essential to America. It was focused on avoiding the divisions that drive people apart and stressed the need for unity, justice, and equality. But, he said, "More importantly, we have an opportunity. Due to our friendship with Taylor and his family, we find ourselves in a unique position."

Nick wasn't sure he understood completely. He knew they were good friends with the Washingtons and that they supported them many times. "Dad, what do you mean? We always . . . (he couldn't find the words) . . . we always stick up for them, don't we? Especially when people pick on them because they're Black."

"Yes, we do. And we should continue to do that. But . . . "

"Dad, but what?"

"While we do that, 'stick up' for them; we can never 'walk in their shoes,' so to speak."

"What does that mean?"

"As much as we love the Washington family, we can never experience their history of racial discrimination and their personal feelings that come from that hate. We may think we can, but we can't. While we can show that we care, have empathy, and understanding, we can never truly feel their experience with the prejudices and realities of the injustices they face every day."

Upon hearing his father, Nick felt a mix of emotions. He was confused as he tried to grasp what living in another's reality meant. He did show empathy when his friend and his family faced injustice. Still, he wondered if he would be responsible or show that he cared enough if he couldn't feel what they felt. He turned to another question that perhaps status should provide some admiration.

"Well, Mr. Washington does pretty good, doesn't he? He has a good job as a pharmacy guy, doesn't he? Don't people like him? Respect him?"

"I think many people do, but he's an exception. Most Black fathers don't have that kind of education and job as he does. But he still gets discriminated against. We just don't always see it." It provided Nick with powerful learning and encouragement that could strengthen his bond with Taylor.

Jonathan and Isaac had gone fly fishing together several times over the last few years, and it offered undisturbed opportunities to discuss racial discrimination candidly in a secluded atmosphere. Isaac shared some stories with Jonathan that he had never told anyone else. This mutual respect was especially important to them because their sons were good friends. They recognized that they would need explanations beyond what they had already received from past encounters.

Jonathan told Isaac that he wanted Nick to understand how Taylor and his family might feel when they are the object of injustice just because they are Black. Isaac greatly appreciated Jonathan's concern, which immensely strengthened their friendship. They agreed that the boys were maturing in many ways, both physically and mentally, and they wondered about the right time to have a more intelligent conversation with them. The historic day of August 28, 1963, offered that opportunity.

Just before dinner, Jonathan called Isaac to get his reaction to the capital's events and remind him of their conversation from one of their fly-fishing trips. "Hey, Isaac. Remember our discussion when we went to Westchester last fall to fly fish? When we said we would talk to our sons when they were a little older about all this racial discrimination crap?"

"Yeah, man! I think today gives us a perfect opportunity. I have already started talking with Taylor, and he has some questions. I told him we could watch King's speech on the TV news in a little while. I think hearing the 'I Have a Dream' speech will help the discussion."

"Great minds think alike! I did the same with Nick. We plan to watch it too. Say hello to Makena for us, and I'll catch up with you later." Isaac told him it sounded good, and he looked forward to seeing the Greene family soon.

Isaac and his family assembled in the TV room. *The CBS Evening News*, anchored by Walter Cronkite, was about to begin in about ten minutes. It was the perfect time to prepare Taylor for what he was about to experience. "Taylor, I want you to listen carefully when Martin Luther King Jr. gives his speech. He spoke to thousands of people who were present in Washington, and millions more, like me and your mom, watched from all over the country today. He shared something very personal—his hope for every person, not just Black people. He did discuss their struggles, but more importantly, emphasized that every person deserves respect and equal opportunity."

Taylor listened as his father had asked. Isaac continued. "Even when there is injustice, people can speak up and have their voices heard. Today was an example of people doing just that peacefully, hoping their voices would matter and could create change for the better. Listen to King's dream. It's what he hopes for America, for all people, for uniting them."

That was as much as Isaac thought Taylor could take in before hearing the speech, which he believed would answer some of his son's questions. He was prepared to talk with him for as long as he needed.

Before running King's speech in its entirety, Cronkite described the March on Washington as a watershed moment in the civil rights movement and pointed out the diversity of the masses assembled and that it included people from all walks of life—Black and White, housewives, Hollywood stars, senators, clergymen, and even a few beatniks. He commented on the peaceful and organized nature of the march, as well as its significance in the fight for equality and justice.

His detailed reporting was informative about the significance of the day and captured the diversity, passion, and spirit of the march, which played an essential role in bringing the full impact of that historic day into the living rooms of millions of Americans. He emphasized that in a matter of minutes, King's speech provided a vision of racial harmony and justice that resonated deeply across the nation and the palpable emotional energy that radiated from the Lincoln Memorial. Cronkite's summary gave his viewers a shared experience of hope, struggle, and the promise of a better tomorrow.

The news ran King's speech for all to hear again. Taylor and Nick, sitting in their respective homes with their parents, had heard of the importance of the speech from their fathers and watched and listened in silence. They would hear about the Emancipation Proclamation, slavery, the urgency of the civil rights movement, police brutality, and the segregation of the Negro in many forms. Much of this was blended for them in a way that there was no real message to latch onto, yet.

However, the message seemed to be clarified when King spoke of his dream. The boys heard him talk about slaves and former slave owners sitting together, about Black children joining hands with White children, about working, praying, struggling, and standing up for freedom together. They heard him call out several states where freedom would ring loudly and that when all his dreams became reality, all God's children would finally be free.

The repetitive words "I have a dream today" would be hard to forget. After hearing the news, Taylor and Nick briefly discussed what they had heard with their parents, then turned to doing their homework, followed by reading or engaging in a hobby activity before getting ready for bed. The words continued to be an obsession. It was like listening to a Christmas song, "Jingle Bells", that had become intrusive. It was a brain-centered focus, a mental persistence. It would play over and over again. They finally went to bed, and "I have a dream today" repeated until they drifted off to sleep.

Chapter 48

"We Can Never Walk in a Black Person's Shoes."

Rivera started the day's history lesson with a question. "How many of you saw the news about the March on Washington, DC, yesterday?" About half the class raised their hands, with a majority of them Black students. Her students had been learning about the Civil War and the issue of slavery. Although there was an established curriculum, she thought it would be beneficial to spend a few minutes on the historical event that had occurred.

"Good, so some of you saw the news where people from all walks of life were peacefully marching for justice and equality. They wanted their voices to be heard, and several civil rights leaders delivered speeches. Martin Luther King Jr. delivered a speech from the steps of the Lincoln Memorial. Does anyone want to share their thoughts on his speech or what they learned from his words?" She had several eager volunteers.

James Jones, one of Taylor's Black classmates, raised his hand, among others. Rivera said, "Yes, James. What would you like to say?"

James and his family had been the target of racial discrimination, like Taylor and his family. He was never assaulted like Taylor or the other boys were, but his reactions and questions begged for better understanding, as they did for most kids through early elementary school.

When James's parents spoke with him about King's speech, they used words that he remembered and repeated in his answer. He said, "Martin Luther King Jr. talked about a time when people like me could be treated the same as everyone else, and I wouldn't have to be treated differently or unfairly just because of my skin color. He made me feel like my dreams were the same as his, that I could be equal to others, not that I was lower or inferior to other people."

"Very good, James, that's right. You heard his message very well. Anyone else?"

Taylor's hand stood out as it waved more wildly than any of the others. "Yes, Taylor. What did you think of the speech?"

Taylor said that when he was attacked by the White-boy gang and ended up in the hospital, he didn't understand why they would do that just because he was Black, but said that his parents told him that it goes back to slavery, and that he was very interested in learning more.

Rivera wasn't sure where Taylor was going with his initial statement. But then, he said, "Martin Luther King Jr. made me feel like a change is going to happen soon and that equality and justice are not just his dream, but could be real. People wouldn't treat us like slaves or, like James said, like inferior people." Obviously, in thought, he hesitated, then said, "No, that's all."

He was going to mention that as he drifted off to sleep last night, King's words, "I have a dream today," took over his thoughts, and he couldn't get them out of his head or focus on anything else, and that it took him to a place he couldn't describe. He kept that to himself. Nick knew Taylor well and sensed that he was going to say more.

Rivera was intrigued and said, "Okay, one more before we get back to the Civil War. Anyone?" Nick popped his hand up, and Rivera called on him for his perspective.

"You know that Taylor and me . . . I mean, Taylor and I are good friends. I know that he and his family were picked on a lot because they are Black. I always knew that I would fight against racial discrimination because I learned how wrong it is, and I always thought I was doing the right thing. But my dad told me something I didn't know. He said, 'We can never walk in a Black person's shoes.' I didn't know what he meant, so he explained it to me. We can't walk in their shoes, which means we can't experience what they experience. We can't wear their skin color." All eyes widened at this statement.

Nick said, "My dad said the best we can do for our Black friends when we see racial discrimination is to stand beside them, listen, and support them. This would help to erase inequality and help make Martin Luther King Jr.'s dream of equality, justice, and unity among all people come true. His speech gave me a better understanding of the civil rights movement. At least that's what I remember." Nick's maturity was evident to the class and Rivera. She was very proud of those answers and that many others wanted to share their thoughts as well.

She said, "Let's give them a round of applause, then we need to move on. Thank you, boys." Everyone clapped, and a couple of the Black girls in the class looked at Nick and smiled shyly, but he didn't notice them. He continued to dwell on Taylor's hesitation.

The immediate political aftermath of the March on Washington and Martin Luther King Jr.'s speech was multifaceted, marked by symbolism and the country's approach to civil rights. It was a galvanizing force through the immense and peaceful demonstration of 250,000 people on the National Mall, sending a clear message to the federal government. It influenced news media broadcasts and reports through respected journalists like Walter Cronkite. This helped to form the narrative of civil rights and altered the public's perception, making the struggle for equality an urgent and moral imperative for millions of Americans.

Before the march, incidents that sparked civil rights discussions were more abstract, lacking a broader mandate for change. The unity and clarity expressed by the crowds, along with compelling speeches, reframed the debates as if there were a collective call for action. This would create momentum to overcome inertia and opposition from Congress, with its lack of any comprehensive civil rights legislation.

It demonstrated to activists that large-scale, peaceful protests could be an effective driver of social change. It also helped set a precedent for future rallies and campaigns, stressing the power of a united front in the struggle for equality.

The understanding and pursuit of civil rights in America underwent a significant redefinition. President Kennedy acknowledged the profound impact of King's words, and it pressured his administration to take more decisive action on civil rights legislation. It led to the president's meetings with civil rights leaders to discuss the proposed Civil Rights Act, which aimed to address racial discrimination and segregation.

In academia, the march and speeches marked a transformative moment that defined the movement from the teachings and research of the past to the urgency and relevance of future narratives. It promoted a rethinking of academic approaches to Black history. Dr. Reed and his colleagues recognized and advocated for narratives of Black challenges and the history of the civil rights movement to be a core element of the American story. They began to establish the academic legitimacy of Black studies programs, with the goal of developing dedicated courses and even departments fully committed to Black studies and African American history.

The erudite group would utilize the march and speeches to strengthen their commitment to mentorship and to leverage these historical moments to empower students, especially those from marginalized backgrounds, to view themselves as active participants in shaping their community's future.

They recognized that historical events, such as the one on August 28, 1963, provided a robust foundation for advancing social order by enabling us to learn from the past, understand the systemic roots of inequality, and foster social justice. That foundation allowed individuals to see beyond a skewed narrative and become more educated and critically aware. They realized that academics could profoundly impact policy reform, fostering empathy and community solidarity and inspiring and empowering future generations to transform entrenched systems of injustice.

There was a lot to learn, digest, and act on across many sectors of the nation, not only in public opinion, political developments, and academic discourse but also in cultural and artistic expression, spirituality, global human rights, international movements, labor, economic reform, and grassroots empowerment—shaping a more interconnected and just world.

A foundation was laid for Nick's and Taylor's future education in high school and college, encompassing history, economics, other relevant classes, and social studies.

Chapter 49

WHERE TO FOCUS

The second half of 1963 contained notable changes in American history and personal changes in Nick and Taylor. It was not simply a collection of isolated events but a nexus of historical, cultural, artistic, and technological shifts that redefined America.

It was a period of gradual but significant escalation in the United States' involvement in the Vietnam War, not by any sudden increase in combat troops but by a steady buildup of military advisors, increasing tactical challenges on the ground, and growing political instability in South Vietnam. Viet Cong forces effectively employed guerrilla tactics against the better-equipped Army of the Republic of Vietnam (ARVN), the main ground force of South Vietnam.

The forces adapted to counter the conventional military technologies deployed by the United States, highlighting the need to reassess the numbers of ground personnel and the strategy in a terrain environment where enemy tactics were vastly different. This sharpened US awareness of both tactical and political challenges in the region.

Just a few months after the march and demonstration in the nation's capital, President John F. Kennedy was assassinated on November 22, 1963. This stunning event set the stage for significant policy shifts under his successor, Lyndon B. Johnson, who inherited a nation grappling with racial inequality and the momentum of the civil rights movement. It set the stage for Johnson to take more decisive action on associated legislation.

The tragic loss of a president and the empowering rhetoric of the civil rights movement motivated nationwide calculation of the issues of inequality, justice, and what it means to be an American.

These influences found their way into academia, activism, and the everyday conversations of many citizens.

The cultural environment was also dynamic, as a diverse array of sounds of various forms held powerful messages of social change. Artists such as Bob Dylan began shaping a new, protest-driven musical narrative. New movements, such as pop art, emerged and challenged traditional forms of expression in galleries and museums.

Technology, particularly represented in the space race with the Soviet Union, underscored America's commitment to technological leadership on the global stage. In November 1963, the Bell System introduced a more universally adaptable technology when it transitioned from rotary dial phones to the first push-button phones equipped with dual-tone multifrequency (DTMF) signaling. Instant replay technology made its groundbreaking debut in early December 1963, when it could call up replays of the Army-Navy football game broadcast by CBS Sports.

Taylor experienced his replays, enabling him to recapture his thoughts of the "I Have a Dream" speech. He didn't think of it every day or as he was about to fall asleep every night. It occurred occasionally over the next few months, but he did not share it with anyone (yet). He had many other distractions from the portions of the speech that occupied his thoughts.

These diversions were very natural for a boy his age. Twelve going to thirteen is a significant milestone for a tween, marking the end of an era and the cusp of entering teenhood. He embarked on a journey of transformation, undergoing a range of changes that impacted his body and inner world of cognition and emotion. He and Nick had experienced growth spurts that were closely matched in height and weight over the last few years. The onset of puberty, marked by the development of new body hair and a change in his voice, often caused him concern, with his voice cracking before it deepened.

With the growth and pubertal changes, Taylor felt more energetic. His enhanced physical capacity, motor skills, and coordination were still adjusting to work well together. His participation in sports over the years contributed to his ability to adapt more effectively than his peers of the same age.

His emerging identity and self-awareness prompted him to reflect more deeply on who he was and his place in the world, a process significantly enhanced by the ongoing civil rights movement and the call for justice. With hormones shifting, his emotions became more complex and often took center stage. He was reasonably well-grounded due to his parents' excellent and caring upbringing. Still, like most kids his age, he would occasionally experience mood swings as he navigated new social and academic pressures. It was nothing that overly concerned his parents.

His parents' support for his cognitive growth showed he was prepared to think abstractly and solve more complex problems. This enabled him to understand and appreciate multiple perspectives, which helped him form his own opinions and moral values. The surge in his cognitive skills led Taylor to heightened empathy and ethical reasoning. It prompted him to question the world around him as he tried to balance the interplay of physical and emotional developments with the guidance of his parents.

Isaac and Makena understood Taylor's evolving self-identity. After all, they went through it themselves. They would continue supporting Taylor, building his self-esteem and helping him navigate personal and societal changes. Their recent discussions about the march and speeches addressing equality and justice for all were perfectly timed for him at this stage in his life. They observed his maturity and were very pleased with how life was evolving for their family. *Someday, we'll need to do the same for our little Ava!*

Nick was in lockstep with Taylor's physical, emotional, and cognitive development. He felt proud of how he explained to his class what he had learned from the demonstrations of civil rights and his first-hand experiences of racial discrimination. His parents supported him with a holistic, caring approach through open and active listening that fostered honest communication and validated Nick's feelings.

They would listen without judgment and acknowledge his experiences. Jonathan was a role model for Nick, who now had a new appreciation for his dad from the way he explained what he could do to help the Black community by standing next to them with his support. Jonathan and Mary guided Nick's interests, values, and worldview, especially in the context of family and broader social issues. They consistently emphasized values of empathy, respect, and diversity, which were in harmony with what Nick learned at PS 91 from the very beginning in first grade. The messaging between home and school provided a support network that reassured Nick that he was not alone in his adjustment to social environments and his emotional state of mind.

While Taylor's and Nick's development proceeded along reasonably predictable paths for physical, emotional, and cognitive changes, another element of their growth—gender awareness—took hold in the brains of the two young studs. Their body awareness and increasing consciousness of how they looked, and perhaps more importantly, how they were perceived, became dominant quickly. A heightened sense of self-awareness introduced them to concepts of masculinity, physical fitness, and athletic prowess. *Girls! What could be more important?*

Self-identity would extend to the question, *"What does it mean to be a man?"* It was too early for Nick and Taylor to have the answer to this most essential question. They would learn over time as they worked their way through the complex mix of heightened emotions, identity formation, social influences, peer dynamics (and competition), media and cultural influences, family and role models, teachers, coaches—and every other aspect that could define what it meant to be a man. Their foundation for this journey of understanding was established much better than most.

Despite the distractions that defined "growing up" for young boys, Taylor had more discussions with his father and mother about being Black in society and how that would hopefully change as a result of the collective efforts of the civil rights movement. He felt energized by his occasional thoughts about King's speech. He gave it attention when the distractions—school, homework, sports, and family get-togethers in addition to growing up—were not in play.

"I have a dream today," "I have a dream today," would repeat in his mind until he fell asleep. Still, it didn't extend into rapid eye movement (REM) sleep, where the brain is busy consolidating memories and integrating new information. His daily activity simply exhausted him, causing him to succumb quickly and sleep soundly through the night. The following day, he would repeat his daily routine and not think much about his state of mind as he lay awake in bed the night before. There were enough other things for this curious, energetic, developing young man to focus on.

Chapter 50

MORE OF A MATTER OF HORMONAL INFLUENCE

Despite the powerful impact of the March on Washington and King's speech in highlighting the urgent need for change, the fight for civil rights faced violent opposition and systemic challenges, spurring further instances of racial discrimination. It was just weeks after the march when the bombing of the Sixteenth Street Baptist Church in Birmingham, Alabama, killed four young Black girls and injured many others. The march was a turning point, but it also revealed the depth of the struggle ahead. At the same time, segregationists and opponents of civil rights continue to challenge, by legal means and violence, any efforts to discredit racial inequality.

Television and newspapers reported ongoing discrimination, especially highlighting in detail the bombings of churches, violence against civil rights activists, and other racially motivated acts. It served to identify the gap between calls for equality and the often-lived experiences of the Black population. It offered the public a glimpse into reality in America during the 1960s, providing an opportunity for comprehensive coverage that catalyzed the mobilization of public support for legislation and held institutions accountable.

The Black group meetings attended by Isaac, Dr. Reed, and others continued, especially after vivid descriptions of racial violence in the news. One evening, Isaac, Makena, and Taylor witnessed the gruesome details of the church bombing by the Ku Klux Klan, which continued its campaigns of intimidation and violence across parts of the United States but mainly concentrated in the South.

Deep-seated racism still existed with similar acts of violence against Black communities, which galvanized further support for the civil rights movement. These images disturbed all Blacks, and Taylor often thought he had a responsibility to be more active in the fight. He just didn't know how to do it beyond hearing what his father and Martin Luther King Jr. said about standing up for justice and equality. Taylor thought more about the beginnings of his dream, which would always cut out after the words, "I have a dream today." It lingered in his head more often; he felt it would lead him somewhere. He just couldn't control it.

He was thinking about the day at school and remembered seeing two upper-class students walking together after school was over for the day. They walked, holding hands, talking, and laughing. Nothing unusual there. However, what stood out most of all, and as clear as day, was that the boy was White, and the girl was Black. He hadn't noticed anything like this before at his school, or anywhere else, for that matter. It immediately reminded him of the part of King's speech where he talked about White kids and Black kids joining hands as brothers and sisters. Only the two were not siblings. *That was obvious. What they had going on was more of a matter of hormonal influence.*

He thought about it on the way home and knew this would be important news to share with Nick. Maybe he should ask Nick if he observed anything similar. This was big news. He wondered how many other Black and White combo-couples existed. *Was this about to become a trend? Do their parents know about this interracial handholding?* As he thought more, he arrived at a well-established conclusion, leveraging his developed ability to employ deductive reasoning. The Black and White handholding was a good sign that moved in the right direction of better relations between the races. To him, this was more like equality than inequality, more in line with getting along than fighting one another. *Did Martin Luther King Jr.'s speech include boyfriend-girlfriend handholding?* As advanced as his reasoning was for his age, he could not yet envision the backlash that could come from interracial relationships that eventually led to marriage.

At home, Taylor remained quiet about what he had seen. He acted like it was a regular day, telling his parents about his classes that day, doing homework, having dinner, watching TV, reading, finishing his homework, and then going to bed. Only this time, he had some fuel for his bedtime thoughts. The Black and White teen couple holding hands generated so much curiosity. *His dream began to form.* Taylor had no idea how multidimensional his dream would become. He only sensed that there was a lot more to it than he had thought so far.

He fell asleep quickly, just as he did on other nights. Only this time, images that would become memorable formed in his head, in his subconscious. It started with the usual repetition, *"I have a dream today."* But after a few echoes of this well-entrenched string of words, he envisioned the White boy and Black girl holding hands. *Brothers and sisters, Black and White; boyfriend and girlfriend; families and potential families, Black and White.*

He woke up, startled, and looked around his dimly lit room. It took him a minute to realize he was dreaming. It was 10 p.m., and he was tired. He turned over, pulled the covers over his head, and fell asleep, not waking up until the following day.

At breakfast, Taylor was unusually introspective. His father asked, "Son, is everything okay? You seem very quiet this morning."

"Uh, yeah. I'm okay. Just tired."

"Tired? Did you sleep okay last night?"

"Yeah, pretty much. I woke up one time from a dream I had . . . but I can't remember what it was now." He did remember but didn't want to talk about it. He finished his breakfast and got ready to go to school. He made a mental note to look carefully when other kids came to school to see if Black and White teenagers were holding hands. He couldn't wait to tell Nick what he saw the day before.

He headed out to school as usual each morning, only this time, his antennae were on alert for any mixed pairs. He didn't notice anyone who would qualify for his attention, and he felt a little disappointed. He wondered if what he had seen previously was an isolated case or if he had seen it correctly. *Maybe it looked like they were holding hands, but they really weren't!* A slight sense of self-doubt crept in, but he quickly dismissed it. *Nope, they were holding hands!*

He saw Nick and ran over to him. "Nick, guess what I saw when I left school yesterday."

"What?"

"There was a guy and a girl who are in eighth grade, and they were holding hands while walking home."

"Yeah, I seen some kids doing that too."

"But this was a White guy and a Black girl!"

"No way, really?"

"Yeah, really. I looked for them this morning, but I didn't see them or anybody else doing that."

In the South, the outward display of affection between a teenage White boy and a Black girl would most probably be considered taboo or unacceptable. However, this was a more progressive and integrated area within a population actively involved in the civil rights movement. In the broader cultural context of the present, when civil rights challenged racial prejudices and interracial relationships were viewed as an equal and just expression of friendship or love, it may be more acceptable. On the other hand, it would be no surprise that such Black-and-White relationships would face societal challenges.

Nick and Taylor settled in their classroom seats, and their attention turned to a typical day of learning. Taylor's thoughts devoted enough time to the Black-and-White situation last night and this morning. *Enough confusion already!* It was nearing the Christmas break when many kids' attention shifted to the holidays. School, homework, and even White boys and Black girls holding hands took a back seat. But Taylor's dream kept him on a journey, as if it had a mind of its own.

Chapter 51

"I'm Still Black!"

nick and Taylor walked a few blocks together as usual after school, before they parted on one street corner to their respective apartments. The walk from there for each of them was only about eight minutes more. Nick walked at his usual pace, swinging his empty lunch box, when he suddenly stopped and quickly stepped into an alley. He peeked around the building to see more of what he noticed: students he recognized from PS 91. They were a White guy and a Black girl tucked into a small carved-out section of a brick building. They weren't holding hands. They were kissing!

Nick pulled his head back as he saw the White guy look around to check for any onlookers. Not seeing anyone, he went back to his extracurricular, after-school activity. Nick peeked out again and ran in the opposite direction as fast as he could to catch up with Taylor. He dropped his lunchbox, picked it up, and increased his pace until he saw Taylor almost at his apartment.

"Taylor, Taylor!" Taylor quickly turned and, when he saw Nick, he ran to him.

"What? What happened?"

"I . . . I saw them!"

He was trying to catch his breath, and before he could say more, Taylor asked him with a puzzled look, "Saw who?"

"The White guy and the Black girl!"

"You ran all the way here to tell me that? Why couldn't you tell me tomorrow or call me? Were they holding hands?"

"No, they were kissing. Long kisses!"

"Oh man, really? Did they see you?"

"I don't think so. I was hiding in an alley!"

"Last night, I was thinking about them, and I thought, maybe I didn't see it right, but you did, right? You saw it! Oh, man. I bet some other kids are doing that, but we just don't know it yet!"

"Yeah, I guess. Uh, I better get home before my Mom thinks something happened to me. See ya tomorrow!"

He sprinted home, hanging onto his lunchbox. On the way, he tried to understand what this meant for America. Whites kissing Blacks and vice versa. *Did civil rights cause this to happen?* Witnessing what Taylor had told him and what he had observed was like striking gold. It was valuable information, shared only with the closest friends that he and Taylor hung out with, Black and White.

As Taylor was walking home before Nick bombarded him with this news, he was thinking of the holidays, winter fun, sledding, gifts, singing "Jingle Bells," no homework, and maybe a subway ride and visit to Rockefeller Center to see the big Christmas tree. But now, the update on the racial activity of the pleasant kind in Brooklyn directed his mind to the civil rights movement and all it represented, especially treating each other as equals, walking hand in hand with our brothers and sisters, and boyfriends and girlfriends. *Were they kissing just because Martin Luther King Jr. spoke about . . . ?* He couldn't finish this thought as his mother met him at the front door.

"Taylor. You're home a little late. Is everything okay?"

"Uh, yeah, Mom. I was talkin' with Nick for a while about . . . uh . . . about the Christmas holidays. Will we do some things with him and his family?"

"Probably. I have been talking with Nick's mother, so we might plan something with them soon. Do you have any homework?" She didn't wait for his answer. "Go get some homework done. I'm going to prepare something for dinner." Taylor didn't say anything more; no more conversation was needed.

The evening proceeded as usual, except for the residual effects of the previous interruption of Taylor's holiday thoughts. After dinner, he finished his homework and watched one of his favorite television programs, *Bonanza*. He then said he was tired and would read in bed before going to sleep. His parents didn't think this was unusual, as he often headed to bed early after an exhausting day. It was exhausting absorbing all the White and Black handholding and kissing information over the last couple of days, and how that might be related to the civil rights movement.

He was reading one of the two books assigned by Rivera, *To Kill a Mockingbird* by Harper Lee, and *The Adventures of Tom Sawyer* by Mark Twain. He chose to continue with Lee's book, which had gained popularity, illustrating moral courage in the fight against racial injustices. He was reading about the court case of Tom Robinson, a Black man falsely accused of assaulting a White woman, and even with overwhelming evidence of Robinson's innocence, the deep prejudices in Maycomb County's White community led to a guilty verdict.

Rivera looked forward to asking the class what lessons of courage, integrity, and fighting for justice they learned. But for now, Taylor was fighting to stay awake as his eyelids slowly closed, and his book fell to the floor. Isaac heard the noise, peeked in, and saw Taylor motionless, out cold. He picked up the book and smiled proudly that his son was reading a classic of American literature. He reflected. *Yep. There is a lot of powerful stuff in this one—morality, empathy, racial injustice, and the segregated South.* He remembers reading it when he was a young boy.

Several phrases and images emerged in Taylor's head as he fell into a deeper sleep, creating the perfect conditions for vivid dreaming. His circadian rhythm, relaxing reading, healthy diet, and routine physical activity all contributed to a proper mental state for an ideal dive into the dream world. It started slowly, almost at a whisper, before it became rapid and louder.

"I have a dream today," "Black kids holding hands with White kids," "Tom Robinson, Guilty," "Injustice," "Struggle," "White boys holding hands and kissing Black girls," "Sit down together at the table of brotherhood," "I have a dream today," repeating over and over.

He heard a voice, "Taylor, Taylor!" It was distracting at first, but he quickly returned to the recesses of his mind, the hidden, less accessible parts of his subconscious, where memories, thoughts, desires, and feelings lingered. The phrases and images got stronger. "All God's children," "Free at last," "Free at last," "All men . . . Black men, White men . . . unalienable rights of life, liberty, and the pursuit of happiness, freedom, and security of justice." His mind was racing to keep up with the steady flow of reminders that all was not right in America, and something needed to be done.

"Taylor, Taylor!" He sat up abruptly with his eyes closed and listened. "Taylor, Taylor Washington!" He did not recognize the voice at first. "Taylor Washington!" It sounded familiar. He now recognized the voice. It was Martin Luther King Jr.'s voice! "Taylor Washington! Taylor, you have a dream today! You and your White brothers and sisters will sit together at the table of brotherhood. Justice is coming for you and all God's children . . . all God's children." He envisioned himself smiling as he thought, *Martin Luther King Jr. is talking to me!*

Taylor's thoughts drifted to his friend Nick and his parents. *A White family and my Black family.* He thought of them as one family because of the years of socializing with them, their support during times of racial discrimination, and the growing friendship they shared. And then a shocking part of the dream hit him like a lightning bolt. It was vague but startling, nonetheless. He suddenly felt that Jonathan and Mary Greene were his parents and Isaac and Makena were Nick's parents. The whole concept of a Black boy with White parents and a White boy with Black parents caused his mind to go blank as he woke up in a sweat.

It was now close to 11 p.m. His parents and Ava were asleep. He looked around the room. It was quiet. He ran to the bathroom and looked in the mirror. A sigh of relief calmed him as he confirmed, *I'm still Black!* He grabbed a towel to dry off the perspiration and slowly walked back to his room. Exhausted, he fell asleep quickly, and his mind gave him a break—no more dreams, at least for this night.

When Taylor woke up the following day, he saw the book he was reading on the clothes dresser across the room. He remembered reading it, but didn't remember putting it there. He wondered how it got there. Sometimes, when Taylor had a dream, he might recall it the following day. It was hit or miss. But his dream last night had such emotional intensity that he remembered most of it. Waking up during the dream and running to the mirror to confirm he was still Black enhanced his chances of remembering. He didn't tell his parents about the dream, but he pondered whether to tell Nick, especially since he and his family were an essential part of it.

Nick might think I'm weird. It was a weird dream. Yeah, he probably would say that it was weird, that I'm weird. How could a Black kid have White parents, and a White kid have Black parents? He decided not to tell Nick, although part of him wanted to, just because of how close they were. He was torn. He went back and forth. *I'll tell him. No, I won't tell him. It's crazy! He won't believe me. He'll think I'm joking with him.* It made him lose his marbles. It got him all wound up. *Maybe I'll tell him later!*

Chapter 52

"WOWZA!"

The holiday break started with the usual fanfare for school children citywide. The mix of excitement, tradition, and energy put the daily routine of school and homework into the dwindling category, as visions of holiday decorations everywhere generated anticipation of joyful activities, celebrations, gift exchanges, sing-alongs, and fun trips to Manhattan.

Taylor had a few more episodes similar to that one memorable dream, but they were not as intense as before. Perhaps he was getting used to the idea that he could have White parents, at least in a dream. Not for real. He didn't need to run to the bathroom mirror to see if he was still Black, but he occasionally glanced down at his arms and legs to verify his skin color. *It's always good to ensure he was who he thought he was!* He kept his dreams to himself out of fear of appearing silly or foolish and to avoid anyone calling him "weird." After all, it was a very weird dream.

The weather was not too cold right after Christmas, and Nick's and Taylor's families decided to take a subway ride to Lower Manhattan to visit Greenwich Village, often just called "The Village." It was a vibrant cultural and intellectual hub known for its artists, writers, folk musicians, and social activists. It was situated in a charming neighborhood of tree-lined streets, coffeehouses, and historic brownstones, all of which contributed to its unique character. It would differ from the museums, libraries, and parks they typically visited during the past holidays.

There was no lack of activism and protests connected with the civil rights movement. The community's progressive mindset was a breeding ground for ideas favoring justice and equality. As they walked through the streets of The Village, they would hear peaceful but powerful rhetoric in small gatherings of like-minded people who wanted to be part of "all God's children" and enjoy the dignity and freedom meant for them in America. It confirmed the fight they had heard about a few months before, which was delivered on the steps of democracy in Washington, DC.

Taylor decided it was time. He had to tell someone about his dream. The language at the neighborhood rallies prompted him to revisit his dream. He needed to find the right place to share his most important revelation with his closest and most trusted ally. This was no small matter to him. He couldn't hold back any longer. He pulled Nick to the side to show him some squirrels nearby. The parents saw that and ignored them as they were immersed in the orations on civil rights. It was a diversion tactic to keep the parents from asking where they were going.

Taylor whispered, "Nick, I had a weird dream a couple of weeks ago. I wasn't gonna tell you about it because I thought you would say it was stupid."

Nick was all ears. "What was it?"

"I dreamed your parents were my parents, and my parents were your parents!"

"You're kidding me, right? You didn't really dream that, right?"

"I did. I had to run to the bathroom and look in the mirror to make sure I was still Black! It freaked me out!"

Nick was silent for a moment, then asked, "Wowza! Why do you think you had that dream? That's wild!"

"I don't know. It happened a few more times and seemed more real each time."

"What did your parents say about it?"

"I didn't tell them about it. I don't think I will. Maybe it'll just go away!"

"What if it doesn't go away?"

"Do you think it won't?"

"I don't know. It's your dream. I think it will go away soon. There's lots of other stuff to dream about."

"Like what? What do you dream about?"

"I dreamed a few times about flying like Superman and having his superpowers. You saw all my Superman comics, right? Sometimes, I dream I can hit home runs like Mickey Mantle. One time, I dreamed I came out of my body and was looking down at myself in bed. That was very weird. I dream of all kinds of weird stuff, but never tell anybody. I guess . . . now . . . you know. Oh, one time I dreamed I was an astronaut and flew in a rocket ship to the moon." Nick didn't mention that he also dreamed about girls. He wasn't ready to tell anyone about that yet.

Taylor was mesmerized by the breadth of the weird dreams Nick had. Suddenly, he didn't feel too bad about his "weird dreams." They were interrupted. Isaac called out. "Hey boys, what are you doing over there? You guys hungry? We're gonna grab some lunch." They were starving for food and a change of conversation. That was enough about dreams for one day. It was almost too much to digest. Digesting food would be easier. They found a nearby deli with sandwiches, hot soups, and sumptuous desserts. No one went home hungry.

Later, Nick told Taylor he could lend him some of his Superman comic books. He said that maybe he would dream of flying and have all the superpowers of the action hero, and wouldn't think he had White parents so much.

That night, none of the dream episodes Nick shared during the city trip with Taylor worked to redirect his friend's mind. The Black boy with White parents was at it again. The dream grew exponentially in terms of its potential meaning. It seemed to have a message for Taylor.

"Taylor! Taylor Washington! All God's children, Black and White, Jews and Gentiles, Protestants and Catholics, will join hands. They will be one family. One family of love across America. In Alabama, Mississippi, Georgia, Colorado, and Pennsylvania. All across the land, where no one will judge the color of their skin. Freedom will ring from everywhere. We will work together, pray together, and overcome struggles together." This was more pleasant and less startling than before.

"Taylor, it won't matter if your parents are White or Black. They will love you without reservation, unconditionally, and without limitations. There will be harmony among the races in an environment of mutual respect, understanding, and cooperation. All individuals will be treated fairly and have equal opportunities, regardless of their race or ethnicity. There will be empathy and appreciation for the experiences and perspectives of others. We will celebrate our diversity, cultures, and traditions. We will avoid conflict and violence and turn to open and honest dialogue to address any misunderstandings. We will collaborate toward shared goals and avoid anything dividing us."

In his dream, Taylor heard a random mix of words from Martin Luther King Jr.'s speech, words that came together with this young Black boy's knowledge about injustice, inequality, peace, and harmony among diverse people to deliver a simple message: We can hope for and work toward a better America.

In Taylor's mind, it was complex because there still was racial discrimination and bombings of churches where Blacks attended services, despite the marches and speeches. Yet it was simple, just like his and Nick's relationship. Friends from the first time they met. But it remained somewhat of a paradox. *How could something be both complex and simple at the same time?*

It was simple. It was complex. He went back and forth in his dream. *How might people, all God's children, hold hands and sit at a table with one another? People from all faiths and backgrounds, with different colored skin, cultures, and ethnicities?* The more he dreamed, the more questions surfaced. *How do we get to "free at last?"* His journey through his dream made him conclude that if all the demonstrators, speakers, and government officials couldn't find the answer, how could he find it? *This is tougher than I thought!*

The next day, Taylor decided he needed to get another opinion on all his thoughts, but to do it without revealing his dream. During breaks, he briefly talked with Nick at school to update him on the latest voices and conclusions. But when he got home, he waited for the authoritative source of knowledge he had always depended on— his father. After dinner, he told his father that he needed to talk with him about something important and that he wanted to do it in his room.

Isaac responded as Taylor knew he would. "Sure, son. What's going on?"

Taylor was careful and avoided saying he had a dream. "Dad, I was thinking about the civil rights movement, the marches and speeches, and what you told me about why people have racial discrimination, and some do violent things, like the church bombing that killed some little Black girls."

"Okay. Did you want to ask me something about all that?"

"Yeah. Why is it so hard to get people to respect one another, like us with Nick's family and them with us? Why does it take so long for people to stop hurting one another? It seems simple, like Nick and me. We met at school and became friends. We never did anything to discriminate against each other. But then, it seems like it's not so simple."

Isaac was glad Taylor was asking these questions. It indicated that he was concerned and wanted to find solutions. "Taylor, these are very good questions. And you are right. It could be simple, and yet it is complex." He thought for a few seconds, searching for an analogy.

"Think of it this way. This is not a perfect world. There's imperfection everywhere. Yet we try to improve things by removing the imperfections. It's like trying to run faster, hit more home runs, and get better grades in school. We always strive to do better. When you go to the park, you see grassy areas that look pretty, but some places have ugly-looking weeds. The weeds grew there over time, generating more weeds because that's what weeds do best. If we want the weedy area to look better, we need to pull the weeds and remove them. It's the same way for deep-rooted racial hate. Hate continues to generate hate because that's what they are used to doing. Many kids, especially in the South, grew up in families that hated us Black folks. Maybe they saw us as a threat to their jobs or power over us. If your mother and I taught you to hate White kids, do you think you and Nick would be such good friends?"

This was a lot to digest, but Taylor said, "I guess maybe not, but why did you and Mom teach me the way you did?"

"Because that's how my parents and your mother's parents taught us. We should respect and treat one another as we would like to be treated. It's a behavior that's passed down through generations. It takes time to remove all the weeds, change attitudes that have been there for ages, and convince people that everyone should be treated fairly. It's hard work sometimes to change attitudes and years of injustice and inequality. So we must keep up the fight and especially get the government to recognize that we don't yet have the America everyone dreams about."

Taylor thought about his father's last statement, *"We don't yet have the America everyone dreams about."* "Thanks, Dad. That makes a lot of sense."

"Taylor, I'm glad you asked these kinds of questions. It tells me you are considering some very important issues and are concerned. I think you and I know that you and Nick have something special, and we also have that with his family. Other kids are not so lucky. Someday, if it's part of your plan to have a family, I hope you can pass on good behavior to your kids and make the world better."

Taylor was happy that he and his father had this talk. His dad always made him feel comfortable in their conversations. But Taylor wouldn't touch the subject of Black kids with White parents and White kids with Black parents. It was way too early to broach that part of his dream, or if it could ever be a reality. *Maybe Dad didn't answer everything, but he sure helped a lot!*

Chapter 53

The 1964 World's Fair . . . and So Much More

The first half of 1964 contained significant political, social, technological, and cultural development. North Vietnam increased its support early in the year to assist the Viet Cong insurgency in the south with personnel and resources. They intensified their guerrilla warfare, defeating the South Vietnamese Army in numerous battles. The United States took action to initiate covert operations against North Vietnam, which included propaganda dissemination and economic destruction.

The US Congress held extensive debates on the Civil Rights Act of 1964 with civil rights leaders who advocated for the end of segregation and discrimination. Activists prepared for the Freedom Summer campaign, which aimed to register Black voters in Mississippi. Protests and demonstrations continued nationwide, setting legislative change as a goal. The KKK was on a murderous rampage as they sought to counter the campaign. In one incident, they kidnapped, brutally beat and murdered two civil rights workers who were hitchhiking. In another, three civil rights leaders, released from a Mississippi jail, were brutally murdered and their bodies weren't found for weeks.

The attitudes toward interracial relationships and marriages remained complex as societal prejudices persisted, but they were evolving in more progressive and culturally advanced melting pots like New York City. Miscegenation laws, which were designed to maintain racial segregation and uphold discriminatory social hierarchies, were first introduced in the late seventeenth century in the

United States and prohibited interracial marriage and, in some cases, interracial sexual relationships. The laws were historically enforced in various parts of the world.

The space race and space exploration were primarily a competition between the United States and the Soviet Union. The United State's Ranger 6 Mission was launched to capture images of the moon before impact, but failed due to a camera malfunction. In April '64, the National Aeronautics and Space Administration (NASA) launched Gemini 1, the first in the Gemini program, an uncrewed mission to test the structural integrity of the spacecraft and its compatibility with the Titan II launch rocket booster. The Soviets launched Zond 1 in April for a flyby of Venus. Even though its communication system failed, it established progress in interplanetary exploration.

"Beatlemania" began with the band's arrival at JFK Airport on February 7, 1964. Two days later, after they performed on *The Ed Sullivan Show*, songs like "All My Loving," "She Loves You," and "I Want to Hold Your Hand" could be heard by people singing them all across America. New York City's vibrant art scene flourished, with galleries and museums hosting groundbreaking exhibitions. The World's Fair opened in Flushing Meadows-Corona Park in Queens, showcasing futuristic innovations and cultural exhibits that drew millions of visitors.

The city's residents, especially in Brooklyn and neighboring Queens, read and heard about racial discrimination at the 1964 World's Fair. Members of CORE organized protests to highlight the discriminatory hiring practices at the fair and among exhibiting companies. They demanded equitable representation and economic justice. They emphasized that the fair should reflect diversity, not merely a single racial perspective. It was part of the broader civil rights efforts during the 1960s to address systemic inequalities.

The Washington and Greene families went to the fair on a weekend day in May. They had a great time seeing something different that comes along only periodically. The "Expos," as they are also known, began with the Great Exhibition of 1851 in London, showcasing industrial achievements. The two families considered a trip to the fair a once-in-a-lifetime opportunity. Taylor and Nick especially enjoyed "Ford's Magic Skyway," a ride in a Ford convertible that featured scenes from prehistoric times and futuristic cities designed by Walt Disney.

They also liked "NASA's Space Park" and "The Panorama," a detailed model of all five boroughs of New York City, and they took many photos of themselves in front of the massive steel globe called the Unisphere, symbolizing global unity. It was something that Isaac had researched and commented on. "This Unisphere represents a united world. Hopefully, we'll all witness that someday!" It was apparent to the adults that he had the civil rights movement and its goals in mind.

Jonathan, Mary, and Makena all responded with a mixture of "Amen to that," "God, yes," and "Hope so." Taylor, Nick, and Ava weren't listening as much as they were looking in all directions. Their vision was in sensory overload. *Where to go next?*

One month remained before the completion of seventh grade at PS 91. Taylor's dream did not intensify, nor did it happen as frequently as before. He was too distracted and focused on finishing several projects that were due in class. He had borrowed a few *Superman* comic books from Nick, which caused him to join the "I can fly club" in his new dreams. Although they would have one more year before they started high school, he and Nick occasionally talked about where they would go to high school. They wanted to remain together, and the thought of going to different schools was something they wanted to avoid at all costs.

President Lyndon B. Johnson signed into law the Civil Rights Act of 1964, a landmark legislation, on July 2, 1964, two weeks after the school year ended. The bill survived a seventy-five-day filibuster, one of the longest in US history. When the most comprehensive civil rights legislation was first proposed in June 1963 by President Kennedy, it survived strong opposition from southern members of Congress. Kennedy stated that the United States "will not be fully free until all of its citizens are free." One of the speakers against the act, Senator Robert Byrd of West Virginia, a former Ku Klux Klan member, spoke for more than 14 consecutive hours. The filibuster was broken, and the bill passed 73–27 to provide the two-thirds vote necessary to end the debate.

Its details were captured in several key provisions. Title II prohibited discrimination in public accommodations engaged in interstate commerce. Title III encouraged the desegregation of public facilities and authorized the attorney general to file lawsuits for enforcement. Title IV addressed desegregation in public schools. There were other provisions, but perhaps the most important was Title VII, which banned employment discrimination based on race, color, religion, sex, or national origin. The Equal Employment Opportunity Commission (EEOC) was established to enforce these provisions.

It was a monumental step in empowering the federal government to intervene in discrimination cases. It led to the desegregation of many public spaces and workplaces. However, discrimination persisted despite the act. The law provided a legal framework to combat inequality, societal attitudes, and systemic racism, but it didn't change things overnight. Resistance was strong in the South, where businesses and local government sought ways to circumvent the law.

To ensure compliance, continued activism and judicial enforcement were essential. In his first State of the Union address, President Johnson stated, "Let this session of Congress be known as the session which did more for civil rights than the last hundred sessions combined." The act was the moral imperative called for by many activists and most assuredly by Martin Luther King Jr., the year before in Washington, DC.

After another summer of fun for Nick and Taylor, they turned thirteen and entered Donna Sweeney's eighth-grade class. As the school counselor, Sweeney was familiar with most PS 91 students, especially Nick and Taylor. The story of how they became friends in first grade, by Lopez, was unforgettable and served as an example for several teachers to share with their students about children of different races and backgrounds and how they can build friendships.

The boys had a comprehensive year of learning ahead with core subjects: English language arts, mathematics, science, and social studies. The latter will include US history, including the Civil War, Reconstruction, and the Progressive Era. The civil rights movement would emerge again as an important topic, not only because of the recent Civil Rights Act of 1964 but also when slavery was examined as a central topic while exploring the causes of the Civil War.

Taylor learned a lot from his parents over the years as he witnessed and survived racial discrimination. Nick would learn the same by association. They would learn about the economic, social, and political tensions between the North and the South in the eighth grade. The picture of slavery would become clearer when the boys would hear about the Missouri Compromise of 1820 and the Fugitive Slave Act of 1850.

The Compromise was a legislative agreement to maintain the balance of power between free and slave states to preserve balance in the Senate. Missouri was admitted as a slave state, and Maine was a free state. This was a temporary solution to the growing sectional tensions over slavery north of the 36°30' parallel, except for Missouri. The Slave Act was designed to strengthen the enforcement of laws requiring the return of escaped enslaved people, even if they were found in free states. These new dimensions of slavery and the root causes of the civil rights movement would provide a deeper understanding of what they witnessed in public demonstrations of racial discrimination.

The boys looked forward to the additional subjects, some more than others—foreign languages, art and music, physical education, and industrial arts—primarily focusing on physical fitness, building muscles, and some ideas for woodworking projects. Nick wanted to make a birdhouse for his mother. She liked to feed birds that visited their small rear apartment balcony, where she placed birdseed in a dish. Taylor had his heart set on making a planter box with painted designs for his mother's tiny flowers and her small garden on her balcony.

Entering eighth grade marked a significant transition for Nick and Taylor, with the academic rigor of more complex subjects like algebra, advanced science, and in-depth historical analysis. It would require critical thinking and problem-solving skills. They needed to develop more independent learning and self-directed study habits while balancing extracurricular activities like sports and clubs. The social dynamics of evolving friendships, peer pressure, and a growing sense of identity could be both exciting and challenging.

While schoolwork would envelop their everyday lives and consume much of their mental activity, it would be difficult not to recognize the developments in the second half of 1964. During the Gulf of Tonkin incident, where North Vietnamese forces allegedly attacked the US Navy vessel USS Maddox twice, President Johnson sought the Tonkin Gulf Resolution, granting him authority to use military force in Vietnam, where previously the United States had been primarily in an advisory role. North Vietnam sent its People's Army into South Vietnam, causing the United States to escalate the number of its military personnel who were now actively engaged in operations.

Race riots occurred in Harlem and Philadelphia, demonstrating the strained relationship between African American communities and local law enforcement. The FBI foiled a KKK bombing plot in Philadelphia, Mississippi, where civil rights workers from the Council of Federal Organizations (COFO) planned to meet in a hotel. On the positive side, peaceful desegregation in restaurants, lodging establishments, and theaters in McComb, Mississippi, was a significant milestone. Also, Martin Luther King Jr. received the Nobel Peace Prize, at the time the youngest recipient, for his groundbreaking work in the American civil rights movement through peaceful means.

NASA significantly improved its space technology after the failed Ranger 6 mission by launching the Ranger 7 spacecraft toward the moon. It successfully transmitted 4,308 high-resolution images back to Earth, providing unprecedented, detailed imagery of the lunar surface necessary for future missions.

Culturally—and perhaps more in tune with Nick and Taylor's interests—music, fueled by the Beatles' "British Invasion" and Motown artists such as the Supremes and the Temptations, was gaining widespread popularity. New film and television shows provided a variety of entertainment, the Mod style provided a new wave of clothing, and baseball marked the end of an era for the Yankees with their World Series loss to the St. Louis Cardinals. From 1949 to 1964, the Yankees had dominated Major League Baseball, appearing in fourteen of sixteen World Series and winning nine. Nick and Taylor were sad, but they still loved the team.

Despite what was happening in the world in 1964, with its achievements and setbacks, Nick and Taylor had a full plate to digest as they began life as teenagers. And they would continue to grow in their understanding of civil rights because racial discrimination and violent acts continued, and so would Taylor's dream.

Chapter 54

SOMETHING WAS HIDDEN IN HIS POCKET

Toward the end of the school day on Tuesday, November 10, 1964, a young Latino man drove to the PS 91 parking lot, turned off the engine, and sat there for a few minutes. He looked in the rearview mirror and took a deep breath. After leaving his car, he checked his pocket for something he had hidden, approached the school, and entered through the main door. He came upon the janitor, Jamal Brown, and asked, "Excuse me, where is the principal's office? I have an appointment with Principal Carpenter."

Brown smiled and said, "It's down this hallway on the left." He looked the man up and down and returned to his janitorial chores. The man slowly walked the hallway, observing the numerous showcases that exhibited the educational focus and culture of the time. Displays of drawings, paintings, and students' crafts demonstrated their curiosity and learning. Some displays featured school concerts and posters, while others reflected the students' diverse backgrounds, showcasing photos of teachers with their classes. The man focused on one particular photo and smiled before he continued to the principal's office.

He knocked on the door and entered. Carpenter's assistant, Jenny Wilson, asked, "Sir, may I help you?"

"Good afternoon. My name is Sergeant Rafael Vargas. I'm here to see Dr. Carpenter."

"Oh, uh, yes! She's expecting you. Just a moment, please." Vargas stood there and scanned the portraits of national leaders, the school motto, and photos from local events that connected the school with the community. He had heard about some of them through a trusted source.

Wilson came back from Carpenter's office. "Sergeant Vargas, you may go in now. Dr. Carpenter is ready for you." She looked him over and smiled as he entered the office.

Dr. Carpenter stood up from behind her desk and came around to greet the young Marine sergeant. "Sergeant Vargas, good afternoon, and welcome to PS 91!"

"Thank you, Ma'am. Thank you for allowing me to come here today!"

"You are most welcome!" She shook his hand and said, "I'll be right back. Please have a seat."

As she left her office, Vargas said, "Thank you, Ma'am," but he remained standing and looked at the US flag in Carpenter's office. He recalled his five years as a Marine, following completion of rigorous physical and mental training at Marine Corps Recruit Depot (MCRD) Parris Island, South Carolina. He excelled in physical fitness, marksmanship, combat skills, and classroom instruction that taught military history, customs, and basic tactics.

Carpenter told Wilson to go and relieve Garcia from her second-grade class and have her report to her office. She sprang up, exchanging big smiles with Dr. Carpenter, and went to complete the mission. *The military was here; they were on a mission!* Within a few minutes, Miss Izzy Garcia entered the principal's office, ran to Sergeant Vargas, and hugged him.

"Oh, Rafael, I am so excited! How are you doing?" Dr. Carpenter and Miss Wilson looked on; their faces lit up with a slight trace of blush and formed huge smiles.

"Hi, Izzy. I'm a little nervous."

"Oh, Rafael, you can't be nervous. You're a Marine!" Everyone laughed.

Vargas said, "Right, I'm a Marine! I'm good. I'm good!" The laughs repeated.

Dr. Carpenter went to her desk and flipped a switch that turned on the school's public address system. It was now 3:15 p.m., approximately thirty minutes before the end of the school day.

"Attention, everyone. This is Principal Carpenter with an important announcement."

This surprised most of the teaching staff and the entire student body. *What could this be about?*

Carpenter continued, "Everyone, please finish any last-minute work and assemble in the school gym in ten minutes. This is important, but nothing to worry about, I can assure you." She wanted everyone to remain curious but not distraught. Wilson quickly left the office to set up a microphone in the gym.

As teachers and students arrived, they asked each other, "What is going on?" When they saw Wilson setting up the mic, they asked her, "Jenny, what is going on? Is everything okay?"

Wilson said, "I have no idea. Suddenly, Dr. Carpenter told me to set up the mic here. She's going to tell everyone something, but she didn't say what it was." (But she did know.)

In a few minutes, the gym was packed. There was a lot of buzz, with one question after another, and puzzled faces that conveyed both excitement and concern. The nail biters were busy. As she looked around the room, Lopez asked Rivera, standing beside her, "Gloria, where is Izzy? I don't see her."

Rivera said, "I don't know. I saw her earlier, so I know she's here or was here."

Lopez remained curious. "Hmmm." Nick and Taylor were standing side-by-side with the same jaw-dropping, wide-eyed expression of confusion, just like everyone else except Jamal Brown. He was sitting in a chair off to the side, wearing a huge grin. He knew exactly what was about to happen. He was honored to be part of the plan that strategically placed him near the school's front door when Sergeant Vargas entered.

Dr. Carpenter arrived with a sheet of paper in her hand. She approached the mic and said, "Everyone, thank you for being here on short notice. This won't take long." Everyone was dying to hear what was next. Just before she continued, Garcia snuck Sergeant Vargas into a small room adjacent to the main gym. Dr. Carpenter glanced around the room to ensure everyone was there, but this tactic ensured that Garcia and Vargas were in place.

Carpenter continued, "As you know, tomorrow is Veterans Day, a national holiday to honor veterans who serve our country. There will be parades, ceremonies, and community events all across the country. So, in honor of those in the US Armed Forces, it is my honor today to present someone from our community serving in the US Marine Corps to speak to you."

There was complete silence as everyone looked around the gym, but no one noticed anyone from the military. "Teachers and students, please welcome Sergeant Rafael Vargas from the United States Marines!" Cheers and clapping erupted from everyone except Maggie Lopez, whose hands covered her face in astonishment. She had not seen her boyfriend of three years, Rafael Vargas, for several months while he was away on a special assignment. Izzy joined, standing next to her best friend and holding her close. Lopez did not know why or how Rafael was there.

Sergeant Vargas walked up to the mic and smiled at Lopez. Everyone noted his impeccable uniform, complete with several service ribbons and medals on his chest. He said, "Dr. Carpenter, thank you for the honor of my being here today and addressing your students and teachers. I am proud to be a United States Marine and to serve our country. And I hope that, in the future, some of these kids will also serve in the military. I will be happy to come here and speak with them whenever I can and answer any questions." There was another round of cheering and clapping as some tears formed in Lopez's eyes. She thought that was the extent of the surprise.

Vargas left the mic, walked over to his girlfriend, smiled, and just as he was moving to hug her, he dropped to one knee. He reached into his pocket, pulled out a small, black velvet-covered box, opened it, and displayed its contents to Lopez. "Maggie!" She covered her eyes. *What is happening right now?* "Maggie Lopez, I love you with all my heart! Will you marry me?" The crowd was silent. All eyes were fixed on one of their favorite teachers, who meant the world to them and had taught them respect, love, and much more.

"Yes! Yes," Lopez answered without hesitation. Teachers were chanting for them to kiss. The crowd erupted in the loudest clapping and cheers of the day. Rafael rose, hugged, and kissed Maggie. Nick and Taylor jumped up and down with hundreds of other students who would remember this day.

Dr. Carpenter was delighted when Sergeant Vargas called her several weeks earlier to ask if he could propose to his girlfriend at the school. He told her how much Maggie loved the school and her students, how dedicated she was, and all the hard work she put into teaching them every day. When they discussed the plans, Dr. Carpenter was the one to suggest the Veterans Day idea. To keep it a secret, she only shared the plan with her secretary, Wilson, the janitor, Mr. Brown, and Garcia. This was one of the happiest days that the school personnel and students would remember. *The mission was accomplished!*

Chapter 55

Free and Equal Only in Our Graves

The six-day period of the Harlem Race Riots of 1964 started on July 18 in the upper Manhattan neighborhood when an off-duty police officer fatally shot a Black teenager. It left an aftermath of unrest that later spread to other city sections, especially Bedford-Stuyvesant and Brownsville in Brooklyn and South Jamaica in Queens. These were the first of several race riots that spread to major American cities, including Rochester, New York; Jersey City, New Jersey; Elizabeth, New Jersey; Dixmoor (near Chicago), Illinois; and Philadelphia, Pennsylvania.

These social disruptions, which continued to plague civil rights movement efforts, would provide more fuel for Martin Luther King Jr.'s and Taylor's dreams. It was unavoidable for Taylor not to revisit his dream due to the focus of his eighth-grade class on the Civil War, slavery, and the racial tensions of the day in nearby neighborhoods, often broadcast in the news media. He would also hear his father talk about it as he continued to meet with his Black group, including Dr. James Reed from NYU.

Isaac had asked Reed for any recommendations for Taylor, who had expressed interest in more books about the Blacks' struggles. He explained that he was learning more in school now about the Civil War, slavery, and the civil rights movement, and that one of the school reading assignments was *Uncle Tom's Cabin* by Harriet Beecher Stowe.

Reed had commented, "That's a powerful depiction of the horrors of slavery and what Uncle Tom endured in the face of cruelty. It's a historical awareness of the experiences of enslaved people, and it also shows that Tom's character demonstrates the strength of compassion and faith. I'm glad he will read that. I can also recommend *To Kill a Mockingbird* by Harper Lee."

"He already read that one last year. He liked it."

"Okay, then, let me see. I would start with a couple that I think would be good: *Up From Slavery* by Booker T. Washington and *Black Boy* by Richard Wright. He might enjoy reading a book by Washington because they share the same last name. It's an autobiography covering Washington's path from his enslavement to becoming a renowned educator. The other is Wright's memoir, telling his experience growing up in the segregated South."

"Dr. Reed, those are great recommendations. I'll let Taylor know. Maybe we can visit the library this week. I'll have to check his homework load. His teacher is laying it on thick for these kids getting ready for high school."

"Sounds good, Isaac. I always tell my history class students, 'You can never read enough, and just keep learning.' " They hung up. Isaac always felt good staying in touch with Reed for discussion or advice. He considered both valuable.

Over the next few weeks, Taylor consumed an extraordinary amount of civil rights–related material through school reading and assignments. He and his father had taken a weekend subway ride to the Grand Army Plaza at the north end of Prospect Park to visit the Brooklyn Public Library's Central Library. They returned home with several books, including those recommended by Dr. Reed.

The multisource racial material saturated Taylor's mind as he tried to spread his focus over the range of school subjects that required his attention. As he transitioned to sleep each night for the past few weeks, pieces of his previous dreams, which recalled some of Martin Luther King Jr.'s phrases and his own generated mixture of words, wove into an ever-growing quilt of subtle and indirect communication.

"Taylor! Taylor Washington! This is Uncle Tom!" Taylor recalled something he had read in *Uncle Tom's Cabin*: that all men are free and equal only when they are in their graves. His subconscious fought this thought and steered him toward equality. "Taylor! We cannot wait until we get to our graves to be equal. We must do something while we are alive. We need to act now. Hold the hands of our brothers and sisters as we sit at the table of justice. Stand among our Black and White family, our Black and White mothers and fathers. All God's children. Be one family."

Taylor then saw his parents, Jonathan and Mary Greene. *No, that can't be right!* He saw Nick with his parents, Isaac and Makena Washington, and he held his sister's hand, Ava's. Everyone was smiling. It felt just and . . . *No, this can't be right! How is this possible?* The images of White kids with Black parents and Black kids with White parents overwhelmed him. They were everywhere. His REM sleep triggered high brain activity resembling wakefulness. His heart rate and breathing became irregular as these vivid images consumed his emotions, memories, and problem-solving ability.

In his sleep, the visions and voices diminished for a while, only to return to cycles during the night that seemed like forever. They were so strong he felt as though he was awake. This lucid dreaming caused Taylor to realize that he was, in fact, dreaming. And in the realization, he tried to exert control over his dream, to change what he envisioned as impossible. But his dream was in control, not Taylor. His false awakenings caused him to dream that he was waking up to perform routine activities, but he later realized he was still asleep. The lines between his dream and reality were blurred.

The depth of his dream caused Taylor to tell Nick again, especially because Nick's parents were Taylor's parents in his dream. And Ava was Nick's sister! During class, Taylor's mind drifted to his dream, no matter how hard he tried to concentrate on Sweeney's explanation of solving fundamental algebra problems: ($2x - 5 = 15$) for linear equations and ($x + 2y = 20$) and ($2x - y = 15$) for multiple variables. She followed the steps to solve the x and y values on the blackboard. Taylor struggled between Sweeney's, "And by doing these steps, you will see that x = 10 and y = 5," and "Taylor! Taylor Washington! This is Uncle Tom!" He couldn't give either his full attention.

Sweeney gave her class some algebra homework to practice similar problems. Taylor told himself he'd better do the practice problems (maybe with Dad's help—he was very good at math).

After school, Nick and Taylor set out for home. They always looked for the White guy and the Black girl, but hadn't seen them lately. *Maybe somebody caught them kissing and stopped it!* Taylor couldn't keep it in any longer. He had to tell Nick about the latest part of his dream, its vividness, realism, and added scenes. The dream was evolving with more emphasis on the togetherness of Black and White people, and it was good, but also disturbing.

"Nick, I had more dreams for a couple of weeks. They are getting weirder."

"Like how weirder?"

"Well, I almost finished the book Mrs. Sweeney told us to read, *Uncle Tom's Cabin*."

"Yeah, I'm reading it too. It lets you know how bad slavery was. My dad said it might help me understand about justice and humanity. So what's the book got to do with your dream?"

"Well, remember I told you that Martin Luther King Jr. called to me in my dream before?"

"Yeah, I remember."

"Well, now, Uncle Tom from the book was calling my name!"

"You're just making that up. Right? You're just joking with me. Right?"

"No. It happened. I could hear his voice. He called me. He said something about how we can't wait to get to our graves to be equal. We have to do something now. Then he said . . . I remember the exact words. He said, 'Hold the hands of our brothers and sisters as we sit at the table of justice. Stand among our Black and White family, our Black and White mothers and fathers. All God's children. Be one family.'"

"He said all that?"

"Yeah, but that's not the weirdest part. Then I saw myself with my parents, but they were your parents. Then I saw you with your parents, but they were my parents. In my dream, I kept thinking this couldn't be right, but it seemed so real! You were even holding Ava's hand, and I saw you as brother and sister. It all seemed so real. I thought I was awake, but I wasn't. Why would I dream all that? I kept thinking, how is this possible?"

"Wow! Anything else?"

"I'm afraid to fall asleep! I don't know if it can get weirder than that!"

"Did you tell your parents yet?"

"No. They might think there's something wrong with me, you know, mentally."

They arrived at the corner where they would split up to go home. Nick didn't know what to say at first. Then, just before they parted, he said, "Don't worry. If it's a dream, then you know it's not real, even if it felt real, right, Taylor?"

"Yeah. I guess so. See you tomorrow. Hey, did you talk to your dad about going fly fishing yet? Your dad and my dad keep saying we're all going soon. They said that last year, but we didn't go, did we?"

"Oh, I forgot. I'll ask him tonight."

"Okay, cool. Alright, see you tomorrow." They walked for the next few minutes as their minds shifted from fly fishing to the added complexities of the dream. It had a grip on them and wouldn't let go.

Chapter 56

THE PLAN

nick worried about his best friend. Even though he tried to assure Taylor that it was only a dream, nothing real, he hoped that it would disappear soon and that Taylor would completely return to reality. He agonized over whether to tell his father, but he wasn't sure how to do so without breaking Taylor's trust in him not to tell anyone. *What if I didn't tell him it was a dream, Taylor's dream?* After careful consideration, he decided to ask his father some questions without mentioning Taylor.

The next day at school, Nick shared his plan with Taylor. At first, Taylor hesitated but said, "What are you gonna ask him?"

"I was thinking I could just ask him if Black people could have White parents and if White people could have Black parents."

"He's gonna think you're nuts! He might ask you why you're asking that question or ask if I told you anything."

"I'll just say that I thought of it while we were learning about the Civil War and slavery. I won't say anything about your dream. I promise."

Taylor showed signs of nervousness—fidgeting by tugging his clothing, slightly sweating, and avoiding eye contact with Nick. He said, "I'm not sure that's gonna work."

"Why not?"

"I don't know. I'm just not sure."

"Taylor, trust me, man. Maybe my dad knows something we don't know about it. Maybe your dad knows something."

After pensiveness, Taylor said, "Okay, you ask your dad first. Maybe after we hear what he says, we might ask my dad."

Nick smiled and put his hand on Taylor's shoulder. "I'll try to ask him tonight after dinner." *It was a plan!*

Taylor had an idea during class and waited for the lunch break to share it with Nick. "Nick, I thought of something while we were in history class. Why don't we ask Mrs. Sweeney if she thinks . . . you know . . . what you will ask your father?"

Nick was initially enthralled by the question. "Hmmm." Then, after a few seconds, he said, "Then our whole class might think we're nuts! I think we stick to our plan. I'll ask my dad."

"Yeah, okay. I didn't think of that. Yeah, just ask your dad." *Yeah, our whole class will think we're nuts!*

On the way home, the boys reviewed the plan again, but then shifted to indecision about whether to ask the crazy question. They finally convinced themselves it had to be done. The day was Friday, November 13. They realized they might have to wait until Monday to talk about it again and find out what Nick's father had said. Someone might overhear them if they spoke on the phone over the weekend. And that might lead to more questions! They accepted the agony of waiting through the weekend.

"We're having take-out tonight for dinner," Mary said. She and Jonathan decided on pizza for dinner. They had it delivered and added a homemade salad to complement the meal. They didn't want to cook, as they had other plans that hadn't been disclosed to Nick yet. Nick loved pizza. It was one of his favorite foods, and he was starving as usual. His stomach always took over his mind when it was near dinner time.

The delivery guy rang the bell and handed over the hot pizza box. Jonathan tipped him as the aroma from the pizza permeated the apartment. After he consumed two slices, Nick was mentally prepared to ask his father for some time to talk about something. He was hesitant. He decided to ask him about the possibility of fly fishing first before turning to the other subject. His father had told him that fall was one of the best seasons to fly fish.

"Dad, Taylor, and I were talking about all the times you and his father said when we got older that we would go fly fishing. We talked about going last year, but . . ." His father interrupted him.

"Nick, you're right. We had planned to go, but something came up. I don't remember what it was, but you know, we're way overdue. We should go. This is a good time of the year. I'll call Taylor's father over the weekend. Maybe we can go next weekend!" He looked at Mary for some sign of approval. She smiled and nodded her head. She had something else on her mind.

Nick replied with excitement. "Oh, alright! I hope we can go. I wanna catch some trout!" He ate two more slices of pizza before he was about to ask his father for some father-son time to talk. But Mary spoke first.

"Nick, after dinner, we are going to Grandma and Grandpa's apartment. Aunt Julie, Mikey, and Jenny will be there too. So finish your pizza, wash up, and get ready to go in a little while." This threw a curve at Nick's (and Taylor's) plan for questions that needed answers.

"Why are we going to Grandma and Grandpa's?"

Mary smiled at Jonathan. Jonathan said, "Nick, your mother has some news, and she wants to tell you first. Then we'll tell Grandma, Grandpa, Aunt Julie, and your cousins the good news." Nick was all ears for the good news.

"What is the good news?"

Mary smiled at Nick. "Nick, you're going to be a big brother! We wanted to tell you first before we tell the rest of our family!" Nick looked at his mom and dad. All he could immediately think of was the day Taylor whispered in his ear about how babies get inside their mother's tummies. The visual took over momentarily before he displayed a broad smile and a flushed face, followed by a loud cheer of enjoyment.

"Yeh! I'm gonna be a big brother! I thought I would never be a big brother!"

Jonathan said, "Well, we've been trying for a long time, and it finally happened! You will have a little brother or sister! We'll have to wait and see!"

Nick's thoughts went back to the visuals again. The flush deepened, but he quickly asked, "When, Mom?"

Mary said, "Next May, late in May!" Mary had informed her family the day before, since they lived in Pennsylvania and would not get together until Christmas.

Nick completely forgot about his conversations with Taylor and his important assignment to query his father. He could only think of a new little Greene in the family and couldn't wait to tell Taylor.

"Did you tell Taylor's parents yet, Mom?"

"No, not yet, but we will after we tell the others in our family. We know how much you enjoy playing with Ava when you see her. Maybe you'll have a little sister of your own!" Nick just looked off into the distance, letting the news sink in. "Okay, let's get ready to go to Grandma and Grandpa's. We told them we just wanted to drop by and see how they were doing, and to catch up with everyone since it's been a while. We knew Aunt Julie and the kids were going there for dinner tonight."

Nick darted off to the bathroom. Jonathan and Mary smiled at one another as they cleared the table. Jonathan grabbed one more slice of pizza. Somehow, spreading good news made him hungry again.

Right after they left the apartment, the Greenes's phone rang . . . and rang. Taylor called to talk with Nick. Isaac, Makena, and Ava left their apartment briefly to shop for groceries. They asked Taylor if he wanted to go, but he quickly thought this would be a good opportunity to call Nick to ask how everything went with his questions to his father. "No, I'll stay home and watch some TV." They told him they would be back soon.

When no one answered the phone, Taylor thought the worst. *Maybe he asked his father those questions, and his father figured out something about my dream!* He called again—no answer. *Crap, where are they?* Now, he wished he had gone with his parents and Ava. At least he could have salvaged the evening by getting snacks or candy at the store. Anxiety was escalating. A weekend with no answers about White and Black this and that and when they would go fly fishing. And then there was algebra homework to do. His head hurt.

He was so physically and mentally drained that he fell asleep while watching television. The dream returned with the same scenario—calling out his name, drawing his attention to how the world should be, and encouraging him to act now and be part of a unified Black and White family. We cannot wait until we get to our graves to be equal. The door opened as his parents and Ava returned. Ava ran over to her brother to give him some candy, shook his arm, and Taylor shouted, "Uncle Tom, we can't wait, we can't wait!" He woke up. Isaac heard this and approached Taylor.

"Son, who is Uncle Tom? Are you okay?"

Startled by these last few seconds, he said, "What? Uncle who?"

"Uncle Tom. You said, 'Uncle Tom,' then something like, 'We can't wait.' Were you dreaming?"

"Yeah. I guess so. I was watching TV, and I guess I fell asleep. I don't remember anything. What did I say?" (But he did remember.)

Isaac said, "Nothing. I think you just had a dream. Did Ava give you some candy?"

"Yeah, I got it, thanks."

Isaac thought about what Taylor said. He knew his son was reading a book assigned by his teacher, Sweeney. *I wonder if that dream had something to do with the book* Uncle Tom's Cabin. *Who else could be Uncle Tom?*

Chapter 57

THE WRONG QUESTION

Jonathan and Mary announced the news of another little Greene due next May to the senior Greenes, Julie, and her two teenage children. Jonathan called his other sister, Kathleen, from his parents' apartment. The whole family was excited and looked forward to getting together, as they did every year for Thanksgiving, and to celebrate this future addition. Nick was having fun catching up with his cousins, Mikey and Jenny, about school, activities, and interests. They didn't see each other too often, with everyone's busy schedules. Holidays and special announcements made up for that.

After a couple of hours, Jonathan, Mary, and Nick returned to their apartment. On the way home, they discussed possible baby names for a boy and a girl, the preparations for a nursery they would need to make at the apartment for their new little one, and setting up a schedule of regular prenatal check-ups. They had plenty of time to ensure they would be ready when he or she came into the world.

Jonathan told Mary and Nick, "We might as well tell the Washingtons the news since I need to ask Isaac about fly fishing next weekend. They'll be excited to hear the latest about us."

Nick asked, "Dad, after you talk to them, can I talk with Taylor for a little while?"

"Sure."

Jonathan made the call. Makena answered. "Hey Makena, it's Jonathan; how are you all doing?"

"We're all okay here. Isaac ran out for a minute to pick up something. He'll be back soon. Did you want to talk with him?"

"Uh, yes. I wanted to ask him if he and Taylor would be available next Saturday to fly fish. Nick told me that he and Taylor were talking about it, and that Isaac and I had promised to take them last year, but we didn't go. Those guys remember everything!"

"I'm sure Isaac would love to go. I don't know of any plans for the weekend after Thanksgiving. We'll get together with family at his brother's house in New Jersey for the holiday. Do you want him to call you back when he returns?"

"Yes, please, but hold on for one second. I have to ask Mary something." Makena said she would hold. Jonathan held his hand over the phone while he asked Mary, "Isaac is out but will be back soon. Do you want to tell Makena the news? Maybe after you talk with her, Isaac will be back. She said he'll be back soon."

"Okay, yeah, let me talk with her."

"Hey, Makena, Mary wants to talk with you for a minute."

"Oh, sure. Thanks."

"Hi there! How are you guys?"

"Hi, Mary! We're all good. What's happening with you!"

"Well, we just returned from a quick visit with Jonathan's parents and his sister, Julie, and her two kids."

"Oh? Is everything alright with them?"

"Yes, they are very excited about something we went to tell them, and now we want to tell you all!"

"Oh, please! What is it?"

"I'm expecting! Due in late May next year!"

"Oh, my God! What great news! You guys have been trying for so long. I've kept you in my prayers! I am so happy for you, Jonathan, and Nick! What did Nick say when he found out?"

"He found out when we had pizza for dinner tonight, just before visiting Jonathan's family. He was blushing with joy. He's very excited about being a big brother, like Taylor!"

"Did he say whether he wants a brother or a sister?"

"No, but we were considering several names on the way home tonight. Got plenty of time to figure that out!"

"Yes. I'm glad you won't have to go through the summer months. That was tough for me toward the end with Ava."

"How is that sweet girl doing?"

"Oh, she loves kindergarten! Oh, Isaac just came in."

"Okay, I'll get Jonathan."

"Okay, stay in touch."

"I will!" Jonathan took the phone. "Jonathan, I'll give the phone to Isaac, but first . . . congratulations . . . a baby on the way!"

"Hi, Makena! Yes, finally! Thanks!" She said goodbye and handed the phone to Isaac.

Isaac, overhearing his wife, said, "Jonathan, I just heard the news! Congratulations, man! That's great to hear. Uh, Makena just handed me a note. Due in May! You guys have a preference, boy or girl?"

"We'll be happy either way; we just want a healthy baby. Thanks. Hey, there's another reason for the call today. Nick said he had talked with Taylor about fly fishing and that we hadn't taken them last year. They're eager to go. Are you and Taylor up for going the Saturday after Thanksgiving?"

"I think that's open. Let me just check with Makena and . . . hang on. Uh, she's nodding her head, so I guess, yeah, that sounds good."

"Okay. Great! I have extra rods and reels for the boys. They won't have waders like us, but we can find plenty of access areas to the streams where they can fish from the banks. We can assist them if they hook some trout. I mean, not if, but when they hook one! They'll be excited with the way trout fight!"

"I look forward to it; I can't wait. Let's touch base a few days before for any final preparation."

"Okay. We might want to go to the park the night before to pick up some night crawlers. We can use a trick my dad taught me to catch the worms. Remember how much the trout loved them last year?"

"I do! This will be a whole new experience for the boys. I'll call you on Friday, after Thanksgiving, right after I get home from the pharmacy. Sound good?"

"Sounds good. Talk with you then. Bye for now."

"And congratulations again!" They hung up. The fathers immediately told their sons they would all go fly fishing and that they would go to the park on Friday night to search for worms. He forgot that Nick wanted to talk with Taylor.

Nick said, "Dad, I wanted to talk with Taylor, remember?"

"Oh, sorry, son. Why don't you give him a call tomorrow? It's getting late, and I need to make a few more calls tonight about our good news." Jonathan did not sense the urgency that Nick felt internally to talk with Taylor. He picked up his phone directory to look up the first of several friends' phone numbers. Nick was upset but didn't say anything more to his father.

Taylor was also frustrated because executing Nick's plan was taking way too long. When he called Nick earlier, there was no answer. Now that his parents had called to tell them about the new baby, he still had had no chance to talk with Nick. He could feel the despair overcoming him, contributing to another restless night of weird dreams. *Waiting! Waiting! I hate waiting!*

Nick's attention turned to the coming week. It would be a short school week due to the Thanksgiving holiday. But thoughts of days off from school, Thanksgiving, and fly fishing made his evening a little brighter. Then, as he thought further, he wondered, *Why do we need worms if we're going fly fishing? Why do they call it fly fishing anyway? Worms don't fly!*

He walked up to his father, immersed in a newspaper article. "Dad?"

Jonathan slowly turned his head toward Nick as he finished reading the last few words of a sentence in the article. "Yes, son."

"Why do we need worms if it's called fly fishing? Don't we need flies? You showed me some fake flies when you and Mr. Washington went fishing for trout."

Jonathan completely forgot he was reading the business section of the paper. His love of fly fishing could easily overtake his mind, no matter what subject competed with it.

"I wondered when you would ask that question. It's a good question. Many people who go fly fishing use other things to catch trout, like worms, grubs, and insects. Trout like a variety of food depending on what's available in different seasons, like spring, fall, or winter, on hot and cold days, whether it's raining or not, and many other conditions."

He also said, "A long time ago, when men first fished for trout, they used live and artificial flies as primary bait to attract trout. Some would float on top of the water; others could be used under the water's surface. The whole strategy is to make the fly look as natural as possible to attract the trout. Trout are very smart, and there is always something new to learn about fishing for trout. But, over many years, anglers—those people who fish—adapted using other natural baits, like worms, grubs, and insects."

He had Nick's full attention as he became absorbed in this tutorial. "My father, your grandfather, taught me a lot about fly fishing, but he said he could never learn everything in his lifetime, so just keep learning. He doesn't fly fish anymore because of his severe arthritis, but he's always excited to hear about my fishing, and he'd love to hear about your experience. The more you learn and practice, the better you will do. I will pass on anything I have learned, and maybe someday, you can do the same for your children. It's like a special tradition."

Nick said he couldn't wait to go and thanked his father. Just as Jonathan was about to return to his newspaper again, Nick said, "Dad, I have to ask you something else." Jonathan was a patient man. He put the newspaper down, realizing he might not return to it anytime soon.

"Nick, I sense something is bothering you. What is it?"

"Uh, well, you know, we're learning about the Civil War and slavery and all that stuff in history class. And remember when we talked about the Martin Luther King Jr. speech he gave and the civil rights movement and fight for justice, equality . . . " He hesitated.

"Yes, I remember. What about it?" Suddenly, Nick, who was so sure he knew how to handle the issue, couldn't come up with the right way to ask the question he and Taylor wanted answers about.

He said, "Well, this is weird, but what if Black people could have White parents, and if White people could have Black parents? Wouldn't that help everyone feel more equal and get along with each other?"

He realized he had asked the question the wrong way. It was not the question he and Taylor agreed to ask. They wanted to ask if having Black and White parents was possible. But as he thought about it, it was actually a better question. It assumed that this situation could happen, and if so, wouldn't that make people feel more equal, get along better, and be more like one family? It suddenly didn't sound like a crazy question out of the blue. It was putting deductive reasoning to the test. He was tapping into Aristotle, the father of logic, who established foundations for "if-then" reasoning.

Jonathan sat up, more attentive, and had to think for a second, more like a minute. "Son, that's a good thought. They probably would get along better now that I think about it. Where does this come from? Are you talking about this in school?"

"No, no. I was just thinking about it. It's weird."

"Did you mention this to anyone else? Taylor, maybe?" Nick didn't want to lie; he only had a few little white lies in his portfolio, but this didn't seem to fit that category for him. He needed a quick out.

"Dad, I have to go to the bathroom!" Jonathan watched him run off like he wouldn't make it in time. He sensed there was much more to this than Nick's, "I was just thinking about it." Jonathan eventually returned to his business news, and Nick snuck off to his bedroom after the bathroom visit and an unnecessary toilet flush. Mary was getting tired after spending the last hour looking over a spare bedroom and imagining how it might look several months from now.

Chapter 58

It Was Near a White Lie

Jonathan thought about calling Isaac regarding Nick's question and finding out if Taylor had asked anything similar. He suspected that the curiosity could have come from both boys. He didn't think Nick would ask a question as he did on the subject of Black and White people with different racial parents on his own, or simply out of thin air.

However, as he reflected carefully, he recalled that Nick occasionally came to him for a conversation that only a father and a son might share. He didn't want to break that trust and compromise his relationship with his son by revealing something sensitive to Nick, only to have it shared with someone else. He spoke with Mary about it, and she agreed with his decision not to call Isaac. She felt that over time, the real source of the question might unfold without undue interference.

The weekend was coming to an end, and it was Sunday evening, with no communication between Nick and Taylor. Taylor's frustration grew, especially after revisiting his dream, which made him restless and fidgety. His anxiety interfered with his ability to focus on his schoolwork. Isaac and Makena noticed his abnormal behavior and queried him.

Makena said, "Taylor, you seem upset about something. Is anything wrong? Are you okay?"

"No. Nothing's wrong." His usual smile was gone, his face reflected stress, he avoided eye contact, and his voice cracked—perhaps a sign of a young boy maturing through puberty. But Makena knew her son well, especially that the voice cracking was not due to hormonal changes. She probed further.

"You don't sound like nothing is wrong. Is there something you want to talk to your father about, instead of me?" She thought this was the age when a son would rather talk to a man, even if he loved and trusted his mother.

"I, uh . . . I just couldn't sleep last night. I'm just tired."

"Were you waking up from dreams, or something bothering you in your dreams?"

Taylor, like Nick, had a threshold for lies. His white lie list was short, but he didn't want to deceive his mother. Unlike Nick, he didn't think of running off to the bathroom, so he quickly concocted a simple answer. It was near a white lie, but not quite there. He said, "Yeah, it was some dreams, but I can't remember them all. I'm okay, Mom." According to the quick-thinking ability of a young man named Taylor Washington, this was more true than untrue. This seemed to dissuade any further questions from his mother. He was proud of himself, even if only for a moment.

Sensing something remained off, she didn't want to push it further and simply said, "Okay. Please come to me or talk to Dad if anything bothers you." After additional thought, she said, "In a few days, we'll celebrate Thanksgiving with Grandma and Grandpa, your aunt, uncle, and cousins, and you'll go trout fishing for the first time!" A smile broke through as Taylor embraced his mother's change of subjects.

"I will, Mom." He gave her a hug, which was akin to dotting any i's and crossing any t's on that conversation. He quietly went to his room to read some books and comics. Makena pondered whether to alert Isaac to her conversation with Taylor, but that fleeting thought was replaced by seeing her list of to-dos in preparation for their trip to New Jersey to celebrate Thanksgiving with Isaac's family at his brother's house.

Nick was also anxious after a long weekend. However, a surge of eustress came from his conclusion that the question he asked his father was less likely to compromise the closely held secret discussion between him and Taylor. He was excited as he looked forward to seeing Taylor at school on Monday morning. He was determined to make this coming week a good one. It would be tough to beat a short school week, Thanksgiving with extended family, and fly fishing!

It was a time right smack in the midst of what would become a memorable decade of revolution and change across politics, music, and society in America. It was a tumultuous period of distinct characteristics in the country's history, marked by turbulence, violence, and also a certain colorfulness. There were memorable moments, national crises, cultural and social evolutions, the emerging generation gap, and divisiveness. There were flower children, civil rights movements, pop fashion, anti-war protests, and the space race.

On the political scene, Lyndon B. Johnson won the presidential election earlier in the month, securing his position for a full four-year term. He had focused his campaign on promoting his vision for a "Great Society" that addressed social issues such as poverty, education, health care, and civil rights. He highlighted the importance of the Civil Rights Act of 1964, which he signed earlier that year, and a push for further legislation to combat racial inequality.

Johnson realized that one of the biggest failures of the civil rights movement was in addressing poverty and economic discrimination. Despite laws that were passed, there was still widespread discrimination in employment and housing. Businesses owned by people of color were still denied access to markets, financing, and capital.

The voter registration efforts led by civil rights activists in Alabama began organizing as early as 1963. Still, despite the passage of the Civil Rights Act of 1964, local officials in Selma obstructed Black citizens from registering to vote, using tactics such as literacy tests and intimidation. This provided a basis for further violent conflicts in the future.

Technologically, the United States was in high gear with the Gemini program. Having launched its first uncrewed flight, Gemini 1, on April 8, 1964, it began testing critical technologies that would lead to spacewalks and orbital docking. The first crewed mission was scheduled for the first quarter of 1965, supporting plans for the Apollo moon landings. These efforts supported space exploration and had broader applications in defense and communications.

The war in Vietnam continued to slowly shift in character, transitioning from a majority of advisory roles to more operations on the ground. The North Vietnamese continually increased their support for insurgency in South Vietnam, creating political chaos, protests, and competition for power.

The baby boomer generation was coming of age. Their rebellious actions influenced the surge of music, fashion, and attitudes that challenged traditional norms. The women's liberation movement, sparked by the publication of Betty Friedan's *The Feminine Mystique* in 1963, was gaining momentum.

And, the most important thing on the minds of Nick and Taylor, with the definition of a dynamic decade unfolding, was that *we need answers about this dream thing!*

Chapter 59

"I Hate Waiting!"

Taylor waited for Nick at the school entrance on Monday morning. They had ten minutes before class started to cram in all the details they couldn't talk about over the weekend. Both boys were anxious, but in different ways.

Taylor said, "What happened? I called you on Friday when my parents went shopping for food. There was no answer, and when they came home, my father woke me up. I fell asleep, and I felt him shake my arm. He asked me who Uncle Tom was, and that I was saying 'Uncle Tom' in my sleep."

"What did you say?"

"I told him I didn't remember anything, but I did. I was dreamin' about Uncle Tom from the book. Did you talk to your father? Did you ask him if Black people could have White parents, and White people could have Black parents?"

"Yeah. I was gonna talk with you. My parents said they would call your parents to tell them that my mom will have a baby next May. I told my dad I wanted to talk with you after he finished talking with your parents, but he hung up. He forgot. First, my dad called and was on the phone. Then he gave the phone to my mom, and she was talking with your mom. Then my dad got back on the phone and talked with your dad about the baby and fly fishing after Thanksgiving. It just went on and on. When he hung up, I reminded him that I wanted to talk with you, but he said it was getting too late and that I should call the next day. I wanted to tell you that with all the news about my Mom having a baby and going to my grandma and grandpa's apartment. There was no time to talk with my dad until very late on Friday after we got back from seeing my grandparents, and after he told me about fly fishing, what my grandpa taught him, all that stuff."

"So what did your father say? Did you ask him the question?"

Nick was ready to tell Taylor how the question had come out and how much better he felt about it when the warning bell sounded, alerting everyone to get to class. The boys looked at one another, Taylor with more frustration on his face, and they darted down the hall to get seated at the last moment. Taylor would have to wait a little longer. *Waiting! Waiting! I hate waiting!*

Taylor couldn't concentrate in class. His mind was locked in the question that had no answer (yet). Sweeney didn't notice Taylor was a million miles away, but Nick was keenly aware that his buddy was not really in class. He worried about him and was anxious to get to lunch break to share the news that he knew would make Taylor feel a little better, at least. He knew that Taylor's dream was taking a toll on him. He didn't completely realize how much of a toll it took. He recalled something his father said. "We can never walk in their shoes." He knew one thing for sure. He would stand by his friend no matter what.

By the end of the lunch break, Taylor did feel better. After listening to Nick about how he posed the question to his father and the answer he got back, he smiled for the first time in a while. He asked, "He really said that was a good question? That Black and White people would get along better?"

Nick said, "Yeah, he said that's a good question . . . or a good thought; I can't remember, but he wondered if we were talking about it in school or if I told you about it."

Taylor's worried look returned. "What did you say?"

"I just told him it was something weird that I was thinking about. Then I told him I had to go to the bathroom, so we didn't talk about it after that. I went to my room after I went to the bathroom."

Taylor consumed this update with guarded interest. It was not as bad as he expected. When class resumed, Taylor's concentration gradually shifted from the big question and the not-so-bad answer to focus on Sweeney's teaching. He hoped the rest of the week would progress along a positive path.

Tuesday was a good day at school with no problems from the night before. He did his homework, watched television, and read before bed. He slept well, and a half-day at school on Wednesday flew by. Everyone wondered why they even had school on Wednesday before Thanksgiving. *Why don't we get Wednesday and Friday off with the holiday?* It made sense to everyone except the New York State and the local educational administrators. They made the rules.

On the way home, Nick and Taylor didn't talk much about anything other than meeting after Thanksgiving to go to Westchester County to fish for trout. Taylor said he wanted to find worms with Nick and his father next Friday evening. Taylor said, "See ya Friday!"

Nick responded, "Happy turkey day! I like drumsticks. I always get one of the drumsticks! And my two cousins and I play rock-paper-scissors to figure out which two of us will pull on the wishbone. Sometimes I get my wish; sometimes I don't."

Taylor quickly added, "Yeah, I like the drumstick too, but I don't have to play anyone for it. I always get one!"

Nick quickly considered telling Taylor he hoped he would win and that he would make a wish to figure out the answer to his dream question, but he decided to remain silent. Taylor was in a good mood, and Nick wanted him to stay that way.

Instead, he said, "Our whole family, my parents, Grandma and Grandpa, my aunt Julie and her kids, and my aunt Kathleen decided that my mom and dad would make a wish since Mom was gonna have a baby. I asked them what they might wish for, but they said it's a secret. It might not come true if they told anyone. They always say that." Taylor had no comment. He didn't want to hear anything about any secrets.

As the temperature dropped, they each proceeded to their homes. The forecast for the next few days was for the lower fifties and clear skies, perfect for Thanksgiving and fly fishing for trout.

Families usually rise early on Thanksgiving to finalize any preparations they need before the big meal celebration. Jonathan's sister-in-law, her two teenagers, and his sister, Kathleen, had arrived at William and Sarah Greene's apartment the night before to help the elderly couple prepare the Thanksgiving meal, and for Jonathan, Mary, and Nick's arrival, scheduled for 2 p.m.

Isaac and his family left their apartment at noon to drive to his brother's house in New Jersey. Traffic was terrible, as usual, but they arrived in the early afternoon and planned to stay until early evening. Isaac's older brother, Kenneth, and his wife, Samira, usually host Thanksgiving and Christmas. Their house could comfortably accommodate everyone, including the senior Washingtons, Darnell, and Sadie.

It was a time for the families to catch up with everyone, especially the grandkids, who looked like they had grown a foot taller since the grandparents last saw them just a few months earlier. William and Sarah were amazed at how Nick had filled out with budding muscles and a long crop of thick, light hair. They noticed his voice changing and expressed excitement about attending his elementary school graduation next summer.

Nick told them he was looking forward to graduating and attending high school, but didn't know where he might go. He wanted to discuss high school with his cousins, Mikey and Jenny. Mikey was a senior, and his sister was a junior. Nick also said he hoped he and his friend, Taylor, would attend the same high school.

Nick's grandfather, William, had followed Nick's growing relationship with Taylor since the two boys met in first grade. He occasionally talked with his son, Jonathan, when he heard that Nick had befriended a Black student, and some of his prejudices surfaced. He was "old-school" with his discriminatory remarks and attitudes. He held on to traditional stereotypes and biases, which reflected the influence of William Greene's parents and their extended families, who had established a foundation of racial discrimination that was carried forward. His comments would draw everyone's attention.

Jonathan realized that his father came from a close-knit family that treated outsiders, and especially Blacks, with distaste. This was a common societal behavior that infiltrated many families and helped to perpetuate racial discrimination and all its ill effects. He explained the relationship with Taylor's family, its merits, and no downsides.

Gradually, over time, Jonathan would meticulously convince his father, in addition to Sarah's constant scolding of William for his racist language, that he needed to change. William adjusted to the idea of a harmonious community among Black people, especially as he recognized the importance Taylor held for his grandson and how the Washington family maintained close ties with his son's family.

It took time, but his attitude and behavior changed. His hurtful rhetoric diminished, resulting in much better family get-togethers. There were enough other problems in the world to complain about.

The family held hands and said grace before they enjoyed a fabulous meal. Grandma and Grandpa loved the interaction with their grandchildren, who showed respect for their elders as they were taught. They had fun together, telling stories, playing games, and discussing the future for their grandkids, as well as the future for their parents and grandparents, and the future of the country. They were in the present, which was always fleeting, moving faster than desired, but they did their best to enjoy it and plan for the best to come. Their Thanksgiving holiday was everything they had hoped for.

Kenneth, Samira, and their son, Kenneth Jr., happily greeted Isaac, his family, and the men's parents, Darnell and Sadie, who lived about thirty minutes away in a city on the Jersey shore. They were also eager to catch up with all the family news, especially with Taylor and Ava, who they claimed are "growing like weeds."

From the 1940s to the present, Darnell and Sadie occasionally experienced racial discrimination when they faced barriers in accessing public spaces, including beaches and restaurants. The Public Trust Doctrine was the legal measure that established the government's responsibility to manage natural and cultural resources for the benefit of the public. These resources often include navigable waters, shorelines, and submerged lands.

Despite the doctrine, Darnell and Sadie were victims of discriminatory fees and restrictions that disproportionately affected Black communities. However, since the passage of the Civil Rights Act of 1964, conditions on the Jersey shore and in the North had generally improved.

Isaac kept his parents informed of his meetings with Dr. James Reed from NYU and other members of his Black discussion group. Darnell's grandfather was a slave who, after the Emancipation Proclamation, moved to the North to escape the horrible memories of the South. Darnell would tell stories, passed down from his father, of his grandfather's journey, fraught with challenges of hostility and limited resources upon arrival. The former slave settled in the rural areas where he and others could establish churches, schools, and mutual aid societies.

Thanksgiving was always a memorable holiday for the Washingtons as it allowed them to express their sincere gratefulness for the freedom to build independent lives despite systemic racism and often limited opportunities. Darnell and Sadie felt very blessed and were especially proud of their sons, Isaac and Kenneth, both pharmacists. Their hopes were high for Taylor and Ava's future, and for the generations of their family to follow. They said grace before dinner in the most solemn manner.

As the family held hands, Darnell led the family in prayer. "Let us take a moment to give thanks. We are grateful for this food, those who prepared it, and the love of our family. Our God, we thank You for Your grace and provision. May this meal nourish us and strengthen our bond of unity. And may the Washington family, present and future, enjoy a life of justice and equality. Amen."

"Amen," was the family's unified response. Darnell closely followed the civil rights movement and was hopeful that the efforts, especially the March on Washington and Martin Luther King Jr.'s speech, would continue to influence change in America. The family settled into their meal and joyful conversation. Taylor's quiet and calm demeanor, with a distant gaze, indicated he was focused inward due to his grandfather's reference to the civil rights movement goals of justice and equality. But only for a moment when he heard his mother.

"Taylor, would you like this drumstick?" He shook his head up and down as the family laughed. They knew his answer would always be, "Yes!"

Chapter 60

THE REVEAL

"**W**orms! Worms! Look at all these worms!" Taylor and Nick shouted as they held their flashlights focused on the ground. Isaac called Jonathan on Friday evening after their families had enjoyed the Thanksgiving holiday. Nick's parents had completed the ceremonial wishbone event, keeping their wishes a secret. In a novel version of spin-the-bottle, the Washington family had selected Taylor and his grandfather to make a wish. Taylor had won but would not reveal his wish after everyone asked him what it was.

The fishing team arranged to meet shortly after dusk on Friday at a designated location in Prospect Park to gather a few dozen worms. The nightcrawlers were long, smooth worms that could grow up to 8 or 10 inches. Their bodies were covered in slimy mucus, aiding their movement. They are nocturnal and only emerge from their burrows at night to feed on organic matter, such as decaying leaves.

Jonathan told the boys they needed to act fast to grab the worms because they could quickly retreat into their deep burrows when threatened. The worms' size and movements make them popular bait, and trout love them. The men and the boys managed to catch enough for the next day's fishing contest: *Who can catch the biggest trout?*

Nick and his father arose at 5:30 a.m. and planned to pick up Isaac and Taylor at 6 for the drive north of Manhattan. They hoped to arrive there between 7:30 and 8 a.m. On Saturdays, city traffic was usually light, allowing them to arrive within this window. The morning was cool, but it was forecast to warm up with clear skies. They met, packed the car with all their fishing gear, lunch, and a cooler with some ice to keep any trout they caught fresh for the ride home. Having reviewed his checklist, Jonathan stated, "Okay, guys. We have everything. Let's go catch some trout!"

They had planned to arrive near the Kensico Reservoir, and the towns of Pleasantville and Chappaqua, where Jonathan knew of several excellent trout fishing streams. The reservoir had some large lake trout, but for an initial indoctrination, the streams and their smaller trout would be best for the boys. The streams attracted many anglers, but the landscape and winding nature of the streams allowed them to spread without interference. Nothing is worse for a trout fisherman than to have someone else crowd your space. Trout fishing, in part, is to avoid crowds. It's a time for seclusion, remoteness, and a lack of social action, unless it's with your friends and family.

They arrived as planned and parked near one stream at a clearing with picnic tables. It remained chilly as the men drank coffee from a thermos, and the boys had chocolate milk. They all consumed the breakfast sandwiches Isaac had prepared as they observed the gentle flow of the inviting stream. A gentle breeze aided the sway of the trees, contributing to the serene atmosphere. They could benefit just by sitting there and doing nothing else, but . . . they came to fish!

Jonathan and Isaac donned their waders and boots, and the boys watched every detail leading to setting up their fly rods and reels. Nick said, "How do I put this worm on the hook? It's huge!" Jonathan explained that they are too big for the hook and the trout sometimes, so he showed them how to cut a worm to a smaller size, then thread it onto the hook with a small length trailing. Nick said, "Oh, yuck!"

"Yeah, it's pretty gross, but it's what trout consider a gourmet meal! Okay, you guys, give it a try!" Nick and Taylor squeamishly handled the giant worms and used their pocketknives to trim them down to eatin' size. Once their gear was ready and they had all the necessary fishing supplies and implements, and they were about to embark on a trail that paralleled the stream, Nick said, "Dad, I have to pee!"

Taylor jumped in, "Me too!"

Jonathan and Isaac laughed. Isaac said, "Okay, boys, there's the bathroom," as he pointed to a tree.

Taylor and Nick looked in that direction and simultaneously said, "Where?"

"Behind that tree! You're in the wilderness, boys . . . have to adapt!" They both ran behind the tree and did their thing. When they returned, Isaac asked, "You guys ready? The trout are calling us!" They stepped into the cool, quiet forest where the sun dipped through the trees, creating patterns on the ground. The scent of earth filled their nostrils as they listened to the sound of crystal clear, flowing water cascading over rocks, creating eddies and pools that Jonathan pointed out were good hiding places for trout.

Taylor asked, "Why do the trout want to hide? Hide from what?"

As they continued to walk on the soft carpet of pine needles and moss, occasionally over a fallen log, they could hear birds chirping overhead and the rustle of leaves, hinting at a nearby squirrel or even a deer. Jonathan and Isaac both began to answer when Jonathan said, "Isaac, please go ahead. You answer."

Isaac said, "Well, here's what I learned from Mr. Greene. Trout hide for several reasons. One, they use shadows of underwater rocks, vegetation, and deep pools to avoid birds, bigger fish, and sometimes other animals that prey on them. I also learned that they are sensitive to water temperature and look for cooler water, such as shaded areas. They try to blend in with their surroundings and find slower moving water to conserve energy. How'd I do, Jonathan?"

"I could not have said it any better!"

They found the trail opening to a quiet spot where the stream widened into a pool, shaded by nearby overhanging trees that were not low enough to interfere with novice line casting. The surface was calm, a perfect spot to teach the boys to roll-cast their fishing line. Just then, they heard the splash of water as a trout rose to the surface and grabbed an insect flying a few inches above the water. "Holy cow! I saw that," said Nick. "Did you see that?" Taylor had just missed seeing it, but he heard the splash and saw the circular effect it created in the pool.

Jonathan said, "Well, now we know trout are in there. Let's hope they want worms as much as dry flies! The first thing we'll do is teach you how to roll-cast your fishing line. There are different ways to cast, but today we'll use one technique that is not too hard to learn." The boys were all ears. They wanted that trout that just jumped!

Jonathan was about to demonstrate the cast when they heard some rustling nearby. It was three White men who approached their area from the trail. Jonathan and Isaac looked up and said, "Good morning!" Jonathan added, "Nice day for trout fishing!"

The three men did not immediately reply as they stared at the group, especially Isaac and Taylor. They were older men who probably thought someone was encroaching on their fishing territory, or they may have harbored some prevalent prejudices, even in these remote areas, during a time of rising civil rights achievements. Jonathan sensed trouble but quickly said to the men, "I know there are some great spots up ahead on the trail. I've been there many times and always caught trout. Good luck today! I hope you all do well!"

The men did not say a word. They simply continued their walk. If they thought about creating a scene, it quickly vanished. Hearing Jonathan's well wishes, and more likely the fact that they came here today to fish rather than get involved in a crisis, caused them to disappear.

After they were out of sight, Jonathan and Isaac looked at each other briefly before Jonathan said, "Okay, back to our lesson for today!" He demonstrated the maneuver by letting out a little length of fly line in the water in front of him. He said, "Now watch, boys. You bring the rod tip up slowly to right behind you to the one o'clock position and form a curve behind you called the 'D-loop,' because it takes the shape of a 'D.' Now watch what I do. Push the rod tip forward smoothly, then stop hard at the ten o'clock position. See how the energy from snapping the rod forward sends the line and the worm out there?"

He demonstrated again, then asked each boy to spread apart and try the cast. They attempted it, but the line remained stuck behind them. Jonathan said, "Don't get frustrated, boys. This happens to everyone. It happened to me, your father, too, Taylor, and just about everyone I know who learned how to roll cast." After a few more tries, the boys improved enough to get the worm in trout territory. After ten minutes and a little impatience, Taylor's strike indicator whipped off through the water.

"Dad, I got one! I got one!" Isaac rushed over to help Taylor with the proper technique to keep the fly line taut and slowly bring the trout into his net. Nick was watching anxiously. It wasn't long before he got a similar hit on his fly line. Jonathan helped him catch his first trout. The boys were ecstatic. Jonathan and Isaac took out their Kodak Instamatic cameras to capture the moments.

After the lessons and success, the men told the boys to continue fishing. They would proceed a little further upstream using their waders, but would remain within visual and audible distance from the boys. As demonstrated by their fathers, Nick and Taylor had threaded a line through the trout's mouths and gills and attached the lines to a tree branch, keeping the trout alive and fresh in the cool water. Over the next hour, they each added a couple more trout to the stringer. They could hear the hoots and shouts from their fathers, who were also doing well.

The day was off to a great start as the warmer temperature crept in. After a couple of hours trying new locations, the trout were biting less, so they decided to break for lunch. They returned to the parking area and picnic table to find it was occupied by the same three men they had encountered earlier. Jonathan was annoyed since there was a vacant table near the car that the men drove to the site. He couldn't help himself as he said, "Hi guys. Hope you had success this morning." They remained quiet as they swallowed their beer and subs.

"Is something wrong with the picnic table right next to your car?" He was trying to be as sarcastic as possible while attempting to make it a legitimate offer for a confrontation.

They smirked, slouched at the table with their beer bellies protruding under the table. One of them said, "Nothin' wrong with it. We wanted to use this one. You got a problem?"

Jonathan walked over to them and said in a calm voice, "Gentlemen, and I'm not so sure I should call you gentlemen, but of all the men who I have met during my years fly fishing, I have always found them to be kind, courteous, friendly, and respectful of other people's space. You can sit wherever you want, but I will remember this day as the day I met you earlier and wished you all good luck fishing, and you still turned out to be morons."

The guy who spoke earlier stood up, almost falling over, and said, "Who the hell . . . " Both Isaac and Jonathan walked up to him, inches from his face. They stood there, looked the jerk in the eye, and held up their hands. The others looked on as their stupid, fearless leader fell back onto the bench. He could only see two very physically fit younger men standing over him.

"C'mon, boys. I don't like the company here." They gathered their mess, went to their car, and drove off after a few minutes.

Jonathan said to Isaac and the boys, "Sorry for that. I just couldn't contain myself. What idiots. I suppose we'll face this every once in a while. But, hey, they're gone now, let's enjoy the rest of the day."

Isaac touched Jonathan's shoulder and whispered, "Thank you, man. I appreciate it. I know their behavior was meant for me and Taylor."

Jonathan said, "Well, if it was meant for you and Taylor, then it was also meant for me and Nick. We stand together." Isaac smiled, and they all had lunch, telling quick stories of their morning catches. So far, Isaac caught the biggest trout, a fifteen-inch rainbow. Nick recalled what his father told him about standing together, and he had just witnessed it in action.

They returned to the stream at a different location. The boys, satisfied now with nourishment, were eager to return to see if they could catch the biggest fish. They all caught more trout with an adequate supply of worms, but Isaac's trout kept the record for the day. They had a cooler filled with enough trout for both families for a while. They planned some for dinner the next night and would have more in the freezer for later meals.

To follow a tradition Jonathan's father had kept, they packed up their gear around 3:30 p.m. and drove to one of Jonathan's favorite drugstores for a treat. They stopped at Katz's Pharmacy in White Plains, a beloved local spot where residents could enjoy an ice cream soda, milkshake, or other treat at the counter or a cozy booth. Jonathan usually sat at the counter, but with the four of them, it was a better arrangement at a booth.

Taylor and Nick ordered root beer floats and Oreo cookies, while Jonathan and Isaac opted for milkshakes and apple pie. They were tired from being outdoors, breathing in fresh air, walking through the woods, and pulling in fighting trout. The boys were amazed by how strong even the smallest trout were. Their arms were sore! Jonathan recalled spending a day fishing with his father and suspected the boys would do what he did on the drive home—fall asleep from exhaustion!

The ice cream drinks and desserts arrived at their isolated booth at one end of the drugstore. Only a few other customers were seated at the counter and in one other booth. Nick and Taylor split the Oreo cookies between them and sipped their sodas. Taylor separated the chocolate wafer cookies from the sweet, creamy vanilla filling sandwiched between them. He said, "I love to lick the white filling first, then eat the chocolate part." Nick just put a whole cookie in his mouth and tried to say something, but it came out mumbled. The four laughed loud enough for everyone in the store to hear them.

Nick finally swallowed his cookie, sipped some root beer float, and said, "Taylor, Oreos remind me of us. We are Black and White, and we are good friends. The cookie is like black and white cookies that came together to be friends." Taylor looked at him and processed that thought. He smiled, looked at his father, and had a quick but fleeting image of Black and White kids holding hands.

"Yeah. I never thought of that. I like that. It's like two Black kids holding a White kid's hand." Nick's focus intensified as he thought of the secrets Taylor shared with him about his dream. The men laughed at this seemingly isolated analogy. Taylor's mind got the wheels turning faster. He asked, "What if we had two white cookies with chocolate in between? Like two White kids holding a Black kid's hand, or hugging him?" Their booth went silent as they pondered this unexpected question.

Nick was showing signs of nervousness as the cookie conversation deepened. Isaac was the first to respond. "I think that's a great idea. I had so many Oreo cookies and never thought of that. I don't know what we would call it."

Jonathan said, "Look, guys, nothing will ever replace the Oreo cookie, not even close."

Nick observed that the conversation was light and warm, producing chuckles and smiles, which diminished his concern. He wanted to add to the fun. He said, "We could call it the opposite of Oreos, like 'Soero' or 'Seros.' " No one liked those names, so they tossed around a few more, like "Backward Oreo," "Milkshake Sandwich," and "White Delight." They all decided they needed to think about that for a while. But Nick said, "Anyway, every time I see an Oreo cookie now, I'm gonna think about Black and White kids holding hands, hugging, and being friends. No racial discrimination."

That got the attention of Jonathan, Isaac, and Taylor. Jonathan asked, "You mean like we saw today when those three men sat at 'our picnic table,' and who acted unfriendly?"

"Yeah. That and all the other times we saw people act stupid." The conversation sparked Isaac's attention as it reminded him of some of the things Taylor would say in his sleep; some of which Isaac had observed but had never fully discussed with Taylor. He tried to change the subject casually.

Isaac said, "You know. Today was as close to a perfect day as possible, if it had not been for those three jerks. We just put them behind us and remember all the good from today. I think we'll all dream better tonight." He meant to say, "Sleep better tonight," but the word "dream" was a slip of the tongue.

Jonathan asked, "Why? Is someone having bad dreams?" It was an innocent question that he realized immediately was none of his business. Taylor got very fidgety and broke into a slight sweat, which Isaac noticed, and Nick also reacted with noticeable discomfort.

Isaac said, "What's up, boys? Obviously, something upset you both right now." Jonathan agreed. Nick and Taylor just looked at one another, searching for an escape plan that didn't materialize. They were quiet. Isaac insisted, "Okay, you two are either upset or worried about something. You can tell us. It's okay."

The boys stopped eating their Oreos and sipping their floats. Taylor spoke first. "I been havin' these dreams for a long time."

Jonathan was quick to step in. "Look, Taylor. We'd understand that you only want to tell your dad if this is private. Nick and me, we'd understand. You don't have to say anything here if you don't want to." He looked around to ensure no one was listening to their conversation.

Isaac expressed his appreciation for Jonathan's sensitivity, but Taylor said, "No, it's okay. Nick knows all about it. I told him everything that's been in my dreams all along." The men were all ears as they suspected it would be a bad dream. Taylor took the next few minutes to relate the events from his dream from the beginning—hearing Martin Luther King Jr.'s words, "I have a dream today," which took him to a place he couldn't describe, but he didn't elaborate on the context.

He explained that he had occasional replays of his dream over the course of a few months, and that he kept it to himself, not even telling Nick. He said the civil rights movement leader energized him. He told them that he observed a White boy and a Black girl from the upper class in his school walking holding hands, and that it reminded him of Martin Luther King Jr.'s words about Black and White children holding hands, and that later Nick told him he saw the couple kissing.

Taylor monopolized Jonathan and Isaac's attention. They held their gaze, their focus captivated. He said he asked himself if the Black and White couple holding hands and kissing resulted from the civil rights movement or the speech. He continued with clips of his dream, which contained visions and words from *To Kill a Mockingbird*, and about the guilty verdict for Tom Robinson, about the voices that called out his name, "Taylor, Taylor," about White brothers and sisters sitting at the table together, and that he thought, "Martin Luther King Jr. talking to me."

He then mentioned the shocking part of the dream, when he suddenly felt that Nick's parents were his parents, and that his parents were Nick's parents. He didn't feel comfortable with that weird segment. He said he wanted to tell Nick, but didn't let him know until later, when they all went to Greenwich Village. He told them the dream was so real that he had to run to the bathroom and look in the mirror to make sure he was still Black. There was a moment of soft laughter, quickly followed by undivided attention.

Taylor concluded by relating many of the dream elements that continue to add depth and realism, and that he thought of a paradox: something could be simple—like the friendship between him and Nick—yet be so complex because of racial discrimination, violence, and bombings. He mentioned that he talked with his father about people respecting one another and asked why it was difficult, and how his father had given him the example of weeds that grow over time, and how racial hate was like weeds.

Taylor took a deep breath and paused for a long time. Everyone was quiet for a few seconds, which felt like minutes. Jonathan asked, "Nick, did the question you asked me the other day have anything to do with Taylor's dream?" This made both boys nervous because it leaned into the most sensitive part of Taylor's dream, but it was unavoidable at this point.

Nick said, "Yeah, but my question came out wrong. The question was supposed to be, 'Can Black people have White parents and White people have Black parents?' But I was nervous, and the question came out, 'What if Black people could have White parents and if White people could have Black parents, wouldn't that make everyone feel more equal and get along?' "

Isaac was curious now. He looked at Jonathan and asked, "What did you say?"

Jonathan said, "I had to think about it for a moment, but then said that they would probably get along better. I had to ask where the question came from, whether it was something discussed in school or between Nick and Taylor, but I couldn't remember hearing an answer. I thought about calling you, but, as an afterthought, I didn't want Nick to think our private conversation could be shared with anyone else."

Nick said, "I finally told Taylor how my question came out and how Dad answered me."

Taylor said, "Yeah, and I felt better how Nick asked the question because I was worried about what anyone would think of my dream about having each other's parents, that I was weird or crazy."

Jonathan looked at Taylor and said, "Taylor, any parent, Black or White, including me, would be proud to have you as their son!" Taylor's composure changed from visibly tense to relaxed, and a huge smile formed.

Isaac added, "Nick, that goes for me, too! You would make any parent proud!"

The boys let out a massive sigh of relief. Months of tension, questions, and uncertainties had kept them on edge, often causing daydreaming, anxiety, and lack of sleep. Taylor added one more element that was deeply rooted in his soul. "I feel like the voices—Martin Luther King Jr.'s, and others, like Uncle Tom from the book, *Uncle Tom's Cabin*—told me I had to do something, something to help the civil rights movement, eliminate racial discrimination, and fight for justice and equality. But I don't know what I can do. I can't find ways to do what they did."

Isaac said, "Ah, that's what you were dreaming when I heard you calling out for Uncle Tom the other day when we came home from the grocery store."

"Yeah, he was calling out to me, too!"

Isaac said, "You never know, Taylor. You might be able to do something very important if you put your mind to it."

At this point, the men and the boys had been at the drugstore for an hour and needed to drive back to Brooklyn. They saw four Oreo cookies left on a plate. Jonathan said, "We can't leave those Oreo cookies here. They mean so much to us now that we've discussed what they represent." Each took a cookie, a symbol they will recognize from this day forward, representing their relationship. They were close before, but the black and white cookie meant something much more—a stronger bond, perhaps something sweet. *Physically and mentally exhausted, Nick and Taylor fell asleep on the way home.*

Chapter 61

THE HAUNTING DIMINISHED

The weight of the world was off Taylor's shoulders. The week of Thanksgiving ended in an enjoyable trout fishing experience, despite the brief encounters with unsportsmanlike jerks. He and Nick witnessed how opposition to any hint of racial discrimination could be implemented. The drugstore visit represented a tradition passed on that celebrated catching trout for the first time for him and his best friend, but more importantly, for the opportunity to unload the anxiety that had built up over many months. He was assured of personal support from Jonathan, Nick, and his father. It allowed him to continue searching for answers to his dream, rather than dreading it.

Any future inner voice, "Taylor, Taylor Washington," would represent a calling of encouragement, not a haunting. It would enable Taylor to use his dream as a catalyst for seeking the answer to how he may help the civil rights movement's goals of justice and equality. Furthermore, there was no longer any need to withhold his dream or any new developments. He had several trusted ears at the ready. The week contained a holiday with family and an outing with friends, contributing to Taylor's peace of mind, which he desperately needed. He was a new kid full of confidence, appreciation, and contentment. It was a booster shot of renewed perception.

Before they went to work Monday morning, Jonathan and Isaac dropped off their rolls of 126 film cartridges from their Instamatic cameras. They were eager to see the images that captured their sons' expressions of joy and the trout they had caught. They expected the photos to be ready in a few days. Their wives were happy to hear about their day in nature and the details from the drugstore.

Isaac and Jonathan agreed not to bother telling them about the only "cloud" in an otherwise perfect day, and they assured the boys that it was unnecessary to tell their mothers and spoil the happiness they were experiencing. *What was done was done, and handled perfectly!*

Nick and Taylor held their hands out to show their friends at school how big the trout they had caught were. They inherited the fishermen's tendency to tell tales using the knack for dramatic embellishment. They exaggerated the size by a factor of two. The photos would provide the exact measurements! But for right now, their trout were "legendary!"

The next few weeks led into Christmas break, with plans for more family celebrations and holiday activities, including trips to the city. Taylor tried very hard to think of something other than his dream as he got into bed each night, not because he wanted to avoid anything troubling, but merely as a change, to focus on other things. The dream emerged several times despite his attempts, and the calling continued. Only now, Taylor subconsciously embraced the visions and the words as confirmation and encouragement, as new words were added. The words, "Your family and best friend are with you. They believe in you and trust you," were a welcome addition.

Taylor did not wake up in sweat or become tense as before. His dream enabled him to relax and achieve a sense of calm. It was a boost of confidence that wrapped his mind in reassurance. His body felt light without exertion, and emotionally, he was content, hopeful, and motivated, which refreshed him with new energy and inspiration. The positive episodes prompted him to have another talk with his father.

Makena and Isaac tucked Ava into her bed. Her mother promised she would read a story to her. Isaac kissed his daughter goodnight, left her bedroom, and sat to watch some TV after finishing a crossword puzzle. Taylor approached his father.

"Dad, I wanted to talk more with you about my dream."

He placed the puzzle on the coffee table and said, "Sure, is everything alright?"

"Oh, yeah. It's all good, Dad. I had a few more dreams, but they were not bothering me anymore. They were good dreams, not making me worry so much."

"I am glad to hear that! So, is there anything new?"

"Mrs. Sweeney told us that sometime during the next few months, she's gonna give us a science project that will be worth a lot of points for our grade, you know, with tests and class participation, all that stuff."

"Okay, that sounds interesting, but what does that have to do with your dream?"

"Oh, yeah. I was getting to that!" Taylor laughed. He said, "Well, my dream still tells me that Black kids have White parents and White kids have Black parents. It's really strong . . . sounds real . . . convincing (he searched for the right word). So, I was thinking of doing a project that would be connected with that somehow."

Isaac was perplexed as he could not think of any way to approach Taylor's intent. He remained pensive and quiet for a while. Taylor asked him, "Do you think that's a good idea? Do you think I can do that?"

Isaac said, "I can't think of a project that could relate to that, but let me think about it. I don't think that can happen. It is weird, like you said, but I'm no expert. I know medicine because I'm a pharmacist, but I don't know about how . . . uh . . . how genealogy and race could cause any way for that to happen. Let me think about it, okay?" He was concerned that he would come up short in helping his son. At the same time, he wanted to continue to encourage Taylor's yearning to demonstrate his science project, even if the concept (and reality) only existed in his son's dream.

Taylor was content for now. He had piqued his father's interest, who offered to check and get back to him. He knew he had time to develop his project because it had not yet been assigned. His father's mention of genealogy and race caught his interest, and he decided to look it up in his father's *World Book Encyclopedia*. It contained sections on genetics and human biology. He considered asking his parents to take him to the Brooklyn Public Library near Prospect Park for more information. He was excited that it might be possible to do the project he wanted.

His interest in contributing to the civil rights movement, to move Black and White people, all God's children, toward equality and justice as one family, could be a possible outcome of a successful science project, was a young Black boy's dream. *If only that could be true!* Martin Luther King Jr. did a lot for the civil rights movement. *Why can't I?* But Taylor's father did not know how it could be possible, *but he said he would think about it!* For Taylor, this was a small step of progress.

After the holiday break, Sweeney's eighth-grade class got busy with intensive studies and numerous creative endeavors in addition to the science project. Preparing for high school was a mix of anticipation and responsibility, and she wanted to ensure that her students would be ready in every way possible: academically, socially, and culturally.

She focused her teaching on reviewing foundational subjects, such as English, mathematics, history, and science, to ensure her students' readiness for high school. She suggested visiting high schools or attending orientations that would provide an overview of the layout, rules, and expectations, as well as meeting with older siblings, friends, or neighbors who are already at the school. She encouraged her students to consider joining clubs, sports teams, or participating in the band to emphasize the importance of extracurricular activities.

She also connected with the parents to advise them to actively instruct their children on their responsibilities and encourage hard work to prepare them for their academic and social transition.

After a couple of weeks of searching his brain to help Taylor with his science project, Isaac realized he needed to conduct some research himself or find someone who could guide him in the right direction to assist his son. He thought of some connections he still had at the Long Island University Pharmacy in Brooklyn. Still, he felt they would be too compartmentalized to provide insight into the connection between genealogy and race. He thought of Dr. James Reed, his Black history professor friend at NYU, and wondered if he might be able to recommend some sources with his extensive knowledge of history.

He called the university, identified himself as a friend of Dr. Reed, and asked if he was available for a quick conversation. After a short wait, the receptionist told Isaac that the history department representative had informed her that Dr. Reed had left for a conference at Howard University in Washington, DC, and would not return until mid-January. He asked if she could convey a note to Dr.

Reed that he had called and to please call him when he returned. He emphasized it was nothing urgent, but it had to do with a science project for his son. She said she would try to contact him.

To his surprise, Dr. Reed called Isaac that evening. "Isaac, James Reed. I understand you called. It was something about a science project for your son. How have you been, the family? How can I help you?"

"Hi, Dr. Reed. I didn't expect to hear from you so soon. I heard you were at a conference until mid-January, and I hope I am not interfering with that."

"No, not at all. We are preparing for the conference here at Howard. I am busy during the day and have some social engagements in the evenings, but I'm free tonight. Everything okay?"

"Yes, we are all fine. Thank you. I appreciate you calling me right away."

"Absolutely! I understand your son, Taylor, needs help with a science project. How can I help you?" Isaac did not want to uncover the whole story of what led to the project. That would take some time and compromise the trust established among the Washingtons and the Greenes.

"Well, it's a bit wild, and I didn't know anyone else to turn to for any information."

"A bit wild, huh? I can't wait to hear it!"

"He wants to do a science project focusing on genealogy and race. But the wild part is that he wants to show any connection to . . . are you ready for this . . . how Black children can have White parents and vice versa." There was silence. "Hello, Dr. Reed, are you still there?"

"Yes, I'm here. It is remarkable that a boy his age wants to explore that genetic possibility. How did he think of that?"

Isaac answered as simply as he could, without all the details. "I think he just had a dream, and then told me about it. He said his teacher planned to assign a science project that her students would present later in the year. He'll attend high school next year, so he wanted to make his project special."

"That's very impressive. I'll be glad to help. I'm no expert on genealogy, but I can do some checking for you. NYU has a medical department affiliated with Bellevue Hospital Medical College. However, genealogy is a field that I believe is more commonly associated with historical and cultural studies than with medical research. That being said, genetics is gaining prominence in medical research, especially in understanding hereditary diseases and traits."

"Wow! You said you were no expert, but you know a lot!"

"Well, thank you, but I can also check here at Howard University. As one of the leading institutions for Black intellectuals and activists, and a center for civil rights, Black history, and cultural identity, they may be able to help, or at least point us in the right direction. I also have good connections with Morehouse College and Spelman College in Atlanta, Tuskegee Institute in Alabama, and Lincoln University in Pennsylvania."

"Dr. Reed, I was hoping you wouldn't have to spend too much time on this. You are a busy man, I am certain."

"Isaac, don't worry about that. Your son's science project interests me, and I want to help. I can also check other resources focusing on genealogy in its historical and cultural departments. The University of Chicago explores themes of migration, family structures, and cultural heritage that intersect with genealogy. Harvard and the University of California, Berkeley, have similar departments. Perhaps one of the most renowned institutions, Brigham Young University in Utah, is one of the leaders in genealogical studies."

"Wow! Now I know you're an expert, even though your focus is Black history!"

Dr. Reed laughed. "I think Taylor's science project might make us all smarter. Who knows? When do you need me to call you back?"

"Sir, Taylor told me he would need to begin gathering information in about a month for the project. He also asked me if we could go to the Brooklyn Public Library, so I'll take him there soon. My sincere thanks for your offer to help."

"Okay. Give me a couple of weeks. I need to finish here at Howard, and I'll make some phone calls when I return to New York. Take care, Isaac. Regards to your family." They said goodbye. Taylor now had a pharmacist and a well-known Black history professor to aid the young scientist in his search for data for his wild project.

Chapter 62

DNA

saac told his son that Dr. Reed would call him back in a few weeks with sources that might help him with his science project. Taylor had no solid methodology yet for his loosely defined idea. He didn't want it to come across as crazy or stupid, but his dream kept driving him toward some approach that would make sense. It was a complicated thought process, but he was encouraged to hear that his father's friend, a university professor, would be willing to help. To Taylor, that meant that perhaps his science project idea was not so crazy after all.

Nick was still struggling to come up with an idea for his science project. Unlike in the past, when Nick and Taylor often teamed up to present class-assigned projects, Sweeney insisted that her students research, prepare, and present projects independently, stressing the need to better position themselves for higher education requirements. Over the last few years, while Taylor's interest focused on biology and medicine, Nick drifted toward one of his favorite subjects, mathematics, and decided he wanted to match that with some engineering demonstration. He chose to assess some possibilities over the next few weeks.

The young anglers looked at the photos from their fly-fishing trip that their fathers had picked up. Each family had started a photo album that captured the boys' activities together and their rapid growth as they progressed through elementary school. Baseball games at Yankee Stadium, trips to the city and local parks, youth baseball at Prospect Park, and many other photos preserved happy memories. Still, those memories also reminded them of the unwelcome and unpleasant circumstances that had arisen. As much as the families focused on enjoying the photos, they could not completely erase the scars that remained. *Racial discrimination has a way of screwing up the best of times!*

The newest album section would hold the evidence from the boys' fishermen's tales that would prove their trout size exaggeration. They showed copies of the photos to their friends at school, who were amazed by the catch. However, they also stated to Nick and Taylor, "I thought you said the fish was this big," as they demonstrated by extending their arms and widening the space between their hands. All the kids laughed and wanted to know more about the experience.

Nick and Taylor provided them with the details, including Jonathan's tongue-lashing of the three shady characters they encountered. The boys were proud of how their fathers reacted, first with kindness and then by pointing out the unacceptable behavior of the dimwits. They had to tell someone the *fishing story with a twist.*

By comparison, the middle of the decade was characterized by progress and setbacks for the nation. President Johnson's January State of the Union Address outlined his Great Society program to eliminate poverty, reduce racial inequality, and improve education and healthcare, including Medicare and Medicaid. Later in the month, NASA launched the unmanned Gemini 2 spacecraft from Cape Kennedy using a two-stage, liquid-fueled Titan II GLV rocket, which was adapted explicitly for future human spaceflight. Enhanced safety features included redundant systems and the ability to detect malfunctions, ensuring safety and reliability.

In mid-April, Gordon Moore published a paper in *Electronics* magazine introducing Moore's Law. The law predicted the exponential growth of transistors on microchips, revolutionizing the field of computing.

From a cultural perspective, the movie industry advanced, with *The Sound of Music* being one of the highest-grossing films and winning multiple Academy Awards. The mod fashion style continued to be popular, with bold patterns, miniskirts, and go-go boots.

Military planning for Operation Rolling Thunder was underway to sustain bombing against the North Vietnamese, aimed at weakening their ability to support the Viet Cong troops in the South. The launch occurred on March 2, 1965, with the end goal of pressuring the enemy forces into negotiations. Shortly after the launch, the first American combat troops landed in Da Nang, South Vietnam, shifting from advisory roles to boots on the ground. The growing number of Americans represented a more profound commitment to the war.

Black Muslim minister and human rights activist, Malcolm X, was assassinated on February 21, 1965, during a rally at the Audubon Theatre and Ballroom in Washington Heights in Manhattan, by the Nation of Islam, an organization he left the year before. While the civil rights movement fought against racial discrimination, Malcolm X advocated a complete separation of Blacks from Whites, stating that Whites were "a race of devils."

His remarks, describing the assassination of President John F. Kennedy as a case of "chickens coming home to roost," implied he was killed due to America's history of global and domestic aggression. This sparked outrage from the leaders of the Nation of Islam and others who admired Kennedy. They instructed members to refrain from commenting on the assassination, but Malcolm X did not abide by the directive.

Setbacks in the civil rights movement continued mainly in the South. On March 7, 1965, nearly six hundred civil rights marchers walked from Selma to Montgomery, Alabama, to peacefully protest Black voter suppression. The local police and state troopers brutally attacked them as they crossed the Edmund Pettus Bridge. More than fifty people were hospitalized in what came to be known as "Bloody Sunday." The violence was seen nationwide on the evening news broadcast. After successfully fighting in court for their right to march, Martin Luther King Jr. and others led two more marches that finally reached Montgomery on March 25.

As Isaac watched the evening news on television, which featured King's march to the state capital, he called Taylor from the kitchen table, where he was working on his science project. Now that Isaac understood the context of Taylor's dreams and his motivation to do a science project connected with the dream and the goals of the civil rights leader, he knew his son would be interested in seeing the movement in action. "Taylor, quick! Come see this news on TV!"

Taylor ran to the TV room and sat next to his father. "Dad, what's goin' on?"

Isaac pointed out the news coverage by CBS News reporter Bill Plante, who walked alongside and interviewed Martin Luther King Jr. Plante asked him if all the activities in Selma over the past few weeks had come to fruition. King responded that the march from Selma and the culmination in Montgomery were the high points of the struggle in the state. Taylor was watching the event live. It reinforced the messages in his dream of equality and justice for all, and that his project would be relevant and have merit.

He had already completed a trip to the Brooklyn Public Library with his father earlier in the month and searched the encyclopedia for ideas, but struggled to formulate his project. However, that all changed when Dr. Reed called Isaac back after he had done some professional research. He told Isaac that when he shared Taylor's project with several colleagues, they were amazed that a young boy would even consider such a possibility.

However, they were also very willing to provide current genetics research that would be needed as a basis for any further studies, and stressed that Taylor could demonstrate this foundation of knowledge that could lead to specific parent-offspring dynamics across racial lines. Isaac started to get a headache when he heard this. *What has Taylor gotten us into?*

It seemed overwhelming. Dr. Reed sensed Isaac's tension and reassured him that he received great feedback on helping Taylor structure his project. Dr. Reed said, "Hey, a thirteen-year-old boy leveraging some of the best minds in genetic research and tapping into the emerging importance of DNA in genetic tracing? Your son is in a class of his own!"

Isaac's headache worsened. "D . . . N . . . A? What's that?"

"Not too many folks know much about it currently. It stands for deoxyribonucleic acid. It's a molecule that carries genetic information essential for the development, functioning, growth, and reproduction of all living organisms and viruses. I don't know the details. Let me tell you, I've learned a bit from the conversations I've had over the last few weeks. It's pretty fascinating! My colleagues say this is a whole new world opening up since the discovery of the DNA structure in 1953. The breakthrough revealed DNA as the molecule responsible for heredity, laying the foundation for genetic testing."

Isaac had a full-blown migraine by now. "Wow!"

"Yeah, wow! Sounds like this is right up Taylor's alley, don't you think? Can you imagine if he continues to express interest in this?"

"Dr. Reed, he's a smart, obedient kid who loves school and does all his homework. We look forward to preparing him for high school as he completes eighth grade. What you described sounds like it belongs in a research lab!"

"Isaac, I'm glad you brought that up. I'm firming up some contacts for you, lab researchers dedicated to genetics. My friends have already given them a heads-up!" They finished their call. Isaac could not thank Dr. Reed enough. Reed told him he would call him back in less than a week. Isaac had not yet told Taylor of his call with Dr. Reed. He did tell Makena, who developed a headache of her own.

Chapter 63

PROJECT: GENETIC EVOLUTION

Sweeney reminded her students that their science projects and presentations were due in early May and asked them to give her their project names, purpose statements, or scientific premises. To widen the choices, she had loosely defined science projects to encompass topics such as medicine, biology, chemistry, and engineering. She instructed them to describe the project's goal in terms of aims to investigate or achieve. She was elated to hear her students' enthusiasm and the variety of interests they had for the assignment.

One student selected a water purification experiment, showing methods of filtering water and describing the findings. Another student said he would show experiments he had done with plant growth and sunlight, using incandescent and fluorescent light sources. A female student reported that she chose to investigate the effects of different antiseptics on bacterial growth using petri dishes and a gelatinous substance called "agar."

It was Nick's turn to describe his project, which he said would need to be demonstrated outdoors. Everyone's eyebrows rose, including Sweeney's, as they wondered, *What could that be?* Nick was fascinated with the evolving news of space exploration and NASA's programs, and he worked with his father to gather information and define his project.

He said he would discuss the design and launch of small rockets using baking soda and compressed air, combining chemistry and engineering principles. Sweeney said, "Nick, that sounds very interesting! Let's hope for good weather!" Nick immediately frowned when he heard her and thought that if the weather was bad, he might be unable to present his project. She noticed his expression changed and said, "Don't worry, Nick. We'll pick a day that will be good for your rocket project." He went back to smiling.

"Taylor, how about you? What project have you chosen?"

By this time, Taylor had completed initial research with his father at the library and read through other reference books on genetics, genealogy, and race. He was dismayed by the lack of information supporting any premise for his project related to his dream. He didn't want to tell the class about his dream, as he now considered it a closely held secret among his family, Nick's family, Dr. Reed, and now two scientists. He had to present a credible hypothesis.

Dr. Reed had called Isaac with the lab research contacts he had received from interested colleagues he had spoken with earlier. He mentioned that he had personally spoken with two women who were deeply involved in genetics research. He explained that even though they worked in different facilities, they collaborated on their work. They were very interested in hearing Taylor's idea for a project.

Doctors Clair Cartwright and Zora Caldwell were scientists specializing in genetic research. Cartwright was affectionately known as "Cee Cee," and Caldwell as "Zee Cee." Once their colleagues learned they worked together, they initially used these closely sounding abbreviated names as a joke to confuse people, but the names stuck. Anytime someone mentioned Dr. Cartwright or Dr. Caldwell in a conversation, the response was, "Oh, you mean Cee Cee or Zee Cee?"

The women explained to Dr. Reed that genetics research was in its early stages, and studies were underway for genetics tracing focused on broader population genetics rather than specific parent-offspring dynamics across racial lines (where Taylor's dream pointed him). They further explained that studies explored genetic markers and inheritance patterns, but were limited by technology and societal issues of the time. Detailed studies that traced Black offspring from White parents or vice versa were not widely documented in any scientific literature.

They suggested a title for Taylor's project that would make sense given the current data but also capture the intent of his project and show potential for further research. The simple title of "Genetic Evolution" was basic enough for eighth-grade comprehension, but would allow Taylor to elaborate with elements of the project that could include all or some of the following: family tree analysis, genealogy and identity, genetic trait studies and disorders, DNA, and genetics and race.

After hearing from Dr. Reed, Isaac and Taylor were reenergized by the scientific community's level of information and interest. Taylor responded to his teacher. "My project is called 'Genetic Evolution.' " Eyebrows across the room rose again, as there was a low mixture of mumblings among the students. Sweeney asked Taylor to briefly describe the project.

He said, "I am excited about my project, and I want to tell you what I am learning about genetics, how it has been connected to race and ancestry over many years, and where it could go in the future." That was undetailed enough to get everyone's interest without disclosing that Taylor still had some learning to accomplish on the subject.

Sweeney heard the remainder of the students' projects and commented, "I can hardly wait to hear from all of you! Your projects sound amazing, and I know we will all learn something new from one another!"

Nick and Taylor took advantage of Sweeney's preparation of her students to proceed to high school by strengthening their study skills of time management, note-taking, and test preparation. They would graduate in a few months, which motivated them to search for a school they could attend together. The families independently searched for school options but were aware of the boys' intentions.

After visiting and gathering information from about seven schools, they narrowed the list down to three in Brooklyn and one in Queens. The Brooklyn schools included Brooklyn Technical High School, an all-boys school; Abraham Lincoln High School; and Erasmus Hall High School, all of which were within minutes of each other by subway. Thomas A. Edison Career and Technical Education High School was located in Jamaica, Queens, and a little farther away by subway.

Considering their son's interest in engineering, Jonathan and Mary favored Brooklyn Technical High School and the Edison School in Queens. Still, they emphasized to Nick that any of the schools on their list would provide a strong foundation for what he needed later in college.

Isaac and Makena had learned that genetics research wasn't a specific focus in high schools anywhere, and they weren't sure Taylor would continue to have such a profound interest in the subject. Like most things in a young teenager's life—fads, clothing, hairstyles, girlfriends, and more—interests could change at a moment's notice. So, the best they could hope for was to select a school with the best springboard for his general science orientation. Taylor often asked Nick where he wanted to go during this family process. It didn't help Taylor much when Nick responded, "What high school do you want to attend?" They were locked into a you-go-first dilemma.

Eventually, after long procrastination in both families and careful collaboration between Nick and Taylor, they reduced their list to Brooklyn Tech and Thomas Edison. Both boys had excellent foundations in science and engineering. The decision was on the horizon. Isaac and Makena found that the Black student population at Brooklyn Tech and Thomas Edison was small. However, they also discovered that the schools were experiencing a significant increase in student population due to substantial demographic shifts, which reflected the changing racial and ethnic composition of their surrounding neighborhoods. They could go either way. They left the decision to Taylor.

Isaac told Taylor he had heard from Dr. Reed again and that Dr. Cartwright and Dr. Caldwell would call them one evening during the week to talk for a few minutes. Taylor was excited to hear that and nervous at the same time. He said, "Dad, what if I can't understand them? They must be super smart! How can I do my project if I don't understand what they tell me?"

Isaac boosted his son's confidence: "Just ask them your questions, and I'm sure they will answer you so you can understand. They know that you're in eighth grade, and they have information about the goals for your project." Taylor seemed less stressed but still worried how the calls would go.

On April 14, at 7:00 p.m., Dr. Zora Caldwell called from the Cold Spring Harbor Laboratory (CSHL) on Long Island. She was a Black research scientist who focused on molecular biology and genetics under the mentorship of pioneering scientists James Watson and Barbara McClintock. Watson had co-discovered the double-helix structure of DNA with Francis Crick in 1953, and McClintock was renowned for her groundbreaking work on transposable elements, also known as "jumping genes," which she had discovered in corn.

Isaac answered the phone and heard, "Hello, Mr. Washington? I'm Zora Caldwell, calling to speak with your son, Taylor."

"Oh! Miss Caldwell, I mean Dr. Caldwell. Thank you for calling. Dr. Reed from NYU told me you would call and talk to my son. I really appreciate you taking the time to talk to me. Oh, and please call me Isaac."

"You're very welcome. Please call me Zora, or, as many people call me, 'Zee Cee.' I heard about Taylor's project and am excited to help him!" He asked her to hold while he got Taylor.

"Hello, this is Taylor."

"Hi there, Taylor! I understand you are a very ambitious student who wants to learn about genetics and present your science project in school!" She exuded the energy and enthusiasm that Taylor could feel, making him wonder how she had become so interested in genetics.

"Yes! I want to learn more about it because . . . (he hesitated on his words, but it just flowed out) . . . I want to know if Black people could have White parents, and White people could have Black parents." Isaac, who stood beside Taylor, could not believe Taylor said that. He thought it would be at a much more basic level and not jump right into the end goal of satisfying months of Taylor's dreams. He didn't interrupt.

"Taylor, Dr. Reed explained that you are interested in that. I think that's an excellent thought! We have a lot to learn about genetics and race, and we are doing extensive research here at the lab and working with others. I know that Dr. Cartwright will call you tomorrow evening. What I can tell you is that once we learn more about the elements that carry genetic information, what we call DNA, we'll be able to learn more about your question. I will help you with any information to make your 'Genetic Evolution' presentation successful."

"Okay, that sounds good. Thank you." Taylor asked a few questions that Dr. Caldwell answered in layman's terms so that Taylor could easily present his project elements in class. He now knew how to get the project moving. Isaac took the phone to thank her again and wish her success in her work.

Isaac said, "Wow, she was really helpful, wasn't she? I didn't think you would talk about what you dreamed, but it sounded like she answered you. What did she say?"

Taylor said he hadn't planned to say anything about his dream, but it just came out of his mouth, like he had no control. He explained her answer, and Isaac thought how appropriate it was and how thoughtful Dr. Caldwell was. They looked forward to hearing from Dr. Cartwright, Taylor and Isaac told Makena. She was proud of her son, who sought the expertise of others, and she mentally prepared for the future when her son would share his knowledge with someone just like him.

Dr. Clair Cartwright was a White research geneticist in her early fifties at Rockefeller University in Manhattan. Established in 1901 as the Rockefeller Institute for Medical Research, it was the first biomedical research institute in the United States. Dr. Cartwright was among an elite group renowned for its groundbreaking work in medical and biological sciences. Early achievements included pivotal discoveries in molecular biology, including the role of DNA in heredity. She collaborated regularly with the younger Dr. Caldwell.

"Cee Cee" identified herself to Isaac, and they had a similar exchange as with Isaac and Zee Cee the evening before. Taylor got on the phone and spoke with her. However, he did not bring up the parents of White and Black kids again. However, Dr. Cartwright did, having heard from both Dr. Reed and Caldwell regarding Taylor's interests. She gave Taylor a similar answer to Dr. Caldwell's and, after a short question-and-answer period, urged Taylor to follow his heart and his dreams. Taylor felt like he was already part of the research community and was eager to complete his school project.

The unanimous choice for the high school was Brooklyn Technical High School, located at 29 Fort Greene Place in Brooklyn, near the Brooklyn and Manhattan Bridges, and about six to seven miles from East New York. The Hoyt-Schermerhorn subway station was within a short walk of the school.

The schedule for science projects was determined by picking a number from a paper bag. Nick and Taylor's numbers were higher, indicating that they would present their projects after the students with lower numbers, giving them a little more time to prepare their presentations. Graduation was set for June 23, and their high school was determined. However, another significant event was on the horizon: a precious delivery by Mary Greene.

Chapter 64

MR. DNA

Sweeney's class members presented their science projects during the first week of May. It culminated many weeks of work, including trips to libraries and museums, and even consultation with some of the country's most prestigious intellectuals. Students learned to collect data that supported their defined objective and methodology, analyze it, and organize the results in a clear and presentable form, such as graphs, charts, or images. Sweeney emphasized the importance of these graded elements and students' summary statements. She encouraged them to practice their presentations at home with their parents.

The array of projects and presentations to the class demonstrated exploration and passion, self-confidence, and a sense of achievement among the students. Nick presented his project, beginning with a ten-minute discussion of interest in space exploration, current NASA programs, achievements, and the principles of rocket propulsion. He also mentioned Newton's Third Law of Motion ("For every action, there is an equal and opposite reaction"). The class then proceeded outside the school where students could observe the launch Nick had prepared. Fortunately, the weather cooperated. *He wouldn't need to scrub the mission.*

Taylor and another boy helped Nick carry the launch components, including the rocket assembly made from two-liter soda bottles with cardboard fins, which were mounted with duct tape. He also had baking soda and vinegar to provide chemical reactions that would propel the homemade rockets. Nick ensured everyone was safely away from the launch area. He donned a pair of goggles as an additional safety step. A small wooden crate served as the launch platform. He used his bicycle pump to pressurize the rocket and asked the class to count down from ten so that he could release it.

"Ten . . . nine . . . eight . . . . . . one!" Nick released two rockets, one after the other. The launch demonstration at Nick's own little Cape Canaveral went off without a hitch. They cleaned up the debris and returned to class, where Nick summarized his project with a few words about trajectory, height, and stability data that would be necessary in space exploration. He answered a few questions and received a round of applause. *Mission successful!*

The next day, Taylor's turn came. He dove into his project with energy and enthusiasm, mainly sparked by his parents, Dr. Reed's willingness to help, and the two women scientists who expressed their excitement for him. While his original question about Black and White parents of children of opposite colors sounded unusual at first, Doctors Cartwright and Caldwell offered Taylor a more plausible approach for his project based on current information and analysis.

Taylor began his presentation, "Genetic Evolution," with a question: "Did you know there is a molecule in you called DNA that holds information about where your ancestors lived thousands of years ago?" This caught everyone's attention, including Sweeney's. He told the class what he had learned about genetics from his research, particularly from experts who discover new information every day. He mentioned them by name and where they worked. He said they were nice and made him feel . . . he paused momentarily as he thought to say, "that my dreams weren't crazy." Instead, he said they made him think his project was important.

He used diagrams of DNA strands, images, and drawings of family trees to briefly describe the use of DNA in building the trees and uncovering ancestral origins, as well as how genetics reveals the shared origins of humanity. Flashes of humanity as "all God's children, Black and White, Jew and Gentile," caused him to pause again, briefly. But he took control and focused on his presentation. He stated that genetic research could challenge misconceptions about race as a biological concept and contribute to our understanding of identity, history, and diversity.

He summarized his project by saying, "I learned a lot from my project on genetics. It helps us understand where we came from and how we are all connected. If we continue to learn about genetics, we can trace our ancestry to uncover shared roots and see how similar we all are—whether Black, White, Asian, Latino, and so on. Understanding genetics can also help us solve problems like fighting diseases and improving health." Sweeney and her students gave Taylor a huge round of applause. He hadn't felt this good in months.

Graduation was around the corner. The science projects were the last major hurdle that required extraordinary effort. Sweeney did not want her students to think they could coast through the next few weeks, so she assigned a reasonable homework load to keep them honest.

At 4:00 p.m. on Sunday, May 23, with one month to go until graduation, Mary told Jonathan, "It's time! We need to go now!" She was having contractions. She had done everything possible to prepare for this day by caring for herself, with healthy nutrition, regular prenatal checkups, mild physical activity, and adequate rest. The baby's supplies were ready, and the decorated nursery contained a crib, changing table, small chest of drawers, and a rocking chair.

As Jonathan grabbed a prepared bag containing comfortable clothing, toiletries, identification documents, and other items for Mary, he grabbed her hand and said, "Let's go!" Mary took one last look at the nursery before leaving for the hospital. She realized one more thing was missing. *All we need now is the baby!*

Nick stayed home. At nearly fourteen, his parents trusted he could care for himself if they were out. His father planned to call him from the hospital to check on him and tell him about his new little brother or sister. Isaac had told Jonathan they would take Nick in if needed while Mary was at the hospital.

Jonathan carefully escorted Mary into the Kings County Medical Center, the same facility where Makena had delivered Ava. The hospital staff admitted Mary and took her to the maternity section. "Have a seat in the waiting area, Mr. Greene. Your wife is in good hands. Our doctors and nurses will ensure everything goes as well as possible. We'll keep you updated. We'll come for you when your wife delivers the baby."

Jonathan thought, *"As well as possible? What does that mean?"* Even though he had gone through this before, when Nick was born, he was nervous. He called his parents and Mary's family to notify them that he was at the hospital and would call them as soon as Mary gave birth to the new addition.

Little Lila Greene entered the world three hours later at 6.9 pounds and twenty inches. Her faint coos and delicate little whimpers, accompanied by yawns and a whispering exhale, provoked a sense of fragility and innocence. Mary held her close, her nose against Lila's skin to take in her newborn's delicate, warm, and comforting smell. The peace and tenderness of the moment caused all the pain and agony over the last few hours to disappear.

A nurse came out to be the first to congratulate Jonathan and direct him to Mary's room. He ran down the corridor, entered her room, and saw his wife cradling Lila in a cocoon of warmth and security. She said, "Honey, here is your daughter," as she delicately handed over the bundle that held soft, delicate features, a button nose, pinkish skin—their product of love.

He kissed his wife and then his daughter. He stared at Lila for what seemed an eternity before he asked Mary, "You did an incredible job! I love you! How are you feeling?"

"I feel like I just had a baby!" They laughed, but shortly after, Mary moaned and moved in her bed to find more comfort. After about an hour of bonding with their little girl, they handed the baby over to a nurse who completed the initial health checks that she had begun right after birth. Jonathan told Mary he would call the family and have his parents pick up Nick on their way to the hospital.

Jonathan's parents, William and Sarah, and Nick, arrived within thirty minutes with flowers and tiny teddy bears. Mary's parents, Edward and Susan Moore, lived in Connecticut and told Mary and Jonathan they would visit shortly after their grandchild's birth. Jonathan planned to call them later after he and Nick returned home.

Everyone wanted to hold the cocoon. Nick's grandparents told him to go first. He sat in a chair, and his father handed Lila over to him. Her sweetness completely enveloped Nick's attention. Holding his sister made him recall the time he first held Taylor's sister, Ava. "She's so tiny," he said, as he uncovered one of her arms and gently held her fingers in his hand. The grandparents were eager for their turn, and eventually, the gift was shared by all. No one had Nick's graduation on their mind, but that would soon change.

Graduation day, June 23, at PS 91 had arrived. The venue was the school's gym, decorated with a sign that read, "CONGRATULATIONS, CLASS OF 1965." Balloons were stretched across the entrances, and a photo booth had been set up. There was a display of pictures of the graduating class, showcasing their achievements and projects. Among them were diagrams of family trees and images of genetic markers like DNA, as well as the remnants of a rocket launch with the name "Nicholas Greene, Space Engineer," next to it.

Families, friends, and school staff were seated, and the ceremony began with opening remarks by Dr. Mary Carpenter. She welcomed everyone and spoke of the significance of the milestones and the students' achievements. She noted that she had witnessed the educational growth and maturity of the students through their years at PS 91 and was especially proud of all they represented.

The students began their procession to receive awards and certificates for their hard work. "Pomp and Circumstance" played as the young teens proudly approached the stage to be recognized individually, displaying their best semi-formal attire.

The children were lined up alphabetically, so Nick preceded Taylor. As Nick approached Sweeney to accept his diploma and awards for extracurricular achievements, his family yelled out his name, but what was most audible was his grandfather, William.

"Yeh, Nicky! Go Nicky! Nicky! Nicky! Nicky!" Everyone followed Grandpa Greene's chant. No one had ever called him Nicky. Only his grandfather called everyone that way. David became Davy, Tom became Tommy, Joe became Joey, William became Willie. His wife, Sarah, had called him Willie, and he had liked it, so he adopted the tradition from his wife early on.

Taylor approached the stage, and before he accepted his diploma and awards, his classmates chanted, "Mr. DNA! Mr. DNA!" His parents and grandparents were immensely proud of Taylor's influence on his classmates. This was unexpected yet understandable, given Taylor's passion for the subject.

After a few enlightening and heartwarming remarks from teachers who had taught these graduates, Dr. Carpenter delivered some closing remarks. She congratulated the students and their parents for their dedication to their children's education. She thanked her teachers and all others who contributed to the school's goals, maintenance, and safety. Jamal Brown smiled and nodded a "Thank you" to her. She pointed to some tables set up with refreshments and reminded everyone to take advantage of the photo booth.

As everyone thought this was the end of the ceremony, Dr. Carpenter said, "Oh, one more thing. We have a surprise for everyone that we hope will make this a more memorable day." *What could that be?*

"As many of you know, we had another surprise at PS 91 a while back. Miss Margaret Lopez, everyone here calls her 'Maggie,' was engaged to United States Marine Corps Sergeant Rafael Vargas. They are getting married this Saturday at St. Rita's Roman Catholic Church on Shepherd Avenue. One of your teachers, Miss Izzy Garcia, will be her matron of honor. You are all welcome to attend the ceremony scheduled for 11:30 a.m. Maggie and her fiancé hope that many of you whom she taught can be there. But she would like to take a photo with all of you here today. So, graduates, please come up to the stage for the photo and wish them many years of happiness."

Nick and Taylor rushed up. They were the first to arrive and stood on either side of Lopez. Taylor had asked Vargas if he could move so he could be next to her. Vargas smiled and said, "Of course!" They stood next to their first-grade teacher, holding her hand, and looking and smiling at her, now at eye level. She recalled how she had looked at them when they were much shorter, younger, and less mature. She recalled the instance outside at playtime when she was about to witness a fight between Black and White boys, but was relieved to see them shaking hands. She had been kept informed of their progress through PS 91. She couldn't be prouder.

Chapter 65

THE NEW GUYS ON THE BLOCK

Nick spent a significant amount of his summer months bonding with his little sister. He had heard about a similar experience from Taylor when Ava was born, and when visiting the Washingtons, he even had opportunities to hold Ava and feed her a bottle. But now he was creating and living his own beautiful stories, as Lila would wrap her tiny fingers around his thumb, and react to his gentle cuddles and voice. "Hi Lila. I'm your big brother," would always elicit Lila's pure smile, sparkling eyes, and a soft coo, confirming her awareness of the world around her.

Nick and Taylor felt a sense of freedom as they began a new chapter in their lives. It was a significant milestone, honing their skills in core academic subjects of mathematics, reading, writing, science, and history, and becoming more aware of world events, both good and bad. They embraced the rock 'n' roll explosion and the rise of folk music, adapted to the emerging styles of bell-bottoms and tie-dyed shirts. They attended parties where they did the Twist, the Mashed Potato, and the Watusi, and watched *American Bandstand*, which showcased these dances in action.

Nick's interest in engineering and space exploration prompted him to follow space race events and technology and visit the library. He recalled hearing about President Kennedy's statement about choosing to go to the moon and emphasized America's pioneering spirit. He borrowed a library book, *Exploration of the Moon* by Franklyn M. Branley.

Taylor's interest in genetics and genealogy grew exponentially. The confidence boost from his class science project prompted him to find books in the library that would build on his knowledge in these areas. He began with *The Principles of Heredity* by Laurence H. Snyder and *Before the Mayflower: A History of Black America* by Lerone Bennett Jr. This book provided a comprehensive history of African Americans, offering a broader context for understanding their heritage and identity.

Fuel was constantly added to the fire to keep the civil rights movement moving and Martin Luther King Jr.'s and Taylor's dreams active. King's march to Montgomery earlier in March had led to the passage in August of the Voting Rights Act of 1965, which outlawed discriminatory practices such as literacy tests and poll taxes that disenfranchised Black voters. Despite the legislation, discrimination persisted in various forms, especially in the South.

Blacks were intimidated and harassed, often facing threats, violence, or economic retaliation if they attempted to register to vote, particularly in rural areas of Mississippi, Alabama, and Georgia, where local officials often found loopholes in, or outright ignored, federal mandates. Poll workers used subtle tactics to discourage or disqualify Black voters by providing incorrect information about polling places or hours, and gerrymandering occurred where districts were redrawn to dilute Black voting power and influence. In the North, de facto segregation persisted, fueled by economic inequality and systemic racism.

As he learned bits and pieces of this news, either through his father or by catching a glimpse of TV news coverage—whether national or local—Taylor's dream would occasionally come back. The inequality and the injustice were paramount, and with the more recent development of his understanding of the importance of genetics, his dreams became more complex. He would hear a disorganized series of words and phrases—"All God's children," "Mr. DNA," "civil rights," "hold the hands of your little Black and White boys and girls," "slavery," "let freedom ring"—and there were visions of Black and White parents with offspring of different colors mixed in with the phrases. He had to process the added elements of his dream. He felt perplexed but determined at the same time.

His maturity—coupled with the encouragement and support from his family, professionals, teachers, and peers at PS 91—enabled him to be self-driven. He did not disclose any of the new developments of his dream. He was deeply entrenched in his interests in biology, genetics, and Black ancestry, and was determined to use his time at Brooklyn Tech to delve more deeply into these areas.

Taylor was an example of dynamics in action. He developed good study habits and knew how to research through libraries and visit knowledge centers. He would read the books he borrowed from the library, as well as others. He tapped into experts through his father's connections, adapted to cultural change, and remained cognizant of political ups and downs. He maintained his interest in recreational activities, such as baseball. He continued to nurture his friendships, especially with Nick, while also trying to determine his role in the civil rights movement. His dreams persisted in communicating to him that he did have a role.

Nick and Taylor's summer was jam-packed, and hardly a day passed when they weren't active playing, learning, or being big brothers. Their routine abruptly changed after the Labor Day holiday as they rode the subway together to begin their freshman year at Brooklyn Tech. They had visited the high school earlier in the year with their parents, but as they approached the technical school's towering stone façade and grand entrance, they felt a sense of excitement and responsibility. At the same time, their status as "elders" at PS 91 eroded when they immediately realized they were the new guys on the block.

Brooklyn Tech was renowned for its rigorous academic program, with math, science, and English as primary subjects. Nick and Taylor would share these classes. They needed to rise early, have breakfast, and take the subway to arrive in time for their first class, which started at 8:30 a.m. They were also in other classes together, but the boys gravitated to the particular interest they had developed earlier.

Nick could choose from a variety of Brooklyn Tech's specialized workshops, which offer hands-on training and set the school apart from other high schools. He was particularly interested in the drafting workshop, where the instructor stressed the importance of "precision as the backbone of engineering." Nick reflected on his rocket demonstration and thought, *"If I weren't precise, my rocket would have failed!"*

He also heard about the robotics club, which captured his interest—building and testing mechanical prototypes—*something that sounds like it might be needed on the moon!* He began to understand why he was groomed to become more independent as a student. There were choices to make—his choices!

During his previous vetting of potential high schools with his parents, Taylor knew that Brooklyn Tech did not offer dedicated courses in genetics, genealogy, or ancestry. However, he learned enough about the biology classes, the independent exploration resources available, and the extracurricular clubs and projects he was sure could build upon the basic knowledge he gained while at PS 91.

The biology course material covered the principles of genetics, including Mendelian inheritance, a concept established by Gregor Mendel in the nineteenth century, which refers to the patterns by which traits are passed from parents to offspring. Taylor thought, *"If this doesn't fit right into my dream, I don't know what does!"* He was excited to understand its key principles and their applications to humans. Darwin's theory of evolution might also include discussions on genetic variation and adaptation.

He had previously wandered through the school's library and noted they also had the book he borrowed from the Brooklyn Library, *The Principles of Heredity.* Community elders occasionally offered rich insights into their heritage and cultural identity at special oral presentations at the school. There were science clubs where Taylor could dive deeper into genetics and discuss scientific discoveries. He immediately thought of Doctors Cartwright and Caldwell and wondered if they would be interested in speaking at the school. *Maybe later. I need to get a good start here first.*

Taylor had choices, as did Nick. While they attended standard core classes, they drifted to their special interests and committed to maintaining their friendship. They enjoyed the sanctity of their high school for a new chapter in their lives, but that only went so far, as the struggle for civil rights continued and the Brooklyn environment around them added scars of inequality and injustice to the integrity of the city and the nation.

The period through the end of the year was tainted with episodes of racial discrimination and violence. Brooklyn neighborhoods organized activism to address housing discrimination, police brutality, and educational inequality. Brooklyn Tech and many other high schools were examples of low numbers of Black students. Marches and rallies advocated for better living conditions and equal opportunities. Brooklyn's role in the civil rights movement was part of a broader narrative of Northern cities grappling with systemic racism and the fight for justice.

The Brooklyn Congress of Racial Equality (CORE) focused on housing discrimination and school segregation, staging protests and sit-ins. Activists worked to expose discriminatory practices by landlords and real estate agents, advocating for fair housing laws. There were calls for police reform and accountability, spurred by tensions between the NYPD and Brooklyn's Black community.

Ironically, despite the limited number of Black students in the high school, student activism, inspired by the civil rights movement, established high schools as centers for change through protests, walkouts, and demands for better resources and treatment. They sought to end racial discrimination in their schools. As the new guys on the block, Nick and Taylor looked forward to a new beginning and a whole new world of information for their specific fascinations, but they could not avoid hearing about and witnessing the same old crap produced by a persistent wound that refused to heal.

Chapter 66

"Bang, Zoom! To the Moon, Nick, to the Moon!"

In the first two years of Nick's and Taylor's experiences at Brooklyn Tech, the period was a turning point in American history, with profound impacts on civil rights, war, politics, science, and technology. Each of these was deeply interconnected. President Johnson's decision to escalate US involvement in Vietnam was one of the most consequential political choices of the decade. US troops rose from 184,000 in 1965 to more than 400,000 in 1967. Growing opposition to the war led to widespread demonstrations, including student protests and draft resistance, eroding public trust in the government. This resulted in setbacks for the Democratic Party, as they lost seats in Congress because of growing dissatisfaction with President Johnson's handling of the Vietnam War and domestic unrest.

The war fueled civil rights activists and caused a convergence of the anti-war movement and the civil rights movement. African American leaders protested racial disparities in the draft and military service. They highlighted racial disparities where Black soldiers were disproportionately sent into combat roles while being denied full rights at home. Well-known figures such as Muhammad Ali refused induction into the US Armed Forces; he publicly argued that Vietnam wasn't his enemy, but that racial injustice in America was.

With a strengthening connection between the war protests and activism, Martin Luther King Jr. articulated his opposition to the war in a speech, "Beyond Vietnam: A Time to Break Silence," at Riverside Church in New York City on April 4, 1967. It was collaborative work with his close associate and friend, Vincent Harding, a native of

Harlem. King linked domestic and foreign policy and the need for a "revolution of values" in the country. He called for Americans to prioritize peace, social justice, and compassion over militarism and economic nationalism, and framed his condemnation of the war as morally wrong, saying that it violated the principles of nonviolence and caused immense suffering.

As much as Nick and Taylor would prefer to focus on their particular interests, Brooklyn Tech, like many other schools in the mid-to-late 1960s, was affected by the turbulence of politics, the war, civil rights activism, and social unrest. Teachers would cover current events in their social studies classes, including the Vietnam War and its impact on American society, as well as protests and the draft. However, given the school's technical focus, discussions included technical discussions such as military engineering and weaponry.

Because the civil rights movement was a significant force in New York City, Brooklyn Tech students were not isolated from its influence. Landmark events during the movement included the Voting Rights Act and urban protests against discrimination. The students became aware that the broader New York City student population engaged in anti-war demonstrations and participated in discussions on war and civil rights.

Despite the school-wide conversations and external influences from the war and its connection to the civil rights movement, Nick and Taylor focused on the subjects they liked and knew would best prepare them for college and beyond. They looked forward to meeting for lunch to tell each other about their most interesting classes and workshops.

They were often tempted to visit the local thriving food scene, just a five-minute walk from the school, which featured a variety of Italian and Jewish delis and sandwich shops serving huge heroes. They occasionally indulged in a crusty sub roll at Tony's Deli, slightly toasted and layered with slices of salami, capicola, mortadella, prosciutto, and mozzarella. They added shredded lettuce, ripe tomatoes, onions, hot peppers, and a drizzle of olive oil. If they weren't young teens burning energy every minute, they would be overweight by the end of the school year.

Brooklyn Tech had no tuition since it was in the public school system. However, due to a limited budget for subway fares and lunch, the boys needed to be frugal, so they used the school cafeteria most of the time.

Nick said, "We're talking about principles of flight, propulsion systems, and aerodynamics in our aerodynamics and mechanical engineering courses. It's awesome! Our teacher, Mr. Lefkowitz, is amazing! He's been talking about NASA's Gemini missions and the Apollo program. They studied the docking of space vehicles and how astronauts would walk in space. He said if we want to study engineering in college, we should get our hands dirty in the aeronautics shop and lab to get excellent experience there!"

"Wow! That's so cool! I'm really diggin' my biology class. I told my teacher, Mr. Fanning, about the project I presented at PS 91, and that everyone called me 'Mr. DNA.' He liked that and laughed. He said he was happy I was enjoying the genetics and DNA discussion. He called them the 'blueprints of life.' We'll learn about a new topic called messenger RNA (mRNA), which is responsible for carrying protein information from DNA to cells in the body. I can't wait to learn more about it!"

Nick took a deep breath and said, "I'm glad you are the one who likes this DNA, RNA stuff. It's too much for me to understand. After all, you're Mr. DNA!"

"Yeah, and I can see you goin' to the moon someday, or maybe even a planet. I saw a rerun of the Jackie Gleason *Honeymooners* show the other day. He said something that reminded me of you. It could apply to you."

"What was that!"

"Bang, zoom! To the moon, Nick, to the moon!" The boys laughed so hard they choked on their lunch, but recovered to laugh some more.

Nick talked more about getting involved in the robotics club and drafting workshop. He said that his teacher recommended some books that might interest the class: *Introduction to Space Flight*, by Francis J. Hale, which covered basic aerospace engineering concepts, and *Principles of Guided Missile Design*, by E. Arthur Bonney, Maurice J. Zucrow and Carl W. Besserer, which explored missile and spacecraft guidance systems. "He also said we might take a class trip to the Hayden Planetarium in the city. I went there a long time ago and remember how neat it was."

"Yeah! Yeah! I went there too with my dad one weekend. Our biology teacher gave us some good ideas for books, too. One was *The Genetic Code* by a guy named . . . uh . . . Asimov. Isaac Asimov. I remember it because he has the same first name as my dad. The book explains the role of DNA in heredity, like I talked about at PS 91.

"He also told us about some good scientific journals that are available in the school library. I like the science club. We can discuss all this there and hear everyone's ideas, and where to find more information. They couldn't believe it when I told them about Doctors Cartwright and Caldwell, and how they helped me. Whoa! We're gonna be late for math class!" The boys gulped down their drinks and headed to class.

They considered joining a sports team, either baseball or basketball, but decided to focus on their schoolwork during their freshman and sophomore years. On the way home on the subway, the discussion of Vietnam came up. They had just finished a social studies class, and the hot topic of the war was fresh in their minds. Taylor said, "You wanna hear what happened to my cousin Kenny?"

"What happened?"

"He's in college now, but the Army drafted him and told him he would need to go to Vietnam."

"Oh, is he there now?"

"No, he went to the Army recruiter and told them he forgot to notify them that he was in college. If you're in college, you could get . . . he called it something . . . uh . . . a draft deferment. He was able to postpone military service. Kenny, my Uncle Kenny, and Aunt Samira were very happy about that. Kenny has two more years to go in college. He wants to be a pharmacist like my uncle and my dad."

"Wow! I guess he's lucky he didn't have to leave college and be in the war!" Taylor just nodded. They continued their ride in a crowded subway car that slowly released its passengers as their ride got closer to their destination in East New York. Something had been on Nick's mind for a while, and he wanted to bring it up with Taylor.

"Taylor, I wanted to ask you something."

"Okay, what?"

"How do you like Brooklyn Tech?"

"I like it a lot."

"I mean, there are not many Black students there compared to White students."

"Yeah, I know. So what?"

"Well, do you ever feel you're not wanted there?"

"No, I like it there, and all the subjects are cool, and the teachers are good. Why are you askin' me that?"

"It's not anything in particular, but sometimes I notice some White kids doing things to Black students, and sometimes you."

"What things?"

"Just things. Like casual remarks about how their work is not as good as White kids' work, or just the way they interact with Black students, like staring at them in a certain way. It's discrimination in a subtle way. I'm unsure I can make it any clearer, but I notice it."

"Yeah. I notice it too."

"Doesn't it bother you?"

"Not really. I just ignore it and focus on my schoolwork."

"But, we're in high school now. Kids should be smarter and know that the civil rights movement is all about treating each other equally, not making Black kids feel uncomfortable or left out."

"Yeah, I totally agree with that. But I don't feel left out. Besides, if anyone here at Tech does anything to me because I'm Black, I know I'll be alright."

"What do you mean?"

"I'll be alright because I have you here to stand with me like you always do."

Nick said, "Right on! I can't walk in your shoes, but I can walk with you!"

Nick nodded, smiled, and put his hand out for Taylor to shake. Nothing in the world could break that bond. It was confirmation of their friendship and support—not that they ever needed it, but it was always welcomed. A Black woman sitting right behind them overheard their entire conversation, turned for a quick glance at the boys, turned back, and smiled. She thought, *"Now that's what it's all about!"*

Taylor was comforted knowing that Nick always had his back, and that he could trust him no matter what. Whether he realized it or not, he was a remarkably grounded and self-confident teenager. He was a product of his parents' influence, as well as the confirmation, encouragement, and inspiration he received from his former teachers, Doctors Reed, Cartwright, and Caldwell.

He had all this in his camp, but his ongoing dream was a distinctive source of undeniable strength and drive, a pillar of resilience.

Chapter 67

Orbital Trajectory Calculations; Mendelian Inheritance Studies

"Nick, I'm thinking of trying out for the basketball team. You interested?" Taylor's physique was changing rapidly, adding muscle to his seventy-inch frame, which was two inches taller than Nick's, and weighing 147 pounds. Nick was slightly stockier, weighing 143 pounds. They both considered baseball for this new school year, but had given basketball a slight tilt on the decision needle.

"I thought about it. The team last year had a mix of White and Black guys, but they are way taller than I am. I'm not sure I would make the team."

"We won't know unless we try out."

Nick said, "Uh, let me think about it." Taylor had experienced several times when he asked his parents about something he wanted to do or somewhere he wanted to go. When they said they would think about it, they occasionally would not get back to him, which was frustrating.

"I thought you already thought about it. If you put a decision off, you'll probably forget, and then it'll be too late."

Nick acquiesced. "Yeah, okay. I guess I could try out." A quick thought that Taylor might end up on the team without him, which would separate them to some degree, prompted a quick decision. But, *we won't know unless we try out . . . and he could be on the team without me!*

Nick's focus was not much on basketball. As a student interested in aerodynamics, aeronautics, and space exploration, he was immersed in courses of applied physics, mechanical engineering, drafting and technical drawing, electrical engineering, aerodynamics, and fluid mechanics. The necessary math courses for these studies included calculus, linear algebra, differential equations, geometry and trigonometry, statistics and probability, and numerical methods (for simulations and computational modeling).

The array of special engineering projects gripped Nick's attention as he considered what he might select for his assignment. Drafting projects, wind tunnel experiments, model aircraft designs, rocket propulsion studies, and spacecraft structural analysis were among the contenders. Brooklyn Tech was known for its hands-on technical education. He couldn't be happier surrounded by dedicated teachers and an environment that catered to his interests.

Because he enjoyed discussing the latest NASA missions, especially the Apollo program and the space race, his passion for aerospace often led him to dream about how he might contribute to space exploration. In his senior year, he narrowed his special project to model rocket design (a much more advanced design than he demonstrated at PS 91) and orbital mechanics calculations.

He chose to present "Nick's Orbital Trajectory Calculations," which would demand all his skill and knowledge of math (calculus, differential equations, and trigonometry), physics (Newtonian mechanics, gravity, and fluid dynamics), drafting, and technical drawing (precise schematics for spacecraft components and orbital paths). Nick used slide rules, mechanical calculators, and drafting tools to perform the orbital mechanics calculations manually. His project was well done, earning him an A grade for his technical accuracy, presentation, documentation, creativity, innovation, and hands-on execution.

Taylor's world of genetics, heredity, DNA, and his dream contributed to his choice of science project for his senior year. As a student interested in the exploration of his dream and answers to the deeper question of parents with offspring of a different color, he gave 100 percent effort in his biology studies (cell structure, heredity, and molecular biology), chemistry (understanding DNA and biochemical reactions), mathematics (statistics and probability in analyzing genetic inheritance patterns), and drafting (to document experimental results and genetic diagrams).

He enjoyed discussing early genetic research, inspired by James Watson and Francis Crick's groundbreaking discovery of the double-helix structure of DNA on February 28, 1953, at Cambridge University in England, and exploring concepts in genetic engineering. Rosalind Franklin's X-ray crystallography images significantly influenced their work, providing crucial evidence for DNA's twisted-ladder shape. She did not receive formal recognition at the time, and Watson, Crick, and Maurice Wilkins were awarded the Nobel Prize in Physiology or Medicine in 1963.

Taylor selected his project as "Mendelian Inheritance Studies," where he explained the tracking of dominant and recessive traits in families or local populations. He used Punnett squares, developed by Reginald C. Punnett in 1905 (diagrams used in genetics to predict the possible offspring genotypes based on the parents' genetic makeup). He demonstrated genetic probability for inherited traits, family pedigree charts that mapped traits across generations, statistical analysis that showed the ratios of dominant vs. recessive traits in a sample population, and microscopic observations of cells and chromosomes.

Months before the project, Taylor had contacted Doctors Cartwright and Caldwell again to share his ideas for his high school project. They were delighted to hear from him after these fast-moving years and advised him on the data to research and how to present the material. They both told Taylor they started experiments in gene manipulation, setting the stage for biotechnology advancements.

They asked him where he wanted to attend college, and after hearing about the choices he had applied to, they added their recommendations to help him continue his studies. He illustrated his project using charts, images, microscopes, slide rules, calculators, and drafting tools, and he received an excellent grade of A, consistent with the grades he received for most of his work in high school.

While Nick and Taylor attended Brooklyn Tech for their junior and senior years, American history was more dramatic than their first two years in every respect. There was no loss of essential topics to discuss in class. The era remained both turbulent and transformative.

In Vietnam, there were intense battles intended to wipe out the Viet Cong strongholds near Saigon. One such mission was Operation Cedar Falls, a large-scale, nineteen-day "search and destroy" effort that targeted the Iron Triangle northwest of the city. The attacks were launched in January 1967 and aimed at destroying enemy forces, infrastructure, and intelligence, and to deny the Viet Cong access to the area. Public sentiment shifted as images of burning villages, wounded soldiers, and protests fueled anti-war activism.

In late 1967, North Vietnamese forces actively prepared for large-scale surprise attacks against South Vietnamese and US military and civilian targets during the Lunar New Year (Tet) holiday in January 1968. The holiday was a traditional time of peace and truce. The offensive attacks involved more than one hundred cities and military bases across South Vietnam, including the US embassy in Saigon.

US confidence in the war effort was shaken, anti-war protests and demonstrations intensified, and public opinion of the war shifted. President Johnson announced he would not seek reelection in 1968, paving the way for Richard Nixon to win the presidency. The 1968 Democratic National Convention was marred by protests and police clashes fueled by deep divisions over the Vietnam War and civil rights. Nixon began his presidency focusing on ending the war and addressing domestic unrest. His policy of "Vietnamization" aimed to gradually withdraw US troops and transfer combat responsibilities to South Vietnamese forces.

During this period, science and technology had tremendous advancements and heartbreaking setbacks. Apollo 1 was a tragic accident during the space race, when a cabin fire occurred during a preflight test, which engulfed and killed three astronauts, Gus Grissom, Ed White, and Roger Chaffee. This forced NASA to overhaul spacecraft design, delaying the program for increased safety. Nick's instructor emphasized the importance of precise engineering as technological progress came with significant risks.

The Soviets also experienced disaster when, in 1967, Soyuz 1 cosmonaut Vladimir Komarov died when his spacecraft crashed due to parachute failure.

Apollo missions 7 and 8 in 1968 paved the way for the historic Apollo 11 moon landing on July 20, 1969. This fulfilled former

President Kennedy's 1961 goal of landing a crew on the moon and returning them safely to the Earth. Neil Armstrong and Buzz Aldrin became the first humans to walk on the lunar surface, with Armstrong's memorable words, "That's one small step for man, one giant leap for mankind," observed by more than six hundred million people globally.

Other notable achievements included the first human heart transplant in 1967 by Dr. Christiaan Barnard, as well as the groundwork for developing the first commercial computer networks, which paved the way for more extensive technologies. Color television broadcasts had become increasingly widespread, transforming the way people consume entertainment and media.

The civil rights movement represented advancements and recessions, during which progress faced backlash, often in response to political shifts and societal resistance.

In 1967, a case involving Richard Loving, a White man, and Mildred Loving, a Black woman of mixed African American and Native American ancestry, eventually reached the US Supreme Court, which unanimously ruled that Virginia's law violated the Equal Protection and Due Process Clauses of the Fourteenth Amendment.

They had married in Washington, DC, in 1958 and were arrested in their Virginia home due to a violation of the state's Racial Integrity Act of 1924, which prohibited interracial marriage. The Supreme Court decision effectively invalidated all remaining anti-miscegenation laws nationwide. It was a major victory for civil rights.

However, urban unrest in cities such as Detroit and Newark in 1967 highlighted the tensions and frustrations of Black communities facing systemic inequality. Efforts to address housing discrimination, where minorities were excluded from certain neighborhoods, gained momentum during 1966–67, with protests and advocacy pushing for federal intervention. President Johnson signed the Civil Rights Act of 1968, also known as the Fair Housing Act, which provided equal housing opportunity regardless of race, religion, or national origin.

Black voters in Greensboro, North Carolina, uncovered discriminatory practices in polling places, where they were turned away due to minor clerical errors or being asked to provide unnecessary proof of residency. Some states began removing names from voter rolls under the guise of maintaining accuracy, which affected Black voters who had recently registered. Local officials also strategically relocated polling stations to inconvenient or inaccessible areas to suppress turnout in Black communities.

Due to the growing frustration with the slow pace of civil rights reform, the Black Power movement emerged from a desire for more immediate action against racial injustice. It emphasized self-determination, racial pride, and economic empowerment, and that integration alone was not enough to achieve equality. Stokely Carmichael popularized the movement's name during the Meredith March Against Fear in Mississippi in 1966.

The movement was identified by several groups who played key roles: the Black Panther Party, which focused on community programs, self-defense, and political activism; the Student Nonviolent Coordinating Committee (SNCC), committed initially to nonviolent protests, but shifted toward Black Power; the Nation of Islam, though predating the movement, it influenced Black Power ideals with emphasis on Black self-sufficiency; and the Black Liberation Army represented armed resistance.

The movement encouraged Afrocentric identity in various forms, including Black-owned businesses, Afro hairstyles, African clothing, and Black studies in universities. While Taylor thought the Afro was "pretty neat," he maintained a clean-cut image that was prevalent among all the boys in school.

Much of the civil rights movement focused on the South, but Brooklyn had its share of racial tensions and activism. Communities such as Bedford-Stuyvesant organized to address housing discrimination, police brutality, and educational inequality. Marches and rallies advocated better living conditions. Key Brooklyn figures, such as Sonny Carson and Al Vann, worked to organize protests and advocate for Black empowerment.

The Brooklyn Congress of Racial Equality (CORE) focused on housing discrimination and school segregation issues by staging protests and sit-ins across the borough. The Bedford-Stuyvesant Restoration Project of 1967 was one of the first community initiatives led by local activists to improve living conditions, economic opportunities, and access to education for residents of one of Brooklyn's largest Black communities.

Many of Brooklyn's schools remained segregated, sparking outrage. Teachers' strikes were held in response to efforts to decentralize and integrate schools. The presence of police in Brooklyn high schools was a continuous issue, especially in neighborhoods like Bedford-Stuyvesant and East New York, hotspots where activists and high school students protested. Some argued police presence was necessary to maintain order; others saw it as intimidation, leading to protests and further distrust of law enforcement.

Martin Luther King Jr.'s nonviolent campaign, including the Chicago Freedom Movement, aimed at ending housing segregation in Northern cities. This movement's geographic focus shifted, and later, King addressed broader issues, including economic inequality and poverty, which led to the launch of the Poor People's Campaign in November 1967 to demand economic justice.

King and the Southern Christian Leadership Conference (SCLC) aimed to raise awareness of the plight of the poor and advocate for policies such as income assistance, job creation, and affordable housing through an Economic Bill of Rights. King spearheaded the campaign, with events and actions occurring from May 12 to June 24, 1968. It began with a Mother's Day march and rally on May 12, followed by a major march on Washington, and concluded with a protest encampment in DC, known as "Resurrection City."

Martin Luther King Jr. did not see the culmination of the campaign that was part of his vision. He had come to Memphis, Tennessee, to support the striking sanitation workers as part of the campaign. The civil rights movement suffered a devastating blow when he was assassinated on April 4, 1968, on a balcony of his hotel room by James Earl Ray, who was later convicted of murder. Under Ralph Abernathy's leadership, the SCLC carried out the campaign.

King's assassination sent shockwaves throughout the nation. Those who followed and admired him felt grief, anger, and a profound sense of loss. They saw him as a beacon of hope. Now, they mourned, rioted, and protested in more than one hundred cities, and called other leaders to action.

When Taylor heard the news, he asked his parents for an explanation. *Why did this happen?* But they didn't have anything other than that the fight for justice and equality continues, and some choose violence as their tactics. Taylor went to bed that night with thoughts shifting from his excellent schoolwork to his dream and how that might change. *Who will inspire me like Martin Luther King Jr.?*

Chapter 68

"Our Dream!"

Taylor's reaction to the assassination of Martin Luther King Jr. was one of shock and disbelief. It was a profoundly emotional and disorienting moment, losing one who had been a guiding force, a role model, a symbol of hope, and an inspiring leader who stressed nonviolence and justice. It wasn't just the death of a man, but the loss of a dream for racial equality. It was a betrayal of a system that allowed violence to dominate.

Many who had relied on King's leadership and moral compass wondered how the movement would go without him. They questioned whether nonviolence and peaceful protests were still viable or if more radical action was needed. *Is justice even possible when a country silences its leaders? What now?* Doubt crept in. *Will things ever change?*

The fight for justice underwent a profound transformation as activists began to question whether peaceful protests were an effective means of achieving justice. It led to more militant actions from groups like the Black Panther Party and the continued campaign of the Poor People's Party under Abernathy. The Civil Rights Act of 1968, which included fair housing protections, was passed partly in response to King's assassination. The movement became more diverse in its strategies, with some leaders maintaining a commitment to nonviolence, while others stressed more direct action.

Two months later, Robert Kennedy, who had won the California Democratic primary, was shot by Sirhan Sirhan, a twenty-three-year-old Palestinian, after he delivered a speech at the Ambassador Hotel in Los Angeles. Kennedy was rushed to the Good Samaritan Hospital after multiple shots were fired at close range on June 5, 1968. He died the next day. The murder led to increased Secret Service protection for presidential candidates.

The ensuing shock, grief, and turmoil led to national mourning, political uncertainty, riots, and protests. Many became disillusioned with politics, thinking that violence had become a permanent element in political life (and death). Kennedy's death was a devastating blow for those who believed in his vision for justice, equality, and an end to poverty. His murder, shortly after King's assassination, made 1968 one of the most tumultuous years in American history.

Over the last few weeks, after King's death, Taylor had several episodes in which his dream unfolded. Its scope expanded after watching the news coverage on TV. Listening to Walter Cronkite on the CBS Evening News, other key broadcasts, and President Johnson's remarks emphasized the severity of the impact of losing this civil rights movement leader. He absorbed the images of shock and grief across the country, footage of riots and protests, and King's funeral, where millions witnessed the nation's farewell.

President Johnson did not hold back anything when he planned his special address to Congress. He lamented, "I rarely have felt that sense of powerlessness more acutely than the day Martin Luther King Jr. was killed." He pushed for stronger civil rights measures. "Goddamn it, this country has got to do more for these people, and the time to start is now." In part of his public address, he said, "If I were a kid in Harlem, I know what I'd be thinking right now: I'd be thinking that the Whites have declared open season on my people." Despite calls for harsh crackdowns on protests, Johnson resisted excessive force, saying, "I don't want Americans killing Americans," a response reflecting both grief and determination to channel the tragedy into meaningful legislation.

"Taylor! Taylor Washington!" From the depths of his deep sleep, Taylor heard the familiar call. "Taylor, it's Martin Luther King Jr. I'm here, Taylor." In his dream, he was confused. He thought his mind was playing tricks on him. *How could Dr. King call me? He's . . . he's dead.* He received an answer. "I'm still here, Taylor. I'm still here, and you're still here. We're here together, we're here to continue the fight."

Taylor's mind rapidly went through all the conversations he had heard about the assassination: from his parents, teachers, and television broadcasts. He had visions of Walter Cronkite, President Johnson, riots, and prayer at King's funeral. It was overwhelming.

"Taylor, we can't give up. Our dream must become reality." *Our dream! He said, "Our dream?" No, they're different dreams! Aren't they different dreams, Dr. King?* "Taylor, our dreams lead us to the same thing: all God's children together in love, holding hands in a land of peace, equality, and justice. Standing in a circle . . . Black, White, Black, White. Holding hands in a circle of Black and White beauty, smiling and rejoicing at what we have achieved."

In his dream, Taylor was lifted by these words. They represented a hope that had finally come to fruition. But another side of him told him we weren't there yet. His recollection of the television coverage said otherwise. There is much more to be done. His emotions shifted again as he was inspired by King's "communication" with him. It went back and forth like a pendulum, one end signifying equality and justice, the other drenched in struggle. It resulted in uncertainty, but the image of a circle of Black and White people holding hands was indelible.

Nick, Taylor, and their parents had begun a search for colleges and universities that would allow them to continue studying in their areas of interest. The boys realized they would be separated once they started their freshman year in college. This concerned them, and they steered their choices for advanced education to remain near one another if possible. They intended to stay in the New York City metropolitan area. They understood that this might limit their options for the best institutions of higher learning, but, as they had done for high school, they felt they could manage a solution.

Both boys did exceptionally well in their last two years at Brooklyn Tech, despite Nick's initial reluctance to join the basketball team. They developed coordination and strength of their bodies and minds. Late in their junior year, after visiting some colleges and universities, they submitted their applications to several nearby and remote colleges.

Taylor's interest in genetics, microbiology, and DNA research led him to focus his search on top-tier universities that were nationally recognized. Among them were Harvard, Stanford, the University of California, Berkeley, MIT, the University of Chicago, Johns Hopkins University, and the University of Wisconsin-Madison. Each had strong faculties and programs in biology and genetics-related programs. Taylor applied to all of them.

The New York institutions included Columbia University, NYU (where Dr. Reed was a professor in the history department), the Icahn School of Medicine at Mount Sinai, Rockefeller University, Sarah Lawrence College, and City University of New York (CUNY). Taylor applied to Columbia University, home to the department of genetics and development, as well as NYU for its strong genetics research, and Rockefeller University for its groundbreaking work in molecular biology. Doctors Cartwright and Caldwell gave their thumbs-up approval for each of these.

Nick's interest in the space race, aerospace engineering, and aerodynamics drove his interest in nationally recognized schools such as MIT, California Institute of Technology (Caltech), Stanford, the University of Michigan, Purdue University (the alma mater of Neil Armstrong), the University of Texas at Austin, the University of Colorado Boulder, and Georgia Institute of Technology (Georgia Tech). All had exciting programs related to a wide variety of space-related subjects. Nick applied to all of them.

The New York City area schools included Columbia University, NYU, and the City College of New York (CCNY). Rensselaer Polytechnic Institute (RPI) was located in Troy, New York, 10 miles north of Albany, and Cornell University was situated in Ithaca, in the Finger Lakes Region of central New York State. Nick also applied to Columbia, NYU, and Cornell.

Nick's and Taylor's strong academic performances in math, science, and English, as well as their knowledge demonstrated on the Scholastic Aptitude Test and the American College Testing verified their qualifications. Taylor had submitted letters of recommendation from some of his teachers at Brooklyn Tech, as well as a letter each from Doctors Cartwright and Caldwell, who had been following his devotion to genetics and his performance in high school. He also submitted essays that were required to accompany some of the applications.

Nick also received recommendations from his high school teachers, who highlighted his strong skills in advanced mathematics and his exceptional research in engineering topics related to aerospace and space exploration. The boys would soon make their decision based on the formal letters they each received in the mail in the early spring of 1969. They had a majority of acceptance letters to consider. Their parents were extremely proud of their achievements and eager to celebrate their graduation from Brooklyn Tech, a school that had proved to be a critical foundation for higher learning.

With its strong curriculum—which encouraged critical thinking, problem-solving, time management, and independent learning—Tech developed the skills, knowledge, and habits necessary for success in advanced education. Tech's guidance and mentorship provided invaluable support from its educators. Consequently, Nick and Taylor emerged as confident and capable thinkers, ready to tackle higher education.

Graduation was scheduled for Saturday, June 21, 1969, in the large auditorium, which had been decorated to celebrate the achievements of the seniors, who wore traditional caps and gowns and were seated in their assigned seats. Families, teachers, and alumni gathered in an atmosphere of pride and excitement. Nick's parents, sister, grandparents, aunt, and cousins sat next to Taylor's parents, grandparents, aunt and uncle, and cousin. They briefly met four years ago at PS 91 when Nick and Taylor were so small, uncertain, and full of curiosity. Now they witnessed two young people entering adulthood, taking on responsibility, and embarking on a journey of self-discovery. *How time flies!*

After the opening remarks by Brooklyn Tech's principal, Isidor Auerbach, several class representatives gave speeches on their challenges and triumphs while attending the school. After the graduating class cheered and shouted, Principal Auerbach introduced the keynote speaker, an alumnus of Brooklyn Tech.

"Graduates, families, and esteemed faculty, today, we celebrate your hard-earned accomplishments and the limitless future ahead. Brooklyn Technical High School has always been a foundation for innovation, where curiosity meets ambition. With immense pride, I welcome back one of our very own, a distinguished scientist who walked through these halls, sat in these classrooms, and once dreamed of shaping the world like each of you.

"Through years of dedication, brilliance, and a passion for discovery, our guest speaker has contributed to the pioneering advances that have taken mankind beyond the boundaries of Earth.

As the world prepares for the historic Apollo 11 moon landing, his work at NASA reminds us that the future belongs to those who dare to imagine and strive to achieve their goals.

"Graduates, it is my honor to introduce a Brooklyn Tech alumnus and NASA engineer, Dr. Alvin Hartman, who stands before you as proof that the foundations built here can lead to the greatest heights—perhaps even the stars." Before Dr. Hartman said a single word, the crowd stood, clapping and shouting praise.

Hartman thanked the principal for his introduction. He opened his address to the class and recalled sitting where they were to receive his high school diploma. He began his speech with a few short stories of growing up in the Ridgewood section of Brooklyn, visiting the "greatest city in the world," and telling a few jokes. He had the complete attention and respect of everyone there. He then focused on his message for the next few minutes.

"Graduates of Brooklyn Technical High School, today you stand at the edge of possibility, just as I once did in 1951 when I sat where you are today. The time has gone by very quickly. Brooklyn Tech values precision, problem-solving, and bold thinking—qualities that have shaped my journey at NASA, and will shape yours.

"In just a few short weeks, the world will witness history as astronauts attempt the first landing on the moon. Some of you may have dreams of shaping that future by designing spacecraft, calculating trajectories, and discovering mysteries beyond our planet. The same drive that got you through physics exams, engineering labs, and midnight study sessions will be the force that propels you into greatness.

"Whatever your path—whether in laboratories, on drafting tables, in corporate offices, or the halls of justice—know that the skills you have developed here at Brooklyn Tech will serve as the foundation for change, discovery, and greatness. Brooklyn Tech prepared you well. Congratulations, Class of 1969—go forth and build the future!" Hartman received a standing ovation of prolonged applause and cheering from those who admired him for his encouragement and achievements.

Nick and Taylor waited with several hundred of their graduating class to hear their names called and proceed to the stage to receive their diplomas, marking the official completion of all their hard work. Each graduate listened to his family's shouts and cheers, not the least of which was "Nicky, Nicky," from Grandpa Greene. Once they were all seated and received the final gestures of "Congratulations" and "Good Luck," they tossed their caps in the air, cheered, and were ready to party with their friends and families.

It was a surge of triumph, an explosion of relief, a celebration of everything they worked for. The anticipation of college, knowing where they would go in the fall, and their next adventure confirmed, "They made it!" Nick and Taylor's Class of 1969 looked back at their journey in Brooklyn Tech's yearbook, *Blueprint*, which reflected the innovation and camaraderie of their class.

Nick and Taylor knew where they were going after much discussion with their parents and even more debate between themselves. They would both go to Columbia University, Nick for its strong physics and engineering programs related to space science, and Taylor for the university's strong genetics presence, with the establishment of the Department of Human Genetics and Development earlier in the year. *College! We're ready!*

Chapter 69

SHE'S A ROLE MODEL

The summer after graduation from Brooklyn Tech was filled with nonstop activity for Nick and Taylor. After several graduation parties, it was a delicate balance of get-togethers with family and friends; day trips to New York City, Coney Island, and Long Island beaches; and hands-on experiences before heading off to college. They also had some orientation scheduled at Columbia before the fall semester began on August 18. The highlight of the summer for them and the rest of the world was observing the moon landing on July 20, 1969.

Television broadcasts, radio announcements, and crowds in public gathered at places such as Times Square, London's Trafalgar Square, and Tokyo's streets to watch it live. Across the world, there was a collective cheer at humanity's achievement. Nick was "over the moon" as the event was carved into his heart and mind, with his goals set on someday being like Dr. Alvin Hartman or even Neil Armstrong.

The Brooklyn Navy Yard remained active, offering opportunities in mechanical and aerospace engineering. Nick spent part of his summer observing some of the work there. He figured, *I better start building my resume!* Taylor was elated when he heard from Dr. Zee Cee. She offered to mentor him for a few days over the summer at the Cold Spring Harbor Lab on Long Island, where she worked. He took the subway from East New York to connect with the Long Island Railroad (LIRR) and then took the Port Jefferson Branch train to the station near the lab. By this time, Nick and Taylor had the New York City subway map imprinted in their brains.

Dr. Caldwell had graduated from Columbia and decided she would like to follow Taylor's college experiences if he agreed. With the world of genetic information expanding rapidly, she was drawn to the excitement of this young Black man, who demonstrated his interest and passion for the subject in numerous ways. She offered Taylor any assistance he wanted beyond the excellent education she knew he would receive at Columbia. Taylor and his parents expressed their appreciation to her for the time and effort she offered.

"Taylor, welcome to Cold Spring Harbor Lab." Dr. Caldwell met Taylor at the lab entrance. He observed this thirty-year-old woman, who was wearing a pressed white lab coat and a huge smile. Her skin was warm and smooth, the color of espresso, and her hair was styled in a short Afro. She was the epitome of brilliance, resilience, and trailblazing ambition.

"Hi, Dr. Caldwell. Nice to meet you, finally." He immediately admired her, not only for her beauty but also for her sixty-nine-inch stature, the intellectual image she projected, and his recognition that she was proof that the world has room for people like him. She was doing important work in important places. That's what he wanted to do.

"Taylor, we're not so formal here. You can call me Zora or, as most people call me, Zee Cee."

"Oh, okay . . . uh, Zee Cee." Before they entered the lab, he caught a glimpse of the serene view of the water from the campus. They walked down the hallway of this historic and cutting-edge science building, which gave Taylor vibes of tradition and innovation. It was a not-for-profit research and education institution at the forefront of molecular biology and genetics.

"Taylor, we focus on several major divisions here at the lab. Please don't hesitate to ask any questions at any time. I can get carried away talking about the lab here. I love it so much." Taylor nodded his head. Her charisma captured him.

"Our primary purpose is to research and gain general knowledge that will lead to better diagnostics and treatments for cancer, neurological, and other significant diseases. We explore the genetic basis for cancer development and study how mutations lead to tumors."

"Wow. That's what I'm interested in: genetics. I learned a lot at Brooklyn Tech, and from your and Dr. Cartwright's suggestions for my project there. Thank you again for helping me."

"Anytime, Taylor. You can always depend on us." She continued with the other areas of CSHL. "Regarding genetics, we focus on chromosome studies, hereditary diseases, and mutation analysis. We investigate DNA replication, gene expression, and protein synthesis in the field of molecular biology. This contributes to breakthroughs in genetic engineering."

"Wow! I have a lot to learn. I can't wait to go to Columbia University!"

"You will love it there. There is so much to learn, and as you know, it is among the leading institutions in the country focused on genetics. Columbia has very close ties with Cold Spring Harbor Lab. I'm certain you will hear about us in some of your classes. We also conduct quantitative biology, where we apply mathematical models to biological systems, helping us understand complex genetic interactions. Ultimately, we investigate the genetic factors that influence neurological disorders. This field is just emerging and is very exciting."

"I didn't know the lab here did all that. I guess that will help in many ways to understand human genetics."

"Not only human genetics. Think about everything from medicine to agriculture. Genetics research applies to all living organisms: humans, animals, plants, bacteria, and even viruses."

"Wow! Now I just learned there is much more to learn than I thought!" Zora was thrilled with Taylor's attention and thirst for knowledge and discovery. She had mentored others, but observed some hidden drive in Taylor that was hard to describe. She looked forward to watching him grow in his undeniable interest and zeal.

Dr. Caldwell gave Taylor a tour of the open labs for display and discussion. Much of the lab work required strict security and sterility to ensure safety, accuracy, and integrity in the scientific work. He was excited when she gave him a lab coat and some protective gear as they progressed through cleanroom protocols, as some areas required air filtration systems to keep the environment free from dust and other pollutants.

After a couple of hours with Dr. Caldwell, Taylor shook her hand and thanked her for her time and information. He said that he couldn't wait to learn more. Before he departed the lab, she said, "Taylor, I thoroughly enjoyed our time together today. There's something I just thought about that you should know." His eyes widen slightly, eager to hear more.

"Here at the lab, we are organizing plans to establish archives in a few years to house a rich depository of rare books, manuscripts, photos, and scientific reprints that document genetic research. Some of the archives will be from the faculty here that go back to 1890."

As Taylor rode the LIRR back to connect with the subway, he reviewed everything Dr. Caldwell had shown him and discussed. He viewed her as the embodiment of possibility, the future in motion. She was passionate. She belonged in the lab, breaking barriers. She was a role model.

He saw some promise that all this information, his future studies at Columbia, and his ongoing communication with the deceased—but very much alive in his dreams, Martin Luther King Jr.—would eventually answer the question that continued to plague him. *Can Black and White people have kids of the opposite color?*

Chapter 70

Columbia University: Incredible Education/ Contentious Environment

A few days after hearing about Taylor's visit to the Cold Spring Harbor Lab and visit with Dr. Caldwell, Isaac contacted Dr. Reed to tell him, "I never thought Taylor would end up with her offering to mentor him and follow his progress at Columbia. I have to thank you again for making that introduction years ago."

Reed said, "I am so happy this is working for Taylor. I have many friends and colleagues at Columbia. He has demonstrated a yearning that is vital to university students, and I hope to hear more about his progress through his years there."

Isaac and Dr. Reed spoke for a few more minutes about scheduling the next discussion group meeting and then caught up on recent news about the civil rights movement. Their conversation drifted to student activism on university campuses. Dr. Reed commented, "I don't know if you recall this in the news, but last year there was a series of protests at Columbia. It was one of the many student demonstrations that occurred around the globe."

Isaac said, "Yeah. I recall something about the country's involvement in the Vietnam War and another issue . . . I can't quite remember . . . having to do with a gymnasium?"

"Yes, students discovered links between the university and the institutional apparatus supporting the war. Apparently, Columbia had an affiliation with the Institute for Defense Analysis (IDA), a weapons research think tank connected to the Department of Defense. The nature of the association had been kept secret. A few magazine articles on the IDA appeared between 1956 and '67, and the IDA was mentioned in a few books for academic specialists published by university presses. The RAND Corporation, not IDA, was the military-oriented think tank that received the most publicity prior to early 1967. But links were found leading to the Columbia-IDA relationship, which touched off an anti-war campaign between Columbia and the Students for a Democratic Society (SDS) activist group."

"Very interesting. What happened?"

"There was a peaceful demonstration inside the Low Library administration building in Columbia in March last year. It ended with the Columbia administration placing six anti-war Columbia student activists on probation for violating its ban on indoor demonstrations. The group was called 'The IDA Six.'"

"You said 'indoor demonstrations'?"

"Yes, students barricaded themselves inside the Low Library, Hamilton Hall, and several other university buildings during their protests, and the NYC police were called onto the campus to arrest or forcibly remove the students. This series of protests was right around the time of the assassination of Martin Luther King Jr."

"Ah, yes! I remember that now. What about the gymnasium?"

"Yes, that was another complex issue. Students demonstrated against Columbia's plan to construct a gymnasium in neighboring Morningside Park. Activists perceived it as a 'segregated gym' in city-owned property, with limited access to Harlem residents. Part of the issue, as I recall, was the design, where the upper level would be used as a gym for Columbia, and the lower level as a community center. The plan included east and west entrances as an attempt to circumvent the Civil Rights Act of 1964, which banned racially segregated facilities. Harlem opposed the construction because its residents would only get limited access, even though it would be on public land and a park."

Dr. Reed also told Isaac that since 1958, the university had evicted more than seven thousand Harlem residents from Columbia-controlled properties—85 percent of whom were African American or Puerto Rican, and that many Harlem residents paid rent to the university.

"I guess racial discrimination is alive and well, even at our universities."

Dr. Reed was well-connected with colleagues from numerous universities nationwide and was attuned to the challenges faced by Black students. "I'm afraid so. There continues to be overt racism, exclusion from social spaces, and resistance from faculty and peers. It's a disgrace. Blacks have limited representation. They continue to organize protests, sit-ins, and other forms of action to demand educational equity. They've even created Black student unions to seek support for advocacy and cultural affirmation. Universities are shifting, recognizing the need for diversity and inclusion, but it's a slow process."

"I guess I'll need to alert Taylor to what he could expect at Columbia. I had forgotten the racial issues there. Thanks for reminding me. He's got a good head on his shoulders, but he is still maturing and learning the depth of racial discrimination and how difficult it is to eradicate it."

"I hear you, Isaac. Good luck to him, and please give my regards to Makena. I look forward to meeting with you again soon. Let's make that happen." They said their goodbyes. Their conversation was always expressed with genuine interest, warmth, and reciprocity, never with competition or power struggle. It was two people, fully engaged, listening, and sharing freely. And they were always informative. This time, Isaac learned more.

Isaac spoke with Taylor about the issues Dr. Reed mentioned are happening at university campuses across the country and what he could expect from student activists at Columbia. He also thought it would be worth calling Jonathan to share what he had learned and about his conversation with Taylor, so that Nick would also be informed.

Jonathan was very grateful for the information, and he said he would discuss it with Nick when he returned from the Brooklyn Navy Yard, where he was observing engineering practices with some mentors.

Nick visited the Brooklyn Navy Yard several times a week to meet with his mentor, Richard Morris, an industrial engineer who had graduated from Rensselaer Polytechnic Institute. Morris was a personable man in his forties with young boys of his own who had interests similar to Nick's. In their conversations, he would cover general principles of construction and load-bearing frameworks that would translate into spacecraft durability and aerodynamics.

He had a solid background in other related features, such as propulsion and fluid dynamics, materials, and heat-resistant alloys for thermal shielding and spacecraft protection against extreme temperatures. He emphasized the importance of precision manufacturing and systems engineering in aligning with the rigorous standards of NASA's programs.

Nick ate up this information as if it were one of his favorite foods. He recalled his Brooklyn Tech science class, specifically the drafting workshop, where the instructor emphasized the importance of "precision as the backbone of engineering." Everything made sense. When it comes to engineering, especially for space programs, precision and safety are top priorities. Otherwise, accidents happen, like the one that took the lives of astronauts Gus Grissom, Ed White, and Roger Chaffee.

The subway ride from the Navy Yard to the station nearest his apartment in East New York was a little over an hour, so he had time to absorb everything he was learning from Morris. Brooklyn Tech has helped connect Nick with Morris through a program designed to provide graduates with hands-on experience before their first year in college. Jonathan and Richard Morris also connected by phone to discuss the goals for Nick at the Navy Yard. The conversation between an accountant and an engineer could not have gone better.

Nick arrived home tired and hungry, but eager to tell his parents about his day at the Yard. After he unloaded for about an hour, Jonathan said, "Nick, it sounds like you and Mr. Morris are getting along great, and you're getting a good education from him. He's got some great experience." Nick, with a mouthful of food, just nodded.

"I got a call from Taylor's father. He spoke to Dr. Reed from NYU. I think I told you at some point that they have a discussion group that meets to update on civil rights." Nick nodded again. He was nowhere near finished eating.

"They talked about what's happening at many of the universities across our country, and especially some racial discrimination incidents at Columbia. Some students are heavily involved in activism, from peaceful protests to police intervention and arrests. Isaac spoke with Taylor and wanted to tell me so I can tell you."

Jonathan and Isaac followed up with one another a few weeks before the boys would begin their first semester. They were excited for them but also concerned about the diverse environment they were about to enter—one of incredible education and building a foundation for their futures, and the other, a contentious one, where conflict, disagreement, and tension exist.

They could expect enlightening discussions and presentations in class, as well as arguments and ideological clashes that lead to polarization, and competitive, power-driven dynamics. *Welcome to college in the era of racial discrimination and the fight for equality and justice!*

Chapter 71

UNSTOPPABLE COLUMBIANS

Manhattan sweltered under a relentless stretch of heat and humidity in mid-August 1969, when Nick and Taylor rode the subway together to attend the first day of their freshman year at Columbia University. They had been there with their parents to get a campus tour, meet faculty and advisors, and explore the study spaces and the surrounding area. The boys returned together a few times to observe student life and ask questions without any parental influence.

They had become familiar with the many common meeting places where students gathered to sit, talk, or take breaks between classes. They selected the Low Library Steps, the Sundial College Walk, and Morningside Park, just off campus, to link up whenever possible.

Nick had a mix of core technical engineering courses and general education requirements, including history, philosophy, and literature. Taylor's courses focused on fundamental sciences, laboratory work, and similar general education courses. They carefully selected their schedules to allow them to take a few classes together.

They exited the subway, packed like a can of sardines with students and faculty. Nick and Taylor walked through the campus and entered Columbia University, which was in an era of scientific breakthroughs, space exploration milestones, Cold War-driven advancements in aerospace technology, and groundbreaking discoveries in genetics, DNA research, and molecular biology.

Their nervous excitement was a mix of anticipation and uncertainty as they scanned the sprawling campus, with its towering libraries and historic buildings that represented monuments of intellectual prestige, rising within the grandeur of New York City. They were about to enter a university, grand not only in size, but in its influence and ability to look beyond into the depths of knowledge.

They observed many students, not realizing that collectively they reflected a lower enrollment at the university due to the 1968 protests and occupation of multiple buildings. Over time, they would hear all the details from their peers and be reminded that the Vietnam War and the civil rights movements were key components that triggered coalitions of anti-war and civil rights activists that often worked together.

On campus there were no lack of demonstrations or resistance to the military draft, often involving the burning of draft cards. There was also motivation to form Black student unions and organizations, such as the Student Afro-American Society (SAS). Students faced a complex balancing act of managing their academic responsibilities and navigating a campus that was a hotbed of political engagement, ignited by the pressures of the Vietnam War protests and civil rights activism.

Columbia University was at the forefront of these engagements, mirroring the broader unrest seen across American campuses, such as Cal-Berkeley, Harvard, and Wisconsin, where sit-ins, strikes, and building occupations seemed to be part of the curriculum. Nick and Taylor were smack dab in the middle of it.

Considering all the current events that caused academic turbulence and the collision of activism and scholarship, Nick and Taylor felt a moral responsibility to engage where necessary, yet still navigate their coursework, research, and future aspirations. It was a dual pursuit of justice and knowledge. The priority was their education and groundwork for life ahead, yet they could not ignore life's other significant issues.

Nick plunged into his courses in mathematics, calculus and differential equations, physics, engineering fundamentals, computational methods using the recently developed programming language FORTRAN, and numerical analysis. He quickly learned that he would have no spare time, as he used breaks between classes to work in the library and spent almost all his weekends at home doing research and homework.

He was hoping that he and Taylor would be able to fly fish again with their fathers in the early fall, but they would need to postpone that possibility to the academic break at Thanksgiving.

Taylor had done extensive reading on genetics and biology in his later years at Brooklyn Tech, as well as in some of the recommended readings provided by his teachers and mentors. But when he began his courses in general biology, chemistry, physics for life sciences, mathematics, genetics foundations, and lab work, it was as if everything hit the fan, creating chaos. He quickly reacted by establishing a nonstop work ethic to navigate his academic challenges.

When the young college students met at Morning Side Park at the end of their first week, they expressed frustration. Nick told Taylor, "Man, this is like drinking from a firehose!"

Taylor added his similar reaction. "I'm already behind, and it's only been one week! I can't even fall asleep right away at home. I have so much coursework on my mind. This is crazy."

"It's exciting, but pretty overwhelming. We can do it. If other students can do it, we can."

"Yep. We have to stay positive. I heard it gets tougher later, more specialized, advanced coursework, higher expectations, and responsibility," Taylor said. "We have to adapt." They agreed that they were resilient, capable, and determined, as their mental fatigue began to fade. They decided to call themselves the "Unstoppable Columbians." They were determined to prove their ambition in the pursuit of excellence. They did what they had always done since first grade at PS 91. Nick wouldn't walk in "genetic shoes," and Taylor wouldn't walk in "space shoes." They just stood beside one another for support.

While the shoe-walking description held firm, it did not prevent them from occasionally discussing the interdisciplinary connections between their areas of interest. They contemplated the exploration of astrobiology and space microbiology, where microbial life might survive in space, as well as materials science, a field of study focused on the structural integrity of both spacecraft and biological membranes. They were fascinated by the possibilities.

As the weeks passed, Nick learned of Columbia's collaboration with NASA's Goddard Institute for Space Studies (GISS), housed in the university's Armstrong Hall, near West 112th Street, which offered exposure to planetary atmosphere, astrophysics, and climate research. The recent moon landing had greatly influenced coursework, research projects, and lectures on lunar exploration and future missions. Nick also learned about internships, networking with the Institute, and other nearby New York City scientific organizations, such as the American Museum of Natural History and local aerospace firms. In a short time at Columbia, it was as if a whole new universe opened up for him.

Taylor knew that the Cold Spring Harbor Laboratory was affiliated with Columbia University. He was happy about that as he looked forward to keeping in touch with Dr. Caldwell. However, he also discovered that the university had connections to Rockefeller University, where Dr. Cartwright worked, as well as other local biotech firms that offered internships and networking opportunities. He made a mental note to contact Dr. Cartwright later in his first year to tell her of his visit with Dr. Caldwell and his study program at the university.

In his courses on cell biology, microbial genetics, molecular biology, and biochemistry, each contributed to the understanding of how organisms transmit hereditary traits. He thought, *"This is where I will get the answer to my dream question!"* He often heard how the CSHL was a rising force in genetics research, where faculty and students actively engaged in groundbreaking DNA studies. *I already have a connection with a lovely lady at CSHL!* He had a universe of his own to explore.

During Nick and Taylor's first year at Columbia, numerous political events, scientific advancements, and cultural activities diverted their attention from their studies. In August 1969, though not directly tied to Columbia, the Woodstock Festival took place on Max Yasgur's dairy farm in Bethel, New York, about sixty miles southwest of Woodstock. It symbolized the era's counterculture movement and had a profound influence on student activism. Jimi Hendrix, Janis Joplin, The Who, The Grateful Dead, and others performed at the festival.

The Apollo 12 mission, launched in November, marked the second successful moon landing, further advancing lunar exploration and research. Nick was amazed to learn that Columbia researchers contributed to seismic experiments on the moon that helped analyze its geological structure.

In April 1970, Apollo 13, intended to be the third lunar landing, suffered a near-catastrophic failure. An onboard liquid oxygen tank explosion in the service module forced NASA to abort the landing and to focus on safely returning the crew to Earth. Despite the crisis, the mission became known as a "successful failure," displaying ingenuity and teamwork that saved the astronauts. It demonstrated problem-solving abilities, leading to improved safety protocols for future missions.

While the United States experienced advancements and setbacks in space, there were other significant achievements, such as in laser technology, where optical trapping techniques were developed, enabling scientists to manipulate individual atoms using lasers. The Apollo missions helped shift perspectives of Earth's fragility, contributing to the rise of environmental movements. Key computing achievements included ARPANET, in October 1969, the first large-scale computer network; the UNIX Operating System, developed at AT&T Bell Labs; the first widely recognized supercomputer (CDC 6600) released in 1964; and Intel's first commercial product, the 3101 Schottky TTL 64-bit SRAM, making its entry into the semiconductor industry.

Vietnam War protests intensified as the war escalated and expanded into Cambodia under President Nixon. On May 4, 1970, the Ohio National Guard troops, reporting they feared for their lives, opened fire on anti-war protesters at Kent State University, killing four students and wounding nine others. It was a defining moment in the war protests. Graphic images and news media footage by major networks, including Mary Ann Vecchio crying over Jeffrey Miller's body, fueled anti-war sentiment and questioned the government's use of force against students. The song "Ohio," written by Neil Young, of the group Crosby, Stills, Nash & Young, became an anthem for the anti-war movement. The immediate aftermath led to nationwide student strikes, forcing hundreds of colleges to shut down temporarily.

As they navigated their way through their freshman year at Columbia, Nick and Taylor experienced a mix of awe, excitement, and apprehension. They were caught between the intellectual rigor of Ivy League academics and the tumultuous era unfolding beyond the university gates. The challenge of academics and observing a changing world gave rise to moments of wonder and questions about the country's future.

The boys sat at their usual Morningside Park bench just before taking the subway home to start their summer. They needed a well-deserved break and discussed ways to make the most of it. But these comments came first. Nick said, "Man, I'm glad it's over. I can't count how many nights I couldn't sleep with worry about my coursework, and how many nights I fell asleep exhausted."

Taylor said, "Yeah, me too. Some of those courses and labs were brutal, but the camaraderie and study groups were lifelines for me. I respect what people like Dr. Caldwell are doing in their research." The boys had done well. Their accomplishments, ambition, and resilience reflected their motivation to complete the hard work. It gave them confidence in their future and their personal and intellectual growth. *The Unstoppable Columbians: Year one down; three more to go!*

Chapter 72

WILLIE—HOW LONG DOES HE HAVE?

Columbia University had excellent ties with organizations in many research areas, with apprenticeships and other programs that allowed its students to learn from experts in the field. Nick and Taylor explored where they might be able to spend part of their summer of 1970 in a program, but discovered that there was fierce competition for the slots taken up by more senior students. Freshmen rarely get an opportunity to engage. At the end of their first year, exhausted from physical and mental fatigue, they quickly rationalized that taking a break was best for them.

Nick and Taylor both turned nineteen in June, and each family got together to celebrate but were more motivated to hear about their progress in college. The senior Greenes and Washingtons had always envisioned their children and grandchildren pursuing higher education, something they had not had the opportunity to obtain.

Darnell Washington said, "Taylor, I heard you did very well at Columbia. I am so proud of you!"

"Thanks, Grandpa. It was really tough, but I worked hard, and we had a good group that helped one another whenever anyone had trouble understanding something. Did you hear I went to the Cold Spring Harbor Laboratory and met with a research scientist there?"

"Yes, your father told me. Is that someplace where you would like to work?"

"I would love it there." He immediately thought of Dr. Caldwell. *Who wouldn't love working there?* "Columbia has a good connection with them and many other places. I still have three years to go, so we'll see what happens." His grandpa smiled and gave him a thumbs-up, his chest expanding slightly in pride, signaling strength and accomplishment.

"Do you have any special areas of your genetics study that you are interested in?"

Taylor wished he could tell his grandfather all about his dreams, his special connection to Martin Luther King Jr., and the quest to answer his lingering question of mixed races and the children they could have. But he determined if it was too early to even bring it up in class (yet), why would he bring it up with his grandfather? His traditions and beliefs might cause him to question why Taylor would consider such a situation. He gave a generic answer and changed the subject by asking how he and Grandma were doing. The birthday celebration took priority as the family sang "Happy Birthday," and the birthday cake was brought out with twenty candles, one of which was added for his age to bring good luck.

Nick had a similar celebration with his extended family in June, but it was without his grandfather, William. His grandma said, "Nick, your grandfather wanted to be here today to wish you a happy birthday and hear about your year at Columbia. We want to hear all about it." Then Nick found out from his father that William was in the hospital due to congenital heart failure. He never knew his grandfather had heart defects at birth. The surgeons considered open-heart surgery, which had become more common thanks to the development of the heart-lung machine, which allowed surgeons to perform complex repairs. The treatment for his grandfather's condition was advancing but still relatively limited.

Nick's happy expression rapidly turned as a flicker of disbelief passed through his eyes. He swallowed hard and asked, "Is Grandpa gonna be okay?"

Jonathan said, "He's stable and doing well so far. The doctors considered surgery, but did not want to risk it. They did a shunt procedure to improve Grandpa's blood flow, and they have him on some medications to strengthen his heart and reduce fluid buildup in the lungs and tissues. That helps to ease the strain on his heart."

"Can I go see him at the hospital? I wanna see my Grandpa."

Jonathan said he would take Nick with him and his mother the next day, while his Grandma watched over Lila. The family celebrated

Nick's birthday, but his heart wasn't entirely devoted to happiness. A considerable part of it contained sadness as he thought about his grandfather. Jonathan did not want to tell Nick what the doctors told him—those patients with congenital heart conditions had a shorter life expectancy. Still, his father had lived to seventy-two, which was considered better than average.

The next day, the visit to see Grandpa Greene resulted in good news. He was doing well, but weak, and needed to remain stabilized for another week or two before the doctors would release him from the hospital. William's spirits lifted when Nick and his parents entered his room. He had a tired but genuine smile.

In a weak voice, he said, "Look at you, a year at Columbia under your belt. I heard you did very well there. I am so proud of you, Nicky."

"Thanks, Grandpa. I hope you're feeling better. How are you doing?"

"I'm okay, Nicky. I'm okay." He reached out with trembling hands to gently hold his grandson's face. "I am so proud of you. You will go far. I just know it. Don't you worry. I'm gonna do my best to be around when you graduate." At that point, Mary, Jonathan, and Nick's eyes welled up with tears. William did not notice as his eyelids fluttered, his hands fell to his side, and he slipped into sleep. The family lingered, their quiet presence of love, hope, and prayer filled the room.

As the family returned to their apartment, there was silence, as each searched their minds for answers to the question, *How long does he have?* Sarah had been reading a story to Lila. She jumped from her chair; her face held a fragile tension. "How is my Willie doing?" Jonathan gave her an update from the doctors and told her about Nick's emotional visit with his grandfather. The family remained hopeful even though they could not release the anxiety within them.

Two weeks later, Grandpa Greene was released from the hospital and returned to the care of his wife and family. His recovery was slow, as expected, but his progress was undeniable, fueled by his energy to stay alive for so many reasons, not the least of which was to witness Nicky's graduation from Columbia. He had visions of his grandson as an astronaut or a space scientist, having kept up with all the space race-related news and marveled at what the country could accomplish.

As summer approached the Labor Day holiday, Nick and Taylor prepared their minds and schedules for the next year of rigorous college work. While they thought their freshman year was tough, they realized it was just the tip of the iceberg. They thought of all their professors and experts in the field, as well as the knowledge they possessed. *We don't know anything yet! We have a long way to go!*

In the second year at Columbia, Nick's courses covered foundational engineering and specialized subjects in fluid mechanics, to understand airflow and aerodynamics, propulsion, and aerospace systems. These would provide him with knowledge of aerodynamics, including the study of lift, drag, and flight mechanics. The space vehicle dynamics covered orbital mechanics and spacecraft control. He would receive an introduction to turbomachinery, which is crucial for understanding propulsion systems in aerospace engineering and rocket and jet engine mechanics.

He was excited to hear that his professors would introduce additional relevant topics in human space flight, materials for aerospace design, and finite element analysis, which is useful for structural integrity in aerospace engineering. The Apollo missions and their advancements in space exploration had had a profound influence on the Columbia engineering program.

Speakers, typically from the Goddard Institute for Space Studies, NASA's research center, and aerospace engineers from the Apollo program, would provide a welcome break from class, offering a steady flow of real-time applications of the course information.

One NASA engineer spoke to several hundred students assembled in a lecture hall. He had worked on the Apollo lunar module and explained the trajectory calculations that guided Apollo 11's descent. The students listened carefully and took notes. The engineer commented that the goal in space is not just about getting there but about pushing to explore what we think is possible. He said, "That's what makes aerodynamics amazing. It's the science of breaking limits."

Nick and his student peers began to understand that as they focused on engineering precision. Space travel isn't just science;

it's vision, imagination, and human persistence that ask the question, "What's next?" The engineer closed his presentation by saying, "We're just getting started." Guest visits like this fueled the desire of those who will serve our future space programs.

Taylor looked forward to his study of bacterial genetics, mutation analysis, and chromosome structure, which would provide the foundation for hereditary research. He contemplated that these core studies would push him closer to understanding his most curious question. He felt, *"Maybe this year, I can ask my question without ridicule or laughter. Maybe other students, Black or White, have the same question."*

The other courses would cover DNA development and molecular biology, which included the biology department's deep research in DNA replication, gene expression, and genetic engineering. He heard again about the connections to the lab in Cold Spring Harbor and Rockefeller University, as well as the emerging genetic technologies from the late 1960s and early 1970s that would shape the future of genetic studies. Scientists from these two centers debated the future of molecular genetics.

He also attended lectures by leading geneticists, discussing mutation analysis in medicine and evolutionary biology. He thought about evolutionary biology, and it brought back memories of his eighth-grade science project, titled "Genetic Evolution," where he earned the name "Mr. DNA." He felt even more convinced that his question could be answered soon.

There was no lack of significant events in politics, technological and scientific breakthroughs, the war in Vietnam, space exploration milestones, the civil rights struggles, and campus activism.

President Nixon continued his efforts to Vietnamize the war, reducing American troop levels while escalating bombing campaigns, perpetuating the war's unpopularity. Campus protests at universities nationwide continued activism against the war, racial injustice, and environmental issues. The National Environmental Policy Act, passed in January 1970, marked a significant step in environmental protection through environmental legislation. Although medical innovations had advanced in heart disease treatments and organ transplantation, they were still experimental.

On February 5, 1971, Apollo 14 landed on the moon with astronauts Alan Shepard and Edgar Mitchell. Shepard famously hit golf balls in the Fra Mauro lunar highlands, where they collected valuable geological samples. Nick was "over the moon" again.

Taylor postponed his nagging question again. While lectures and discussions on genetics seemed to approach an opportune moment for him to ask, something always caused him to be hesitant, resulting in his silence. He hadn't had his dream for months. His mind was so focused on his work and exam preparation that lingering thoughts of his multiple course subjects took priority. There was no room for Martin Luther King Jr. and his messages.

It was another firestorm year for Nick and Taylor as they traversed the College Walk at Columbia University, with book bags tucked under their arms, as they proceeded off campus to The West End Bar on Broadway between 113th and 114th Streets to hang out and celebrate with their student peers. There was relief, pride, and exhaustion—another year of lectures, late-night study sessions, and cramming for exams in the rearview mirror. The Unstoppable Columbians became a household name among their friends.

Chapter 73

ATAVISM

nick started his junior year with a mountain of coursework on his plate, but one less concern. His grandfather was improving slowly after his release from the hospital in July. The treatment and medications helped him gain strength as his heart's function became more efficient. Nick went to visit him a week before his classes began.

"Grandpa, you are looking better. I'm glad you're home."

"Ah, Nicky. It was rough for a while, but I feel better and stronger. Grandma says I'm complaining too much and tells me that because I complain, it tells her I'm feeling better." They both laughed.

Nick said, "Well, then just keep complaining, Grandpa." They laughed even harder, and Nick knew if he could make him laugh like he always did, he must be feeling better.

His grandmother overheard them from the kitchen. "I heard that." Now all three of them had a good laugh. Nick's grandmother wouldn't let him leave before he finished the lunch she had prepared for him. They wished him good luck and told him they were looking forward to the day he graduates. He hugged them and told them he would try to stop by again to "check on them." The moments with Nick and Lila were not as frequent as they would like, so every encounter was savored to the max.

Nick and Taylor were now in the year when their specialty rarely allowed them to be in the same class. A class in mathematics, like linear algebra, or political science and history, was the exception.

Taylor started his junior year in "lab heaven" or "lab hell," depending on his perspective. His core courses in genetics, microbiology, and biochemistry all had associated lab work and specialized labs in molecular biology techniques, human physiology, and immunology. While he needed to do well in all of them, his interest intensified with the genetic lab, where he would study inheritance patterns, DNA analysis, and mutation experiments.

Taylor felt certain that his courses and lab work in his junior year would enable him to query his genetics professor, Dr. Phillip Whitmore, about genetic mutations that might cause Black parents to have a White child or vice versa. Once he completed some assigned tasks in the lab, he would spring the question that had lingered in his mind for years. Hearing from the biology and genetics guest speakers, experts on DNA research and heredity, would also provide him with the proper basis to delve into the mystery of his dream. *I'm almost there! I can feel it!*

Nick's courses multiplied in complexity, as orbital mechanics included planetary motion in addition to spacecraft trajectories, astrophysics, and planetary science, focused on understanding celestial bodies and the space environment. His aerodynamics and aerospace engineering courses covered advanced fluid mechanics, the aerodynamics of supersonic flight, structural mechanics for aerospace applications, and turbomachinery and jet propulsion.

Computer-aided design (CAD) and programming were on the rise, with early applications in aerospace engineering allowing computational techniques to solve engineering problems.

Nick always looked forward to hearing from NASA engineers, planetary science experts, and guest speakers who would discuss past and future Apollo missions. Apollo 16 and Apollo 17 were scheduled to be the last of the moon landings in April 1972 and December 1972, respectively. Researchers would discuss their study of potential missions to Mars and Venus.

Early in their junior year, Nick and Taylor discussed their plans to strategically position themselves for internships or mentorship programs for the summer of 1972, a year before graduating from Columbia. It seemed like the right step to take at the right time. They would need to achieve academic excellence and research experience in their labs, engage in networking, and obtain faculty advocacy.

Taylor had his eye on the lab in Cold Spring Harbor. Nick considered programs at the Goddard Institute for Space Studies, the Langley Research Center in Hampton, Virginia, a key NASA facility for aerodynamic research, space technology, and atmospheric studies, and the Marshall Space Flight Center in Huntsville, Alabama. Marshall played a crucial role in rocket development, space exploration, and propulsion systems, particularly during the Apollo program. Their ambition consumed them.

Because networking was necessary for the programs, Taylor would not want to miss the Cold Spring Harbor Symposia on Quantitative Biology. This major annual event would provide exposure to leading researchers and, undoubtedly, Dr. Caldwell. He made it his priority to mention his interest in the symposia to his professors at every opportunity.

Nick worked on his application to NASA's internship program early with guidance from his engineering professors. He ensured he was visible in the numerous student engineering groups and projects that Columbia offered as societies and aerospace research clubs.

The influence of faculty could not be overstated. Nick was profoundly shaped by professors engaged in NASA collaborations, research, and computing applications in aerospace. The genetics and microbiology faculty ensured that students with Taylor's passion were immersed in both theoretical and lab-based exploration of heredity, mutation, and molecular sequencing.

The moment between the Thanksgiving and Christmas holidays presented itself after an intense discussion exploring genetic mutations, pigmentation inheritance, and rare genetic phenomena related to human traits. Taylor raised his hand. He was one of fifteen students: the White students consisted of eight men and three women, while the Black students comprised three men and one woman.

Professor Whitmore said, "Yes, Taylor."

"Professor Whitmore. I have been thinking about this for a long time, but now seems like the right time to ask."

"I'm all ears. What's your question?"

"I've been thinking about genetic mutations and how they affect traits like skin color. Is it theoretically possible for Black parents to have a White child—or vice versa?" *There, I finally asked it! Why did it take me so long?* Everyone in the class sat up a little straighter and gave 100 percent of their attention to Dr. Whitmore.

"Taylor, that is a fascinating question. While it's highly uncommon, genetic variations can lead to unexpected traits in offspring." This first response was not what Taylor expected. He thought he would hear something like it was impossible. "The expression of skin color is influenced by multiple genes, primarily those that control melanin production. However, mutations, genetic recombination, and rare conditions can sometimes result in atypical pigmentation."

Taylor's following question displayed his level of knowledge and how it related to Whitmore's explanation. "So it wouldn't be a typical Mendelian inheritance, but rather a complex interplay of multiple genetic factors?"

"Exactly. Skin color inheritance follows a polygenic pattern, meaning multiple genes contribute. But, in rare cases, mutations such as albinism can result in a child with little or no melanin, regardless of parental skin tone. There are also cases of genetic recombination where ancestral traits can resurface." This topic was racing to the top of "the most interesting pile," as all thirty ears were entirely in reception mode.

Taylor had encountered a term related to human traits in his studies in developmental biology. Although it was not yet a mainstream study topic, some evolutionary biology faculty members explored genetic regression and inherited traits in human development.

He said, "Does that mean 'atavism,' where traits reappear after skipping generations, could play a role?"

Whitmore explained, "Atavism is a debated concept in genetics, but yes, ancestral traits encoded in DNA can sometimes be expressed due to recombination or mutation. If a child inherits specific genetic combinations that were dormant for generations, it could lead to an unexpected phenotypic outcome."

"Wow! So while the probability is extremely low, genetic diversity makes it possible. Are there any documented cases?"

"There have been reports, some linked to mixed ancestry and genetic variation across populations. In science, we always approach such cases with careful genetic analysis before making any assumptions."

Taylor was quiet for a moment as his mind drifted to his dream with Martin Luther King Jr., reminding him of the circle of Black and White people holding hands.

"Taylor, that was a fascinating question and discussion. Is there anything else?"

Returning from daydreaming, Taylor said, "I would love to explore this further. Maybe a research project focusing on pigmentation genetics?"

"That could be an excellent study! You might look into melanin production pathways, genetic mutations affecting pigmentation, and historical ancestry recombination."

The class ended with Taylor's enthusiasm through the roof. He decided to use the topic of atavism and Dr. Whitmore's suggestions as a basis for his internship program at the Cold Spring Harbor Lab in the summer of 1972. I can't wait to tell Martin Luther King Jr. what I learned in class today! *And Dr. Caldwell!*

Chapter 74

Summer, 1972—Internships

It didn't take long before Taylor's dream was revitalized. His "communication" with Martin Luther King Jr. could not have gone better. It was purposeful and precise. It represented understanding and direction. "Taylor! Taylor Washington! I understand you have some clarity to share. You know where *our dream* is headed. You're approaching the end goal of justice and equality for all God's children, Black and White, Jew and Gentile, all holding hands in freedom and love."

Taylor felt his connection with the civil rights leader was better than ever. He did not wake up in sweat or run to the bathroom to check the color of his skin. He was now much more intelligent and envisioned that his studies and research could lead to a better understanding of how Martin Luther King Jr.'s dream could become a reality. He was hopeful and determined to maintain his concentration and attentiveness, keeping them precisely focused on his research.

"Dr. King. Your dream is within our grasp. I will do everything in my power to make it happen. My professor told me I should continue my studies so that my dream, your dream, will become real."

"Good, Taylor. It's our dream, remember? Our dream. We can make it happen. Keep working on it. It will happen."

Taylor woke up with a smile, and it remained there when he met his parents and Ava for breakfast. Isaac said, "Taylor, you look very happy this morning. Not your usual 'I have a heavy schoolwork load' look. What's up?"

"Dad, I finally got an answer to my question of Black and White parents having different colored offspring and Dr. King and I discussed it . . . in my dream, of course."

Makena and Ava looked on with anticipation. Isaac said, "Oh, wow! I can't wait to hear this."

Ava, now fourteen years old, said, "Yeah, me too!"

Taylor explained his conversation in class with Professor Whitmore and how he "discussed" it with Martin Luther King Jr. in his dream. He said the dream was so different. It was not confusing or tense. It was clear . . . to him, and Dr. King. Makena and Isaac finally observed years of anxiety extinguished from their son's face. It was refreshing as they felt extreme pride in Taylor's accomplishments at Columbia and his potential.

Ava laughed at Taylor's explanation and said, "How is that possible? My friends are gonna think I'm crazy if I tell them that."

Taylor said, "Well, don't tell them. It's too early for them to understand anyway. I thought it was crazy too, and didn't tell anyone for a long time." Ava just looked at him, not knowing how to respond.

Nick and Taylor utilized every resource they could muster to land their internship programs for the summer of 1972. With one more year to go at Columbia University, they finally cracked the code and statistics that had previously prevented them from enrolling in a program, and they rationalized that they needed that time off to recover their sanity after all the hard work. Now, as seasoned students with research experience and faculty endorsements, they had found their niche.

Nick was scheduled for two fifteen-day visits: one at the Langley Research Center in Hampton, Virginia, where he would work alongside experts in aerodynamics and spaceflight systems, hear about Apollo program contributions, and observe wind tunnel testing and computational simulations; the other at the Marshall Space Flight Center in Huntsville, Alabama, to learn NASA's rocket development and propulsion systems, and meet with engineers who were developing Skylab, NASA's first space station scheduled to launch in 1973.

Taylor obtained his other dream: to work alongside geneticists, including Dr. Caldwell at the Cold Spring Harbor Lab, on projects related to polygenic inheritance and skin color, genetic mutations and rare phenotypes, atavism and ancestral trait reemergence, and epigenetics and environmental influence. He couldn't wait to get started. He had heard there were documented cases of genetic conditions that led to unexpected pigmentation inheritance. *What could be any closer to what matters to my dream?*

The internships were a phenomenal experience for both boys. The personal attention and variety of scientific substances kept them engaged and motivated to learn more. They thanked their mentors, who told them that they would go far, and promised to send their official reports to the university, which would contribute to the resumes the boys would prepare in the future. Their foundation in science had gained a crucial element from these internships, which will enhance the durability of their knowledge.

After a few weeks of relaxation at the beach with some mutual friends, the senior year at Columbia was upon Nick and Taylor like a relentless tide, pulling them forward with unyielding force. There was no turning back, no slowing down. The expectations and challenges would be ever present to the finish line of their academic journey—Commencement Day on May 16, 1973, an early graduation under the university's revised academic calendar.

During Nick and Taylor's final year of undergraduate work at Columbia, the period was marked by political scandal, scientific progress, and social movements. Students continued to engage in activism against the Vietnam War, racial injustice, and environmental issues, reflecting broader national concerns.

The Paris Peace Accords, an agreement to end the Vietnam War, were signed on January 27, 1973, by the United States, North Vietnam, South Vietnam, and the Provisional Revolutionary Government of South Vietnam (Viet Cong). Even though it ended direct involvement by the United States in Vietnam, fighting continued between the North and the South. Despite US troop withdrawals, war protests persisted, especially on college campuses.

Columbia University's student activists pushed for greater inclusion of Black and Latino students, protesting admissions policies and urban development projects that disproportionately affected Harlem residents. The Women's Rights Movement gained momentum as feminist activists pushed for equal pay, workplace rights, and reproductive freedom.

The Watergate scandal that began in June 1972 with the break-in at the Democratic National Committee headquarters intensified, leading to Senate hearings in 1973, exposing corruption in Nixon's administration. The impact on Columbia University resulted in student protests, with many demanding greater transparency in government.

The evolution of microprocessors paved the way for more powerful computing. Research into organ transplantation and heart disease treatments gained momentum. Astronaut Eugene Cernan led the final Apollo Moon landing on December 11, 1972, ending forty-one months of crewed lunar landings. NASA launched Skylab, the first US space station, on May 14, 1973, marking the beginning of long-duration space missions. Genetic research expanded with the development of DNA sequencing and molecular biology, laying the groundwork for future genetic engineering.

Space exploration and genetic advancements provided an ideal playground opportunity for Nick and Taylor. But first, they needed to get through their senior year. Nick had the usual stack of complex key courses, with new challenges of adapting to new computing methods and balancing theory and practical applications.

Taylor's key courses in molecular genetics, DNA research, developmental biology, and atavism studies faced challenges due to rapidly evolving techniques and complex data analysis. The 1970s marked a pivotal era in the ethical debates surrounding genetic modifications, as breakthroughs in DNA sequencing and genetic engineering raised profound questions about scientific responsibility, human intervention, and social consequences.

The effort Nick and Taylor exerted in their senior year was one where they pushed themselves to the limit, knowing their next step was graduate school. They had already discussed it and determined that a program at Columbia made the best sense. They were familiar with the programs and the faculty and had built good reputations through their research and mentorship programs.

Nick immersed himself in aerospace research, computational modeling, and propulsion studies to secure a spot in Columbia's master's in space engineering, which required academic excellence and technical expertise. Taylor was laser-focused on genetics research, molecular biology, and faculty mentorship to ensure he could transition to Columbia's master's in genetics program.

By the end of April 1973, they were over the hump. They had labored through the intense coursework, which they both loved and hated simultaneously. Deep down, they knew they loved it more than they hated it, because while it was grueling work, it was also a passion for knowledge and excellence. All the research, lab work, faculty collaboration, and networking paid off. They were primed for the master's degree programs at Columbia as they began to see their future evolving. As the final weeks drew to a close, they and their families were excited about the commencement ceremony.

Columbia University's graduation was a moment of tradition and transition, taking place on Low Plaza, the iconic heart of the university's campus. The mass of friends and families were seated as the graduates, in their caps and gowns, were ready to follow the faculty they came to know and respect. Nick and Taylor stood proudly and tall, the weight of their final moments pressing against their chests, a culmination of sleepless nights, endless exams, and relief.

Nick's grandfather was in a wheelchair at home with his wife. Due to his weakened condition, he could not travel but would celebrate when the family reunited after graduation. He had kept his promise to do his best to see Nicky graduate.

They had grown intellectually and physically over the last four years. Nick was just under six feet tall, weighing 170 pounds, with a full head of rich light brown hair and fair skin, all mounted on a moderately athletic frame. Taylor was taller, at six feet one inch, and weighed 180 pounds, with a strong brow, short hair, and a moderate brown skin tone, all on a well-proportioned frame. They were two handsome young men with ambitions for more scholarly work.

The procession, guest speakers, and recognition of academic excellence in aerospace, computing, and genetics research all helped maintain the excitement that reflected the students' years at Columbia. During Nick's and Taylor's years at Columbia, expertise, mentorship, and exposure to cutting-edge developments in engineering and genetics prepared them well for their next chapter in the two fields that were advancing at blazing speed.

After the graduation and family celebrations, Nick and Taylor looked forward to a well-deserved respite before embarking on a few weeks of additional mentorship, followed by their master's degree programs. Taylor continued research and learning at the lab in Cold Spring Harbor. Nick secured an industry mentorship with Northrop Grumman in Bethpage, Long Island, New York, for a few weeks in their aerospace development facilities. *Their resumes continued to develop and shine.*

Chapter 75

"HE WILL DO THINGS I COULD NEVER DREAM OF DOING."

Monique Langford and Tanya Winston were two women who had graduated from Columbia University's undergraduate program. Their paths mirrored those of Nick's and Taylor's through four years of intense study and research, as well as similar mentorship programs in genetics and aerospace engineering. The guys knew them and occasionally socialized with them in a larger crowd of students with similar interests.

Monique had been fascinated by genetics from an early age and had pursued her dream of becoming a research scientist. She and Taylor got to know one another better when they spent time together in their mentorship program at the Cold Spring Harbor Laboratory over the summer. She came from a family of two older sisters and a younger brother, living in Queens. Her parents had met in school, where they majored in biology, and their passion for science was passed down to the whole family.

Tanya's father was an airline pilot whose stories of flight always inspired her. Only she established her goals beyond the lower stratosphere. She was interested, like Nick, in the moon and beyond. They were in several classes together and shared experiences in their mentorship programs. She had two older brothers in pilot training, one with United Airlines, the other in the US Air Force's undergraduate pilot training at Vance Air Force Base in Oklahoma, all devoted, in one form or another, to "Oh! I have slipped the surly bonds of Earth," in reference to the poem *High Flight* by John Gillespie Magee Jr.

Nick, Tanya, Taylor, and Monique found themselves in the same master's degree programs at Columbia. They would work through the new challenges of study and research together and among their peers through a two-year program to earn more than forty credits.

Nick's studies focused on planetary motion, exploring shock waves and high-speed aircraft design, using emerging computing technologies, and applying numerical techniques to aerospace problems. Taylor was knee-deep in the study of DNA replication, transcription, and gene regulation. He had other core courses but was most interested in evolutionary biology, focusing on genetic variation and adaptation.

One late afternoon in a study lounge on campus, Taylor and Monique were seated at a table with stacks of research papers and analytical data. Their conversation turned to the ethical dilemmas of genetic modification, which stirred debate among scientists and the public.

Monique said, "Every time I read about gene manipulation, I hear someone say scientists are 'playing God!' Do we really think that's what we are doing? We're identifying sequences, correcting errors . . . but isn't that just the progression of science?"

Taylor thought momentarily, then said, "I think people see it as an unnatural interference with life. It raises moral questions about human control over evolution. It's progress, sure. But that's the concern. The moment we alter genetics beyond disease prevention, we're designing traits. What happens when people start wanting 'perfect' children?" He then thought, *Or Black parents want White offspring or vice versa.*

Monique was always one to push the limits of knowledge. "It's unsettling. Right now, we're studying how mutations affect heredity, but what's stopping someone from using that same knowledge to dictate intelligence or eye color? When does research become manipulation?"

"Scientists are already discussing limits. They know what's at stake, safety, ethics, consequences we can't predict."

"Yet we work under Cold Spring Harbor's shadow, the place once tied to eugenics research (referring to the belief that human traits could be improved through selective breeding). Have we really learned from history?"

Taylor became more serious. "I think what we are doing matters, and we are at the edge of something big. But who decides the boundary between curing disease and genetic enhancement?"

"And if we can prevent genetic disorders before birth, wouldn't parents want that option? Wouldn't we, if given the choice?" Monique always had a way of adding one more question to prompt further thought. They closed their notebooks and collected their papers before moving on.

Taylor contemplated what Monique said at the end of her question. *"Wouldn't we, if given the choice?" What did she mean by "we"?* There was no doubt that Taylor and Monique shared a high interest in genetics and all its possibilities, and that an interest in each other seemed to be forming.

In late January 1974, after the Christmas holiday, Jonathan received word that his father was back in the hospital, much weaker this time, and the prognosis was not good. He rushed to his father's side and, after speaking with the doctors, realized his father was probably not going to recover. His heart was very stressed, and the years had taken their toll on him. Jonathan notified Mary and the other members of the extended family. He called Columbia University's Public Safety Office, which handled emergencies and could locate students if necessary.

When Nick received the urgent message to contact his mother at home, Nick immediately sensed it was about his grandfather. Tanya was sitting next to him in class when he received the note asking him to call home. She observed the anxiety on Nick's face and whispered, "Is everything okay?"

"I don't think so. I have to leave. I'll contact you as soon as possible." He excused himself from class as his professor and student peers looked concerned.

His professor commented, "Okay, everyone. Let's hope it's not too serious for whatever Nick is going through here." However, everyone sensed it was serious and hoped for Nick's best (or whoever needed it).

Nick rushed from the campus to take the subway back to East New York and then immediately to the hospital. He couldn't imagine not seeing his grandfather again and telling him how much he loved and admired him. As he rode the subway, he recalled many of his conversations with his grandfather—the stories of immigration to America, marrying Grandma in 1920, working in the coat factories, and the long wait to become an American citizen. Grandpa Greene always had Nicky in stitches, laughing at his jokes and asking his grandfather more about his early life. William Greene loved that about his grandson, someone who wanted to know more about his ancestry.

Nick arrived at the hospital to find his father and mother, his grandmother, his aunts Julie and Kathleen, and his cousins in the room with his grandfather. Lila, now eight, was still in school; Mary had notified the school that she needed to go to the hospital for Jonathan's father and that her friend Makena would pick Lila up after classes ended.

Nick observed the family in tears. He was too late. His grandfather passed away less than thirty minutes before. They said that some of Grandpa's last words were, "Tell Nicky, I love him, and I am so proud of him, and that he will do things I could never dream of doing." Nick broke down in tears as he hugged his grandfather for the last time.

Nick notified his professors and some classmates, including Tanya, about his grandfather's death and that he would be out for the remainder of the week to be with family through the funeral and burial of his grandfather.

Tanya said, "Nick, I am so sorry. I know how much your grandfather meant to you. I loved hearing about him from you, how much you admired him. If you need to talk or just sit silently with me, I'm here . . . for you." Nick thanked her, and although he didn't see her and only heard her voice, he felt warmth and understanding in this difficult time. The effect of her tone and steadiness lingered with him long after they ended the call.

Mary picked up Lila at the Washingtons' apartment, and after giving all the sad news about Jonathan's father, learned that Isaac's father's health was declining. Darnell had cardiovascular issues with hypertension and diabetes, and fit perfectly into the higher mortality rates group for stroke victims. His condition was compounded by worsening kidney disease and neuropathy over the last few years.

When Taylor heard the news about Nick's grandfather, he immediately went to comfort his friend. Taylor had become closer to Nick's grandfather, who, over the years, had finally come to accept that this young Black man was a blessing to Nick. Grandpa Greene had never used a single word of racial discrimination in a long time, which the family noticed and appreciated.

Tanya spent extra time with Nick to help him in two ways: to catch up on the lectures and research requirements and to offer him comfort. They walked through the campus to Morningside Park, sat on a bench, held hands, and remained quiet.

It was not long before Nick needed to focus entirely on his studies. The occasional vision of his grandfather emerged, and his last words, which were spoken through his family, gave Nick all the motivation he needed to "do things I could never dream of doing." The silence on the park bench ended. Nick said, "Thank you for all your help and understanding," as he squeezed her hand. He decided to change the subject.

"Tanya, do you think NASA will have room for us? Apollo's finished. Skylab is interesting, but I've read funding is shaky. I mean, getting into Langley or Marshall would be a dream, but . . ."

"NASA's always going to need engineers. Space exploration will not stop. Why would it? The programs will just shift. They will always need people who understand orbital mechanics, propulsion, and thermal control. We fit right into that."

"So, you see us designing rockets for Mars and beyond?"

"Yes, I do. Let's be realistic. Skylab, satellite development, space probes. That's where it's at. Northrop Grumman's got contracts everywhere. TRW does the satellite work, and Lockheed is looking at deep-space telemetry."

"You're right. TRW is interesting. Their Pioneer missions are incredible. Imagine working on interplanetary spacecraft."

"Yeah, and what about Boeing? They're pivoting from Apollo to shuttle concepts. Columbia has some faculty consulting with them. Maybe we should check that out."

Nick said, "I always thought of myself as a NASA guy, but maybe defense and aerospace contractors make more sense."

"If you had to choose right now, NASA or industry?"

"NASA is my dream, but I suppose industry has more stability. We should both keep our options open." Regardless of the direction they might take in the future, they knew they would cross that road when they got there, and either way, the future for two devoted engineers was wide open. They also knew that holding hands on a park bench in New York City's Morningside Park was more than just someone comforting the other.

Chapter 76

JOBS (AND A DOUBLE WEDDING) SECURED

During Nick and Taylor's graduate program, Columbia University remained a hub of intellectual and activist engagement, responding to global shifts in the war in Southeast Asia, political events, scientific and technological advancements, and civil rights and social movements. As a result, protests and academic discourse continued, and institutional reforms were debated.

After US combat involvement in Vietnam ended, Columbia's anti-war movement slowed but didn't vanish. Student groups pushed for supporting Vietnamese refugees and demanded accountability for war crimes. There were protests about the fall of Saigon (April 1975), where some students viewed the war's end as a failure of US foreign policy and organized teach-ins about Cold War geopolitics.

The Watergate scandal and Nixon's resignation prompted Columbia law and political science students to dissect the constitutional crisis, holding forums on executive overreach. Students debated whether Gerald Ford's pardon of Nixon was an attempt to heal the country or a betrayal of justice.

Like Nick and Tanya, engineering students studied Skylab's experiments and other developments in space exploration. Columbia's computer science department analyzed Intel's 8080 microprocessor, exploring early computing advancements.

Columbia's Black student organizations pushed for faculty diversity, equitable housing, and greater representation in academic leadership. In the women's rights movement, the landmark decision of Roe v. Wade (1973) and the enforcement of Title IX led students to demand more equitable gender policies on campus.

At the Asilomar Conference on Recombinant DNA, held in February 1975 at Asilomar Beach, California, scientists gathered for a landmark meeting to discuss the potential biohazards and ethical concerns associated with recombinant DNA technology. It represented the rare instance of scientists proactively regulating their own work, setting a precedent for ethical oversight in genetic research.

Most students, like Nick and Taylor and their female friends, devoted more time to their fascinating scientific studies rather than being active in protests, sit-ins, or formal debates. Generally, Columbia's history, political science, and social studies majors were more involved in civil rights activism, political movements, and historical discourse.

Science and engineering students addressed systemic issues by applying technology, ethics, and policy frameworks. World events and the active reactions to them were not necessarily as important as the heads-down work in their master's degree courses, which took up most of their time. Taylor, Monique, Nick, and Tanya devoted the rest of their time to each other. They double-dated as often as their schedules allowed, usually spending their free time in the city visiting numerous places or having a meal. Their classmates and faculty members noticed a gradual change in their behavior, tell-tale signs of their budding relationships—the shared glance, the small gestures.

Despite the challenges of higher education for each couple, their romantic relationships began as a few sparks and evolved into an undeniable flame over the course of the two-year program. They used their time wisely to earn and utilize faculty mentorship and research guidance, aligning their work with industry needs. They maintained connections with industry and government, securing letters of recommendation that carried strong endorsements for positions in biotech firms, aerospace companies, and national research laboratories. Nick and Taylor turned to another priority as they saw the light at the end of the academic tunnel and the potential jobs ahead. They applied for jobs at several research centers they had become familiar with over the years at Columbia.

They secured their jobs, beginning in late summer. Taylor would be at the Cold Spring Harbor Laboratory as a molecular geneticist, focusing on evolutionary biology, and Nick at NASA's Goddard Institute for Space Studies as an aerospace engineer, contributing to NASA's space missions and satellite development. The women secured employment at the same facilities: Monique at the lab in Cold Spring Harbor as a research associate, assisting with DNA sequencing and molecular biology experiments, and Tanya at GISS as a planetary scientist. They were all elated with how the jobs and locations synced up with each other.

The day that seemed so distant was now here. Columbia University's Commencement Exercises for its 221st academic year took place on May 14, 1975, with more than sixty-six hundred students receiving their degrees. Nick and Taylor, who had shared so much since they were six years old, who stood up for one another (or stood next to one another in silent support), now stood proudly as they received their advanced degrees, having completed some of the most challenging academic work imaginable. Their families sat with pride and excitement at the beacon of intellectual energy and cultural vibrancy in the heart of the Big Apple—Columbia University—a prestigious institution that seamlessly blends history, academia, and urban dynamism.

After graduation, Nick and Taylor decided they needed to declare independence and looked for a temporary apartment in East New York to share the rent and utility payments. The neighborhood experienced a significant decline in the mid-1970s, marked by an economic downturn, rising crime rates, deteriorating housing conditions, and social instability. Despite these hardships, community activism emerged, with residents fighting for better housing, safer streets, and improved city services. They selected a location near their parents, which happened to be near Angelo's grocery store, making food shopping easy.

One day, searching for the apartment, they stopped at Angelo's, hoping to see him. It had been years since either was there. They were happy to see the little man, older and weaker, but still vibrant and friendly. "Buongiorno, Angelo!"

He looked up from behind the counter, where he was stocking some shelves. He paused before he realized it was Taylor and Nick. His expression changed from "Who are these guys?" to "Ah, *Buongiorno, come stai?*" The boys remembered that it meant, "How are you?"

They responded in unison, "*Tutto bene,*" meaning everything is good. They talked for a while, and Angelo told them in his broken English how proud he was of them, how much they had grown, and to come and see him often. They responded that they would because they would be moving into a nearby apartment and shop at his store. He looked tired but happy.

When they asked Angelo when he would retire, he said, "Retire? Whosa gotta time for that? The tomatoes, they still needa to be sorted, I gotta to bake some bread, whosa gonna pick the best oranges? No, thisa store isa my life. They carry me out before I leave on my own!"

They all laughed. Nick and Taylor shook Angelo's hand and wished him well, "*Stai bene!*"

Once settled in their apartment and into the routine of hopping on the subway to work—in Taylor's case, via the subway followed by the LIRR to Cold Spring Harbor—they discussed their work and how they had adjusted to their new roles and responsibilities. They also kept their social lives intact with Monique and Tanya as they addressed the fascination of their work and the fascination they felt for each other.

Throughout the grueling graduate degree program, each couple had supported one another academically and personally during the most difficult times. The men and women always had their priorities in check at Columbia, and now at their jobs. It was time to look ahead a bit further. Nick and Taylor confided in one another about their futures as they sat in a coffee shop one weekend.

Nick sat with his arms crossed, had a huge grin, and said, "I am going to ask Tanya if she will marry me!"

Taylor sipped his coffee, looked at Nick, and said, "I was waiting for you to tell me. I figured it would be soon, and here we are. I am ready to ask Monique the same question."

Nick laughed and jokingly said, "Oh, you mean if she will marry me?"

"No, wise guy. If she will marry me, Taylor Washington, distinguished geneticist who works at the renowned Cold Spring Harbor Lab!" They both enjoyed a good laugh over that.

Nick came back, "Well, wonders never cease! Who would have thought?" They sipped their coffees, then Nick proposed an idea. "Hey, what do you think . . . (he paused, as Taylor's face turned to "think what?") . . . what do you think . . . let's say we don't just do two weddings. What if we do one? Together."

"A double wedding? You serious?"

"Think about it. Our lives have been intertwined since first grade. We have been through everything together, good and bad. Now we're getting married, assuming, of course, the women say yes."

Taylor said, "How could they not say yes. Look at us, man. We're the best."

Nick said, "Well, I can't disagree with that! So, why not make it special, something unforgettable? Can you imagine the energy in the room? And it's less stress, fewer logistics, and twice the fun!"

"Ah, now I see the engineering side of Nicholas Greene! I like it, but when Tanya and Monique say yes . . . when they jump right into yes . . . we should discuss that with them, don't you think?"

"Absolutely, I'm with you on that, just like everything we've done together."

Nick proposed to Tanya, and Taylor proposed to Monique on the same day, Christmas Eve 1975, under the Christmas tree, in private, in the women's respective homes, while the family was in an adjacent room. The women said, "Yes!" Nick and Taylor got on the phone after the families congratulated their sons and future daughters-in-law. Nick and Taylor didn't immediately discuss a double wedding with the women or a date yet, but asked them to consider a day in the fall of 1976. The planning would begin.

The families had met the women, their future daughters-in-law, a few months after Nick's grandfather passed away. Jonathan, Mary, and Lila quickly welcomed Tanya, as they observed her support and affection for their son and their commitment to one another. Taylor's parents and sister initially reserved their feelings, but that changed quickly when they learned of Monique's passion for the same goals as their son, how happy she made him, and witnessed a growing relationship that was built on respect, understanding, and mutual support.

Nick and Taylor would serve as best man for each other, being the groom in their own vows and standing beside their best friend in theirs. Shortly after their engagements to be married, the couples decided that a double wedding was a great idea to bring all the families together. They envisioned a shared celebration of love, unity, and cultural exchange, where they could incorporate food, music, and traditions from Black and White heritage.

The wedding date was set for October 30, 1976, in Brooklyn. *Black and White coming together to hold hands and rejoice!* Taylor thought, *Martin Luther King Jr. would be proud!*

Chapter 77

EPHEMERAL TIME, 1957–1976

Loyal friends, Nick and Taylor, grew up in a dynamic neighborhood that underwent major transformations, shaped by economic shifts, racial demographic changes, discrimination, urban decline, and grassroots activism.

The Brooklyn community saw White flight and racial transition, characterized by a shift from a predominantly White neighborhood to a Black and Latino community. Many White residents moved to the suburbs, driven by real estate speculation and racial tensions. As city services declined, local activists formed groups, united community centers, and advocated for better housing, education, and safety.

Banks and real estate developers denied loans to people of color, leading to widespread housing abandonment and decay. Many landlords abandoned properties, leading to arson-for-profit schemes, where buildings were deliberately set on fire for insurance payouts. Local factories and small businesses declined, resulting in high unemployment and worsening poverty.

Crime surged in intensity due to gang activity, drug trade, and rising homicide rates, fueled by economic hardship. Scandals within the NYPD, including bribery and misconduct, weakened public trust in law enforcement.

Local leaders fought for fair housing, school funding, and racial equality, challenging discriminatory policies. Schools suffered from overcrowding, outdated materials, and high dropout rates.

Despite these challenges, community resilience remained strong, working to rebuild neighborhoods, demand better services, and push for policy changes.

In the nearly twenty years that had transpired, many people connected directly or remotely with Nick and Taylor, and experienced inevitable change. It was a period of "goodbyes, karma, restitution, and sad farewells."

Dr. Mary Carpenter retired from PS 91, having served as the school principal with integrity, compassion, and unwavering dedication to the students, staff, and community. She passed the reins to Donna Sweeney in a ceremony marked by deep appreciation and respect in recognition of her years of dedication, wisdom, and lasting contributions to PS 91.

Maggie Vargas (formerly Maggie Lopez) became the matron of honor for her close friend Izzy Garcia at her wedding. Maggie and Izzy continued teaching at PS 91, and each had two children attending the school. After several remote tours of duty, Maggie's husband, Rafael, served in a US Marine Corps recruitment center in Brooklyn, enabling him to be with his family after many years of devoted service to his country.

Jamal Brown, janitor and staff member at PS 91, passed away after a year-long illness with cancer. The entire school staff attended his funeral.

The 75th Precinct of the NYPD changed with the retirements of Shamus O'Reilly and Captain Francis O'Rourke. The boys in blue presented Shamus with a plaque holding his famous nightstick with the words "Shamin' Slammin' Sam" underneath. Conan McGuire progressed through his career and became the captain at the precinct. Marty O'Shea became the head of the NYPD's Bureau of Special Services and Investigation.

Reggie "Smokes" Johnson, the Black man who worked at a grocery store as a night watchman and as a janitor, was attacked by several White men again. This time, he didn't survive. The men were never caught.

The hellbent group of racial discriminators, who thought intimidation and violence were justifiable pastimes, were under the cloud of Sanchia karma that accounted for the total sum of all their piled-up criminal actions. Henry Mason (aka Sabre), Jethro Paine (aka Cue Ball), Butch Brady (aka VenoM), Rhett Walker (aka Cyclone), and Brian Savage (aka Bullet) were all still serving lengthy sentences behind bars. Ricky Miller (aka Deadman) "lived" up to his name. He was now a real dead man.

Buddy Mason, Henry's son, served time in jail, only to return shortly after his release. His indoctrination by his father warped his mind so much that he could never accept accountability and lived a life of racial discrimination. His younger brother, Sonny, was without parents or extended family, which required him to be in a structured, compassionate program of rehabilitation. He was placed in therapeutic foster care with a group that provided stability, mentorship, and emotional support for at-risk youth. He was on a good path, mentally and physically, as he put his past in the past.

Once a 75th Precinct administrative clerk Tyler Barnes, turned spy with the code name of X-ray, sought to make amends after serving time for his crimes. With the help of his parents and Sergeant McGuire, now captain, Tyler engaged in sustained, meaningful efforts to rebuild trust as he contributed positively to the community. Tyler's parents, Annie and Thomas Barnes, were extremely proud of their son.

He actively volunteered in grassroots civil rights organizations that had been negatively impacted by his actions. He often spoke in schools to teach young people about the consequences of their actions when they unlawfully take the law into their own hands or seek revenge. His actions were genuine, and the tremendous weight on his shoulders dissipated, although not entirely. He would always regret being X-ray.

Mrs. Daniels and her dog, Damon, lived together for nearly twelve years in Yonkers before they both passed away within weeks of one another. Their time together was most rewarding for both, as they shared devotion and love, which would not have happened had it not been for Tyler Barnes' information on Henry Mason and others.

Jack "Big Man" Henderson was in a New York upstate penitentiary, not as a prisoner, but as an FBI informant to continue his craft of getting real criminals to reveal important information, leading to further arrests. Even though he was promoted to run the division that led these informant tasks, he could not completely avoid the occasional opportunity to get in a cell and scare the hell out of someone, while he conned them into telling their secrets.

Dr. James Reed, a distinguished professor of Black history at NYU, had witnessed dramatic changes in the civil rights movement and was instrumental in making the department he served more robust and influential, thereby enhancing the university's prestige. He retired from full-time service but continued to guide students through mentorship and advice.

He occasionally gave public lectures and supported workshops that hosted Black history, activism, and social justice. He invited the Black discussion group, which included Isaac, to these community engagements. Although retired, he continued to write books and articles that inspired discussions on Black history and contemporary issues. He was delighted to learn of all the success Taylor had achieved through his education and would not miss the wedding he was invited to attend.

Doctors Clair Cartwright and Zora Caldwell maintained close contact with Taylor through their professional, scientific work, agreeing that Taylor and Monique had bright futures ahead.

Bright futures ahead! For Nick and Tanya, for Taylor and Monique. It would be here soon, as time moves relentlessly forward, an endless current carrying everything with it. The present is always fleeting and ephemeral, with barely a chance to exist before it's pushed into the past, dissolving into a memory. People will be promoted, retire, and pass away as the world evolves socially, politically, technologically, and scientifically. They, like everything else, will come and go.

Nick and Taylor's relationship was a perfect example of embracing and enjoying experiences as they happen. A deep appreciation for the present and for each other allowed them to savor life, its challenges, and its opportunities with mindfulness and gratitude. Despite the chaotic and frenzied demands of the world, with the weight of uncertainty always present, they found sanctuary in their friendship. They always had, from the earliest days.

Chapter 78

GENETIC MELTING POT

Taylor's dream was undeniably linked with the dream of a civil rights leader who captured the attention of a nation through a combination of moral clarity, strategic activism, and powerful oratory. Their "communication" motivated Taylor to take responsibility for the action that would lead to justice and equality, that would eradicate racial discrimination and violence, and would enable a nation to rise and live the true meaning of its fundamental creed: "We hold these truths to be self-evident; that all men are created equal."

The twist in his dream, where he wondered about the possibility of Black parents having White offspring and vice versa, prompted his interest in the genetic fundamentals that might answer that question. However strange as it seemed, the support from his closest friend, Nick, and eventually from the boys' parents incentivized Taylor to stay the course, leading to his growing interest and devotion to learning as much as he could about genetics.

He eventually envisioned a future where genetic research could bridge divides, where mapping our biological connections might inspire more profound unity. If genes could reveal the shared stories within us all, then perhaps science could reinforce the idea that no person is truly separate, and that every generation is intertwined with those who came before—and those yet to come.

The "genetic melting pot" concept aligns with the theories suggesting that genetic diversity increases as populations intermix over generations, potentially diminishing the significance of racial distinctions. Evolutionary genetics highlights how human populations share a vast majority of their genetic makeup, emphasizing our common ancestry.

Research indicates that all humans share a common maternal ancestor, known as "Mitochondrial Eve," who lived approximately 150,000 to 300,000 years ago, supporting the "Out of Africa Theory." It emphasizes the interconnection of all humans from a genetic perspective, allowing "gene flow," the transfer of genetic material between populations. This suggests that historical migration, trade, and intermarriage have led to a blending of genetic traits across continents, supporting the idea of diminishing biological distinctions between racial groups.

Taylor's studies at Columbia University, and now at his and Monique's work at the Cold Spring Harbor Laboratory, can address the "melting pot" idea in evolution, specifically the Hybrid Vigor concept, which suggests that genetic mixing leads to greater diversity, resulting in stronger, healthier populations. Genome-wide studies have shown that humans are genetically more similar than different. Observable variations, such as skin color or facial features, make up a tiny fraction of genetic differences.

From a social and cultural perspective, education and awareness of genetics demonstrate that race is a social construct rather than a strict biological reality, and that increased globalization and cross-cultural interactions continue to expand genetic mixing, fostering a melting-pot society where race becomes less significant.

Having personally been a victim of racial discrimination and violence, Taylor, now educated and mature, understands that while genetics reveals the shared humanity and potential diminishing of racial divides, addressing racial issues ultimately requires societal changes in attitudes, policies, and education. Science can be a powerful tool for encouraging dialogue and understanding about our shared origins.

For Taylor, studying genetics became more than an academic pursuit. It was an exploration of origins, an attempt to decode humanity's shared inheritance. It was a means to an end—to satisfy a dream—for justice and equality.

Chapter 79

WHITE LAKE, 1980

The early evening air of June cooled, as a slight breeze swept through the trees surrounding White Lake. The lake, according to local lore, also had a Native American name of Kauneonga, meaning lake with two wings, because it had a figure-eight layout resembling wings. The nearby town of Bethel was a postcard image of a hamlet in Sullivan County, approximately one hundred miles from East New York, making it a two-hour drive by car.

Rustic wooden cabins were scattered around the lake and nestled among towering pines and oaks, adding to the serenity of the relaxing environment. The moon was full as it spilled its light across the still water, which appeared almost glass-like and haunting. It provided a weightless, timeless aura of quiet contemplation that Taylor and Nick enjoyed as they sat in their Adirondack chairs facing the water.

Nick said, "I can't believe our fourth wedding anniversary is coming up in just a few months."

Taylor gazed at the water. "Yeah, man. When they say, 'time flies,' it's no lie."

"You know, I love times like these, when there are no distractions, no pressing work, no immediate obligations, where you have time to reflect and recall the memories."

"Amen to that. I can use more time like this. It's an opportunity to recharge the batteries, body, and mind."

Nick said, "I can't argue with that. I've been so busy, I forgot how to relax."

"This was a great idea coming up here. Your family did a good thing by purchasing this place last year. You'll be able to enjoy it for years to come. And, thank you for inviting Monique and me."

"Of course. We should make it a tradition . . . every year . . . we meet here to recharge our batteries."

"I like it! Especially since our jobs have not allowed us to get together as often as we would like." Taylor and Monique were on the cusp of monumental advancements in genetics research at the Cold Spring Harbor Lab, integrating analyses from several major projects by the scientific team there.

"Good! We'll make it a priority among priorities. You're right, we haven't gotten together as much as Tanya and I would like with you two." He knew that the work he and Tanya were doing at the Goddard Institute was becoming increasingly intense, as climate modeling, atmospheric research, and planetary studies became more critical in studying Mars and Venus.

The Cosmic Background Explorer (COBE) was another key effort that would help confirm the Big Bang theory. First formalized in 1927 by Georges Lemaître, a Belgian physicist and Catholic priest who proposed that the universe expanded from a "primeval atom," the theory gained strong support in 1929 when Edwin Hubble discovered that galaxies were moving away from each other, indicating cosmic expansion.

Taylor reminisced. "Almost four years ago! Wow! Brings me back to the wedding of weddings!"

"Yeah, no kidding. It was a plunge into the unknown at first with our two families. Remember the circle of Black and White that we asked everyone to join on the dance floor?"

Taylor said, "How can I forget? It was not only a test of our two families, Black and White, getting together, but it also immediately reminded me of my 'conversation' with Martin Luther King Jr. in my perennial dream. Remember? 'Taylor! Taylor Washington!'"

He called out his name in the eerie manner that he "heard" it.

"Taylor, keep working on our dream. All God's children, Black and White, Jew and Gentile, holding hands for equality and justice. He kept pushing me."

Nick said, "Yeah, and you know what? Our double wedding was a symbol of that."

They both took a pause, looked out at the water that could cast a spell on them, before Nick said, "Taylor, as I look back on all the years you and I have known each other, what we've been through together, how we've supported one another, during the chaos of the civil rights movement, with all its verbal hate and physical violence, with the war in Vietnam where we could have been drafted, with political unrest, assassinations, you name it. Who could have ever known we could last as friends this long? Think about it. A White guy and a Black guy. What are the odds?"

Taylor was about to answer Nick's question when Natalie, Nick and Tanya's three-year-old daughter, interrupted them as she approached the men in their chairs. She was wrapped in her cotton pajama set, which displayed a pattern of tiny stars. Its long sleeves kept her warm against the night's cool breeze.

Nick said, "Oh, hi, sweetie. Are you ready for bed?" Tanya and Monique were not far behind, approaching arm-in-arm, and quietly listened to Nick and his daughter's conversation.

Her voice was soft and sweet. "Yes." She rubbed her eyes and put her hands out in a gesture for her father to pick her up so she could sit on his lap.

Natalie said, "Mommy read me a story. And Aunt Monique did too."

"Oh, how nice. Did you like the story? What story was it?"

"*Clifford the Big Red Dog.*"

"And what was the other story?"

"It was *Clifford the Big Red Dog.*"

"You mean, Mommy and Aunt Monique read you the same story? You heard the story two times?" He held up two fingers.

"Yes. I like that story. I like Clifford."

The women thought it would be a quick "Night-night, Daddy," but they observed there was no rush for Natalie to exit the scene for bed, even though her fists were getting a workout rubbing her eyes. They sat in vacant Adirondack chairs facing the men. Monique was now seven months pregnant with Taylor's and her first child, and sitting became necessary.

"Daddy," she asked as she looked at Taylor, her father, her mother, and Monique.

"Yes, sweetie."

Natalie pointed at her father's face and said, "Daddy, why do you have that color skin, and Uncle Taylor have that color skin?" She pointed at Taylor's face. Taylor smiled and thought, *"Oh boy, I can't wait to hear this!"*

Before he could answer his little girl, Natalie pointed to her mother and then to Monique, asking the same question. It was a very valid question because everyone had different shades of skin color. Then she pulled up one sleeve and pointed to the skin on her arm.

"See my skin, Daddy?"

"Yes, you have beautiful skin."

"Why do we have different color skin, Daddy?"

This was a very observant little girl. Nick thought, *"We have a budding scientist in the family, very inquisitive, searching for answers!"*

Tanya, Monique, and Taylor all looked at Nick with a silent, "Well?"

Nick said in his quiet, confiding manner, "Sweetie, we all have different-colored skin because that's how God made us, so we can all be interesting to one another, all be our own selves. What if we all looked the same? That would be pretty boring, right?" Natalie looked at her skin and shook her head, but still a little perplexed, she just shrugged her shoulders, hugged and kissed her father, and motioned to get down.

Nick told her, "Night-night, sweetie, I love you."

"Night-night, Daddy. I love you." She rushed over with open arms to Taylor, who picked her up and sat her on his lap.

She hugged and kissed him and said, "Night-night, Uncle Taylor. I love you." He returned the same gestures and words of love and lifted the pajama package so she could run to her mother and Aunt Monique. The night air filled her little lungs, and she would be asleep before her head hit the pillow.

Tanya helped Monique out of the Adirondack chair, as her baby bump and the angle of the seat did not offer any easy exit, then lifted Natalie into her arms, and they headed back to the cabin. Turning her head, Tanya said, "We're pretty tired, guys. We might turn in soon and get some rest. Don't stay out too late."

Taylor said, "She's a real cutie, that Natalie. I can't wait to see what our baby will be."

"Me too. It won't be long now. You'll wake up every four hours through the night before you know it." They both laughed.

"Natalie is so curious. Those questions. I think she's a little scientist already!"

Nick said, "I was thinking the same thing."

They took a deep breath, looked out over the water, and were quiet for a minute, which seemed like an eternity. Nick said, "I'm not ready to go in just yet, you?"

"Nah, I'm good for a while. It's hard to even think of getting up. It's so comfortable and peaceful out here. I want to soak in a little more. So what were we discussing before such a beautiful interruption?"

Chapter 80

A COMMEMORATIVE TOAST

"Who could have ever known we could last as friends this long? Think about it. A White guy and a Black guy. What are the odds?" When Nick asked Taylor this question, he was thinking of probabilities, the likelihood of an event occurring, rather than comparing the number of successful outcomes to the number of unsuccessful ones. As a scientist, he knew these were related but not precisely the same question mathematically. He was on vacation. He didn't want to make it too scientific. It was just light conversation that led to a lengthy narrative by each of them.

Nick and Taylor knew what they observed from the first day of first grade: a new environment with many kids, some similar to them and some not. They may have gone through school, never having their parents meet, had it not been for the racist attack at PS 91 that prompted the school principal, Dr. Carpenter, to call a meeting for the parents with local police participation. The Greenes and the Washingtons met at that meeting, and what had followed intertwined the lives of Nick and Taylor, as well as their parents.

One could debate whether the influence of loving, caring, and understanding parents was greater in forming their sons' lasting relationship or the other way around—their sons' strong bond that resulted in a Black family and a White family coming together.

Nick did not recall his question immediately. Instead, he said, "Our double wedding. Yeah, as we asked everyone to assemble in a circle in no particular order for a short prayer at the reception, other than alternating Black and White, Black and White."

Taylor said, "You know, given the times, when the civil rights movement had been through so much, with progress and setbacks,

I wasn't sure exactly if we would have any concerns, worry, resistance, or disapproval. We took a risk."

Nick said, "You know, I give a lot of credit to our parents. Number one, they set an excellent example for others, the way they accepted each other, knowing how close we became. They always supported our relationship and influenced some family attitudes. My Grandpa Greene, rest his soul, he didn't show any deep-rooted hatred for Blacks, but he always discriminated against them in subtle ways. Ways and attitudes he had learned from his parents. You knew him before he passed. He was a different man."

Taylor agreed. "Yes, he was. He treated me and my family very well. Mutual respect emerged from growing acceptance of us as individuals."

"I think once people recognized the change in him and others, they accepted our cultural and traditional differences more easily."

"Yeah, I'll say. Remember how we mixed the Motown and soul music with the classic rock and jazz, and the Southern comfort food with the American dishes." The guys laughed as they recalled how many were reluctant to engage in it until they tried it.

Nick said, "And Tanya and I really loved your and Monique's suggestion to alternate members from our families in the seating. After a few minutes of staring at one another, you couldn't break their conversation if you tried."

Taylor added, "Well, it's no surprise that Monique and I loved Tanya's idea of lighting a unity candle to symbolize the merging of our families. And do you remember how Ava and Lila were dancin' together all night? They had the time of their lives."

Nick crossed his arms and looked at Taylor. "Here we are. We survived in an area where racism was terrible—much worse in the South, of course, but still terrible. The gangs in Brooklyn. Heck, the discrimination you and your family experienced. I remember the incidents on the subway on the way to Yankee Stadium and at the ballpark, and the time that White group beat you up when you were on your way to Angelo's and ended up in the hospital."

"I know, Nick. What stands out in my mind is your support and understanding. The way you said you can't walk in a Black person's shoes, but you can stand beside them. That is powerful, man. When

I heard you say that, I knew I could depend on you no matter what. And you know what I hate?"

"What?"

"I hate when Black people call all White people 'White supremacists,' and throw them into a category like that. That's racism also."

Nick turned his conversation to what he learned from Taylor. "I learned a lot from you, Taylor."

"What do you mean?"

"I learned the reality of racial inequality. Like I said, I witnessed it firsthand through your experiences, just because of your skin color. But I also saw how you stood firm in those challenges and your resilience. I watched you embrace the civil rights movement and learned how you found guidance from one of your role models in the fight, Martin Luther King Jr. I genuinely believe your dream was meant to be. Look how far you've come, working in a complex science, and seeking the answers you have worked so hard to find—your determination, steadfastness, and devotion. I'm proud of you, man, and I feel so fortunate that you're my friend."

Taylor choked up as he listened to Nick's praises. He had to swallow a few times. "Nick, thank you. Your friendship means everything to me. It always has. You always stood by me, listened, and never made fun of my dreams. You showed me that our relationship can endure anything. You are as Black as I am White, if that makes any sense."

"It does. It makes perfect sense. But what troubles me is that we are the exception. Even though society is changing, and progress is being made in terms of civil rights—not only for people of color, but also for women's rights—there remains racial discrimination in many forms, economically, and in housing, for example. When does it stop? Will it ever stop?"

"That's the question we all want the answer to. I sense that discrimination will be around for a long time, way past our time and perhaps our children's. I hope I'm wrong, and I know that hope is never intended to be the only answer to the problem, but it is still important. One of the things that drives Monique and me to do our work is to help find how the genetic melting pot will affect the outcome. Will racial identity disappear over time? I guess we can go all night on this."

"I'm sure we could. This is the perfect place for a conversation like this. I feel very fortunate. We both have dreams: the best for each other."

"Amen to that, and for all those who still yearn, and dream, for justice and equality."

"When I met Tanya, I did not see the color of her skin as anything other than beautiful. I loved her from early on, and we have a beautiful daughter whose skin is the perfect tone that reflects us both. Some day she will understand how beauty can come from parents who are Black and White."

Tanya was a beautiful woman who carried effortless grace. Her soft brown complexion was rich with warmth, and her skin was as smooth as satin. Her eyes were dark and expressive, revealing wisdom and kindness that spoke volumes without a word. Natalie was a bundle of joy and curiosity, a beautiful fusion of her parents. Her light caramel skin was a seamless blend of two histories, two families intertwined. Her big, inquisitive eyes sparkled as she soaks in every detail around her.

Taylor said, "And when I met Monique, who has the fairest skin I've ever seen, the predominant—I like using the word 'predominant' because it comes up so often in our work—the predominant thing I noticed was her warmth and love. I can't wait to see the color of our baby!"

Nick said, "Tanya and I can't wait either. He . . . or she . . . will be a beautiful representation of you two. You know what this means, don't you?"

"What? What does it mean?"

"You are fulfilling the dream you and Dr. King have fought for. You are doing your part to reach racial equality and justice."

"I guess you're right, in a sense. But I just thought, you never gave me a chance to answer your question."

Nick was getting tired, and the bed was rapidly calling out to him. "What question was that? Oh, wait, I remember now. Who could have ever known we could last as friends this long? Right?"

Taylor said, "That's the one." Before answering, he went to a picnic table that held a few items to make their most cherished drink. A cooler was beside the table, filled with ice that kept some half-and-half and coffee ice cubes. He mixed them with some Amaretto, vodka, and Kahlua to make a drink they have shared on the most special occasions, including their double wedding—a Black and White Cocktail representing their relationship. It was symbolic and became a tradition they would enjoy that locked in lasting memories.

Nick and Taylor's friendship reflected America's evolving social landscape through the decades. They supported one another and learned from each other, proving that understanding wasn't just about education. It was about experience, empathy, and the willingness to grow. Their relationship demonstrated an example of what was achievable amidst racism. Their mutual support expressed uplifting each other during tough times, shared growth and courage, and a symbol of change that represented hope and progress in a community or society that's grappling with division and transformation.

Taylor returned, gave Nick a glass, and said, as they clinked glasses, "That answer is easy, Nick. That person is me. I knew we could be friends. Something inside me assured me my sense was right. I knew from the moment I raised my hand to say hi to you in first grade that we would be good friends for a long time." He raised his glass again. Nick did the same. "Here's to our friendship and for all those who need friends and inspiration like us."

Acknowledgments

To Fran, my first editor, my first "go to" confidant. She has consistently demonstrated an aversion to racial discrimination and a genuine appreciation for diversity through her teaching, student counseling, parenting, and everyday life. She has been a tremendous influence on our family, teaching us critical values that benefit us in society.

To my children, Bill, Joe, and Jeannie, and their families. I have been privileged and proud to witness their embodiment of diversity, not as a slogan, but a way of life, in their friendships, their choices, and their convictions, which reflect a deep respect for others, regardless of background or belief.

To Lonzer Tynes, a fellow retired United States Air Force officer, a patriot, a neighbor, a dedicated family man, and an African American who graduated from Howard University. I entrusted this story to him, valuing his lived experience, thoughtful review, and the insight I deeply appreciate. This was extremely important to me, as I could never walk in his shoes, but will always appreciate his perspective.

To Mike Sager, founder of The Sager Group, publisher of this book. Mike's impressive career as a staff writer for *The Washington Post*, *Rolling Stone*, *GQ*, and *Esquire* reflects the depth of experience he brought to his thoughtful feedback and encouragement for my book. He is a bestselling author and a lecturer in journalism at Columbia University, New York University, and several other institutions. Mike is an inspiration. His expertise and personal one-on-one guidance have made me a better writer.

To the men and women I served with during my military and civilian careers. I worked alongside teams that prioritized diversity and upheld a culture of mutual respect, valued dignity, and where racial discrimination was actively discouraged and rarely tolerated.

To Gloria Nkanka, Partnerships Specialist at the Association for the Study of African American Life and History (ASALH), the Founders of Black History Month. Thank you for your invitation to participate in an annual author's book signing event for this book in Washington, DC, in February 2026.

ABOUT THE AUTHOR

William A. Cimino is a native of Brooklyn, New York. He brings nearly six decades of leadership excellence, marked by 26 years of distinguished military service, and an equally accomplished career spanning over three decades as a senior manager and executive in aerospace and information technology. Cimino entered the literary world in 2023 with his book, *Manifestations of Apprehension: A Memoir*, and now turns to historical fiction, driven by a zeal for accuracy and storytelling.

About the Publisher

The Sager Group was founded in 1984. In 2012 it was chartered as a multimedia content brand, with the intent of empowering those who create art—an umbrella beneath which makers can pursue, and profit from, their craft directly, without gatekeepers. TSG publishes books; ministers to artists and provides modest grants; and produces documentary, feature, and commercial films. By harnessing the means of production, The Sager Group helps artists help themselves. For more information, please see TheSagerGroup.net.

More Books from The Sager Group

Chains of Nobility: Brotherhood of the Mamluks (Books 1-3)
by Brad Graft

The Deadliest Man Alive: Count Dante, The Mob and the War for American Martial Arts
by Benji Feldheim

Death Came Swiftly: A Novel About the Tay Bridge Disaster of 1879
by Bill Abrams

Sing Sing Follies (A Maximum-Security Comedy): And Other True Stories
by John H. Richardson

Going Home to Die No More: A True Kentucky Story about a Train Robbery and a Hanging after the Civil War
by Russ Witcher

Who She Was: My Search for My Mother's Life
by Samuel G. Freedman

On the Run with Mad Bombers, Outlaw Lovers & Movie Stars: True Stories
by Daniel Voll

Lifeboat No. 8: Surviving the Titanic
by Elizabeth Kaye

Hunting Marlon Brando: A True Story
by Mike Sager

Miss Havilland: A Novel
by Gay Daly

Our Washington, DC: America's Hometown in Transition
Edited by Susan Sheehan

Saloon Man: A German Immigrant Battles the Limits of Liberty, 1870 to 1915
by Robert Mugge

See our entire library at TheSagerGroup.net